D0599482

Death on
the Lizard

Death on
the Lizard

by ROBIN PAIGE

BERKLEY PRIME CRIME, NEW YORK

THE BERKLEY PUBLISHING GROUP
Published by the Penguin Group
Penguin Group (USA) Inc.
375 Hudson Street, New York, New York 10014, USA
Penguin Group (Canada), 90 Eglinton Avenue East, Suite 700, Toronto, Ontario M4P 2Y3, Canada
(a division of Pearson Penguin Canada Inc.)
Penguin Books Ltd., 80 Strand, London WC2R 0RL, England
Penguin Group Ireland, 25 St. Stephen's Green, Dublin 2, Ireland (a division of Penguin Books Ltd.)
Penguin Group (Australia), 250 Camberwell Road, Camberwell, Victoria 3124, Australia
(a division of Pearson Australia Group Pty. Ltd.)
Penguin Books India Pvt. Ltd., 11 Community Centre, Panchsheel Park, New Delhi—110 017, India
Penguin Group (NZ), Cnr. Airborne and Rosedale Roads, Albany, Auckland 1310, New Zealand
(a division of Pearson New Zealand Ltd.)
Penguin Books (South Africa) (Pty.) Ltd., 24 Sturdee Avenue, Rosebank, Johannesburg 2196, South
Africa

Penguin Books Ltd., Registered Offices: 80 Strand, London WC2R 0RL, England

This is an original publication of The Berkley Publishing Group.

This is a work of fiction. Names, characters, places, and incidents either are the product of the author's imagination or are used fictitiously, and any resemblance to actual persons, living or dead, business establishments, events, or locales is entirely coincidental. The publisher does not have any control over and does not assume any responsibility for author or third-party websites or their content.

Copyright © 2006 by Susan Wittig Albert and Bill Albert.
Cover illustration by Teresa Fasolino.
Cover design by Annette Fiore.
Map illustration © Peggy Turchette.
Text design by Kristin del Rosario.

First edition: February 2006

Library of Congress Cataloging-in-Publication Data

Paige, Robin.
    Death on the Lizard / by Robin Paige.—1st ed.
      p. cm.
    ISBN 0-425-20779-X
    1. Sheridan, Kate (Fictitious character)—Fiction. 2. Sheridan, Charles (Fictitious character)—
Fiction. 3. Great Britain—History—Edward VII, 1901–1910—Fiction. 4. Lizard, The (England)—
Fiction. 5. Marconi, Guglielmo, marchese, 1874–1937—Fiction. 6. Inventors—Fiction. 7. Telegraph, Wireless—Fiction. 8. Women novelists—Fiction. I. Title.

PS3566.A3396D47 2006
813'.6—dc22

            2005053676

CAST OF CHARACTERS

Charles, Lord Sheridan, Baron Somersworth, amateur forensic detective and wireless enthusiast

Lady Kathryn Ardleigh Sheridan, Baroness Somersworth, author (under the pen name Beryl Bardwell) of numerous novels

*Guglielmo Marconi, Marconi Wireless Telegraphy Company

Bradford Marsden, director, Marconi Wireless Telegraphy Company

Miss Patsy Marsden, photographer, world traveler, and lecturer; sister to Bradford Marsden

*John Nevil Maskelyne, well-known magician and amateur wireless inventor

Residents and Visitors: Mullion, Poldhu, Bass Point, and the West Lizard

Miss Pauline Chase, friend of Mr. Marconi

Tom Deane, constable, Mullion Village, Helston Bureau, Devon-Cornwall Constabulary

Daniel Gerard, chief assistant, Poldhu Wireless Station

Dick Corey, second assistant, Poldhu Wireless Station

Jack Gordon, operator, Bass Point Wireless Station

Edward Worster, operator, Bass Point Wireless Station

Bryan Fisher, American golf enthusiast

Major Robert Fitz-Bascombe, secretary, Lizard Peninsula Preservation Committee

Mrs. Claudia Fitz-Bascombe, member, Lizard Peninsula Preservation Committee

Miss Agatha Truebody, member, Lizard Peninsula Preservation Committee

Residents and Visitors: Penhallow, Helford Village, and the East Lizard

Lady Jenna Tyrrill Loveday, mistress of Penhallow

Harriet Loveday, deceased child of Lady Loveday

*Sir Oliver Lodge, physicist and physic investigator

Niels Andersson, sailor and adventurer

Alice, Harriet's friend

Andrew Kirk-Smythe, major, Military Intelligence; a.k.a John Northrup

---

*Historical Persons

Dedicated to all the wireless operators in our family:
Charles P. Albert, Robert R. Wittig,
Robert L. Wittig, Robert K. Wittig, and Michael Wittig

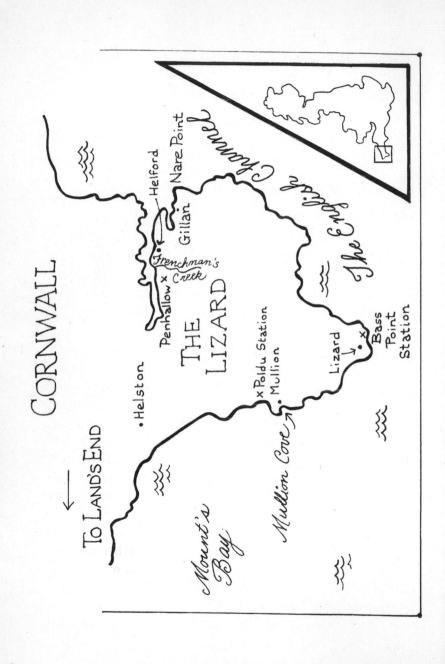

PROLOGUE

Saturday, 20 June, 1903
Lizard Village, Cornwall

They came through the blustery night carrying lanterns, the men of the wide Lizard downs. They came to the Drowned Boy from the farms scattered across the moor like peas spilled across a barn floor, and from Church Cove, and from the coastguard station. They came from up Chapel Lane and down Housel Bay and across Gwendreath Quarry. They walked, most of them, or clattered into the cobbled pub yard on shaggy ponies, or in wagons and carts. They were men who made their living with their hands—farmers and shepherds and miners and fishermen and stone turners. For the rich and idle tourists who came from Europe and America to play golf and bask in the beauties of nature were gathered at the hotel on Housel Bay, eating the crab and lobster brought in by the local fishermen and drinking fine wines and champagne and seducing one another's wives.

More of these wealthy tourists were coming all the time, for nature had been generous in the variety of her beauties on the high plateau of the Lizard. To the west, magnificent cliffs stood like a bulwark against the brutal gales of the Atlantic, and wide beaches of sand gleamed like gold at low tide. To the east, toward the Helford River, the sheltered countryside was divided into irregular fields bounded by Cornish hedges and woodlands, the landscape brightly colored with exotic subtropical plants, the sky like blue silk. To the north of the village, across the center of the Lizard, ranged the bleak heathland and peat bogs of Goonhilly Down, pocked with Bronze Age barrows and hill forts and home to many rare species of plants and animals and birds. To the south flowed the waters of the Channel, guarded since the early 1600s by Lizard Light. And on the cliff above the Channel, the village was a picturesque cluster of thatched and whitewashed cottages arranged around a handsome green, their doors open to the sea air, their window ledges and tiny gardens bright with summer flowers.

It was not just these natural beauties which brought people to the most southern point of England. Over the centuries, drawn by its resources, men had come to mine the tin and copper and china clay; to fish the rich waters of the Channel and build boats for the fishing fleet; to raise cattle and sheep and build and run the railways which took the meat and fleece to market. As wreckers, they had plundered the ships which had come to grief on the treacherous coastal rocks. As privateers and pirates, they had robbed Channel shipping and raided the towns along the Channel coast. And now, some men had come to the Lizard for a new reason. They were employed by the Marconi Wireless Telegraphy Company. They had come to send wireless messages across the Atlantic.

Jack Gordon—that was the name he went by—was one of those wireless telegraphers. With two other operators, he was responsible for the wireless station at Bass Point, just to the east of Lizard Village. Tonight, he had joined the revelers in the main room of the Drowned Boy, but not in a spirit of comradeship. A small, wary-looking man in his forties, he sat alone in a far corner, biting his nails and brooding over a mug of ale, the candle on the table casting flickering shadows over his darkly bearded face.

After a time he was joined by a younger man with blond hair and a fresh complexion, dressed in a rough Cornish jerkin, who stopped by the table and casually pinched out the candle flame as he sat down. In the darkened corner, the two of them fell into a murmured conversation, the younger man doing most of the talking, Jack answering only briefly. Their conversation, however, became contentious, and as it went on, Jack's brows lowered belligerently, his mouth set in an increasingly stubborn line, and he shook his head to every question. The evening's merriment flowed around them, cries of laughter and shouted stories, clouds of tobacco smoke and clinking of glasses, but for all the attention they paid, the pair in the dark corner might have been alone in an empty room.

After a while, their discussion came to an end, and they sat in silence. Then the younger man gave a careless shrug of his broad shoulders, as if saying "Enough, I'm done with you," and got up and left the pub. Jack fetched another half-pint from the bar, returned to his corner to drink it alone, and then left too, a bit unsteady on his feet. The table was immediately seized by three men with a deck of cards, a match was put to the candle, and a rowdy game got underway.

Once outside, Jack took his lantern from among those lined up on a shelf, and hesitated. It was past ten and a full moon had risen, silvering the Cornish heath. The rocky path gleamed whitely, like the Milky Way. He was only a little drunk, and he'd walked the path along the sea cliffs of

Housel Bay a good many times in the eight or nine months he'd lived and worked at the Bass Point wireless station. No need to light the lantern.

Head bent, shoulders hunched against the wind which buffeted the Lizard, Jack trudged along the clifftop path, thinking angrily about the demands Wolf had made. It wasn't fair, wasn't right, that's what it was. He'd already given them more than he'd signed on for. In the circumstance—and a bloody difficult circumstance it was, too—anything more would call attention to him, which would make the situation difficult, dangerous, even. And Wolf hadn't mentioned paying him any more, had he?

Jack grunted scornfully. Of course he hadn't. This one was just like the other one they'd sent, wanting something for nothing, playing on his patriotism. It was all a load of rubbish, that's what it was. He wasn't in this business because of loyalty to his native country, or his family, or any of that fancy stuff. He was in it for himself, pure and simple, and it was time they recognized his value and paid him what he was worth.

And what was more, there was no way to get his hands on the bloody thing. Even when Gerard brought it to Bass Point for testing, he never let it out of his sight. And as soon as the test was completed, into the box it went and back to Poldhu. You'd think it was a pot of gold.

Well, that was that, and an end of the bloody business. Within the fortnight, he'd be gone on holiday, and well out of it. This place was beginning to get on his nerves. End of the earth, the local folk called it, and by damn, they were right. He paused to look down at the silver surf pounding on the glittering black rocks at the foot of the cliff, far below. End of the earth, that's what it was. Nothing beyond the toe of the Lizard but a great lot of water, and America somewhere out there beyond the western horizon. Standing there on the edge of the cliff, facing the silver sea, he might have been the last man in the world.

But he wasn't.

Some fifty yards behind, a man in a dark jacket and hat was picking his way along the same cliff path. He went gingerly, for the moon's quicksilver light was pure trickery and the rock-strewn path was brushed with deceptive shadows. A shorter distance ahead of him, along the headland path, a man in a Cornish jerkin watched as well, the tip of his cigarette glowing briefly in the shadow, then vanishing, ground underfoot. If either of them saw what accident befell the wireless operator, no one else knew. If either of them—or someone else—was involved in the accident, no one else knew that either.

All that was known was what was discovered by a fisherman the following morning: A lantern abandoned in the path, and a man's broken body sprawled face-down on the rocks at the foot of the cliff, just out of reach of the greedy sea.

CHAPTER ONE

Tuesday, 30 June, 1903
Chelmsford, Essex

And what is so rare as a day in June?
Then, if ever, come perfect days . . .

James Russell Lowell

The electric spark is the true Promethean fire which is to kindle
human hearts.

The Victorian Internet
Tom Standage

Charles Sheridan was whistling as he left Bishop's Keep and drove his Panhard down the narrow lanes and through the hamlets which lay between the village of Dedham and the town of Chelmsford. On this last day of June, he felt himself to be a happy man. The sky was clear and blue, the sun was bright and the temperature mild, the road's grassy verges were lavished with purple thistle and foxgloves and wild mignonette. His life was rich and enormously full. He had been born to a station which provided a splendid living with no effort at all on his part, a circumstance which (though no fault of his own) still cost him occasional pangs of guilt. He loved a beautiful and talented woman who returned his love without reservation and who, after nearly eight years of marriage, responded to him just as eagerly as she had in the beginning. He patiently (more or less) fulfilled the obligations of his seat in the House of Lords, and did what he could to effect changes in government policies—not an easy or comfortable effort, since most of the other Lords did not agree with him on any point.

But while his idle friends might complain that life was an endless bore, Charles, Lord Sheridan, fifth Baron Somersworth, enjoyed tuning his fancy to new and interesting challenges. And as he drove into the outskirts of Chelmsford, he was pursuing his latest and most compelling interest: wireless telegraphy. He had studied Morse Code while he was serving in the Royal Engineers and had learnt at first hand that swift and reliable communications were vital to the success of military operations. Telegrams were a great improvement on signal lights, semaphore, and carrier pigeons, but were fine only as far as they went—as far as the end of the telegraph wire, where the message was turned over to the uncertain mercies of the dispatch carrier, and might or might not reach its ultimate destination. Telephones had a similar limitation, and more: the instruments had to be connected through an exchange. Wireless, on the other hand— now that was a concept which looked to the future.

In Hall Street, Charles turned at a two-story brick building which had once been a silk factory but now proclaimed itself, in letters three feet high, to be Marconi's Wireless Telegraphy Company. For the past ten years, a dozen or so scientists and inventors, among them a young Italian named Guglielmo Marconi, had been experimenting with electromagnetic waves (called Hertzian waves, after their discoverer) which seemed to travel through the air in the same way that waves from a stone thrown in a pool rippled in concentric circles through the water. Professor Hertz had demonstrated that these waves lent themselves to the transmission and reception of the telegraphic code invented by Samuel Morse a half-century earlier. A clever young Italian, Marconi had improved upon Hertz's "resonator," a device used to intercept the signals, and then used his mother's connections (Annie Jameson Marconi's Irish family had made its fortune in whiskey) to raise enough capital to set himself up in business in England. In a scant few years, Marconi's Wireless Telegraphy Company had secured the necessary investment capital, obtained patents, built experimental stations along the coast, produced equipment, and installed it on numerous ships.

Then, in December 1901, Marconi did the impossible. He transmitted the Morse letter "S"—*dit-dit-dit*—from a wireless station in Cornwall all the way to Newfoundland. Now there was a daily wireless news service between England and America, and the Marconi Company seemed—to all appearances, anyway—to be supremely successful.

Charles took off his goggles and motoring gloves, climbed out of the Panhard, and went into the Wireless Company by the rear door. He had met Marconi shortly after the young man's arrival in England in late 1896, and three years later had helped him set up this factory in Chelmsford, only eight miles from Bishop's Keep. Charles had his own wireless receiver, so he and Marconi kept in frequent touch and occasionally saw one another when the inventor came down from the City to visit the Company.

When Charles entered the office, however, it was not Marconi who greeted him, but a fair-haired, heavyset man with florid cheeks.

"Ah, there you are, old chap," Bradford Marsden said cordially, with the air of a man who had expected an earlier arrival. He transferred his cigar to his left hand and extended his right. "Good of you to come. Will you join me in a brandy?"

"Hullo, Marsden," Charles replied in some surprise, taking the hand. "No, no brandy for me, thanks. It's good to see you."

"You too, old man." Bradford went to the sideboard and helped himself, clearly an announcement of proprietary rights. "And how is our spirited Kate?" he asked, over his shoulder.

"As irrepressible as always," Charles replied, thinking that his wife would smile at the phrase. He had known Bradford Marsden since they were boys, and it was through him and his sisters that he and Kate had first met. Marsden Manor was only a few miles from Bishop's Keep, the estate Kate had inherited from her aunts and where the Sheridans preferred to live, but they had not seen Bradford since the King's coronation the previous August. Charles was unaware that his friend had any connection to Marconi, but the knowledge didn't surprise him. Bradford, who spent all his time thinking of new ways to make money, owned an investment brokerage firm, sinking money into everything from diamond mines in Rhodesia (his wife, Edith, was Cecil Rhodes's goddaughter) to the new Royce automobiles. He no doubt viewed the Marconi Wireless Company, and Marconi himself, as an extraordinarily promising investment.

The door opened and Guglielmo Marconi—youthful, slender, lightly mustached and flawlessly dressed—entered the room, followed by an assistant with a large silver tea tray.

"Pleased to see you, Sheridan," Marconi said. He nodded at Bradford. "I understand that you and Mr. Marsden are already acquainted. Has he mentioned that he is one of the directors of Marconi Wireless?" Marconi's English, while correct and unaccented, was couched in a formality which made it seem slightly foreign.

"He hasn't mentioned it yet." Charles grinned at Bradford. "But I'm not at all surprised to hear it. The company looks to have an exciting future."

"Remains to be seen," Bradford replied cryptically.

Charles would like to have known what was behind Bradford's remark, but Marconi intervened. "Very well, gentlemen," he said, gesturing to the tea tray left on a table. "Let us be seated. We shall have a cup of tea and catch ourselves up on what is new."

Charles knew that Guglielmo was not yet thirty—he was still in his teens when he began his wireless experiments in the attic of his family's Italian villa—but his aloof, calculating manner and the controlled precision of his speech made him seem much older. Charles had always found him to be modest about his work and reticent when it came to trumpeting his achievements, so he was a little surprised when Marconi began their discussion of "what was new" by reciting a list of the last few months' accomplishments: the adoption of the Marconi system by the British and Italian navies, the construction of four new American Marconi stations, and the outfitting of another five transatlantic liners with Marconi equipment operated by Marconi-trained telegraphers from the school at Frinton, in Essex.

Marconi's glance at Bradford was an odd mixture of deference and defensiveness. "And not least," he added, "we have got the Maggie perfected and production geared up to satisfy any demand."

"Maggie" was the magnetic receiver the Marconi Company had patented the year before, reputedly the best of its kind—although Charles knew that the knotty problem of tuning out interfering signals had yet to be solved.

"I must say, that's all very impressive," Charles remarked. "But I have the feeling that it isn't why I'm here today."

"I was the one who asked Marconi to invite you, old man," Bradford said, flicking his cigar into an ash tray. His sidelong glance at Marconi gave Charles to understand that there was some considerable tension between the two of them. Perhaps Bradford was not impressed by the recital of achievements, or he felt that his position as a director gave him the right to be Marconi's minder. He sipped his brandy. "We've encountered some rather serious problems, you see, and I thought of you."

Ah, here it is, Charles thought with some resignation: the reason he had been asked to come.

"I doubt that one would call them *serious* problems," Marconi began in an offhand tone, but Bradford interrupted.

"The company has been the victim of several very dirty tricks," he said vehemently. "And they've got to stop before . . . well, they've got to stop, that's all."

"What kind of dirty tricks?" Charles asked. "How long have they been going on?"

"Since before the transatlantic signal was sent," Bradford said grimly. "Nearly two years ago. The Poldhu aerial came down, and very nearly put an end to everything."

"It was blown down in a gale." Marconi gave a dismissive wave of his hand. "Inadequate engineering, nothing more."

Bradford put down his brandy glass, now empty. "The guy wires were cut nearly through. Someone wanted to make sure that the experiments would not go forward. And that's not the whole of it." He ticked items off on his fingers. "The fire in the generator building at Poldhu, equipment thefts, and outright sabotage. And less than a fortnight ago, the death of one of the Bass Point operators—"

"An accident," Marconi said hastily. "It was an accident,

I assure you, Sheridan." Perspiration had broken out on his long upper lip. "The fellow was intoxicated. He fell off a cliff."

"No one knows how he went off that cliff," Bradford said. "He had taken that path hundreds of times, in all weathers. An accident does not seem likely." His voice grew harsh. "And with Royal visitors coming in just over a fortnight, we simply cannot afford to take any chances. The company's reputation hangs in the balance."

"I don't know," Marconi said nervously, "that I would put the matter in quite such strong terms, Marsden. It is serious, of course, but—" He broke off and began to pour himself more tea, the cup rattling in the saucer.

Charles looked from one of them to the other. "Royal visitors?"

"The Prince and Princess of Wales are to visit the Poldhu station shortly," Bradford replied. "It was arranged by—"

"I was not consulted," Marconi said frostily. "If someone had asked me, I should have refused. I do *not* think it a good plan to invite Prince George at a time when Gerard and I are working on such an important project. I—"

"It was *necessary,*" Bradford put in, with emphasis. "And it was damned difficult to arrange, believe me. All manner of strings had to be pulled. But now it's settled, and the Prince is eager to have a look for himself, and he insists on bringing his wife—a nuisance, of course, but there it is. And where the Royals go, the Press follows. It's a great opportunity to get the company's name in the newspapers and cement our relations with the Admiralty—George is Navy, you'll recall. It won't hurt the price of shares, either." He stubbed out his cigar in the ashtray. "But the visit *has* to go smoothly. We cannot afford another so-called accident." He paused and looked straight at Charles. "That's why I thought of you, Sheridan."

"Ah," Charles said regretfully.

Marconi's smile was thin and cool. "Marsden seems to imagine that you are another Sherlock Holmes, my friend. He reports that from time to time you have undertaken investigations for certain individuals, on an unofficial and confidential basis." The corners of his mouth turned downward and something like distaste came into his voice. "I have told him that this . . . this sleuthing business is a side of you I have not seen, but he insisted on imposing upon you this foolish, ill-considered—"

"Damn it, Marconi," Bradford exploded angrily, "there is nothing foolish or ill-considered about it! The directors have made it clear that something has to be done, whether you like it or not. If one of these 'accidents' should occur when the Prince and Princess are at the station, I can promise you that the company will *never* recover. You can forget about the Admiralty contract, and any other governmental investment in your wireless."

This outburst was followed by a tense silence. Marconi tented his fingers under his chin and stared out the window. He looked like a man held at bay by a savage dog. Bradford got up and went to pour himself another brandy.

"What is it you want me to do?" Charles asked, at last.

"Go down to the Lizard with me," Bradford replied, returning to his seat. "Have a look around. See if you can find out who is behind these acts of sabotage. Is it someone local, or one of the company's competitors? God knows there are enough of them, and none of them are very particular as to the methods they use to ferret out others' secrets. Or perhaps there is something else going on—something we don't understand. Above all, we want you to make damned sure that nothing happens to Prince George and Princess May while they're at Poldhu." He took out another cigar and lit it. Between puffs, he added, "It would be splendid if Kate could come, too. May is quite her admirer, you know. Reads all her books, that sort of thing."

Charles frowned. "The Prince and Princess will have their usual bodyguards, won't they?"

"And they'll be the usual careless, incompetent sort," Bradford replied with a shrug.

Too true, Charles thought regretfully. After a fiasco or two, the Royal bodyguards had come in for some finger-pointing in the newspapers. He pursed his lips. "And why can't you ask the Cornwall Constabulary to investigate the sabotage?"

Marconi, still staring moodily out the window, gave a snort of derision. "The village constable is a fool. The district police are nincompoops."

"Because," Bradford said bluntly, "the information would be bound to leak out, and that would be disastrous. Any suggestion that Marconi Wireless has been targeted in this way will be reported in all the newspapers, and trumpeted with glee around the world." He shook his head as if he were half in despair—an uncommon gesture for Bradford, who was self-confident to the point of cockiness. "You are a scientist, Charles, and you may think of wireless as a science, engaged in by gentlemen who are all on amicable terms. That might have been true once, but no longer. There's too much money involved. It's become a dog-eat-dog business. That's why we can't use the police. That's why we're asking you to find out who's behind this, and stop them. Will you do it?"

Charles sat for a moment, thinking. It was true that he had carried out several investigations, but most of them had involved an interesting forensic problem—fingerprints, ballistics, toxicology, forensic photography—which he was eager to solve. It was the science of criminal investigation which captured his interest, and not the business of catching criminals and bringing them to justice. What's more, he was not at all comfortable mucking about in the swamps of speculative investments and stock brokering, much of which (he suspected) involved crooked dealings and outright chicanery. On the other hand, he had been fascinated by wireless technology since he had first read Professor Herz's work ten years before. And although Marconi was not an easy fellow to like, Charles admired and respected his intellect and abilities. It looked as if the man were in serious trouble and did not want to admit it.

Without answering Bradford's question directly, he addressed himself to Marconi. "You'll be at the Poldhu station for the Royal visit, will you, Guglielmo?"

Marconi nodded. "I'll be there on Thursday. I'm to give a lecture at the Royal Institution tomorrow night, and meet with a group of potential French investors." He cast a hopeful look at Bradford. "Although Professor Fleming could certainly do the lecture as well as I. In fact, I could go to Poldhu tomorrow with you, Marsden. That would give me a few extra days to work with Gerard on our project. If we're to demonstrate it to the Prince of Wales and Admiral Fisher—"

Charles shifted in his chair, feeling a new curiosity. Admiral Fisher? Jackie Fisher, who had just been appointed Commander-in-Chief at Portsmouth? What did he have to do with—

"The investors don't want Fleming," Bradford said roughly. "They want *you.* You're the brains of this company, Marconi, and its newsmaker. It's your name and face which have to be kept in the press. You agreed to do the lecture, and it's been widely advertised. What's more, we've arranged for the investors to come from Paris. So we will proceed as planned."

"But the tuner," Marconi objected. "Admiral Fisher will want to see exactly how it works, and what—"

"You said yourself that Gerard has the thing nearly finished. Don't worry about it. It'll be ready when you get there."

With an air of defeat, Marconi sighed and looked out the window again, his shoulders slumped. But he turned his head as the door flew open and his assistant burst in, a horrified expression on his face.

"Mr. Marconi, sir!" he blurted out. "There's just been a wire. A terrible accident, sir, at Poldhu. Daniel Gerard is dead!"

Marconi leapt to his feet. "Gerard—dead?" he gasped wildly. "No!"

"How?" Bradford barked. He hoisted himself out of his chair. "What happened? When?"

"Last night, sir. We would've heard earlier, but they've had to shut down the Poldhu station while they sort things out. Gerard was—" He gulped, his face white. "He was electrocuted, sir."

"Sweet Jesus," Marconi whispered, his eyes bleak. "Gerard has been with me since I came to England. So reliable, so intelligent, such a friend. I will never find another." He dropped his head into his hands. "What's more, he was working on . . . ." The rest of his words were lost in a despairing groan.

Bradford wheeled upon Charles. "Well, Sheridan?" he demanded brusquely. "Another accident, another man dead. What do you say now?"

Charles looked at Marconi, who sat with his shoulders slumped, his face buried in his hands. He had, it seemed, no choice but to agree. "When do we leave?"

"As quickly as we can," Bradford said. "Tomorrow is the first of July. The Royals will be at the station Saturday fortnight." He turned back to Marconi. "You can finish the tuner you and Gerard were working on? That's what the Prince and Admiral Fisher are coming to see, you know. That's what the Admiralty is interested in."

"I suppose I can finish it," Marconi said dully. "But without Gerard . . ."

"Good," Bradford said. He nodded to Charles. "We should leave as early tomorrow as we can get away. Is that agreeable to you?"

"Yes," Charles said, and thought once again, curiously, of Admiral Fisher.

CHAPTER TWO

Bishop's Keep, near Chelmsford

A Lady an explorer? a traveller in skirts?
The notion's just a trifle too seraphic:
Let them stay home and mind the babies, or hem our ragged
*   shirts;*
But they mustn't, can't, and shan't be geographic.

Punch, 10 June, 1893

Kate Sheridan finished reading the letter from her American cousin and began to study the snapshot Meghan had sent, a smile curving her mouth. Meg O'Malley was sixteen now, and very pretty, with Kate's exuberant auburn hair, intelligent eyes, and firm features. The girl had been a scrawny seven when the two of them had said goodbye at the New York dock where Kate had taken leave of her Irish-American family and begun her journey from America to England. She had thrown her arms around Kate's neck and cried, although her tears had probably been forgotten in the excitement of watching the enormous ship slip its moorings and head out to sea.

Nine years. It had been a momentous time, during which Kate, using the pseudonym Beryl Bardwell, had established herself as a successful novelist. Even more importantly, she had married an Englishman: Charles, Lord Sheridan, the fifth Baron Somersworth. But while Kate's life had changed dramatically since she left America, she had not forgotten her family. They exchanged letters and gifts, and she had made sure that Aunt and Uncle O'Malley, who had reared her after her mother died, had a comfortable home and that the numerous younger O'Malleys were able to continue their education. Now that Meghan was old enough to travel alone, Kate thought, it was time to invite her to England.

Kate looked fondly at the snapshot and inserted it into the corner of a silver picture frame on her writing desk. The frame displayed the photograph of a handsome, smiling young man, holding a horse. She and Charles had no children of their own—the only real sadness that had overtaken her in the past nine years was the loss of her child, and a pain which seemed to become even more poignant as she grew older—but they had adopted a young waif named Patrick, now nearly seventeen, and passionate about horses. He was currently working at Newmarket with George Lambton, one of Britain's leading horse trainers. He and Meghan might enjoy one another's company.

And Meghan would certainly enjoy Kate's favorite project, her thriving School for the Useful Arts. Kate had created it several years before, here at the Essex estate she had inherited from her aunts. Now, the school enrolled over two dozen young women, some coming daily from nearby Dedham village, a few living in a recently completed residence under the stern surveillance of Mrs. Bryan, who oversaw the year-long practical courses in horticulture, market gardening, dairying, beekeeping, and orchard management. Kate's school was one of only a few in England organized to help the women of rural districts (including the more famous one established by the Countess of Warwick near Dunmow), but she hoped that as more women began to seek ways to make their own independent livings, other schools would spring up. Hers, happily, was nearly self-supporting, but when it needed help, or when she wanted to add something new to the curriculum, she was able to use the income from her writing.

Kate had abandoned her earlier sensational novels for historical fiction, for there were a great many fascinating characters whose real lives offered more twists and turns than any sensational plot a fiction writer might conjure up. The current project on which she and Beryl were working—Kate thought of the writer-part of herself as a kind of alter ego, an intimate and trusted friend—was a novel about Fair Rosamund, the mistress of Henry II. Kate pulled out the chair and sat down at her typewriter. She had hoped to have the book finished by now, but the going had been slow. Beryl was enthusiastic about the project, but Kate's other projects had got in the way. The manuscript was due shortly, though. It was time to settle down.

Kate had barely put her fingers on the keys when she heard a light tap at the library door and glanced up as Hodge, her butler, came into the room. "Miss Marsden to see you, m'lady," he muttered, his dry tone revealing his ambivalence. Hodge himself was rigorously correct in all ways, and while he approved of Patsy Marsden's family connections, Patsy herself was quite clearly a New Woman. Her modernity was evident in her dress, if nothing else, and as Hodge admitted her, he kept his eyes carefully averted.

Patsy was wearing a neat white blouse, a short woven vest striped in a rainbow of colors, and a dark skirt radically shortened to reveal trim, dark-stockinged ankles. A narrow-brimmed red felt hat decorated with a pair of yellow feathers perched jauntily on one side of her sleek blond hair, and her pretty face was much more deeply tanned— sunburnt, some might have called it—than current fashion permitted.

"Patsy!" Kate exclaimed happily, rising from her desk and embracing her friend. "It seems an age since I last saw you! How well you look." She fingered the fabric of Patsy's striped vest. "And how stunning this is. It suits you beautifully."

"I think so, too," Patsy replied. "The wool is hand-spun and woven by the Bedouin women of the Negev desert from the fleece of the local Awassi sheep. I've brought back several bolts of it to show to an importer in London. The women need a wider market for their work." She took off her hat and kid gloves and tossed them on a chair. "Perhaps you'd like a vest for yourself."

"I'd love one," Kate said promptly. "When did you get back?"

In her mid-twenties, Patsy Marsden was already a world traveler who spent as much time as she could abroad, touring with her camera and portable typewriter. She loved going to exotic places where women did not usually venture, seeing (and photographing) strange sights which women did not ordinarily see. Kate had last been with her the year before, when she and her friend Gertrude Bell had left on a daunting and dangerous trek through the Middle East. Gertrude had gone on to India and America, but Patsy had fallen in love with the desert. She wrote to Kate that she was staying in Haifa, taking photographs, meeting the local Bedouin, and studying both Persian and Arabic.

"I returned two days ago," Patsy said. "I would have come here straightaway, but you know Mama. She insisted that I stay and pay court to her." She tilted her head. "How wonderful you look, Kate. Life must be agreeing with you."

"It is, I think," Kate said. "I'm quite content, although there has been rather too much traveling lately. Not your kind of travel, of course," she added with a little laugh. "Charles and I spent part of April at Blenheim, and May in London. It's very good to be at home again." She looked over her shoulder. "Tea, please, Hodge. And ask Mrs. Pratt to send up some of her marmalade cake. Miss Marsden and I will be in the solarium."

Kate took Patsy's hand and led her through the French doors into the glass-roofed conservatory, which she and Charles had just built, adjacent to the library. "I hope you can stay for the rest of the day, Patsy. Charles has gone off to Chelmsford to visit Signor Marconi's wireless works. He would be very sorry to miss you."

"I know where he's gone," Patsy said. "Bradford went over to Chelmsford to meet him. My brother is one of the Marconi Company directors, you know," she added in a wry voice. Patsy and her brother had not been on the best of terms since Bradford had married Edith, who had taken exception to Patsy's unconventional occupations. "You've just built this, haven't you?" She turned around, taking in the expanse of glass and green plants. "I do love the desert, but tropical plants are such a nice relief. They give one the feeling of being in a luxuriant jungle." She laughed, glancing toward a large bamboo cage. "And there's your aunt's parrot, of course, to add to the tropical ambiance."

"Death and damnation," the parrot remarked conversationally. "God save the Queen." Kate had inherited the bird, named "Rule Britannia," from her Aunt Jaggers, who had got it from her husband. He had served in the army in

Egypt and amused himself by teaching the bird to talk—and to swear.

"Britannia doesn't understand that the queen is dead," Kate explained. "And the conservatory will be nicer when the plants, especially the vines, have grown up." She pulled up two chairs beside a fountain which sent a sparkling cascade into a small goldfish pool. "And how is your mother?" Lady Marsden, who still ruled the family roost, lived at Marsden Manor, only a few miles from Bishop's Keep.

"Well, and fully occupied." Patsy made a face. "Meddling in my affairs, directing poor Eleanor's life, and managing Bradford and Edith—as much as anyone can manage Bradford, of course." She chuckled dryly. "My sister is still doing exactly as Mama says, and has the misery to prove it. Mama approves of neither Bradford nor me. I'm not home enough to suit her, and Bradford has more of a nose for profit than she thinks someone of our station ought. Unseemly, you know, in spite of the fact that she's living on Bradford's earnings. Or more properly put, on Edith's inheritance. I'm not sure that my brother is as clever as he thinks when it comes to business."

By "our station," Patsy was referring to the fact that the Marsdens were County, although there was precious little left of the original family fortune, the late Lord Marsden having squandered it all on fine horses and an extravagant lifestyle before he could pass it on to his only son, Bradford. But while Lady Marsden might be a penniless dependent, she put on a good front, and took it as an insult that her son actually seemed to enjoy working in the City.

Privately, Kate thought that it might not be hard to dislike the way Bradford Marsden did business. From all she had heard, he had become quite obsessed with making money, without demonstrating a very high regard as to means and methods. But while Patsy and Bradford did not get along, he was still Patsy's brother, so she kept her criticism to herself.

"I imagine your mother finds it rather a challenge to meddle in your affairs," she said. "The deserts of Arabia are a world away from Marsden Manor. Will you be staying with your mother for a while?"

"That's what I intended. I've brought back a great lot of photographic work to be developed and sorted. Gertrude is just home from America, and she and I are planning to sit down together and see if we might have enough for a book of some sort. Whatever we do needs to be done before she's off to Arabia again. However . . ." She paused. "In the stack of mail waiting for me was a long letter from Jenna Loveday, at Penhallow, in Cornwall. Do you remember her?"

"Cornwall," muttered the parrot. "Death and damnation."

"Jenna? Why, of course," Kate said warmly. She had met Lady Loveday several years before, at a lecture that Patsy had given at the University Club, in London. "What's she doing these days? Is she well?"

"Unfortunately, she's not well at all." Patsy's face darkened. "She's lost her daughter, Kate. In a drowning accident, some three months ago. I don't know the details—Jenna didn't tell me anything, except that the little girl is dead."

Kate felt herself go cold. "Dear God," she whispered. Jenna Loveday had had only one child, Harriet, a girl of about ten. Her daughter had been the center of her life—an isolated life, for Jenna, who had lost her husband some three years before, lived in Cornwall, on an estate which had been in her family for centuries. Kate understood the significance of Jenna Loveday's loss, for it was her own, a mother's loss. "How tragic, Patsy. I am so sorry."

"Yes, it is tragic," Patsy said flatly. "It's horrid. It's appalling. And Jenna is devastated, of course. She has always struck me as—well, a little fragile and other-worldly, you know. She seems to be having a great deal of difficulty accepting what's happened." She leaned forward. "Kate, I feel I must go to Cornwall. Jenna has asked me to come for a visit. I want you to go with me." She took Kate's hand between her own, her voice urgent. "You and Jenna seemed to like each other very much, and I know you'd be a great comfort to her. After all, you know how she feels. And with both of us there, perhaps we can distract her from her grief."

Kate understood what Patsy had not quite said: that she and Jenna Loveday shared a bond of loss, and there would be some solace in that. But she quailed at the thought of trying to comfort a woman who had lost her only child. She knew the bitter truth from her own experience, which had occurred exactly six years ago this week. This was not a loss which could be eased by the distraction of visitors, or soothed by a few quiet words. It was a raging loss, an over-mastering grief as fierce as a lion, an agony as wide as a world of wilderness, so savage that it could never be tamed. And to have lost both daughter and husband in the space of three years was unthinkable. Wordlessly, she shook her head.

"You're not saying no, I hope," Patsy said with a frown. "Please, Kate, *please*. It's a mission of mercy."

Kate looked down at her hands. "I can't."

"But why?" Patsy persisted. "Are you too busy? Are you writing?"

"That's certainly part of it," Kate replied. "Charles and I were both away in April and May. I'm working another

novel—a historical novel requiring a great deal of research—
and I'm terribly far behind. Not to mention that I'm expecting a visit from one of my American cousins. She'll be
arriving in a few weeks, and Patrick is coming home for a
visit. He—"

"In a few weeks, we'll be *back*," Patsy interrupted, in a
firm, brook-no-objections tone. "I'm not suggesting that we
stay all summer, you know, only a week or two. You can
surely manage that much time, can't you?" Without paus-
ing for an answer, she added, "I've already had a look at the
railway schedules. We can take the train to Helston, and
Jenna can send a carriage to meet us. I won't wire her until
the day we leave, so she can't tell us not to—"

"Wait, Patsy, please." Kate put her hand on her friend's
arm. "I really feel I must finish this book before Meghan and
Patrick descend on us. And Charles and I have promised one
another not to do any more traveling for a while. I'm terribly sorry, but you'll have to go down to Cornwall alone, or
find someone else to go with you."

"Cornwall," said the parrot, adding cheerfully, "Tea time!
Tea time!"

Kate glanced up as the butler pushed a cart through the
open French doors. "Oh, thank you, Hodge," she said,
grateful for the interruption. Now they could drop the dangerous subject and get on to something else.

But the minute they were alone with cups of tea and
plates of marmalade cake, Patsy began again.

"I'm not going to leave it there, Kate," she said flatly. "Of
course, I respect your need to work. Heaven knows, I feel it
myself. But reading between the lines of Jenna's letter, I
couldn't help thinking that she's in serious trouble. She
didn't go into the details, but it sounds as if she's having
hallucinations of some sort. Seeing things, hearing things.

She blames herself for her daughter's death, of course, which is . . . well, self-indulgent."

"Now, Patsy," Kate began cautiously.

Patsy raised her hand. "I know, I know. You're going to tell me I'm not entitled to make that sort of judgment, and I suppose you're right. But Jenna has to stop drowning herself in her grief and look to the future. She needs to know that others have met their losses and their lives have gone on. You and I can help her pull herself together, I'm sure of it."

Kate was about to answer when the doors opened again. The parrot gave a squawk, flapped its wings, and announced imperiously, "Fourteen men on a dead man's chest!"

It was Charles, back from his trip to Chelmsford, his brown beard streaked with road dust. He bent over to kiss Kate, then greeted Patsy. A few moments elapsed before the flurry of greetings was over and Charles had been furnished with a chair, a cup of tea, and a slice of Mrs. Pratt's cake. The three of them chatted for a while about Patsy's travels and her photography—Charles had introduced her to the art a few years before—and then Patsy returned to her earlier subject.

"I've just been telling your wife," Patsy said, "that she is required in Cornwall. I'm going to visit a friend in difficulty—Jenna Loveday—and I desperately need to take Kate along. Don't you think she should go, Charles? You can spare her for a week or two, can't you?"

Kate was about to remind Charles that they had agreed not to travel for the next few months, but Charles spoke first.

"Where in Cornwall, Patsy?"

"Cornwall," chuckled the parrot. "Cornwall, Cornwall."

"The eastern side of the Lizard Peninsula. Penhallow, her family estate, is very near the Helford River. I've told Kate that we could take the train to Helston and hire someone to drive us to—"

"I could drive you," Charles said. He put down his empty plate, and with an apologetic glance at Kate, added, "It seems that Bradford and I are also going to Cornwall. We're shipping the Panhard by rail, so we'll have it there. The roads aren't good, of course, but Bradford thinks we'll need the motorcar to get around."

Kate stared at him, nonplussed. "Going to Cornwall?" she exclaimed. "Why, whatever for, Charles?"

"Some business having to do with Marconi," Charles replied with a look which cautioned her against asking too many questions. "Too complicated to go into just now. The idea came up rather unexpectedly, in response to something which happened at Marconi's wireless station on the Lizard, and I had to say yes on the spot. We're leaving tomorrow. We'll be staying at the hotel at Poldhu Cove. I can't say how long we'll be there."

Kate frowned. "I certainly understand," she said, feeling distinctly nettled. "It's just that we agreed we wouldn't—"

"Well, that settles it, Kate," Patsy said definitively, setting down her cup. "If Charles is going to Cornwall, you simply have no excuse. You and I can go to Jenna at Penhallow, and Charles and Bradford can drive over from Poldhu when they like—it can't be more than five or six miles—and all of us can go boating on the Helford. Jenna will be cheered up, and we'll have a very jolly time."

"Really, Patsy," Kate began, flustered. "I hardly think—"

Charles cleared his throat. "I don't know about boating, Patsy. I'm afraid that I shall be rather occupied. But we might be able to find a day to get together, and perhaps you could come over to Mullion and visit the Poldhu Station. If you should like to go to Cornwall, my dear, I certainly wouldn't object. In fact, I should be pleased." He slanted a look at her, and Kate had the feeling that there was more to this than was immediately apparent.

"Wonderful!" Patsy exclaimed, and pushed back her chair. "What an agreeable husband you are, Charles. Kate, you are a fortunate wife. Now, if you two will excuse me, I'll just pop on back to Marsden Manor and tell Mama that she will have to do without me for the next week or two. If it's convenient for you, Kate, I really think the four of us should go down on the train tomorrow so Charles and Bradford can drive us to Penhallow. That will be ever so much better than asking Jenna to send a coach." She stood and smiled at them both. "Goodbye."

"Goodbye," remarked the parrot briskly. "Off you go."

"Really, Charles," Kate said, when Patsy had gone. "You've put me in a very difficult position. I had already told Patsy I didn't want to go to Cornwall. With Meghan and Patrick coming, I have a great deal of work to do here. I was looking forward to—"

"I'm sorry, Kate," Charles said. He put his hand over hers. "To tell the truth, Patsy's offer was much too opportune to decline. The Prince and Princess of Wales will be visiting the Poldhu Station, you see, and it would be very good if you were there to—"

Kate snatched her hand away. "*Really,* Charles!" she exclaimed again, dismayed. "You can't have volunteered me to entertain Princess May. You know how I—"

"I know she's not one of your favorite people, Kate. The Royal visit is an important event for Marconi and his company, but there are difficulties. In fact, if the business isn't sorted out, and quickly, the company may not survive." He leaned forward, his voice low, his expression grave. "This is Marconi's problem, and I didn't want to go into the details in front of Patsy. But if you don't mind, I'd like to tell you about it. When you've heard, I think you'll understand."

Kate listened quietly. When Charles had finished his tale, she sighed. "Yes, I see. Of course, if you want me to be there, and think I'll be useful, I'll be glad to come. I can manage the Princess for a few hours, I suppose. It's just that . . . well, I was trying to avoid going to Penhallow." She told Charles what had happened to Jenna Loveday's daughter, why Patsy wanted to go to Cornwall, and why she felt so reluctant.

Charles got up, went behind her chair, and bent over her, wrapping his arms around her shoulders. "I understand," he said, his lips against her hair. "But it's only for a fortnight. And it should be quiet, too—nothing like the chaos of our visit to Blenheim. If you want to write while you're at Penhallow, I'm sure there won't be any interruptions. Cornwall is a very lovely place."

The parrot flapped his wings. "Cornwall," he muttered. "Hell and damnation!"

CHAPTER THREE

Wednesday, 1 July, 1903
Penhallow, near Helston, Cornwall

All the ends of the earth will be wooed into the electric telegraph circuit.

Scientific American, 1852

"A telegram, m'lady."

Jenna Loveday turned from her task of transplanting a clump of rare tropical ferns in the flower border—a self-appointed task, and entirely unnecessary, since it was Snood's job to maintain the gardens and grounds. But she couldn't stay indoors all day, with nothing to do except manage the household and consult with Harry, Penhallow's estate agent, about farm business, or read, or sit beside the window with her lap full of needlework. It was better to keep busy out of doors, walking or bicycling or gardening. Better to be physically active, to tire herself out so she would fall quickly asleep, wouldn't lie awake all night, remembering, imagining—

She dropped her spade and took the envelope from the silver platter. "Thank you, Melrose," she said, and waved the butler away. The telegram might be from Sir Oliver Lodge, whom she was expecting to arrive on Friday, for the

weekend. Or from her mother-in-law, the dowager Lady
Loveday, who constantly beleaguered her with invitations to
go here and there, stay at one country house or another, take
a holiday in the Swiss Alps, or visit one of the German spas
which seemed to attract so many of the best people. Jenna
had turned them all down. She wasn't terribly fond of
George's mother, who always seemed to know what was best
and was determined to make her do it, and she wasn't especially fond of travel, especially when it took her into the
company of the "best people." Jenna loved Cornwall, and
the Lizard, and Penhallow. This was her home.

And now she had another reason for staying. Two reasons, actually, and both equally compelling, both equally
critical to her survival. Before she could finally accept Harriet's death, she had to learn how it had happened. Why had
Harriet gone to the creek? What was she looking for? What
had she known? Jenna wasn't sure that she could live with
the answers to those questions, but she had to know them.
She *had to*!

And she had to have a clearer understanding of what was
happening. Sensory hallucinations, Dr. Michaels had called
them, born of grief and despair. The doctor's scientific explanation had helped a little, and she had begun to hope
that perhaps she wasn't going mad, after all. No, of course
she wasn't mad, Dr. Michaels had said in his most soothing
voice, patting her hand and carefully avoiding the word
"hysteria." He was confident that the images, disturbing as
they certainly were, would fade as time went on. Such phenomena were brought on by the shock of loss and rarely
lasted for very long.

But there were other views on the matter. An old friend
of the Tyrrill family, Sir Oliver Lodge, was a well-known

scientist who also had a very deep interest in psychic phenomena. Jenna happened to see him when she went up to the City to consult Dr. Michaels, and he had suggested that there might be something else at work here, something far more intriguing than mere hallucinations. The two of them had talked, and Jenna had told him all that had happened to her after Harriet's death. At the end of their conversation, she had invited him to come to Penhallow. He could not promise that he would be able to help her, but he was willing to try. She was more frightened than comforted by the idea of the supernatural, but he was persuasive, and she agreed.

She opened the telegram, which was not from Sir Oliver, after all, nor from her insistent, itinerant mother-in-law. It was from her friend Patsy Marsden, who was staying with her mother near Colchester, and it announced (in Patsy's cheerfully definitive way) that she and Lady Sheridan would be arriving that very afternoon. They planned to stay for a week, or longer. No need to send a driver to Helston to fetch them. Lady Sheridan's husband had an errand nearby; he was shipping his motorcar and would drive them to Penhallow, although he would not be staying.

Jenna frowned with irritation and thrust the telegram into the pocket of her jumper. It was exactly like Patsy Marsden to make plans without consulting her hostess, to set a date for arrival without asking whether she was still welcome.

But then, with a sigh, Jenna realized that this was hardly fair. She turned and walked toward the oak woodland bordering the garden. She *had* invited Patsy to come, although it had been an off-hand invitation, a post-script tacked to the end of a rather sad, self-pitying letter, and not extended with any great enthusiasm. And since she had written the letter, the situation had changed. She had something important to do, and another pair of guests was not entirely welcome.

But just now, she thought she would go down to Frenchman's Creek, which drew her to its bank nearly every day. Still thinking about Patsy—she could scarcely blame her friend for accepting her invitation, or choosing her own time to arrive—she stepped into the shadow of the woods. Holding her skirt in her hand, she picked her way carefully down a narrow, mossy path which twisted and turned, dropping steeply downward toward the water shimmering like silver through the trees. She liked her friend a great deal, for Patsy's travels gave her a wider range of experience, and certainly a greater independence, than most other women. And she remembered Kate Sheridan, whom she had met at one of Patsy's lectures, with pleasure. An American, Lady Sheridan had inherited a small estate in Essex and married a title—the man with the motorcar, no doubt—and wrote novels of some merit. Jenna had read and enjoyed several, and felt that they were worth the critical praise they had received. Well, the two women were on their way, like it or not, and she would have to make the best of it.

She smiled crookedly. But so would they. And if they disapproved of Sir Oliver and his attempts to contact the spirit world—well, they didn't have to participate, did they?

The path leveled, the trees thinned, and Jenna stood on the bank of Frenchman's Creek, named for the French ships which sought safe harbor there in the old days of smuggling and piracy. A half-mile or more away, the pretty stream emptied into the Helford River—a wide, five-mile-long

estuary which served as a refuge for small boats, a haven
for fishermen and oystermen, and a paradise for birds and
shore-life. Jenna loved Frenchman's Creek for what it was,
an enchanted, unspoilt wilderness which called to the wildness in herself—a wildness which had often got her into
difficulties—and made her love it more passionately with
every passing season.

But now, this was the place of her life's greatest sadness,
and she came here because she could not help herself. Over
her head a pair of curlews circled, calling sharply. Upstream,
where the falling tide exposed the flats, an oyster-catcher
zigzagged across the glistening mud; downstream, where
the water deepened and widened, a gray heron, hooded and
wary, stood statue-like in the cordgrass, anticipating an in-
cautious frog. And just this side of the bend, a sleek white
sailing yacht was moored a yard off-shore, its mast tall and
straight against the dark trees. Painted on the bow was its
name: *Mistral II.*

Jenna's vision blurred and there was a brief, unsettling
moment of disorientation—the symptoms which usually
preceded her hallucinations. Was she imagining this, too?
Conjuring up this image because she had hoped so long
and so desperately for it? Had hoped, and yet feared, to
see——

A man dressed in sailing whites emerged up the galley
way and turned in her direction. Seeing her, he froze for an
instant. And then he simply stood there, his yachting cap
pushed back on his blond hair, his hands on his hips, smiling faintly, waiting.

Jenna hesitated, still only half-believing that he was real.
They had said goodbye months before. She should not go to
him, she knew. It was dangerous. *He* was dangerous. But she
had no choice.

She took one hesitant step toward the boat, and then another. And then she flung caution to the winds, picked up her skirts, and began to run.

She did not see the small, silent figure slipping quickly through the trees, watching her as she went.

CHAPTER FOUR

Here on the Lizard, amongst the fishermen and sailors, there is a belief that the dead in the rivers and the sea will be heard crying out if a drowning is about to occur. I know of a woman who went to a clergyman to have him exorcise her of the spirit of her dead child, which she said appeared in the form of a white pigeon. And I have heard of farmers believing that white moths are spirits.

Miss M. A. Courtney,
Cornish folklorist 1893

Kate and Charles met Patsy and Bradford at the Colchester train station early on Wednesday morning. The railway journey to Cornwall was uneventful, the sometimes-temperamental Panhard started promptly when it was off-loaded from the baggage car, and the drive from Helston Station to Mawgan Cross to St. Martin, where Charles turned off toward the Helford River, was far more beautiful than Kate had expected. She had never been on the Lizard Peninsula, and in spite of the fact that she was a reluctant visitor, she immediately liked what she saw. The farther they drove into the moors, the more enchanted she became.

The narrow road, bordered on both sides by stone walls, wound its serpentine way across the rough, wide landscape. With its granite tors and broken trees and seeping bogs, the moor seemed to Kate to be a wild, fantastic sweep of unique and timeless beauty. It was a dreamer's landscape, an enchanted landscape which delighted Beryl Bardwell's imagination. The inventive, fanciful Beryl found it very easy to picture King Arthur and his knights riding full tilt across Goonhilly Down toward the sea, and Tristram and Isolde seeking a shelter from the wild winds and driving rain.

And don't forget the pixies and little people, Beryl whispered in Kate's ear, *the gnomes and trolls and fairies who live in the trees and rocks and rivers and dance all night along the seacliffs. Oh, Kate,* she sighed ecstatically, *I'm so glad we've come!*

As they reached the eastern edge of the moor, along the Helford River, the fields became greener and there were more woodlands. And then, following Patsy's directions, they drove up the long lane through the thousand-acre estate which had belonged to the Tyrrills, Jenna's father's family, since the time of King Henry VIII. The manor house stood at the end of the lane. It was built of the local gray granite and roofed with gray slate. It had a rectangular Georgian facade, regularly interrupted by tall leaded-glass windows which gave it a cloisterlike look.

Kate was somewhat surprised, for both she and Beryl had imagined Penhallow as a grand and imposing manor house, in the tradition of large British estates. Instead, this Cornwall farmhouse put Kate in mind of a comfortably dowdy lady, a bit down-at-the-heel but not in the least concerned about it, as though she had seen better days and didn't mind that her time was past. Or—since the house was clearly designed as the hub of a large working farm—perhaps its owners and occupants had always been too busy tending the land, or too heedless of the neighbors' opinions, to bother with grandness.

As the Panhard pulled up in front and Kate and the others got out, an elderly manservant came down the broad stone steps. He introduced himself as Wilson and explained, apologetically, that Lady Loveday had gone for a walk. She was expected momentarily, however. He would be glad to show them to the drawing room, where tea would be served and—

But at that moment, Jenna Loveday appeared around the corner of the house, flushed and breathless, her hair loose around her shoulders. "Oh, dear," she said distractedly, tidying the collar of her blouse, "you've arrived already and I wasn't here to greet you! I'm so sorry, Patsy. Lady Sheridan, do forgive me." She spoke in a light, lilting Cornish accent.

"Kate, please," Kate said with a smile, extending her hand. "And we'd only just got here, really."

There were some who claimed that the people of Cornwall had inherited a special kind of magic from their Celtic ancestors, an ability to see further and deeper and feel more keenly than other people, a reputation no doubt connected with the old Cornish tales of pixies and fairy-folk. Seeing Jenna Loveday, Kate thought of this, and found the idea utterly convincing, for there was something in Jenna's delicate features and wide-spaced gray-blue eyes—quite remarkable eyes, large and luminous and almost silvery—which made Kate think of charms and enchantments.

Patsy stepped forward and kissed Jenna on both cheeks, then turned, with a gesture, to introduce the men. "This is Charles, Lord Sheridan, and Bradford Marsden, my brother."

"Gentlemen," Jenna Loveday said. "So very glad you're here." Then she put up a hand, realizing that her long, fair mane of hair was rippling down her back. She pulled out a pin, twisted it quickly, and repinned it into a knot at the back of her neck. "I was walking in the woods and I completely lost track of the time. Wilson, please see to the ladies' luggage." To Patsy and Kate, she added, "We'll all go in and have some tea."

Charles and Bradford opened the Panhard's boot and the luggage was taken out. As Wilson went inside with the bags, Charles announced that he and Bradford had to be on their way to the Poldhu Hotel, and wouldn't be able to stay to tea.

"Just a cup?" Jenna Loveday asked, looking from Charles to Bradford. "It may be only a few miles to the coast, but at this time of year, they're dusty miles."

"No, thank you," Bradford said, with an air of regret. "We have business in the Mullion area, and we must be on our way."

"Mullion?" Jenna asked. "You're going to the wireless station, then?"

Charles closed the boot. "That's right," he replied. "I'm to help with a telegraphy experiment, and Bradford—"

"I'm to play golf," Bradford said with a grin, slouching against the car. "It's something I do very well." He glanced at Jenna. "Are you acquainted with the station?"

She lifted her chin, her eyes flashing. "Everyone on the Lizard is acquainted with the station in one way or another. It has brought quite a lot of attention to the Lizard—most of it unwelcome, I'm afraid."

Kate could hear the barely suppressed interest in Charles's "Oh?"

"The inn-keepers and publicans in Mullion and Lizard Village may be pleased," Jenna replied. "The station at Poldhu attracts quite a few curiosity-seekers, and they have to find somewhere to eat and sleep. But the local people would be very glad to be rid of it—the poor farmers, especially, for the noise frightens their cows and keeps them from giving milk, and one of the laborers was injured recently when a horse bolted. The villagers dislike it, too. They complain that it's shattered the peace of the moor. We rather value that, you know," she added with a wry firmness. "We don't think kindly of those who destroy it."

Kate was struck by Jenna's tone. It implied an inner stamina which seemed rather out of character with her delicate features, with the large, luminous eyes which made her seem more than a little fey.

"Noise?" Patsy asked curiously. "I shouldn't think a telegraph station would make a great deal of noise."

"Oh, but it *does*," Jenna replied. "It's the transmitting equipment, you see. The signals are quite loud. It's said that they can be heard as far away as Lizard Village."

"As far away as America," Bradford remarked with a patronizing smile. "That's the point, of course, Lady Loveday. Getting the signal across the Atlantic requires quite a lot of electricity. The noise you hear is the sound of progress."

Patsy spoke with some asperity. "You may not be surprised to learn, Jenna, that my brother occupies a seat on Marconi Wireless's board of directors. He is responsible for promoting the company, a task he takes to heart."

"Progress," Bradford repeated emphatically, ignoring his sister. "Someday, when the Marconi system is perfected, the people of the Lizard will be very proud to say that these first steps, however awkward and faltering, took place here."

"Progress, indeed," Jenna said, and seemed to dismiss the subject. She crossed her arms and tilted her head. "We are having another guest on Friday—Sir Oliver Lodge. I should be delighted if you and Lord Charles would join us for dinner." She paused. "I believe that Sir Oliver has also done some experiments in wireless. If Mr. Marconi would like to come, he is certainly welcome."

Another guest? Kate glanced at Patsy, who looked surprised and a little crestfallen, as if she had expected Jenna Loveday to be entirely alone, friendless, and uncomforted. Perhaps, Kate thought, their "mission of mercy," as Patsy had called it, was unnecessary. Perhaps their hostess had put the death of her daughter behind her and was already in the process of getting on with things.

Bradford's eyes had narrowed. "I regret that I must decline on Signor Marconi's behalf, and my own, as well," he said with a stiff formality. "Professor Lodge is a competitor, and a small unpleasantness has arisen between him and the Marconi Company in recent months. I don't think we three should be entirely comfortable together."

Jenna seemed unconcerned. "If you should change your mind, you're more than welcome." To Patsy, she added, "Sir Oliver and my father were life-long friends. When I asked him for the weekend, I did not know you were coming. It has been lonely here since Harriet . . ." Her eyes darkened and her mouth tightened. "Since my daughter died."

Ah, Kate thought compassionately, watching her expression and hearing the bleakness in her tone. Jenna Loveday is not comforted, after all.

"I am a great admirer of Professor Lodge's studies in electrolysis and X-rays—and wireless, too, of course," Charles said, turning to Kate with a quick smile. "You remember Sir Oliver, Kate. We met at a reception last year."

"Oh, yes," Kate said. Now that Charles mentioned it, she recalled the tall, stooped, courtly gentleman. "I shall be glad to see him again."

Charles smiled at Jenna. "Thank you for the invitation, Lady Loveday. I shall be delighted to join the party." He reached into the motor car for his cap and goggles. "And now, I'm afraid, we really must be on our way."

"Yes," Bradford said. He glanced at his sister. "If you should need anything while you are here, Patsy . . ."

"If I should need anything, I will borrow a bicycle and ride over the moor to get it for myself," Patsy said, raising her chin. Bradford reddened angrily.

Kate sighed, wishing that Patsy and Bradford could mend their frayed relationship, which had been strained since Bradford had married Edith. Patsy's sister-in-law, once a free, frank young woman, had inherited a sum of money and was rapidly turning into a frowning matron.

"Goodbye, Kate," Charles said, and bent to kiss her. Bradford went to crank the Panhard, and in a few minutes the motorcar was clattering down the lane.

"On the whole," Jenna Loveday said, regarding the cloud of dust rising in its wake, "I rather prefer horses." She turned to Kate. "I'm sorry if that sounded offensive. I only meant that—"

"I know," Kate said, with a rueful smile. "Perhaps progress isn't worth it, after all." She looked around at the green fields, with the moor behind. "It would be a great pity if progress destroyed any of this beauty."

Patsy slipped her arm around Jenna's waist. "Thank you so much for inviting us, Jenna. I'm delighted to see you looking well."

"Appearances are often deceiving," Jenna said ambiguously. And then, with a smile and a toss of her head, she said, "Come with me, ladies. I will show you to your rooms, and then, since it's so lovely out of doors, we'll have our tea on the terrace."

She began talking as they walked, in what sounded to Kate like a determinedly cheerful voice. "We're not at all elegant here, I'm afraid. The name "Penhallow Manor" may sound as if it belongs to a grand country house, but we're very old-fashioned, and I fear that you will think us terribly primitive. There's no gas, no telephone, of course, and certainly no electricity. But I think you'll be comfortable, especially since it's July. In the winter—" She laughed gaily. "Well, that's rather a different story. Cold feet and chilblains are the rule."

"What?" Patsy pretended great shock. "Primitive, with the most advanced wireless station in the world not seven miles away?" She laughed. "Just wait until I've told you, Jenna, what it's like to live in a tent in the Arabian desert. Talk about the primitive life!"

A little later, Kate was alone in the upstairs bedroom to which she had been shown, and had completed her unpacking. The room was small but indeed comfortable, the stone floor brightened with woven rag rugs, the walls covered with cream-painted plaster. The windows, a pair of deep-set casements, opened outward into a profusion of blooming roses which flooded the room with their delicate scent. The manor house was set on a high point of land, with the Helford River to the east and Frenchman's Creek to the south. The landscape was green and lush and mysterious, and the warm light of the afternoon sun brushed the rustling trees with gold. At the foot of the lawn, a donkey was pulling a mowing machine across the lush green grass, while in the herb garden, a woman with a basket over her arm was cutting lavender. On the terrace below, bordered with a profusion of blooming flowers, their hostess was seeing to the arrangements for an outdoor tea. The murmur of voices floated on the somnolent summer air.

Ah, said Beryl, with a long sigh, *it's very beautiful, isn't it?* And Kate could see why Jenna Loveday resisted the idea of living in London. It had to do with the light falling like a benediction across the green grass and trees, the woodland sloping down to the creek and the river beyond. And the promise of pixies and elves dancing across the open moors in the moonlight.

And then, just as Kate turned away from the window, she caught a glimpse of something out of the corner of her eye, a pale shape flitting, mothlike, through the shadowy woods. Beryl was immediately intrigued.

Oh, look! she exclaimed. *Is it a fairy? A pixie? Kate, we simply* must *write a fairy tale—and Cornwall is the perfect setting for it!*

"I should think we had better finish the project we're working on before we start thinking about the next," Kate muttered testily. But she reached for the binoculars she had just unpacked, brought in the expectation of watching birds on Goonhilly Down. She put the glasses to her eyes and adjusted them.

The pale shape blurred, and then resolved itself into a small, red-haired girl wearing a blue dress and a plain white pinafore, half-hidden behind an oak tree. Kate could not see her expression, but she seemed to be watching Lady Loveday.

A girl? Beryl asked curiously. *Whatever is she doing behind that tree? Is it some sort of game, do you suppose?*

But there was no answer to Beryl's question, and when Kate looked again, the girl had vanished.

Well, if you ask me, that was no girl, Beryl said firmly. *She was a fairy. They're everywhere here, Kate. On the moors, in the fields, in the woods. Everywhere.*

"Oh, don't be silly," Kate scoffed. But when she put the binoculars down, she was frowning.

CHAPTER FIVE

On the land side our surroundings were as sombre as on the sea. It was a country of rolling moors, lonely and dun-coloured, with an occasional church tower to mark the site of some old-world village. In every direction upon these moors there were traces of some vanished race which had passed utterly away, and left as its sole record strange monuments of stone, irregular mounds which contained the burned ashes of the dead, and curious earthworks which hinted at prehistoric strife.

The Adventure of the Devil's Foot
Sir Arthur Conan Doyle

Jenna Loveday had been right about the road, which zig-zagged across the peninsula from Penhallow on the east to the village of Mullion on the west. It was not a long drive, but it was certainly dusty, and as Charles drove, the Panhard trailed a long gray cloud, like a ragged scarf blowing in the wind. But there was no doubting the beauty of the vast brown moorland, empty of everything but a few dwarfed trees and the ancient stone tumuli built by some vanished civilization.

The road along which they traveled was also empty,

until, not far from Mullion, they encountered a farmer's cart, pulled by a horse which had apparently never before seen a motor car. The stone walls were built so closely on either side of the narrow road that there was no room to pull off, and Charles had to reverse the Panhard for quite a distance to find a spot where it could be stopped and the engine turned off. The horse (now blindfolded) was at last led reluctantly past, the farmer muttering imprecations into his beard and Charles wondering aloud whether bringing the motor car had been a good idea, after all.

"Of course it's a good idea," Bradford growled, climbing back into the car after cranking the engine. "The trouble is that these country folk are so bloody backward." He snorted derisively. "Did you hear what Jenna Loveday said? People complaining about noise from the wireless station!"

"The trouble is," Charles said, putting the car into gear, "that the new ways of doing things disrupt people's lives. You can't blame them for being angry."

Cornwall was the most remote corner of England—one of the reasons Marconi had chosen it, Charles knew, so that he could carry out his experiments out of the public eye. But he also knew that many of the people here still clung to their own Cornish language and spoke reminiscently of the days not long past, when Spanish and Portuguese galleons driven onto the rocks yielded a bounty of gold and goods to those who plundered the wrecks, when smugglers hauled their kegs of brandy up the rocky cliffs to be hidden away in barns and cottages. Except for fishing and mining, there had never been much industry here, and with the decline of the pilchard fishery and the closing of the tin mines, there was precious little employment to be had, except for catering to trippers and tourists.

Charles glanced at Bradford and raised his voice above

the clatter of the car, adding, "Perhaps that's what's behind the trouble at the station—some of it, anyway. People resent the disturbances."

"Well, if that's what it is," Bradford said roughly, "we'll soon put it right. These ignorant country people need to learn that they can't stand in the way of progress."

In another few minutes, they were entering Mullion Village, where they found themselves surrounded by a gaggle of shouting children and barking dogs. As they clattered along the narrow street, the doors of the houses flew open and astonished adults ran out to watch the noisy parade. Bradford shouted and brandished his stick threateningly, and Charles—stopping to keep from driving over a pair of women with baskets of laundry—thought to himself that he had been right. Bringing the car to this out-of-the-way place had been a serious mistake, for it attracted attention when he would rather have come unannounced. Better to park it somewhere and find a pony cart or a bicycle.

At last they were past the square gray stone tower of the Church of St. Mellanus and through Mullion Village. Ahead, as they looked across the windswept plateau toward the sea, they could see four tall wooden towers, odd-looking man-made intrusions. They were huge and ugly, Charles thought. He could see why the local people might not like them.

Bradford shouted over the clatter of the motor car, his voice full of pride. "Two hundred feet high, those wooden towers. We put them up after the first masts were blown over. Those trusses are built to stand up against any storm, even a hurricane. They won't come down, by damn." He pointed. "And you see that aerial wire? That's what transmits and receives the signal, eighteen hundred miles across the Atlantic. *Eighteen hundred miles,* Sheridan! Marconi's miracle, they called that first transmission, eighteen months ago. But that was just the beginning. Why, we'll be flinging signals around the globe in the next decade."

"You're sure the original masts were sabotaged?" Charles asked.

He pulled the Panhard to a stop and cut off the motor at a spot some distance from the wireless station. His ears ringing in the sudden silence, he pushed up his goggles and looked toward the transmitter building, a substantial structure of plastered brick with a roof of gray-blue slates. It had been erected in the center of a fenced compound of about an acre in size, with a wooden tower at each of the four corners. The four wooden towers, one at each corner of the compound, supported the aerial, which was connected to the transmitter building by a radiating web of wires. Not far away stood the Poldhu Hotel, an imposing gabled edifice which looked out toward the sea to the west and a golf course to the north—a challenging golf course, Charles had been told. He didn't play golf, but had heard Conan Doyle talk about its notorious twelfth hole, where the golfer had to drive his ball across a sixty-foot chasm, the white surf churning on the rocks below. A golf ball graveyard, Doyle called it.

"Of course it was sabotage," Bradford replied grimly. "Just damn lucky nobody was killed. When the masts came down, one of them barely missed George Kemp, who was working here at the time. Another inch and he would've been a dead man." He took out a cigar and lit it. "The company, of course, put it about that the damage was entirely due to the storm. They didn't want it known that we'd been the target of sabotage."

"And so it's been on the other occasions? The company covering up?"

Bradford nodded. "Accidents, they say, mishaps, mistakes,

that sort of thing. Never sabotage, for fear of the Press getting hold of the story, and the news getting to the investors. Marconi's oblivious to it all, of course. He's . . . well, he's like other inventors, I suppose. Always scheming for the next innovation, trying to make the product better. And while he spends his time on research, the directors have to keep the company afloat." His voice darkened. "It hasn't been easy, I'll tell you. This is the first year Marconi Wireless has shown a profit—although it has yet to declare a dividend."

Charles was startled. "But I thought—"

"That the investors were already getting something back?" Bradford laughed shortly. "Not bloody likely. And if you want to know the truth, even that so-called profit was produced by juggling the financial report. We've a long way to go before there's any real money to be made, with stations still to be built and equipped, and never enough cash to pay the bills. And the worst of it is that we've got to stay ahead of the pack." His face twisted and he clenched his fist. "Always ahead of the pack, which are nipping at our heels like so many mad dogs."

"There's that much rivalry, then?" Charles asked.

"And more," Bradford said grimly. "The cable telegraph companies—particularly Eastern—have fortunes at stake. Imagine the cost to lay and maintain the undersea cables around the world, all of which will be obsolete once we're in full operation."

Charles pulled his brows together. "You're right about the cost, certainly. But do you really believe that wireless will make cable obsolete?"

"Of course I do," Bradford said. "And then there are the wireless competitors. Fessenden and Tesla in America.

Popov in Russia, Ducretet in France, Slaby and d'Arco in Germany. And the Lodge-Muirhead Syndicate, of course, here in England. You no doubt saw the article in the *Pall Mall Gazette* a few months ago."

"I did," Charles said. "Something to the effect that the Lodge-Muirhead system is more reliable and less likely to suffer signal interference."

"Beastly lot of rubbish," Bradford muttered.

"As I remember it," Charles went on, "one of the cable companies had signed an agreement to use the Lodge-Muirhead equipment. There was something about a contract with the Indian government, too, wasn't there?"

"Yes, unfortunately," Bradford said bitterly. "We were after that Indian contract too, you know. I can't think it's a coincidence that Oliver Lodge is coming to the Lizard. The man has something up his sleeve. He's here to spy, I'll wager."

"I doubt that, somehow," Charles said. "Lodge is a gentleman." Still, he could understand Bradford's feelings. All this rivalry—and especially the very real threat posed by the Lodge-Muirhead Syndicate—must be giving the Marconi Company nightmares. And with the Royal visit looming, no potential source of trouble could be dismissed, no matter how far-fetched it might seem.

Bradford got out and cranked the Panhard again, and they drove down the long slope to the Poldhu Hotel, where they parked and went toward the compound. A guard opened the gate when Bradford identified himself and watched them as they walked to the transmitter building. A rusty bicycle was propped against the wall.

Bradford rapped twice on the door, then twice again, saying over his shoulder to Charles, "I'm afraid we've had to adopt Draconian measures—the guard, coded knocks, passwords—to keep the curious out. They're a bloody nuisance, and it's impossible to separate the sightseers from the spies of other companies and foreign governments."

Charles was about to ask which governments Bradford suspected, but they were interrupted by a wary voice from within. "Station's closed. Who's there?"

"Marsden. Double-ought-nine. Open up, Corey."

Double-ought-nine? Charles hid his amusement. The whole thing was beginning to feel like one of those penny-dreadfuls Kate used to write. But a man was dead, and that was nothing to smile about.

There was the sound of a bolt being slid back, and the door opened. "Glad you're here, Mr. Marsden," the man said with relief in his voice. "It's been . . . well, it's been bad, I'll tell you that. To think that Gerard is dead! Why, I just can't seem to get the fact of it into my mind. I can't—"

"Hold on, Corey," Bradford said, raising his hand to stem the flow of words. "This is Lord Charles Sheridan. He and I have come to have a look around." To Charles, he added, "Corey—Dick, is it?—is the assistant manager of the station."

"Dick, yes," the man said eagerly. He was about forty, with dark, thinning hair and a receding chin only partly masked by a straggling beard. "I've been here for nearly two years now, and—"

"Right," Bradford said. "Corey is responsible for keeping the generator going. It's a big brute of a thing, Sheridan. Thirty horsepower, capable of generating twenty-five kilowatts and some fifty thousand volts. When the thing is operating and the door's open, it can be heard for miles."

"A monster if I may say, sir." Corey took a large blue handkerchief out of his pocket and wiped his sweaty neck. "Beastly and dangerous. Oh, yes, dangerous." He replaced his handkerchief, shaking his head sadly. "I pity Gerard, poor chap, but he had nobody to blame but himself. He was usually careful, but with all the power we're generating here, it only takes one misstep to—"

"Show us around, Corey," Bradford broke in impatiently. "We'll get to Gerard in a minute."

So for the next ten minutes, Charles followed Dick Corey and Bradford around the station. It was a simple layout, clearly designed for economy and efficiency rather than attractiveness. The power room housed the large oil-fueled generator which powered the transmitting equipment. A doorway led to the transmitter room. At one end stood a rack of great boxlike Leyden jars, or condensers, which stored and stepped up the generator's electricity, next to a wooden cage housing other equipment and bearing a sign: CAUTION! VERY DANGEROUS! STAND CLEAR! The floor was covered with rubber mats designed to reduce the danger of electrical shock. On a platform at the other end of the room stood the sending and receiving tables with their various equipment.

"It's quiet enough now," Corey said, "but when the generator's running and the operator's sending, we have to wear cotton wool in our ears. Every time the key is struck, the spark is as loud as an Lee-Enfield rifle. Sounds like a company of infantry firing in a tunnel." He shook his head. "Deafening, that's what it is."

"And where did the accident take place?" Charles asked.

"Gerard's body was found over there," Corey said, pointing, "beside that bank of Leyden jars. You have to stay well clear, because the generator charges the system to fifty thousand volts, and the current will jump right out to you. A crack and a blue flash, like a bolt of lightning. That's what must have happened. Of course," he added, "I wouldn't know. I was in Helston, visiting my brother, when it happened." He shuddered. "But it's a good guess."

"Must've been like touching a trolley wire," Bradford muttered.

Charles reflected that the great disadvantage of the Marconi system was the enormous amount of electricity required, especially compared to what was needed to power the telegraph and the telephone. It sounded as if the transmitters were fire-breathing dragons, and the transmitter station a singularly hazardous place, where a man had to be constantly on his guard.

He turned to Corey. "Did anybody witness the accident?"

Corey shook his head regretfully. "All by himself he was, poor chap. The key operator was delayed coming onto his shift—we have four telegraph operators at this station, and two electricians. Eight-hour shifts for the operators, twelve-hour shifts for the electricians, twelve for Gerard and me. But there was some sort of mix-up in the scheduling, and the electrician wasn't aware that he was supposed to be on." He paused. "It's not a good idea to be in this room alone, of course. But sometimes we've no choice." He slid a deferential glance at Bradford. "Unfortunately, the company's had to reduce the staff. I'm not complaining," he added quickly. "We're doing the best we can."

Looking around, Charles could see how the accident might have happened. The building was not as well lighted as it might have been—just twin bare bulbs, hanging from the ceiling. It would be tragically easy to step off a mat, or make contact with an object carrying a heavy charge. A split-second's inattention, an instant's carelessness, even an accidental spill of water could lead to a sudden and grisly death.

"The constable's been here, I suppose," Charles remarked.

"Tom Deane, yes." Corey looked again at Bradford. "Mr. Marconi—he'll be coming? We need to get the station operating again and the work sorted out. With Mr. Gerard gone—"

"Mr. Marconi is lecturing at the Royal Institution and meeting with a group of French investors," Bradford said sourly. "He asked me to tell you that you're in charge until he gets here."

Corey's face lightened, as if this were the news he'd been waiting for. "Very good, sir," he said eagerly. "As I'm sure you'll remember, I was the man who got the towers in place and the aerial back up in time to send that first signal across the Atlantic. When Mr. Marconi thinks about it, I'm sure he'll—" He stopped, straightened, and all but clicked his heels together. "You can count on me, sir. I'll do my best for the company. My very best."

"Of course," Bradford said heartily. "That's all we can expect, you know. Your best."

"Has the inquest been scheduled?" Charles asked.

"I b'lieve it's tomorrow." Corey looked glum. "The constable can tell you. Can't see much point in an inquest, but I s'pose the rules must be followed."

"What about—" Charles looked around the room for a desk or writing table. Failing to see it, he said, "Mr. Gerard must have kept a notebook about the operation here, or a diary. Where might we find it, do you suppose?"

"A notebook?" Corey frowned. "Well, I don't—"

"He kept a detailed diary," Bradford said. "It'll be in the station office, at the Poldhu Hotel." And then his eyes widened. "Good God, the tuner! We need to locate it immediately. And the diary, too, of course. Come on." He started toward the door. "Thanks for your help, Corey," he tossed over his shoulder. "We'll talk again, as soon as more of the details are clear."

"What's this about a tuner?" Charles said as they walked toward the hotel. "Is that what Marconi was talking about yesterday? The device Admiral Fisher is coming here to see?"

"Right. It's something Gerard has been working on for the past six or eight months. I'm a dunce when it comes to the technical details of this sort of thing, so I can't tell you much, except that it's designed to reduce interference and secure messages from interception." Bradford gave Charles a sidewise glance. "And of course, it's all quite hush-hush, because Marconi hopes that the Admiralty will be interested. I don't mind telling you, we're pinning our hopes on this thing."

At the hotel, the key was obtained from the desk clerk, who took it off a numbered rack on the wall. Bradford led the way to a second-floor room. "It's impossible to hold any meetings in the transmitting station because of the noise and lack of privacy," he said as they went down the hall, "so we rented these rooms for an office and laboratory. We needed more security, too. Over there, workmen and operators and electricians are coming and going all the time. Hard to work on a secret project when you've got people looking over your shoulder." He unlocked the door.

The office was a large, well-lighted space from which the bed and other domestic furnishings had been removed. There was a roll-top desk in one corner and a conference table and several chairs in front of the windows, as well as a sideboard stocked with brandy, port, and whiskey. There were neat stacks of papers on the table, the walls were covered with maps dotted with brightly colored flags, and wooden shelves held reference volumes and boxes of spare equipment. The door to another room stood open, and

Charles could see a work table, littered with pieces of equipment, wires, and small parts—the laboratory, where Gerard had been working on his secret device. Why, Charles wondered, had the laboratory door not been kept locked?

Bradford pointed to the desk. "The diary's in the top drawer. You'll find the key in the empty inkwell."

But when Charles approached the desk, he saw that there was no need of the key. The top drawer had been pried open, apparently with a sharp instrument. He bent closer, frowning intently. The desk was old, and the thick varnish was crazed and rough, like the skin of an alligator. Not the kind of surface where one was likely to find fingerprints, unfortunately.*

He straightened and said, over his shoulder, "Look here, Marsden. The drawer's been forced."

"Forced?" Bradford looked up from the work table in the laboratory, where he seemed to be searching for something. "Let me have a look." He stopped what he was doing and came to the desk. "By Jove, you're right." His voice was heavy with unease. "Perhaps Gerard lost the key and had to pry it open. It's a red leather diary. It ought to be easy to find."

But it wasn't. After looking through the entire desk, they had to conclude that there was no diary. And a moment later, when Charles and Bradford went into the laboratory, it was equally clear that the tuner—the project Gerard had been working on for the past several months, the project the Admiralty was especially interested in—was not to be found.

Bradford's expression was grim. "This is bad," he said,

---

*Charles Sheridan's interest in the new forensic science of dactyloscopy or fingerprinting is described in *Death at Dartmoor* and *Death in Hyde Park*.

shaking his head, "*very* bad. That tuner—why, it's priceless! And the diary contains valuable proprietary information, which any of our rivals would be delighted to get his hands on. The outer door is kept locked at all times, and when the tuner was removed for testing, Gerard kept it under his tightest personal control. So what the devil did he do with it? And where is the bloody diary?"

"Perhaps," Charles said, "he didn't do anything with them."

Bradford scowled. "What's that supposed to mean?"

"That they've been stolen."

"But the door was locked," Bradford protested. "There was no sign of a forced entry."

Charles laughed shortly. "Think, man! The key was hanging in plain sight behind the hotel desk. Anyone could have taken it."

Bradford stared at him for a moment. "Hell and damnation," he said quietly.

CHAPTER SIX

(Marconi) was under tremendous commercial pressure to claim success, as this would undoubtedly push up Marconi company shares. . . . The sense of urgency was growing every day, as Marconi feared that one morning the newspapers would announce that some other "wireless wizard" had outdistanced him and stolen his thunder.

Signor Marconi's Magic Box
Gavin Weightman

"Really," said the Scarecrow, "you ought to be ashamed of your-
self for being such a humbug."
"I am—I certainly am," answered the little man sorrowfully;
"but it was the only thing I could do."

The Wizard of Oz, 1900
L. Frank Baum

Guglielmo Marconi had demonstrated what the newspapers called his "magic box" all over the world, but his favorite venue was the Royal Institution in Albemarle Street, off Piccadilly. There, he could always count on an interested and supportive audience which would hang upon his every word: amateur and professional scientists eager to learn about the latest innovation in wireless telegraphy; the informed public, which was fascinated by the rapidly changing world of communication; and a substantial number of attractive and wealthy ladies, some of whom were regular habitues. Science, it seemed, was an alluring topic, and a handsome, unmarried scientist—especially one with Marconi's fame and fortune—was a highly desirable prize.

Marconi had always had a sharp eye for the fairer sex, and he especially enjoyed it when women besieged him after his lectures, begging him to autograph their programs, clamoring for a private word. Nattily dressed and faultlessly groomed and quite the ladies' man, he occasionally asked the prettier ones out to dinner, and every now and then something interesting came of it.

Not long ago, for instance, he had become engaged to an American woman named Josephine Holman. A shipboard romance, it had been. They had been introduced on the first night out of New York and Marconi had been immediately smitten. In science, he was cool and deliberate: "I am never emotional," he said, when asked how he felt when he heard that first faint wireless signal from far across the Atlantic. But in matters of the heart, he was a passionate, impulsive lover, given to wild and all-consuming infatuations. By the time the *St. Paul* docked in Southampton, he had persuaded Josephine Holman to accept his proposal of marriage.

Marconi's prospective in-laws, however, held a privileged place in the social world of Indianapolis, Indiana, and were not enthusiastic about the prospect of their Josephine marrying an Italian, even (or perhaps especially) one who cut so dashing an international figure and who appeared so frequently in the newspapers' society pages.

And Marconi had to acknowledge his own ambivalence. He dreamt of marriage, but he knew himself to be a man easily tempted by female charms and hardly discreet in his romantic affairs. He wavered a bit too long, and Josephine broke off the engagement, remarking enigmatically, "There have been disasters on both sides." The commitment at an end, Marconi was forced to console himself with the ladies he met in London. Not a bad alternative, when he thought about it, for while Josephine's American connections would have undoubtedly benefited Marconi Wireless, the London ladies were stunning—and willing, into the bargain. What's more, they were *here,* and not in Indianapolis, which had to be admitted as a distinct advantage.

Marconi had looked forward to the Wednesday night lecture at the Royal Institution, because among the other special attendees (the French investors whom he had wooed that afternoon and who now seemed eager to consummate their affair by investing heavily in his company) he was expecting Miss Pauline Chase. He and Miss Chase had met at dinner at Lord Lonsdale's the previous week and had immediately hit it off, for she was not only exceptionally beautiful, but interested in his work and eager for his attention, a combination which never failed to excite Marconi. By the end of the evening, she was calling him "Marky" and he was calling her "Paulie," and he had been allowed to see her home. After another dinner together, he had asked her to attend his lecture at the Royal Institution and invited her to visit the Poldhu station with him. It would be an opportunity for the two of them to get better acquainted, he said, and she had agreed with a flattering enthusiasm.

But the news of Daniel Gerard's death had changed everything. Instead of being excited about tonight's lecture and the prospect of a new and stimulating love affair,

Marconi was anxious and depressed. He and Daniel had been colleagues since Marconi arrived in England in '96, and Marconi had been closer to him than to anyone else. Daniel had been there when Marconi demonstrated his apparatus to the Post Office and to the War Office in '97. He'd been Marconi's right-hand man on Salisbury Plain, and at the Bristol Channel trials, and on board the *Carlo Alberto*. He had helped to design the "jigger" which had earned Marconi his famous "four-seven" patent, and the new tuner—the device which would revolutionize wireless—was really his idea.

As head of the company, Marconi took (quite naturally, he thought) the credit for the designs and achievements of the men who worked under him. But even though he would never say so publicly, he had to admit to himself that Gerard had been his match—oh, more than his match. Marconi knew himself to be a competent inventor, tireless and extraordinarily patient when it came to details, but it was Gerard who had a truly inventive imagination, Gerard who could see what was needed and make it happen, Gerard who could take the crudest instrument and make it sing and dance and click its heels. Now Gerard was dead, and Marconi was in despair. He felt as if both his arms had been chopped off. But the show had to go on. Customers, investors, other scientists, and the public at large could not be allowed to suspect that there were any problems, or that the company might not be able to deliver what it promised.

So Marconi put aside his fears, assumed a confident bearing, and stepped through the curtains and onto the lecture platform. Seeing that the Royal Institution's lecture hall was full and noticing the French investors and the science writer from *The Times,* he felt somewhat better. Seeing Miss Chase, splendid in a garnet evening suit with an extravagant sweep of garnet ostrich feathers on her hat, a matching boa around her neck, and a delicious smile on her pouty lips, he felt even better. He made a modest bow as Professor Werthen completed the generous introduction, stepped to the podium, and signaled for the curtain, which opened to reveal his assistant, Arthur Blok, who was managing the demonstration.

Marconi was lecturing tonight on the important topic "Resonance and Tuning in Wireless Telegraphy." Everyone knew that the ability to tune a telegraphic receiver to a specific wavelength was the most urgent technical challenge facing wireless science. As long as the signal could be picked up by anyone with a receiver, wireless offered no privacy or confidentiality. This meant that the world's military and commercial enterprises, fearing that their enemies and rivals would eavesdrop on their secret communications, were reluctant to trade the privacy of cable for the convenience and low cost of wireless. And even if it were not for eavesdroppers, there was the problem of interference. As long as there were only a few stations owned and operated by Marconi, there was little chance that their signals would interfere. But wireless stations and wireless systems were proliferating, and so was interference.

The "four-seven" system which Marconi patented in 1900 and the "Maggie" he and Gerard devised in 1902 were supposed to solve the tuning problem—at least, that's what the company had been telling everybody for the past six months. Anxious about the claims being made in England by the Muirhead-Lodge Syndicate and in the United States by the De Forest Wireless Telegraph Company, the directors had decided to announce that the problem had been solved. The newspapers, always ready to trumpet Marconi's latest achievement, were already claiming that selective tuning was a reality at last.

Privately, however, Marconi knew better. The equipment they were currently using could not be reliably tuned, no matter how many claims the company made. But Gerard had been hard at work on the problem for some months. He'd got a new idea for a valve—an oscillation valve, he called it—from Thomas Edison, with whom he had worked some years before, and the device he was working on was close to completion. Then they would have a tuner that would *really* solve the interference problem, both in commercial use and in special applications for the Admiralty. In the meantime, of course, they would all go on making the usual claims.

So tonight, Marconi had to swallow his grief and pain at the loss of his friend and colleague and tell his audience that he had already done what he knew lay in the future. The demonstration was planned so that wireless messages from Poldhu, relayed via the Chelmsford Station, would be received on a Morse tickertape printer set up behind a screen at the back of the platform. As the messages came in, Arthur Blok would deliver them to the podium, where, with due ceremony, Marconi would read them aloud, demonstrating that the Marconi system could send and receive with the utmost reliability and confidentiality.

But as Arthur Blok turned on the receiver and began to adjust it, Marconi—so experienced with Morse that he could decode dots and dashes while he was speaking to an audience—heard a very different message than the one he expected. To his infinite dismay, the tickertape was printing out a rhyme:

THERE WAS A YOUNG FELLOW OF ITALY, WHO DIDDLED THE PUBLIC QUITE PRETTILY . . . This insulting bit of doggerel was repeated several times and was then followed by a single, astonishing, and emphatic word: RATS.

Marconi felt himself go cold. His knees threatened to buckle, and he had to grasp the podium with both hands to stay upright. The message—the appalling message!—was proof positive that his claim of freedom from interference was a lie. If anybody in the audience caught on to it, they would call him a fraud, and they would be right.

Fighting to keep his voice steady, Marconi continued to speak as he scanned the audience to see if the humiliating rhyme had been deciphered. The French investors, who didn't know a dot from a dash, were listening intently to his words. Miss Chase, her eyes fixed on him, her pretty lips pursed, was leaning forward as if enthralled. Everyone else was deeply engrossed in what he was saying. No one seemed to have noticed anything out of the ordinary.

But then Marconi saw someone he recognized, someone who was watching him with amused disdain written across his gaunt, triangular face. It was Nevil Maskelyne, a well-known magician who also dabbled in wireless. Catching Marconi's eye, Maskelyne raised one contemptuous finger and laid it beside his nose. Then he winked, a slow, knowing, and very deliberate wink. There was no doubt in Marconi's mind. It was Maskelyne who had arranged for the intrusive signal.

Marconi's heart sank into his shoes, but he managed to struggle through the rest of the lecture, which was blessedly uneventful. The Morse ticker clicked out the closing message from Poldhu, signing off. Marconi finished speaking, bowed, and the audience burst into enthusiastic applause—all but Maskelyne, who, much to Marconi's great relief, had already made his exit. He did not intend, apparently, to cause any trouble.

But as the applause subsided and Marconi bowed and turned away from the podium, he heard the Morse printer begin again. And this time, the message was much more ominous. *MARCONI IS DEAD,* it said. *MARCONI IS DEAD.*

Arthur Blok handed him the printer tape, his eyes round, his face gray. "Who do you think, sir?" he whispered.

"Don't speak of this to anyone," Marconi said roughly, taking the tape and stuffing it into his pocket. Then he swallowed his fear, turned on his heel, and went to greet Miss Pauline Chase, who was waiting at the foot of the stairs, her plumed hat tilted becomingly, her feather boa tossed over her shoulder.

"Oh, Marky!" she cried, taking his arm and gazing up at him adoringly, "I just ate up every word. You are exactly what the newspapers call you. The Wizard of Wireless!"

"Are you?" spoke an ironic, drawling voice, deep in the shadows behind the stairs. "Are you the Wizard of Wireless, Marky? Or perhaps we should rather call you the 'Wireless Humbug'."

Marconi whirled. "You have some cheek, Maskelyne," he growled.

"Cheek?" Maskelyne gave an unpleasant laugh. He stepped out of the shadows, carrying an ebony walking stick and wearing a top hat and a scarlet opera cape that made him look like Bram Stoker's Dracula. "Don't talk to me about cheek, Marconi. All those claims for proof against interference—they're nothing but a fraud on the public. Pure humbuggery." He laughed again. "That Morse signal didn't come from Poldhu or Chelmsford. It came from The Egyptian Hall, less than a block away, where I perform my magic shows. Your device was completely incapable of tuning it out, and you know it."

"Monkey tricks and scientific hooliganism are one thing," Marconi said low, between gritted teeth, "but a death threat's quite another. That's a police matter, you know."

Maskelyne's eyebrow went up. "Death threat? I know nothing about a death threat, old chap. You mean to say that there was *another* transmitter sending you unsolicited messages?" He barked an unpleasant laugh. "Well, I suppose that's another proof, isn't it? Your receiver is totally incapable of discriminating among transmitters. Scientific hooliganism, eh? I like that. I like it very much. You won't mind if I quote you, I hope—Marky."

Miss Chase was tugging at Marconi's arm. "A death threat?" She gave a bright, brittle laugh. "How utterly fascinating, Marky! Should I be alarmed?"

Marconi started. He had almost forgotten Miss Chase. He patted her hand. "No, don't be alarmed. It's nothing to trouble yourself about, my dear."

"Oh, indeed," Maskelyne remarked nastily. "Don't trouble yourself at all, my dear young lady. But do keep an eye on *The Times,* Marky." He grinned. "You won't want to miss my letter regarding the fun I've had at your expense tonight. Since you didn't see fit to let your audience in on the messages you were receiving on that instrument of yours, I believe I shall do just that." He tipped his hat and twirled his cape around him with a flourish. "Scientific hooliganism, eh? Yes, indeed, I shall quote you. Do watch *The Times.* I'll get the letter off tomorrow—no doubt they'll print it right away."

And *that* remark, more than the unfortunate incident, and even more than the death threat, was what ruined the rest of Marconi's evening. Not even Miss Chase's solicitous flirtations could ease his mind.

CHAPTER SEVEN

Thursday, 2 July, 1903

Piracy, privateering, smuggling, and wrecking—the pillaging of shipwrecks—were for centuries features of Cornwall's maritime life. For one thing, Cornishmen were poor, and these were principal means of employment. For another, the King's coast guards and prevention agents were often elsewhere, or part of the game, or both. Whatever the case, robbery at sea and along the shore gradually evolved from random attempts to a highly organized business, financed by prosperous merchants and the landed gentry. Many of the respectable people of the Lizard participated in the outlawry, in one way or another.

Tales of Cornwall
Lawrence Jenner

A t home, Kate was an early riser, for she always had to settle a certain number of domestic issues and matters having to do with her school. The sooner these things were out of the way, the sooner she could settle down to her writing. But here at Penhallow, with none of her regular responsibilities to meet, she slept later than usual. When she awoke, she stretched and lay still for a while, thinking about the pleasant evening she had shared with Patsy and Jenna Loveday. The three of them had found themselves to be remarkably compatible, and by the time they said good-night and went to bed, they were chattering away like old friends. It had been a long time since Kate had felt that kind of easy, enjoyable companionship with other women, and she was very glad to have found it. She thought Jenna might be glad, too, for there was no evidence that she had any other women friends.

There was a light tap at the door, and the housemaid appeared with a tray of tea and buttered toast. As the curtains were opened to let in the morning sunshine, Kate glanced out the window, half-expecting to see the little red-haired girl perched in the tree. Kate had meant to mention the child to Jenna, but by the time the tea bell had rung and Kate had gone down to the terrace, the girl had disappeared and Kate had forgotten about her. Some village child, probably, playing a woodland game.

Not a child, a fairy! Beryl Bardwell chided. *Where's your imagination, Kate? This is Cornwall, for heaven's sake. The woods must be full of fairies.*

"Always on the lookout for excitement, aren't you?" Kate muttered to herself, and picked up her teacup. Still, Beryl had a point. This was Cornwall, the mythical home of the Little People. Any novelist worth her salt would have to confess to being intrigued.

By the time Kate had dressed and gone down to the breakfast room, Patsy and Jenna were already at the table, where Patsy seemed to be regaling Jenna with a tale of life in the Arabian desert.

"Good morning, Kate," Patsy said, with a cheerful toss of her head. "You're just in time to hear all about the Arabian sheik I fell in love with in the desert. So tall and handsome." She sighed elaborately. "With the face of a god."

"And the hand of a tyrant, I don't doubt," Kate replied

practically. "Don't fall in love with a sheik, Patsy. You'd be bored to desperation by life in a harem. Nothing to do but sit with your embroidery and wait until it was your turn." As Patsy and Jenna giggled, she helped herself to bacon and eggs from the hot plates on the sideboard and sat down across from Jenna.

"You slept well, I trust," Jenna said.

"Deliciously," Kate replied. "There's certainly something to be said for taking a holiday." She glanced out the window, where the sunlit lawn sloped down toward the woodland. "Especially in such a beautiful place, and on such a beautiful morning."

Patsy began to butter her toast. "Harriet's monument has just been put up," she said in a matter-of-fact tone, "and Jenna asked me to walk to the churchyard this morning to see it. You'll join us?"

"Of course," Kate said. She was glad that Patsy had opened the subject. They hadn't spoken about Jenna's daughter the night before, but perhaps they were comfortable enough now that Jenna might be ready to talk about it.

"I'm not terribly fond of the monument," Jenna said. "My mother-in-law ordered it, and I couldn't say no. But visiting Harriet's grave is a comfort. I've somehow felt that I have abandoned her, you know." Her smile was rueful. "I know that's silly, but there it is." She glanced at Kate. "Patsy tells me that you lost a child, too, so perhaps you understand."

"I do," Kate said. She spoke truthfully. "If it hadn't been for Charles, I'm not sure how I would have survived. He couldn't have been more helpful and tender. The experience brought us together."

"You're fortunate, Kate." Jenna picked up a pitcher. "Patsy, would you like another glass of orange juice?"

Kate felt suddenly awkward, and wished she hadn't spoken. Jenna's husband was dead, and there was no one to comfort her.

Patsy held up her juice glass. "Yes, please." She gave Kate a mock frown. "If our Kate will not permit me to have my handsome sheik, I'll have to console myself somehow."

Sheltered by overhanging oaks, the small, gray stone church stood at the edge of a green meadow a half-hour's walk from Penhallow. It was very old and had been built by her family, Jenna said, on a site which had once been a place for pagan worship and ritual.

"The Tyrrills were privateers, you see," she said, with the hint of a smile. "Pirates with a fleet of small, fast ships. They moored them in Frenchman's Creek and sailed out to the Channel to prey on French and Spanish galleons. Penhallow came into their possession as part of a dowry during the reign of King James I, and the family decided to settle down." She gestured. "They built the church shortly after. I suppose they felt the need to be accepted and respectable. Or perhaps it was penance for their piracy."

The morning air was mild but still cool enough for Kate to be glad that she had worn her green shawl. The meadow was softened by wisps of silver fog, and the velvety grass was bright with early summer flowers. Jenna had brought a basket of scented roses from the manor garden to put on Harriet's grave, although the wildings at their feet, Kate thought, were just as beautiful.

They went through the gate into the churchyard. "What

a lovely spot," Patsy said. "It's so very peaceful." She glanced around. "Where—?"

"There," Jenna said, pointing to a spot near the stone wall, beside a large lilac bush. "George's mother wanted to bury her on the Loveday estate in Kent, with George. But all the Tyrrills are here, and I wouldn't have my daughter anywhere else." Her voice was firm. "This is where she belongs. Where *both* of us belong."

The small grave was covered with a thick marble slab and marked by a tall, white marble pillar which had been made to look as if it were broken off, topped by a statuesque stone angel in flowing robes, wings spread wide, arms lifted to heaven. An inscription was carved on the face of the monument:

HARRIET
Beloved Daughter of George and Jenna Tyrrill Loveday
4 February, 1893–15 February, 1903

"It's very . . . impressive," Patsy murmured. Kate thought that it was not exactly the sort of monument one might erect to a child.

"Harriet would have been amused by the angel," Jenna said dryly. "But I think a fairy would have been more to her taste." She stopped, staring down at the grass. "There," she said. "It's happened again."

"What's happened?" Kate asked.

"The flowers," Jenna replied helplessly. "I don't know where they come from, or who leaves them there. It's very strange."

Kate looked down. In the grass around the marble slab lay drifts of loose blossoms—daisies, meadow sweet, bluebells. "They're lovely," she said.

"First it was the doll," Jenna said in a troubled voice. "Lately, it's been flowers. They're always here, and always fresh, every time I come." She laughed a little. "I thought I was seeing things, but they're very real."

"The doll?" Patsy asked.

"One of Harriet's. I hadn't noticed it in the nursery for quite a time, and then—" Jenna shook her head. "Then it was here. I have no idea how."

Fairies! Beryl whispered, but Kate paid no attention to her. "Harriet's governess, perhaps," she hazarded.

"There was no governess," Jenna replied, putting the basket of roses down at the foot of the monument. "I wanted Harriet to go to the school in Helford, as I did, when I was growing up here. The teacher is a young woman, very well thought of and unusually good with the children. In another year or two, a governess, perhaps, for French and drawing—" She took a deep breath, steadying herself. "But childhood is so short, so fleeting. I wanted her to have the freedom to enjoy it."

Kate understood Jenna's feelings. She herself violently disagreed with the practice of consigning young children to nannies until the little boys were old enough to be sent off to boarding school and the girls handed over to governesses. It was ironic, she often thought, that the children of wealthy people often grew up with fewer freedoms, and certainly a narrower view of the world, than the children of their parents' servants.

"My mother-in-law didn't agree with me, of course," Jenna added. "She came last year, bringing a governess from London, but I sent her away. And she thought it was scandalous that I would let Harriet go into the woods alone. She said I was letting her run wild." She waved her hand toward the trees beyond. "But I grew up here, and I think I must have inherited some of my ancestors' adventurous spirit. My mother allowed me to explore as I liked, to learn the birds and the plants. To climb trees and play in the woods. I wanted my daughter to have that same sense of freedom." Her voice grew thin and her face twisted. "The . . . the only place she wasn't supposed to go was the creek. I don't understand why she disobeyed. Oh, God!" she cried suddenly, and buried her face in her hands. "I wish I knew what happened! What was she doing there? How did she die?"

Without a word, Patsy gathered her into her arms and held her tight, rubbing her back and whispering comforting words. Kate saw the tears streaming freely down Jenna's face and understood. If Jenna could have guessed the future, she might have been more strict, more watchful. With a cold shiver, she remembered a horrible thing which had happened when she was a child in New York, an accident which had led to the death of her best friend. Children weren't always mature enough to use their freedom wisely, and—

And then, over Patsy's shoulder, Kate saw a fair-haired, mustached young man striding around the corner of the church, dressed as if for hunting in a Harris tweed jacket and breeches, woolen stockings, shooting spats, and stout boots—but without a gun. Instead, he carried a walking stick and wore a canvas pack on his back. A pair of field glasses were slung around his neck.

"Andrew!" Kate exclaimed, astonished to see his familiar figure in such an unfamiliar place. She stepped forward and put out her hand. When he did not appear to recognize her, she added, "Kate Sheridan, Andrew. Are you here to help Charles investigate the accident at the wireless station?"

The young man took off his cap and bowed slightly. "I fear you have mistaken me, ma'am," he said in a distant tone. "My name is John Northrop." His eyes went to Jenna and then away again. He slipped off his pack, took out a leather card case, and presented Kate with a card. "I am an amateur ornithologist. I come to the Lizard frequently, to observe the birds. There are quite a few rarities here, you know."

Kate, somewhat surprised, glanced at the card, which indeed confirmed the man's identity as John Northrop, of Colchester, Essex. But she knew she was not mistaken, and Beryl knew it, too.

Why, he's no more an ornithologist than you are, Kate, she whispered excitedly. *That's Captain Kirk-Smythe!*

Andrew Kirk-Smythe had been serving as the Prince of Wales's bodyguard when Kate had first met him at a house party at Easton Lodge, an occasion indelibly marked in her memory, for it was there that Charles had proposed to her. More recently, she and Charles had encountered him again in Scotland, and had learned that he had become expert in codes and ciphers and was serving in Military Intelligence.* That Andrew was here on the Lizard, only a few miles from Marconi's wireless research station, could not be entirely coincidental, a suspicion which Beryl seemed to share.

Does he know Charles is here? she hissed in Kate's ear. *And why is he holding himself out as a birdwatcher? What's his real game?* But Beryl had a writer's imagination and was often needlessly suspicious of even the most innocent motives. Whatever Andrew's game, Kate thought, she would play

---

*These events are described in *Death at Daisy's Folly* and *Death at Glamis Castle*.

along, at least for the moment, and learn as much as she could about what he was doing.

"My apologies for mistaking you, Mr. Northrop. You reminded me of an acquaintance whom I have not seen in several years." She turned to see that Jenna was wiping her eyes with a handkerchief, and Patsy was watching curiously. "I am Lady Sheridan Sheridan, and these are my friends Lady Loveday of Penhallow and Miss Marsden."

With a murmured, "At your service, ladies," Andrew executed a bow. He straightened, replaced his cap, and turned to Kate. "An accident at the wireless station, you say, Lady Sheridan?"

"I understand that one of Marconi's assistants was electrocuted," Kate said cautiously, watching his face.

If Andrew already knew about this, he didn't reveal it. He shook his head as if in disgust. "Beastly infernal equipment, if you ask me. They say that generator produces enough electricity to run a trolley. The transmissions make a ferocious noise, too. Quite destroys the peace of the moor. I cannot but think that it is disastrous to the bird life. A Little Bustard I was keeping my eye on has quite abandoned her nest, leaving her eggs to their fate." He turned to Jenna. "Oh, I say, Lady Loveday. Do forgive my presumption, but I only just heard of your daughter's accident." He bowed again. "Please accept my condolences at your terrible loss."

"Thank you, sir," Jenna said tonelessly.

"Yes, terrible," he went on. "I go frequently to Frenchman's Creek, y'know, to monitor several nests there. The water looks serene, but it is quite treacherous, I fear." He stroked his moustache, drew down his mouth, and spoke with some warmth. "It is no place for a young child, I fear—especially as the boats come from God-knows-where. There *are* still pirates, you know."

The Andrew with whom Kate was acquainted was neither insensitive nor rude, and she was puzzled and offended by this remark. Was he baiting Jenna? No, Kate didn't think it was that, exactly, although there was something in his voice which revealed strong feeling. Perhaps Andrew was merely trying to caution Jenna, and doing it clumsily.

Kate started to speak, but Patsy interrupted her. "I cannot believe, sir," she said stiffly, "that you realize the insulting tone of your remark. It is not only rude and unnecessary, but—"

"Never mind, Patsy," Jenna said. Her face was darkly flushed. "Mr. Northrup's caution is unkind, but I fear quite accurate. The creek is treacherous. It is no place for children. My daughter was not supposed to go there. I don't know why she disobeyed." Her voice broke. "I would give anything if I could have prevented it."

"I do apologize if I have offended, Lady Loveday." There was real contrition in Andrew's voice, and although Kate could not quite make out his expression, his eyes seemed to linger on Jenna's face longer than was polite. "That was certainly not my intention, I assure you." He put out his hand and took the card he had given to Kate, which she was still holding. "I am staying at the Oysterman's Arms," he added, scribbling quickly, "should someone wish to contact me." He put his cap back on his head. "Now, if you ladies will excuse me, I will be on my way. Lady Loveday, your pardon, I implore you. I am a cad." And with that he was gone.

"Well, that is God's truth!" Patsy cried, stamping her foot. "What a rude, horrid man! And what an appalling cheek!"

Kate pocketed Andrew's card without looking at it, not

wanting to attract the others' attention. "I wonder what he meant by that remark about boats in the creek," she said, as much to herself as to the others.

Indeed, Beryl said wonderingly. *What* could *he mean? It seems such a strange thing to say. And that look he gave her. Why, it's as if he's half in love with her!*

"Birdwatchers are often rather strange, aren't they?" Jenna said, with a gesture which seemed to make light of the episode. But her voice had gone thin and reedy, and Kate heard something in it that she could not quite identify. Was it . . . was it apprehension? She looked more closely and saw that the hand that Jenna put up to brush the hair out of her eyes was trembling.

"I think it is time we started back," Patsy said cheerfully. A breeze had sprung up and the fog thickened, and she glanced at the gray sky. "Do you think it might rain? I for one am looking forward to a nice cup of tea when we return to the manor. Aren't you, Kate?"

Patsy linked her arm in Jenna's and drew her away down the path. Kate pulled her shawl more tightly around her and hurried to keep up with them. The three walked back to Penhallow in a gay and spirited conversation, avoiding any mention of Frenchman's Creek and the rude, horrid stranger they had encountered in the churchyard.

But while Kate kept up her end of the conversation, Beryl was mulling over what had just happened and wondering what sort of plot might lie behind it. Andrew Kirk-Smythe would not be here on the Lizard, in disguise, unless he had a mission of some sort. Was he on government business? Did his presence have anything to do with Charles's visit to the Lizard? Was this something Charles should know about?

And what was the reason behind Andrew's remark—

for Beryl felt sure there was one—about the boats on Frenchman's Creek? Pirates were a thing of the past, weren't they?
Or were they?

By the time Kate and Beryl got back to Penhallow and
warmed themselves with a cup of hot tea, Beryl was already
deep in an intricate plot involving a seventeenth-century
lady, a handsome, devil-may-care pirate, and a small wooden
schooner with its sails furled, riding at easy anchor in Frenchman's Creek.

CHAPTER EIGHT

"Everyone tells me exactly what they have done wrong; and that without knowing it themselves," said Mrs. Bedonebyasyou-did. "So there is no use trying to hide anything from me."

"I did not know there was any harm in it," said Tom.

"Then you know now. People continually say that to me: but I tell them, if you don't know that fire burns, that is no reason that it should not burn you. . . . The lobster did not know that there was any harm in getting into the lobster pot; but it caught him all the same."

The Water Babies, 1863
Charles Kingsley

If Kate and the others had turned as they left the church-yard, they might have seen a small red-haired girl in a blue dress and white pinafore slipping through the trees behind them. And if Beryl had seen her, she would have undoubtedly cried out, *Look, Kate! A fairy!*

But the girl, whose name was Alice, might not have been seen at all, for she was pretending that she was invisible. And perhaps she was, for she had seen everything and heard almost everything which went on in the churchyard that morning, and no one at all was the wiser. Alice had watched from the vantage point of the church belfry, where she went each day to feed the pigeons and play at being a pirate's lookout, stationed at the very top of a pitching, plunging mast, with the wavetops whipping white frothy spume in the Channel seas far below and the wind such a fine, fresh gale in her face that it nearly hurled her from her post and into the violent water, which would have been a very great adventure, Alice considered, without giving a great deal of thought to the consequences.

It had been an interesting morning even before the arrival of the grown-ups, for there had been a surprise among Alice's pigeons—a new bird, one which Alice had not seen before, although she thought she knew where it came from. Her usual flock, the ones who met her there most mornings to take the grain from her hand, were all gray-blue, with beaks like gold scimitars and feather capes of iridescent green and purple. This bird was a soft tawny brown brushed with silver, like moor grass in a December frost. Its eyes were rubies and its legs were coral and its wings had been dipped in chocolate. It refused to eat out of Alice's hand like the others, but when she scattered the grain on the dusty floor, it flapped down from its perch in the rafters and strutted, hungry and hopeful, toward the feast.

Alice crouched down, peering. To one coral leg was attached a metal band and a tiny metal canister. She took hold of the bird, which made a soft sound in its throat but did not struggle, and managed to detach the canister from the band. Then she set the bird on its feet again and pulled out a fragment of flimsy paper. Something was written on it, very small, and not in any words Alice could read, although she prided herself on being able to read very well, better than Harriet, even.

She frowned down at it impatiently. What was the use in going to all the bother of writing something if you couldn't spell a single word right? She wadded up the paper into a tight little ball and thrust it into her pocket. The bird gobbled as much grain as it could hold, and then, with a flurry of chocolate-dipped wings and a soft coo which sounded like goodbye, flew out of the belfry and away, toward Frenchman's Creek.

Alice watched the pigeon fly away, thinking about it. She kept on thinking about it until she heard voices and looked down and saw Harriet's mother and the two ladies who had arrived at Penhallow the previous afternoon. Lady Loveday was carrying her usual basket of roses, and Alice felt the way she always did when she saw Harriet's mother: desperately sad and guilty and full of regret for what had happened and for her own part in it—although, she reminded herself again, it hadn't been her fault. The whole thing had been Harriet's idea, hadn't it? and all she had done was to go along. Alice wriggled her mouth and said the sentence again, whispering it sternly to herself, "The whole thing was Harriet's idea, and all I did was to go along." But her disclaimer of responsibility did not ease her guilt, and she was sure that it wouldn't appease Mrs. Bedonebyasyoudid, a stern character in her favorite book, *The Water Babies*. Mrs. Bedonebyasyoudid knew what everyone had done before they even thought of doing it and was ready to hold them all entirely accountable.

Today, it seemed that Lady Loveday had come to show Harriet's new monument to her friends, for there she stood in the path, pointing it out. Alice's mouth curled with a cynical sort of amusement at the thought of what Harriet herself would say to that ridiculous stone angel, flinging its stone pleadings into the empty face of the sky.

Alice, like Harriet, did not believe in God, or angels, or prayers. She believed in birds on the wide, wild moor; and oak trees older than any human, even a Druid, could possibly know; and the lovely storms which raged and roared around Granny Godden's cottage in the long, black winter nights, while Alice curled up in her attic bed with a stolen stub of candle and the ragged copy of *Treasure Island* Harriet had lent her. God, Harriet had said scornfully, was only make-believe and prayers were a lot of empty words. Harriet was so positively negative that Alice had not found a reason to doubt her friend's declaration of unbelief.

Which only made it more difficult, of course. If Alice had believed in God, she might have taken some comfort from the thought that He had whisked Harriet off to the beautiful place that the vicar mumbled about in Sunday sermon, where she would no doubt discover Smutty, the dear old black cat who had died in the shed last winter and whom they had buried under the gooseberry bushes. And that ill-tempered boy who had fallen off the cliff and broke his head on the rocks—although perhaps he wouldn't go to heaven, but to the other place, for in Alice's opinion, he had been truly beastly.

As it was, there was scarcely a shred of comfort, for Alice, who was a practical child, could plainly see that even if Harriet had wanted to rise up, she would be weighted down by that wretched marble slab installed on top of her. So Alice swallowed her loss as best she could, and eased the pain a little by imagining that Harriet (like Tom the chimney sweep in *The Water Babies*), had become amphibious and lived on in the water where she had drowned. And Alice scattered blossoms on the water of Frenchman's Creek, and in the grass around Harriet's grave, and sometimes tiny shells and bird feathers, and she had even brought back the doll, although Harriet hadn't much liked it. *Treasure Island* was another matter altogether. Alice had no intention of returning *it*.

At that moment, the fair-haired man strode around the corner of the church and surprised the three ladies, to whom he was obviously a stranger. He was no stranger to Alice, of course, for she had seen him more than once down by Frenchman's Creek with his field glasses, watching the boat moored there. In fact, he had been there again yesterday, when Harriet's mother went to the boat. Alice knew this, for she had seen all three of them: the man with the field glasses, who kept himself well hidden behind the large oak tree on the other side of the creek; and Lady Loveday, who had run to climb into the boat; and the man with the white yachting cap who had put his arms around her and held her for a long time.

There were moments, like now, when Alice missed Harriet a very great deal, for she had been clever in ways that Alice was not, and immediately guessed things which Alice had to puzzle over for quite a long time. Harriet would have been able to guess in a flash why her mother's face had turned a dark, dull red when the man with the field glasses spoke to her reproachfully just now—Alice hadn't quite been able to hear what he said—and why her voice had been so thin and trembly when she replied. Harriet had known why her mother went to the boat, although when Alice asked, she had pressed her lips together in a thin line and said she didn't want to discuss it. Alice hadn't pressed, for although the two of them had shared a great many secrets, they both knew that there were some things which were too secret to be talked about. The boat, and the man in it, was certainly one of them.

After a few minutes, the fair-haired man bowed and walked on, and the three ladies began to make their way back up the path toward the manor. Alice said goodbye to the pigeons. They clucked to her softly, and ducked their gray heads, and the boldest flew down to retrieve the last bit of grain she had thrown on the floor. And then she lifted the trap door and climbed swiftly down the belfry ladder, and ran along the path, hunched nearly double, ducking behind first one headstone and then another.

For now, of course, she was no longer a lookout posted high on the mast of a pirate ship, but Jim Hawkins, trailing Ben Gunn across the empty beaches of Treasure Island.

CHAPTER NINE

Is it a fact—or have I dreamt it—that, by means of electricity, the world of matter has become a great nerve, vibrating thousands of miles in a breathless point of time?

Nathaniel Hawthorne

We had an electric phenomenon (at the Lizard station)—it was like a terrific clap of thunder over the top of the masts when every stay sparked to earth in spite of the insulated breaks. This caused the horses to stampede and the men to leave in great haste.

From the diary of George Kemp,
Marconi assistant, 9 August, 1901

Early on Thursday morning, following the hotel clerk's directions, Charles Sheridan located King's Chemist Shop on Mullion High Street, then turned and walked down a narrow alley between two white-painted buildings, and went round the back into a cobbled yard. A sign on the wall announced, in large green letters, that he had reached the office of the Devon-Cornwall Constabulary, Thomas Deane, Constable. A red bicycle with wire baskets fore and aft was leaning against the wall beneath the sign and a wire-haired terrier was sleeping beside it.

Charles rapped lightly on a half-open door. At a man's shouted "Come in!" he pushed it wide and stepped inside.

The constable's office was a small, windowless room, stone-walled and stone-floored and chilly, although the morning air was mild. The constable himself was a tall, rangy man in his mid-forties, his shirtsleeves rolled up, his blue serge uniform jacket slung over a nearby chair. With a reading glass and an air of focussed intensity, Deane was studying an Ordnance Survey map spread out on the table in front of him.

"Good morning, sir." He straightened and put down the glass. "What can I do for you?"

Charles introduced himself and explained his errand.

"Bad business, that," the constable said, shaking his head. "Very bad business." He took his jacket off the chair and motioned to Charles to be seated. "Near as I could tell, poor chap fell into the works." He shrugged into the jacket. "Got a fatal jolt of current."

"So it seems," Charles said, taking the chair. The terrier stood in the door, yawned, scratched, and came to lie down on the rug spread for him in one corner. "When is the inquest?"

The constable glanced at the clock on the wall above the terrier. "In about an hour, in the school. You'll be attending, will you?"

"Yes," Charles said. He removed his hat, put it on the floor, and took his pipe out of his jacket pocket. "I wonder—did your investigation of the accident happen to take you to the Marconi office in the Poldhu Hotel?"

"The office?" Deane rolled up the map and stood it in a corner. "Why, no. I kept to the transmitter building itself, where the accident occurred. Not much to see, of course.

The body spoke for itself, I'm afraid. One flash, and that was it. The best which can be said is that it must've been a quick death." There was a tea kettle on a gas ring on a nearby shelf, and he turned on the flame. "About the office—why do you ask?"

"Because," Charles said, taking out his pouch and filling his pipe, "Gerard's notebook can't be located—the diary in which he kept detailed notes about an experimental piece of equipment he was working on. The equipment seems to have gone missing, as well. The door to the company office does not appear forced, but the desk drawer was pried open with a sharp-pointed tool." He paused, pursing his lips. "I checked the hotel room where Gerard lived, of course. Didn't find the two items there, either."

The constable grunted. "I'll have to let the coroner know about this. You won't object to testifying at the inquest?"

"Actually," Charles said, "I would prefer not, although I am very willing to speak with the coroner privately." And in a few words, he explained why he thought it would be best if the information about the missing items was not made public.

"I can't speak for the coroner, of course," Deane replied thoughtfully, "but I have no objections. What you say makes sense." He paused. "I'm not surprised to hear of the theft. There're several who might like to steal a few of Marconi's secrets, or at the least, cause trouble at the station."

"Several, eh?" Charles lit his pipe and drew on it. "Who might you have in mind?"

The constable sat down in the chair behind his table and measured Charles with a shrewd glance. "I'm not sure why I should tell you."

Charles was silent for a moment. "Because," he said, "the intentions of these troublemakers may bear upon the security of the Royal visit."

Deane stared. "The Royal visit? *What* Royal visit?"

"Oh, then you didn't know." Charles clicked his tongue against his teeth. "I suppose the Palace intended to keep it secret for as long as possible—although that does make things more difficult for you. You'll no doubt have work to do, and the more time you have to do it in, the better."

The constable's eyes narrowed. "Which Royals? When?"

"The Prince and Princess of Wales, on 18 July. Which would be—" Charles eyed the calendar on the wall—"Saturday fortnight. They will most likely be accompanied by a delegation of important people, including Admiral Jackie Fisher. Questions of security have already come up, especially given the recent death of Mr. Gerard and these property thefts. It would be much better if the advance party knew from which quarters trouble might be expected." The Palace was not known for its forward planning and Charles was inventing this, but it sounded good, at least to his ears. He hoped the constable would be persuaded to cooperate.

It did. "I see, I see," Dean said testily. "Well, I'm certainly obliged to you for letting me know." He pushed his lips in and out, frowning. "Where were we?"

"We were discussing those who might steal secrets or cause trouble," Charles prompted.

"Ah, yes. Well, the Marconi people haven't gone out of their way to make themselves popular. The employees keep to themselves out there at the Poldhu Hotel. Oh, they may occasionally drink in one of the Mullion or Lizard pubs, but as a general rule, they have very little to do with either village, or with me. Unless there's trouble, of course."

"There *has* been trouble, I understand," Charles said. "A fair amount of it, so it seems. Two years ago, some of the guy wires were cut and the masts were blown down. Not long after, there was a fire in the generator building, and a great deal of equipment was lost. There have been several thefts, and more recently, one of the Bass Point operators was killed in a fall from the cliff."

"Nobody's reported any thefts to me," Deane put in crossly. "And Jack Gordon spent the evening drinking at the Drowned Boy, in Lizard Village. He'd had a few too many pints, and he went along the cliff path. Everybody knows it's not the safest way, even in daylight. It was moonlight, and treacherous. He took a misstep and fell."

"Witnesses?"

"None." The tea kettle had begun to hiss, and the constable got up to measure loose tea into a china pot and pour in boiling water. "You're not suggesting," he said when he turned around, "that the fellow was pushed?"

"There were no witnesses," Charles said. He paused. "No witnesses to Gerard's electrocution, either. Two recent accidents. Two dead men."

There was silence for a long moment. Deane poured tea into two chipped mugs and pushed one across the table to Charles. He sat down in his chair again, hooked his heels over the rungs, and tipped the back of the chair against the wall. "I doubt any of the local folk would be driven to murder," he remarked. "But it's fair to say that the Marconi people aren't much liked here on the Lizard."

"I thought that likely," Charles said dryly. "Can you tell me what sorts of objections have been raised against them?"

"The usual sort," the constable said, sipping his tea. "They don't hire local people, except for construction work. And when they're transmitting, their apparatus makes an ungodly racket. The discharge sounds like volleys of gunfire, and if you know Morse code, you can decipher the message by listening to the dots and dashes." He grinned crookedly.

"And it seems they can't transmit to America during the daytime, when folks are awake and going about their business. It's got to be at night, when everybody'd like to get their sleep. Something to do with the ether, apparently."

"I can see," Charles said, "why some might object."

The constable put down his cup, took a cigarette from a crumpled pack of Players, and lit it. "And, of course, there are some who worry about these mysterious waves Marconi is generating—electromagnetic waves, or whatever they're called. People can't see them, can't hear them, can't feel them, but they've been told they're there, flying through the air. Some folk have the idea that they're a kind of secret weapon. Some are afraid they're harming the animals and birds—there's quite a lot of rare fauna on the Lizard, and people worry." He pulled on his cigarette. "Might even harm humans, for all anybody knows." His glance fell on the terrier. "And dogs. Mike, here, runs to hide when they start transmitting. Worse than thunder, far as he's concerned."

Charles studied the constable. He had the feeling that Deane was the sort of even-handed, conscientious peace officer who would know every inhabitant of his district by name and be respected by all. No doubt the Lizard folk kept him informed about what was going on in the far-flung corners of his district—although, of course, it was not that large. Only four miles up to Helston, and seven over to the Helford River, and six down to Lizard Point. Small enough to be wholly known, even the out-of-the-way nooks and crannies.

"I wonder," he said, "whether you've noticed many strangers hanging about lately."

"It's summer," Deane replied with a shrug, "and there are the usual tourists and trippers. And the ferrets, of course."

"Ferrets?"

"People from the newspapers, y'know, from the cable
telegraph companies, even a few wireless inventors. They
come to find out what Marconi is doing out here, and they
don't care who they annoy." He raised an interrogative eyebrow. "Why, just yesterday, somebody drove through the
village in a motor car."

Charles drained his cup and set it down. "I've parked it,"
he said with a grin.

Deane nodded. "That's wise. A pony cart will get you
less notice." He paused. "You think it wasn't an accident,
eh? Gerard's electrocution, I mean."

"I prefer to keep an open mind on the subject," Charles
replied, "for the time being, at least." He pulled on his pipe.
"Are any of these ferrets on the Lizard at the moment? Present company excepted, of course."

The constable considered. "Some of them aren't the
Lizard at all, properly speaking. There's an aerial across
Mount's Bay, where the cable comes in from India. It's said
to've been built by the Eastern Telegraph Company, to spy
on Marconi, but it may have other purposes. For all I know,
they may be sending wireless messages themselves."

"Ah," Charles said. Yes, of course. The eastern cable came
in at Porthcurno. The cable companies themselves must
have a great deal of interest in the goings-on at the Marconi
station. They would naturally feel threatened by the recent
successes of wireless. "And ferrets on the Lizard?"

"You might have a look-in at the Housel Bay Hotel,
down at Lizard Point. A man there says he's come all the
way from America to play golf, although he's spending most
of his time nosing about the village. And I've been told of a
man calling himself a bird-watcher, lounging with his field
glasses in places where there aren't many birds worth watch-

ing. He keeps over on the east side of the Lizard, though."
Deane paused, reflecting. "And a foreign sort of chap with a
sailing yacht who comes and goes between Mullion Cove
and the Helford River. I've seen him in the pubs here."

"And that's the lot?"

"That's the lot, so far as I'm aware."

Charles stood. "I'm at the Poldhu Hotel. I'd appreciate it
if you'd get in touch if there's anything you think I should
know."

The constable nodded. "And if there's any more word of
that Royal visit . . ."

"Right," Charles said. "I'll do my best to see that you're
kept informed." He went to the door. "I'll see you at the
inquest."

CHAPTER TEN

Ah, now comes the most wonderful part of this wonderful story. Tom, when he woke, for of course he woke—children always wake after they have slept exactly as long as is good for them—found himself swimming about in the stream, being about four inches, or—that I may be accurate—3.87902 inches long and having round the parotid region of his fauces a set of external gills (I hope you understand all the big words), which he mistook for a lace frill, till he pulled at them, found he hurt himself, and made up his mind that they were part of himself, and best left alone.

In fact, the fairies had turned him into a water-baby.

The Water Babies, 1863
Charles Kingsley

Alice lived with her grandmother, who was a laundress, in a small thatched cottage on the Penhallow estate, not far from the manor house itself. She was old enough now to help with the chores around the cottage—sweeping the floor, feeding the chickens, tending the cottage garden, and every morning, milking the cow which she and her grandmother shared with the head gardener's family, who lived nearby. During the school term, Alice went to school to Miss Stewart in Helford Village, walking the little distance, only a mile or so, with Harriet and the gardener's youngest boy, or riding in the pony cart if Mr. Snood had an errand in that direction. After school, there might be a few chores to do in the cottage, but most afternoons she was free to play games with Harriet or to roam in the woods, or the two of them read out loud from Harriet's books until it was tea-time. Now it was summer, and there was more time for games and roaming through the woods. But Harriet was dead, and Alice was left, alone and lonely, to her own imag-inative dreams and devices.

Earlier that morning, she had been a pirate's lookout and Jim Hawkins; now, an hour or so later, she was Tom the grimy little chimney sweep, from *The Water Babies,* playing leapfrog over the posts (as Tom did before he became a wa-ter baby) because she had decided that she could not climb the fireplace flue (as Tom did when he was still a sweep) without knocking soot onto the fender and tracking it all over the floor and making her grandmother very angry. Alice was leapfrogging down the lane when she happened to turn and look behind her and saw, coming in her direc-tion, one of the ladies who had come to the churchyard that morning with Harriet's mother. She was the tall lady with the auburn hair, who wore a green shawl and carried herself like a queen. She was holding a letter in her hand, and Alice deduced—a word she had recently learned—that she was on her way to the post office in Helford.

"Oh, m'lady," Alice said eagerly, abandoning her leap-frogging and running out into the lane, "I'll take your letter to the post, if you'd like!" Tom the sweep ran errands for people, and occasionally earned sixpence.

"Would you?" the lady asked, looking down at her with a smile. "I'm sure you could do that, and do it very well. I would rather have the walk, though—it's such a lovely morning." She paused. "Do you think you might come along and show me the way? I'm a stranger here, you see, and all the lanes do look rather alike. Perhaps we might find a tea-shop in the village, when we get there, and have something to tide us over until lunch."

Alice nodded, forgetting that she was Tom the chimney sweep and much too dirty to go anywhere in polite company. "That would be Mrs. Skewe's tea-shop," she said authoritatively. "Mrs. Skewe makes splendid apple muffins."

"Apple muffins are *exactly* what I had in mind." The lady smiled again, and put out her hand. "I am Lady Sheridan Sheridan. What is your name?"

"Alice," Alice said, shaking the lady's hand and wondering if she should curtsey, too. But Tom wouldn't have curtsied, so she didn't. "Come on, then. We can go by the lane if you'd rather, but I know a shorter way, across the creek and through the meadow."

So it was that Kate Sheridan and the small girl—she must be nine or ten, Kate thought, with ginger-colored hair plaited in two thick braids, and ginger freckles plastered all over her plain face, and blue eyes which lit the narrow face with such a shining intelligence that its plainness was utterly transformed—went together through the meadow, and across Frenchman's Creek at a place where it became very narrow and shallow and could be crossed on flat, dry stones.

Alice, Kate decided, was the girl she had seen the afternoon before, watching from the woodland as Jenna went about her work on the terrace. She proved to be quite a remarkable child, for she knew the names of trees and flowers and plants, and pointed out spiders and lizards and birds as they went. And then, when they reached the lane (which had curled around in a great loop, and would indeed have taken them quite a distance out of their way), she pointed out the farmhouses and whitewashed cottages, and named the people who lived in them, until they were looking down from the brim of the hill at the village, which lay quiet and peaceful under the late-morning sun beside the wide Helford River, with boats pulled up on the shingle and men fishing along the shore, and not far to the south, the great, gray Channel.

In the village, Kate posted the letter she had written to Charles at the Poldhu Hotel, telling him about meeting Kirk-Smythe earlier that morning. And then she and Alice went along Orchard Lane (she took special notice of the Oysterman's Arms, where Andrew had said he was staying) and across a wooden footbridge to Mrs. Skewe's tea-shop, in the sitting room of a tiny cottage overlooking a garden full of roses and the river beyond, with just enough space for two tables and four chairs. She ordered two cups of tea and two muffins with strawberry jam, and she and Alice had a feast. And when they were finished, and Alice had licked all the strawberry jam off her fingers, Kate asked the girl if they could go to see the village school.

They walked around the schoolyard and peered through the windows into the empty schoolroom, where rows of wooden desks paraded in neat ranks in front of a chalk board. There was a piano in one corner of the room, and a shelf for books and supplies.

"This is where Harriet and I sit," Alice said, pointing. Her mouth turned down at the corners and she corrected herself. "Sat, I mean. Before."

"I see," Kate said gently. "You were a friend of Harriet's, then?"

Alice nodded and jumped down from the window, scattering a flock of sparrows.

"I was sad to hear that she drowned," Kate said. "Were you very good friends?"

"Sometimes." Alice's voice was muffled. "Most of the time. She—"

She pushed her fists into the pockets of her pinafore and kicked at a stone, and her voice became flat and hard.

"But it doesn't matter, does it? She's dead, isn't she? It was . . . it was an *accident*."

Accident. Kate heard a world of pain and loss and denial in that word, and wondered at it. She remembered, as well, the sound of Jenna Loveday's voice that morning, remembered the mother's self-reproach: "I wish I knew what happened! What was she doing there? How did she die?" And she was pulled back to something so painful to think about that she had avoided it for over twenty years, not wanting to be reminded, not wanting to remember. But she had recalled it that morning, and she recalled it again now. Perhaps it was time.

"I had a friend who died once," she said quietly. They left the schoolyard and started back up the winding lane toward the top of the hill. "I saw it happen. It was an accident, too."

There was a silence. Alice darted a look at her, then reached over a fence and yanked the blossom off a daisy. "What sort of accident?"

"We were playing," Kate said. "In a park. We weren't supposed to go there, because my friend's mother and my aunt thought it was dangerous. We were walking along the top of a stone wall."

"What happened?"

"She slipped." Kate was surprised at the sharpness of the pain, after so many years. "She fell in front of a trolley."

Alice pulled a petal out of the daisy. "What did you do?"

"The trolley stopped. A policeman came right away, and lots of grown-ups. They were all taking care of her."

Head tilted to one side, eyes narrowed, Alice regarded her. "But what did *you* do?"

It was, Kate thought, a question with remarkable moral force, a question she had lived with for almost two decades. "I did nothing." She bit her lip, remembering the helpless horror which had shrieked inside her. "I thought there was nothing I could do. Except feel responsible. And afraid, and sad."

"Well," Alice said, in a comforting tone, "It wasn't your fault." Another petal out of the daisy, another darting look. "That she fell, I mean. Unless you pushed her. You didn't, did you?"

"No. But it was because of me that she was there. Or at least, that's what I thought, then. Both of us liked the park, though—it was her idea as much as mine." It had sounded like an excuse then. It still did.

A third petal, and a fourth. "But you didn't do anything to help her."

"I didn't even tell anyone I was there and saw what happened," Kate said sadly. "That's what made me sorriest—after I thought about it, I mean. I should have told somebody. I should have told the policeman. Instead, I ran home, and acted surprised when my aunt told me about it."

The fifth petal fluttered to the ground and Alice stepped on it, hard, as if it were trying to get away. "Why didn't you tell?"

"Because I couldn't explain why we'd gone where we weren't supposed to go. Because I knew my aunt would be very angry at me and might never trust me to go out by myself again. Because . . ." Kate shrugged, not looking at Alice. "I was a coward, I suppose."

The rest of the petals flew away in a furious blizzard, and Alice tossed the plucked stem into the grass with an angry gesture. They had reached the top of the hill, and Helford Village lay behind and beneath them. "I hope you weren't sorry forever." She turned her fierce bright eyes on Kate. "*Were* you?"

"Not exactly," Kate said. "I finally told my friend's mother, you see. She was so desperately unhappy. I didn't want her to keep on thinking that her daughter had been all alone when . . . when it happened. I wanted her to know why, and how. And that it was . . . it was my fault, too. That we were there, I mean."

There was a long pause. "Were you glad you told?"

"Yes. I think she was glad, too. But I'm still sorry I didn't tell right away."

Alice pulled her brows together, as if she were trying to puzzle out a rather difficult question. And then, having apparently come to a conclusion, she said, in a careless tone, "Sometimes Harriet and I went in the woods." She picked up a rock and threw it, hard, at a fence post. "We were *secret* friends, you know. Not because her mother forbade us. Just because."

"Sometimes secret friends are best," Kate said.

Alice nodded. "She would bring her dolls to our secret place. Sometimes she helped me with my chores. Sometimes we read books."

"Oh, books!" Kate exclaimed. "What books did you read?"

"Well, there was *The Water Babies,*" Alice said, "about the boy who drowned and went to live in the sea. And *Treasure Island,* and *A Child's Garden of Verses.*" She glanced at Kate, shyly now. "Do you like books?"

"Oh, indeed I do," Kate said. "Books are my very favorite

things. Speaking of *A Child's Garden of Verses,* do you know 'From a Railway Carriage'?" She began to recite:

> *"Faster than fairies, faster than witches,*
> *bridges and houses, hedges and ditches . . ."*

"Oh, yes!" Alice windmilled her arms.

> *"Charging along like troops in a battle,"*

she cried.

> *"All through the meadows the horses and cattle:*
> *All of the sights of the hill and the plain,*
> *Fly as thick as driving rain."*

And then they recited all the rest of the poem in unison, down to the very last word. When they were finished, they went back to the beginning and did it all over again, just because the words were such fun. And then they linked hands and as they walked they recited as many of Stevenson's poems as they could remember, which proved to be nearly enough to take them most of the way back to Penhallow.

"I wonder," Kate said, when they reached the spot where she and Alice had met, "since your name is Alice, whether you have read *Alice's Adventures in Wonderland*." Kate had seen the book on a shelf at Penhallow, and felt sure that Jenna would not object to a loan. And she wanted to talk to the girl again. She was sure that Alice knew something about Harriet's death, although it might not be easy to get her to tell what it was.

"*Alice's Adventures in Wonderland!*" Alice exclaimed. Her blue eyes were very bright. "No, I haven't."

"If Lady Loveday does not object, I shall bring it to your grandmother's cottage." Kate paused. "How would tomorrow afternoon suit?"

Alice nodded wordlessly.

"Good," Kate said. "I'll see you then." She started toward the manor house, then turned and looked after the girl. Alice was skipping down the lane, chanting the first verses of Stevenson's poem "Looking-Glass River":

> *"Smooth it slides upon its travel,*
> *Here a wimple, there a gleam—*
> *O the clean gravel!*
> *O the smooth stream!*
> *Sailing blossoms, silver fishes,*
> *Paven pools as clear as air—*
> *How a child wishes*
> *To live down there!"*

"What an exceptional child," Kate murmured to herself.

A fairy child, said Beryl, with a happy sigh. *A fairy child.*

CHAPTER ELEVEN

Germany, with Professor Adolphus Slaby, was striking out on its own, endeavoring to secure a position where it could ignore the Marconi patents (and royalties). However, Slaby's devices were far from satisfactory . . . (so) Germany attempted a more direct approach. . . . Relations between Marconi and the German Reich became exceedingly cool, and the company took care not to hire Germans for fear they might be informers.

My Father, Marconi
Degna Marconi

The eerie and alarming appearance of that spark in the rural background of Mullion is something not to be forgotten. When the door of the enclosure was opened, the roar of the discharge could be heard for miles along the coast.

Recollection of Arthur Blok,
Marconi assistant

Charles spent the whole of Thursday morning with various investigative duties. After he left the constable's office, he went to find the coroner, and repeated to him what he had already told Thomas Deane. As Charles had hoped, the coroner, a largish, balding man who seemed to have a very high estimation of his own importance, took the position that there was no clear connection between the missing tuner and diary and Gerard's death.

"No need to testify," he said, with a careless wave of his hand. "The items were undoubtedly mislaid." As far as Charles was concerned, this was a good thing. Word of the thefts was bound to leak out, but the longer that could be delayed, the better.

The inquest itself was the usual presentation of known facts and the drawing of foregone conclusions. Daniel Gerard was said to have been neither mentally nor physically impaired in the days before his death, and was described as a man who normally exercised a great deal of care when he worked with the equipment. It also emerged that the neighbors were increasingly concerned by the enormous amount of electricity generated at the station. A farmer who lived a quarter mile away testified that all the metal gutters and drainpipes on his property ticked and flashed in concert with the station's transmissions, causing the coroner to shake his head and observe dryly, "How very shocking." When the spectators laughed, he gaveled them into silence, but it was clear that he was pleased at their appreciation of his wit.

Following the inquest, Charles walked to the station and spent some time questioning the station employees, one at a time. Gerard was likeable but reserved, he was told, and appeared to have no relationships outside of his professional life. The two wireless operators and the electrical engineer reported that they knew about the red leather diary, for they had seen him making notes in it, and they were aware that he and Marconi had been working on some sort of new device. But none of them seemed to know what it was, or where it was kept, and Charles did not mention that it was missing.

They had all visited the company office in the hotel at one time or another, but all denied ever having been alone there.

Concluding the station interviews, Charles talked to Dick Corey at some greater length. Corey, now the station manager, added the information that Gerard was highly demanding and not an easy man to work for, although the two of them had got on together reasonably well. As far as the diary was concerned, Corey said that it was kept in the desk drawer in the office when it was not in Gerard's possession, and that while he was aware that Gerard was working on some sort of experimental device designed to improve reception, Gerard hadn't discussed it with him. Charles had the impression that Corey's relationship with the dead man was not entirely amicable and that there might have been some competition between them, probably a natural thing in the circumstance.

In the middle of the afternoon, Charles found Bradford Marsden waiting for him, as they had arranged, in the hotel lobby.

"Well, now, Sheridan," Bradford said, greeting him, "what was concluded at the inquest this morning?"

"That Gerard's death was an accidental electrocution," Charles replied, "the result of falling into the electrical apparatus. I spoke to both the constable and the coroner privately about the thefts, and managed to keep that information from coming out at the inquest. I also spoke to the station employees, but learned nothing new. I see no indication that the death was anything other than a tragic accident—except for the thefts, of course."

"Shall we see if we can get a cup of coffee?" Bradford asked, and they started across the lobby toward the hotel bar.

"Oh, Lord Sheridan!" the hotel clerk called, from behind the desk. He raised a white envelope. "A letter for you, sir."

Charles accepted the letter and opened it as he followed Bradford. Since he had left his wife at Penhallow only the afternoon before and was expecting to see her when he returned on Friday for dinner with Sir Oliver Lodge, he was surprised and delighted when the letter proved to be from Kate. It had arrived by the late afternoon post.

"A cup of coffee," Marsden was saying to the man behind the bar. "The same for you, Sheridan?"

Charles nodded absently. He opened the envelope and scanned the brief and somewhat cryptic handwritten note.

Charles, my dear—

I thought you might like to know that I met our friend from Scotland and Easton Lodge in the Penhallow churchyard this morning, although I am sorry to say that he appeared not to recognize me. Of course, I was in the company of Patsy and Jenna Loveday, which might have had something to do with it. He says he is here on the Lizard for the birdwatching and is staying at the Oysterman's Arms in Helford.

All is well at Penhallow. Patsy sends her affection. We are looking forward to seeing you tomorrow evening.

With much love,
Kate

P.S. At the Arms, you might ask for John Northrop.

Our friend from Scotland and Easton Lodge? The man could only be Andrew Kirk-Smythe, Charles thought, as he folded the letter and went to join Bradford at the table in front of the window overlooking the sea. And Kate obviously suspected that he was up to something and was being discreet, in case her message were read by someone else.

Charles sat down where he could have a view of the ocean. John Northrup, eh? An interesting bit of intrigue. When he and Kirk-Smythe had been together in Scotland, Andrew had been working in Military Intelligence. The fact that he chose not to recognize Kate and was masquerading as a birdwatcher named John Northrup suggested that he was on some sort of intelligence mission. But what? Charles frowned. Was he after a foreign agent? That hardly seemed likely, here on the Lizard. There were certainly plenty of secret agents, as the international situation became more uneasy and unsettled, but they tended to cluster in London, where they could listen at the Government's keyholes.

The waiter appeared with cups and a silver pot. When he had poured their coffee and gone, Charles turned to Bradford. "Tell me," he said, "what kind of interest Marconi is attracting on the Continent, particularly from foreign governments."

"A very great deal, in fact," Bradford replied. "There are the Italians, of course—they turned down Marconi's wireless in the beginning, but they're making up for it now. They've contracted for installations on twenty warships. And last summer, King Victor Emmanuel loaned Marconi the *Carlo Alberto* as a floating laboratory. They sailed the ship to Russia, where the Tsar came aboard to see the apparatus. Apparently it was quite an event, flags flying, bands playing, sailors cheering. There is a great deal of Russian interest in wireless, you know—although they are at the present time primarily using Popov's system." He smiled thinly. "But Popov is second-rate. They'll come around. It's only a matter of time before they take the Marconi system."

Charles glanced out at the ocean, where a large ship was steaming across the horizon. Wireless might still be in its infancy, but it had already been of immeasurable benefit to shipping. Steamships could now communicate with one another and with the shore at distances of hundreds of miles. Wireless had saved the lives of the crew of the Goodwin Sands lightship off the coast of Dover, and no doubt it would save many more. And there was the advantage to law enforcement, as well. The summer before, two robbers were arrested in California, the police having been alerted via a wireless message sent from Catalina Island to Los Angeles, where the authorities picked them up as they left the ferry. But the greatest advantage, when the tuning problem could be solved—rather, *if* the tuning problem were solved— would no doubt be military.

"How about the Germans?" he asked. "Is the Kaiser interested?"

"Is the Kaiser interested?" Bradford repeated sarcastically. He looked over his shoulder to make sure that they were not overheard. "Bloody thieves, those Germans," he said, in a lower voice.

"So it's like that, is it?" Charles remarked with interest.

"And more," Bradford said emphatically. "You know the Kaiser."

Charles gave a dry chuckle. "I know what Bismarck said of him. 'The Kaiser is like a balloon. If you do not hold fast to the string, you never know where he will be off to.'"

"Indeed," Bradford said. "And at the moment, he's obsessed with seeing that Germany is ahead of everyone else in every new technology, whether it's weapons, warships, or communications. He's been driven wild by the idea that the Marconi wireless is more successful than the one invented by his own scientists."

"The Slaby-d'Arco system?"

Bradford nodded. "It has a limited range and is quite inferior. The Germans have installed it on a few ships—the *Deutschland,* for instance—but they've purchased Marconi equipment for other vessels, such as the *Kronprinz Wilhelm.*" He chuckled. "It infuriates Willie to have to pay for something when he thinks he should have it free."

"Didn't I read," Charles asked, frowning, "that the Germans attempted to invade a Marconi station? Not here in England, I think. In America?"

"Exactly," Bradford said. "Last summer, the Kaiser sent a naval squadron to the Newfoundland station on Glace Bay. The first day, it was the commander and thirty of his officers, demanding a look around. Vyvyan, the station manager, met them at the gate and told them he'd be glad to show them over the place, as long as they could produce a letter of authority from Marconi or the company. Of course, they didn't have one. The commander huffed and puffed and said that His Imperial Majesty would be much annoyed—as if *that* should trouble anyone!—and they went off. The next day, however, they sent in a mob of 150 sailors. They would have overrun the place if Vyvyan hadn't kept his head. He organized a defensive force of laborers to keep them out."

"And then there was something about Marconi refusing to relay messages, wasn't there? The Kaiser himself made a great deal of fuss about that, I understand."

"Right. Wilhelm's brother, who was sailing on the *Deutschland,* demanded that a Marconi operator relay a message from his Slaby transmitter, which couldn't send the distance he needed. The Marconi operator refused. The Kaiser foamed at the mouth. He called it 'deliberate sabotage,' as I remember, and there were several heated letters in the newspapers. Of course, Marconi said that it was purely a matter of technical incompatibility—"

"Was it?"

Smiling slightly, Bradford shrugged. "Of course not. But why should we relay their bloody messages? If the Germans want to use the Marconi system, they can buy Marconi equipment." He drained his coffee cup and set it down. "Now, though, they've adopted a different strategy. They've been making a lot of noise about standardizing wireless telegraphy. But any fool can see that they're only trying to steal our patents and break our monopoly." He shook his head. "It's come to such a serious point that we've had to make it a policy not to hire German wireless operators. They—"

"I say, old chap," a voice boomed, "you're Marsden, aren't you? On the Marconi Wireless board?"

Charles looked up to see a robust-looking man in tweeds coming toward the table. He had the florid complexion of an outdoorsman, bushy white eyebrows, and a stiff soldierly posture.

Bradford stood. "Bradford Marsden, at your service, sir. And who, may I ask—"

"Fitz-Bascombe. Major Robert Fitz-Bascombe," the major said briskly, lifting his walking stick in a emphatic salute. "I have the honor, sir, of serving as secretary of the Lizard Peninsula Preservation Committee."

"Preservation Committee?" Bradford pursed his lips, frowning. "I'm afraid I don't—"

"Bad show for your side, of course," the major went on, "but rather the better for ours, if y' don't mind my saying so."

"I don't quite take your point, I'm afraid," said Bradford, frowning.

"Oh, that's all right," the major replied benevolently.

"That's all right, to be sure. Best course of action, in the circumstance. Realize that the company faces a loss of revenue, but far better that, I'm sure you'll agree, than—"

"What the devil," Bradford snapped, "are you talking about?"

The major's white eyebrows came together. "Why, about the transmitter, of course. I speak for the other members of the committee when I say that we were shocked, quite shocked and saddened, to hear of the station manager's death." He sighed gustily. "Poor fellow, and such a tragedy—although electrocution is not the worst way to go. Better than being ambushed by Boers, or having one's throat slashed by—" He made a brisk clicking noise with his tongue, as if to herd himself back to his point. "Be that as it may, and forgive me for saying so, sir, but we are pleased that the transmitter has been shut off. The roar was quite deafening, you know. Left my ears ringing." And he smacked the side of his head with the heel of his hand, as if to shut off the annoying bells.

"I see." Bradford shifted from one foot to the other. "Well, I—"

"We are *most* pleased," the major repeated, and added, suggestively, "Be even more pleased when those unsightly towers are pulled down, of course."

"Pull down the towers?" Bradford was astonished. "Pull down the *towers?* Why ever should we—"

"Because there's no profit in leaving them up," the major said with great reasonableness. "They can't be of further use. Quite an eyesore, you have to admit, poking up from the downs as they do. And that aerial is a hazard to flight. Oh, yes, definitely a hazard."

"To flight!" Bradford exclaimed. "But what—"

"Sea birds," the major said sadly. "Four dead last week."

He shook his head. "And one black tern, I am sorry to say. We were all quite alarmed when Miss Truebody brought in that particular fatality. The black terns are declining rapidly, and I should be very sorry if the Marconi Company were responsible for any additional deaths."

Bradford took a deep breath. "Now see here, Major—"

"Fitz-Bascombe," the major said. "Problem's getting quite serious, y'know, with migratory season approaching. Don't want a repeat of last year. Lost a red-necked grebe, two barn owls, a yellow wagtail—"

"I don't give a damn," Bradford said fiercely, "about yellow wagtails. The transmitter is shut down temporarily while repairs are effected and we determine the cause of the accident. Transmissions will begin again as soon as possible. And the towers will stay up. Did you hear that, Major?" In a measured voice, he repeated. "The towers will stay up."

The major looked horrified. "But, my good fellow, a man has *died!* You can't intend to carry on as if nothing has happened. It's a matter of respect. It—"

"You don't go closing the roads every time some poor chap gets run down by the fish man's cart, do you?" Bradford growled. "You don't halt an invasion when the first charge fails. The Marconi Company has tens of thousands of pounds invested in this station. The directors have no intention of shutting it down."

The major pulled himself up, his white eyebrows dancing furiously. "It's not just the birds, y'know, Marsden. It's the noise. Infernal racket, bad during the day, insufferable at night. And the traffic—these roads were never made for dozens of wagons and coaches, one after the other. Why, just yesterday, there was a *motor car*. Next thing, there'll be motor lorries speeding along, no regard for horse nor man." He was warming to his subject. "And more towers, and more building, and destruction of agricultural land and the ancient monuments and the fishing industry and the social harmony of—"

"Excuse me, Major Fitz-Bascombe," said the barman tentatively, "but Mrs. Fitz-Bascombe is inquiring whether you are ready to leave. She is quite anxious to—"

"Of course, of course," muttered the major. He lowered threatening brows at Bradford. "Consider well, Marsden. The Marconi Company's present course is beastly unpopular among the residents of the Lizard. Additional provocation can only result in a dangerous escalation of sentiment and a consequent—"

"Thank you, Major Fitz-Bascombe," Bradford said with a bow. "I am deeply indebted to you for your advice. And please convey my compliments to Mrs. Fitz-Bascombe. I shall look forward to meeting her, at a more convenient time."

Charles watched as the major turned on his heel and marched out of the room. "That sounded serious, Bradford."

"Of course it did." Bradford fell into his chair, chuckling mirthlessly. "But we'll assign Major Fitz-Bascombe the duty of greeting Prince George on behalf of Mullion Village, and his wife can hand the Princess a bouquet of flowers. That will change his tune in a hurry."

"Perhaps," Charles said. "But it won't change the fundamental problem. The wider opposition, I mean."

"Perhaps not," Bradford said, "but opposing the company won't do them any good. The station is here to stay, and that's that." In a softer tone, he added, "Was that a note from Kate you were reading?"

Charles nodded. "It came by the afternoon post. You recall Andrew Kirk-Smythe, don't you? You met him at an Easton Lodge weekend, some years ago."

Bradford pondered. "With the Royal party, wasn't he? Some sort of bodyguard?"

"Yes. Kate writes that he is on the Lizard. If you should bump into him, it would be best if you did not seem to recognize him." He spread his hands. "It appears that he's here on some sort of business he doesn't want publicized."

"What sort?" Bradford asked, scowling. "If he's doing advance scouting for the Royal visit, he ought to coordinate with me."

"I don't know why he's here," Charles replied. "He's not in the same division of the government any longer, so I shouldn't think his presence has to do with the visit. I thought I would hire a cart and drive over to Helford this evening. He's staying at an inn there, Kate says. If it turns out that his business has to do with the Royals, I'll ask him to get in touch with you and fill you in on the details." He paused. "Have you heard from Marconi? When is he coming down?"

"On the late train this evening," Bradford said, adding with a grimace, "It appears that there was trouble at the lecture last night."

"Oh?" Charles frowned. "Trouble with the apparatus?"

"He didn't say. He'll tell us when he gets here, I suppose." He sighed. "He's bringing a guest, which is only going to complicate things, I'm afraid."

"One of the French investors?"

"I wish," Bradford replied with a short, hard laugh. "It's a woman. Marconi is off on another one of his damned romantic adventures." He shook his head grimly. "I hope this one is better than the last. *She* was a disaster, by God." He leaned forward on his elbows, lowering his voice and speaking confidentially. "I say, old man, you're not really going to Penhallow to have dinner with Lodge, are you?"

"Is there a reason I shouldn't?" Charles asked.

Bradford shot him a penetrating glance. "I don't suppose you've heard of the patent challenge, then." When Charles shook his head, he went on. "That patent of his, you know, is a very good one, a strong rival to Marconi's. The company's solicitors fear that when the lawsuit finally comes to court, there'll be trouble."

Charles pushed his chair back. "That has nothing to do with me, Bradford. I'm not an employee of the Marconi Company." He stood, smiling briefly. "And what's more, I must confess that I rather like Sir Oliver."

"Like him!" Bradford said in a disgusted tone. "Well, that's up to you, of course. But I'm telling you, Sheridan, his coming just now is no coincidence. Be careful what you say to him, will you? Don't give away any secrets."

"Oh, come now, Bradford," Charles said. "You know me better than that."

CHAPTER TWELVE

Sir Oliver Lodge has had a remarkable career. From 1881 to 1890, he served as Professor of Physics at University College in Liverpool, where he studied lightning, the voltaic cell and electrolysis, electromagnetic waves, and the ether, a medium permeating all space. In 1894, he became the first man to transmit a wireless signal. . . . In 1900, he accepted an appointment as the first principal of Birmingham University College.

Sir Oliver has for many years been deeply involved with the investigation of psychic phenomena, and has a deep scientific interest in communicating with the spirit world.

"Sir Oliver Lodge Knighted,"
Birmingham Gazette, December 1902

While Bradford was warning Charles against Sir Oliver Lodge, Jenna Loveday was sitting in her bedroom, reading a letter from that very same gentleman. It was only a short note expressing the hope that she was well and letting her know that he would be arriving on the three o'clock train. Enclosed with the letter was an article clipped from *Macmillan's Magazine,* with a note scribbled at the top.

"I thought perhaps you might like to read this,"

Sir Oliver had written.

"It explains in scientific terms the procedure we will be using when we attempt to contact the spirit of your sweet Harriet."

The article was captioned, "Automatic Writing Brings Word from the Other Side."

Nervously, Jenna scanned the article. It contained a description of the way the process worked: the medium seated at a table in a darkened room, a pen in her hand, writing words which came from some supernatural source. "The procedure is very like a spirit trance," the writer went on,

except that the medium conveys the message in writing. This is in fact quite helpful, according to Sir Oliver Lodge, president of the prestigious Society for Psychical Research, for the writing becomes a permanent record of the event.

Sir Oliver, indeed, is the epitome of the psychic investigator, for his well-known interest in wireless telegraphy qualifies him as an expert in messages of any sort, including those received by supernatural means, but which may, when the process is better understood, prove to be quite as natural and normal as sending and receiving a telegram.

In fact, it might be said that the medium herself — mediums are often women, who appear to be more sensitive or susceptible to spirit influences than are men—functions rather like a wireless telegraph key. She transmits words and sentences which come streaking inaudibly through the ether, her consciousness functioning as the aerial which receives and sorts out the signals which are then transcribed by her pen. These

*messages are said to come from the spirit world and convey
the sentiments of the departed, who are urgently bent on getting in touch with their loved ones.*

*These words are the proof which science requires to estab-
lish whether or not personality does indeed survive death.*

Jenna dropped the article into her lap and sat, staring out
the window. It was objective and informative and for that
she was grateful, for she had never even heard of "automatic
writing" until Sir Oliver had told her about it. She would
not have considered doing what he asked had he not been an
old friend of the family, and such a comforting presence, so
sincere in his beliefs and such a well-respected scientist that
it was hard to think ill of him in any way.

But if Sir Oliver hoped the article might ease her nervousness about the séance he planned for tomorrow night,
he was wrong. She was even more frightened than she had
been in the first place, because she understood more clearly
what this was all about and why he was so interested in her.
It was the fact that she was "susceptible to spirit influences,"
as the writer of the article delicately put it: the fact that,
ever since Harriet died, she had been having what Dr.
Michaels called "hallucinations."

Yesterday afternoon, for instance, out on the terrace, seeing to the tea, she had looked up and seen a moving shape
among the trees, a girl in a blue dress and white apron. The
sight had been all the more disturbing because it seemed so
utterly real and because she had not felt the physical sensa-
tions which usually came with her "visions": the bone-deep
chill, the dizziness and disorientation, the voices. And last
night, after she had blown out the candle and gone to bed,
she had seen a dim, translucent shape twisting through the
dark at the foot of her bed and heard a confused chorus of

urgent whispers, like a stream chattering among the rocks, just barely audible beneath the sighing of the wind outside her casement window. She had lain still, unable to move, so frightened that she could scarcely breathe, while the darkness grew icy cold, washing over her like surf freezing on rocks, drowning her in its deathly chill. At last—it seemed like an eternity—the wraith-like shape faded, the air warmed, the whispers died away. But she could not sleep, or perhaps she dared not sleep, for a very long time. And when she finally drifted off, her dreams were dark and dreadful.

Jenna did not have to be a psychic to be aware that these experiences, while they were terrifying for her, made her supremely valuable to Sir Oliver. She was someone who might be able to receive messages from the spirit world, who might be able to produce evidence of the survival of the self after death. Perhaps she should be glad that he didn't think she was losing her mind, that there was another explanation for what was happening to her. But while Sir Oliver's explanation might ease some of her anxiety, it had created a new and even more terrifying fear. What if Harriet *were* able to speak through her? Her stomach turned over and she felt sick, remembering that night, the night Harriet had drowned. What would she say? *What would she say?*

She crumpled the article into a paper ball and threw it on the floor. *No!* she cried silently. *I won't! I'll tell Sir Oliver I've changed my mind. I'll tell him that I'm ill, or that I'm too afraid. I'll tell him . . .*

She squeezed her eyes tight shut and bit her lip, and the welcome pain, the sudden, salty taste of blood pulled her back to her intention. No, she thought dully, she had to do it. She had to know whether she herself could have been the cause of her daughter's drowning. She did not want to think how painful the knowledge would be, how it would twist like a knife in the belly, gnaw like a rat at the heart. But she had to *know* it!

She opened her eyes, rose from her chair, and went to the window to look out toward the garden, where Snood was cutting back the rosebushes, the red roses Harriet had loved so dearly. Beyond the garden and the green lawn, where the wild woodland fell away to the creek, the boat lay quietly in the water, moored against the bank, under the arching trees. Tonight, after everyone else had gone to bed, she had promised to go there, so they could be together. The last time. It would be the last time, she promised herself. She would never go to him again.

But when the clock struck midnight and the house was dark and silent, and she took a light and crept down the steep path to Frenchman's Creek, the boat was gone.

CHAPTER THIRTEEN

*Transatlantic communication was possible but not reliable—
some messages were sent twenty-four times before they came
through. . . . The Marconi Company barely survived falling stock
values and sky-rocketing costs for new stations. . . . Interna-
tionally, (it) was not doing business very profitably.*

My Father, Marconi
Degna Marconi

Charles had gone off to Helford for the evening, and
Bradford decided upon an early dinner. He left a note
for Marconi at the hotel desk, and sauntered into the dining
room, glancing around. At this hour, there were only a few
diners: a couple on holiday, leaning intimately together; an
elderly gentleman with a pince-nez and a book propped under his nose; and a blond, good-looking chap with a bit of
the Nordic about him and a yachting cap hung on the back
of his chair. The couple made him think that perhaps it
would be good to ask his wife Edith to come down when all
the fuss of the Royal visit was over. Perhaps they could hire
a sailboat—an idea recommended by the sight of the

yachtsman—and go out for an afternoon on the sea. Edith would be pleased by that, he thought. And she probably deserved to see the Poldhu station, considering her contribution to the cause.

After a leisurely meal—the wine was excellent and the Poldhu Hotel chef quite good, an import from Paris, someone had said—Bradford was in a mellow mood. In search of solitude, he took himself, his cigar, and a bottle of the hotel's best port onto the terrace overlooking the water.

The terrace was not empty, however. Another man, in golfing tweeds, woolen stockings, and spats, was slouched in a chair with his pipe and a glass of whisky at his elbow. The sun was setting in a bank of burnished clouds on the western horizon, and the fellow seemed to be engrossed in the ocean view. But he looked up and squinted as Bradford took a neighboring chair and set his bottle of port on the table.

"Spectacular sight, eh?" he said. The man was dark-haired and clean-shaven, with a thin dark moustache.

"Yes," Bradford replied. "I trust you are enjoying it." He sat down.

"Oh, you bet," the man said, in that easy, familiar way of Americans. "You bet." Without getting up, he leaned over and thrust out a hand. "Bryan Fisher. Glad t'meetcha, Mr.—"

"Marsden," Bradford supplied. "Bradford Marsden. You're a golfer, I see. What do you think of the course here?"

"Haven't played it yet," Fisher replied. "Been down at the Housel Hotel for a while, and played there." He screwed up his face. "Have to say I didn't think much of that course. Greens're too rough. Chews up my game. You play?"

"Not here," Bradford said briefly.

Fisher barked a short laugh. "Well, hell. If you don't play golf, what *do* you come for? Not much else to do around here, except watch the ships go by." He squinted at Bradford. "Say, don't I recognize you? You're with that Marconi bunch, aren't you?"

"I am a director of the company, yes," Bradford acknowledged stiffly. He had never quite got used to Americans.

"Well, gee whiz!" Fisher exclaimed. "Here I am, staring straight down the old horse's mouth, so to speak. Must congratulate you, Marsden. Fine work you've been doing. Out to put those cable companies smack dab out of business, aren't you?" He gave Bradford an admiring smile. "Yep, nothing but good times ahead for Marconi, from all I read in the papers. People are crazy for wireless, especially in the good ol' U.S. of A. Nothing but wireless, wireless, wireless, everywhere you go, everybody you talk to."

"I'm glad to hear that," Bradford replied, somewhat smugly.

"But I reckon it ain't all sunshine and roses," Fisher said with a grin. "I hear you folks're having some trouble at that station of yours. People dying, transmissions shut off—what the hell's goin' on over there, anyhow?"

Bradford frowned. If there was anything he detested, it was the American habit of assuming too much familiarity. He found it presumptuous and impertinent. "One of our men did suffer an unfortunate accident, if that's what you're referring to," he said in a chilly tone.

"Unfortunate accident?" Fisher hooted, draining his glass. "I'd say! Poor devil fried himself, didn't he? Guess you need one helluva lot of juice to send those wireless signals over to the land of the free and the home of the brave." He wiggled his eyebrows. "How much voltage are you fellas puttin' out, anyway? Must have a pretty powerful electrical plant. Gosh, I sure would like to have a look at it. What say you give me the grand tour, huh? First thing tomorrow?"

"I'm sorry," Bradford said, "we do not give tours, grand

or otherwise." He began to push himself out of his chair. "Now, if you will excuse me—"

"Hey, don't let me run you off," Fisher said, rising. "I'm going upstairs to change for dinner, so you just stay and enjoy the view." He waved in the direction of the sunset. "Mighty fine show you Brits put on for us Yanks. Yep, mighty fine." And with that, he took himself off.

Bradford scowled. Damn the fellow, anyway. He settled back in his chair, poured a glass of port, and lit a cigar, trying to regain the mellow mood the encounter had entirely dispelled. It was too bad that the place attracted fellows like that, the wrong sort altogether.

One thing was certain, though—the view was splendid. The ocean was quiet, the breeze mild, the sky clear. The sun was spilling its last bright rays into a bank of burnished clouds, washing the terrace and the cliffs below with a clear, pure light. The water gleamed a deep aquamarine, and off to his left, the roof and towers of the transmitter station glowed like gold.

Gold. It was a lovely color, a significant color, Bradford thought bleakly, but hardly prophetic. He had got himself involved with Marconi in the hope—no, the expectation— of making a great deal of money, and making it very fast. And that's what should have happened, wasn't it? Commercial wireless telegraphy, after all, was the golden invention of the new century, offering a vision of infinite promise. Wireless messages were now being flashed from London to New York and from London to Paris. Soon it would be possible to send them from Paris to Capetown, Capetown to Calcutta, Calcutta to Sydney, Sydney to San Francisco—all at a fraction of the cost of cable telegraphy, and with a great deal more mobility. Ships at sea, armies at war, the Empire's business in far-flung outposts around the globe—the possibilities were endless. Why, this new communications network, which didn't have to rely on cables and wires, would make it possible to learn, instantly, that diamonds had been discovered in Kimberly, or that the wheat crop had failed in Alberta or New South Wales, or that the Mexican silver mines had been seized by revolutionaries. The advantages to commodities speculators would be enormous. And with the public imagination fired by the "wireless mania" blazing in the U.S. and British newspapers week after week, it was only a matter of time before the money started coming in.

But it hadn't happened yet. Like the other directors, Bradford had originally put some ten thousand pounds into the company, more than he had, much more than he could afford. And still it wasn't enough, and calls for more cash came regularly. The money was borrowed from his wife's fortune, of course; there was nothing left of the Marsden money when Bradford's father had died several years ago. Unfortunately, Bradford's own investments had not worked out as well as he had hoped, and certainly not as well as he pretended. The Marconi investment had to pay off, and very soon. It *had* to, or there would be hell to pay. Bankruptcy was an ominous but entirely likely prospect, and Edith would be understandably angry if he had to tell her that her money had all been lost.

The sun sank behind the clouds and the landscape turned from gold to a bleak, sober gray. Bradford finished his port and chewed on his cigar. It didn't look as if the situation would improve any time soon. Truth be told, the company's cash flooded out much faster than it trickled in. Stations had to be built and equipped, salaries had to be paid, the Chelmsford factory had to be kept producing, research and development had to continue. But the truth could *not* be told, for while the company struggled to stay afloat, it had to turn a confident face to the world, not giving any hint of the difficulties in their financial situation or in the technical problems with wireless itself.

And those problems seemed—at least to Bradford Marsden—almost insoluble. While the company had no undersea cable to maintain at enormous expense, the aerials were constantly at the mercy of the elements. Why, just three months before, in April, the Nova Scotia aerial had been brought down by an ice storm, putting an end to the news service the company had just arranged with *The Times*. Even when the system was working at its best, long-distance wireless was incredibly slow—two-and-a-half-words a minute, on average—and so garbled that the message had to be sent several times, so that one version could be used to correct the other. And there was the continued problem of interference and lack of privacy. Daniel Gerard had believed that he was close to a breakthrough on a new tuner, designed to improve reception—a device with both commercial and military applications. But now Gerard was dead, and both the tuner and his notes were gone. Everywhere, it seemed, there was disaster and defeat.

As twilight fell, Bradford, full of dejection, poured himself another glass of port.

CHAPTER FOURTEEN

Nevil Maskelyne . . . was a self-educated electrician who had been interested in wireless telegraphy since the late 1890s. His demonstration in 1899 that gunpowder could be exploded by wireless control generated widespread public interest. . . . Eventually he became a leading figure in the anti-Marconi faction . . . (and) seemed to be more involved in attacking Marconi than in developing his own practical system.

Wireless: From Marconi's
Black-Box to the Audion
Sungook Hong

It was nearly dark when Marconi and Miss Chase, who had brought an extraordinary amount of luggage, checked into the Poldhu Hotel. The clerk handed a note across the counter. Marconi read it and turned to his companion.

"Go on upstairs and change for dinner, Paulie," he said. "There's a fellow I need to see. I'll be on the terrace. Come out when you're ready, my dear."

Miss Chase nodded sweetly and with one last, flirtatious glance over her fur-clad shoulder, followed her luggage upstairs. Marconi watched her tiny waist and provocatively swaying hips with a mixture of anticipation and apprehension. Of course, he was delighted that Paulie was here. She was a dear, sweet girl who held nothing back, who petted and praised him very agreeably, and their relationship was blossoming in a swift and utterly satisfactory way, and held the promise of leading on to even greater satisfactions.

On the other hand, he was not expecting this trip to the Lizard to be a comfortable or easy one. There were too many unpleasant things going on. He found himself wishing that the two of them might have gone off to some private place, where no company business could interrupt their pursuit of the pleasures of love—chaste love, of course, for Marconi would never stoop to take advantage of a lady. So far, at least, it had been enough for him to woo with words and passionate kisses, although he had to admit that Paulie's deliciously rounded figure was a strong temptation.

With a sigh, he looked down at the note in his hand and went off in the direction of the hotel terrace, where he found Bradford Marsden, a cigar in his hand and an empty glass at his elbow, staring out at the darkening sea.

"Hello, Marsden," he said, without a great deal of enthusiasm.

Marsden looked up. "Hello, Marconi. When did you get in?"

"Just now." Bone-weary, Marconi sank into a chair. It had been a long and troubling day, and his new patent-leather boots hurt his feet. "Miss Chase—Pauline, the lady I've brought with me—is dressing for dinner. Will you join us?"

"Thank you, but I've eaten," Marsden said, adding sardonically, "I'll leave you two lovebirds to your culinary pleasures." He held up the port, raised his eyebrow, and when Marconi shook his head, refilled his empty glass. Then, with the air of a man who wanted to get right down to business, he said, "I got your wire about the problem at the lecture last night. What happened?"

Marconi sighed heavily. "The worst possible thing. Interference, from Nevil Maskelyne."

"Maskelyne!" Marsden exclaimed, scowling. "Why, he's not a serious contender."

True enough, as Marconi well knew. There were serious contenders in England—Oliver Lodge, for one, who (if he were not wasting his time with spiritualist pursuits) could be a serious danger to the company, especially if he made good his threat to sue over that patent. Maskelyne, whose wireless apparatus was incapable of transmitting any great distance, was only a minor nuisance, but certainly an irritating one.

"Of course he's not a serious contender," Marconi said. "But he's a troublemaker of the first class. He set up his transmitter at The Egyptian and got someone to send a message during the lecture last night. The receiver on the platform picked it up."

Marsden stared at him blankly. "A message? What message?"

With a great deal of bitterness, Marconi recited the absurd little ditty. " 'There was a young fellow of Italy, who diddled the public quite prettily.' " He paused, feeling himself flush. "It was repeated a time or two, and followed by the word 'rats.' "

"Rats!" Marsden was incredulous. *"Rats?"*

"I gather that it is some sort of pejorative British slang," Marconi said. "Implying scornful incredulity." He chewed on his lip.

"Diddled the public," Marsden muttered. "Diddled the

public!" He puffed out his cheeks. "Damn. I hope the audience didn't—"

"No." Marconi shook his head emphatically. "I continued with the lecture, and no one seemed to notice anything out of the ordinary. Maskelyne himself did not speak—until after the lecture, that is. At the time, only Arthur Blok and I were aware of what was happening."

"Well, we can be grateful for that much," Marsden said, relief evident in his voice. He puffed on his cigar. "No one knows what happened, so there's nothing to worry about."

Marconi cleared his throat. "Unfortunately, that's not quite true. Maskelyne told me after the lecture he planned to get a letter off to *The Times* this morning, reporting the affair. They'll print it, no doubt, as soon as they receive it, perhaps in tomorrow's newspaper."

"Damn!" Marsden exploded. "*The Times!* What abominable cheek that man has!"

"Right." Marconi sighed again. "But that's not the whole of it, Marsden." He reached into his coat pocket and pulled out a length of printer tape. "As Blok was packing up the equipment, another message came in."

"From Maskelyne's transmitter?"

"He says not."

"What was the message?"

"It says—" Marconi smoothed out the crumpled tape. " 'Marconi is dead.' " He paused, staring down at the horrifying dots and dashes. "Do you think we ought to go to the police?"

"The police!" Marsden's jaw tightened. "Absolutely not! If the police are involved, there'll be no keeping the story out of the newspapers. And we can't afford publicity of that sort, as you are very well aware. One word of a death threat against you and the company stock will fall straight through the floor. No police. I'll ask Sheridan to look into the matter for us, though. He'll find out who's behind it, I'm sure." He scowled. "You're sure it isn't Maskelyne's work?"

"He denied it. And it doesn't seem like him, somehow. He's an irritant, but I don't know why he'd threaten my life." Marconi frowned uncertainly. "Are you confident in Sheridan? I have no doubt about the man's abilities, of course. It's just that I'm not sure he can be fully trusted. He's . . . well, if he got to poking around—"

He broke off, not wanting to say what he was thinking. Charles Sheridan was enough of a scientist and telegrapher to be able to make sense of what he saw. If he became aware of the significant gap between the Marconi Company's claims for their equipment and the unhappy truth of the matter, he might—

"Let's hope he does find out the truth," Marsden said darkly. "The truth of that death threat, that is." He tossed off the rest of his port. "There's worse news here, I'm sorry to say. The device Gerard was working on—it's gone. And so are his notes."

"Gone!" Marconi cried in disbelief, springing to his feet. "But that's not possible! It . . . it can't be!" And then, as the truth sank in, his disbelief turned to despair. "Someone's stolen it, Marsden. We've got to find it! Admiral Fisher is coming to see it, especially—and the Prince, as well! If a competitor got his hands on it, it would be like . . . like stumbling onto a gold mine." He shuddered. "Where can it be? *Where?*"

"How should I know?" Marsden asked huffily. "The office door does not appear to have been forced, but some sort of sharp instrument was used to pry open the desk drawer where he kept his diary."

"Oh, God." A sense of utter hopelessness washing over him, Marconi dropped his head into his hands. "Gerard was so close to a solution. And with his notes . . . with his notes, anyone could replicate all our experiments!" He suppressed a wild groan. "It had to have been taken by someone who wants to pirate our work!"

"That idea did just occur to me," Marsden said dryly. He stubbed out his cigar and stood. "And if that's the case, it would rather seem that Gerard's death was not an accident, wouldn't you say?"

Marconi felt as if his legs would not support him, and he dropped back into the chair. "Not an accident!" he whispered. "You mean, someone deliberately—"

"I don't know," Marsden said. "The inquest was held this morning, so at least we're past that hurdle. No one at the station or in the village seems to suspect that it was anything but a fatal accident. But Sheridan is continuing to look into the matter. He—" He stopped.

Marconi looked around, his attention caught by the seductive scent of perfume. Miss Chase stood in the open French doors, wearing an elegant gold evening dress, daringly décolleté, with a double string of pearls and elbow-length ivory kid gloves, neatly buttoned. The light behind her made a halo of her fair hair.

"Ah, Paulie, my darling," Marconi said distractedly, rising to his feet and wincing at the pain of pinched toes. "I didn't expect you so soon."

"I rushed to change," she said, "because I didn't want to waste a minute of our precious time together. I—"

She caught sight of Marsden and stopped suddenly. Marconi saw her eyes widen, the color flame in her cheeks, and a look he could not read cross her face. But in another half-instant, she had recovered herself. Marconi was about to introduce Marsden to her, but she intervened, stepping forward and extending her gloved hand with a bright smile.

"Why, Mr. Marsden!" she exclaimed brightly. "I was not expecting to encounter you here. What a *delightful* surprise!"

"Indeed, Miss Chase," Marsden murmured, bowing over her hand. "I am . . . astonished to see you here."

Marconi stiffened, an instinctive jealousy—a legacy from his passionate Italian forefathers—rising in him like hot lava. "I had no idea, Marsden, that you and Miss Chase knew one another."

"Oh, not well," Miss Chase said, coming close and tucking her hand into Marconi's arm. "It was rather a long time ago, some years, in fact. In Paris, I believe."

"Paris?" Marsden seemed to reflect. "Yes, it might have been. And then there was Vienna, was there not?"

Paris *and* Vienna? Marconi was not pleased.

Miss Chase frowned and touched the pearls at her throat. "Vienna? I'm afraid I don't recall—"

"Yes," Marsden said decidedly, "we met again in Vienna. I'm sure of it."

"Oh, well, perhaps." Miss Chase tossed her head. "One travels to so many places and does so many things. One does tend to forget, I'm afraid."

"Some things, my dear Miss Chase," Marsden murmured, "one can never forget."

Marconi knew very well that something was going on here, but he did not have a clue as to what it was. He felt as if he were witness to a tennis match, the ball being served and returned and returned again, harder. He frowned as Miss Chase broke into a light, animated laugh.

"Why, what a wonderful compliment, Mr. Marsden!" she exclaimed. "Marky, isn't that a delightful compliment?" She pouted a little, very prettily. "Now, my dear, do you suppose we could claim our table? I am most *frightfully* hungry. I'm sure I haven't eaten for . . . oh, several weeks, at least!"

"Of course," Marconi said, and nodded to Marsden. Then he followed Miss Chase as the maitre d' led them to their table, walking carefully, so as to keep his boots from pinching.

CHAPTER FIFTEEN

The district constable was an essential and valuable part of village life, the eyes and ears of all the people. He generally knew everyone in all the villages in his district and in the countryside roundabout. He knew what was happening, and why, and how, and who was involved, and his thoughtful observations and quiet interventions often made stronger action unnecessary.

"The Local Constabulary in Nineteenth-Century England,"
Clyde Sanderson

In all of Thomas Deane's ten years as the Mullion constable, he had never seen such a fortnight for trouble. Jack Gordon had gone over the cliff down at the toe of the Lizard, and Daniel Gerard had fallen into the electrical works at the Poldhu station. Then there was that disturbing business about the thefts Lord Charles had mentioned and the worse news about the Royals coming, which might polish Mullion's pride but cause everyone concerned a great lot of trouble. And even the usual village affairs had been unusually bothersome: Mrs. Morgan's cow broke into Mrs. Pearson's garden and ate all the rutabagas; Mr. King's new bicycle was pinched by the butcher's lad and ridden to Helston, where it turned up at the railway station with both tyres flat; and there had been another bad row at the Boden place, old Boden drunk as a lord and taking his fists to his youngest son. All things considered, the constable had been a busy man. He had earned an evening at home with his wife Molly and their children.

But Thomas Deane knew his duty, and even though it was not required, he usually stopped in at one or more of Mullion's pubs and inns after dinner, just for a bit of a listen. Tonight he went up the street to The Pelican Inn, which sported a painted sign above the bar:

> THE PELICAN IT STANDS UPON A HILL.
> YOU KNOW IT IS THE PELICAN,
> BY ITS ENORMOUS BILL.

There were no hills in Mullion, but Deane did not doubt the second part of the ditty, especially these days. Derek Faull, the owner, was known for his hospitality, and Mrs. Faull for her savory eel pie, and the Pelican had been the place to stay—until the Marconi Company came along, that is, and the new hotel was built on Poldhu Bay. The Marconi people and the tourists found the Poldhu and its Parisian chef much more to their taste, and as custom fell off, Faull had been forced to raise his prices for food and drink. It was, Deane thought sourly, just another example of the short-shrift and no-favor which the village folk had got from the influx of outlanders.

Still, The Pelican was full tonight. Deane took his half-pint to his place at the far end of the bar, greeting men as he went in the colloquial mix of Cornish and English which was Mullion's work-a-day idiom. From his stool, he surveyed the crowd, the usual gang of fishermen, farmers, laborers, tradesmen, and transients. Jim Barrie, the black-smith, had already had too much to drink—Mrs. Barrie, a proper scold, would be at the door in a few minutes to fetch him. Patrick Mora, the best dartsman in the village, was winning the weekly tournament, and would soon have half poor Mitchell's wages and a fair share of every-one else's. The birdwatcher who was staying at the Oyster-man in Helford was sitting all alone in a corner. Faull was serving behind the bar, one of the Faull daughters was washing up the glasses in the corner sink, and Mrs. Faull was bringing out another tray of pies. And at a nearby table—

With a frown, the constable focussed on the two men, their shoulders hunched over empty mugs of ale. One of the men was Dick Corey, from the wireless station, who had tes-tified at the inquest that morning that he had worked closely with Daniel Gerard and was now the station man-ager. It was a bit of a surprise to see him here, since the Mar-coni men mostly kept to themselves out at Poldhu.

The other man? The constable regarded him thought-fully. It was the foreign chap, the sailor, whom he'd seen several times in the Mullion pubs, and who seemed to spend some of his time on this side of the Lizard, some on the other. He had mentioned the fellow to Sheridan that morn-ing, when he'd been asked about strangers. Tall and broad-shouldered, blond hair, skin tanned leathery by sun and wind. He had the look of a Swede or a Dane, the constable thought. Again, he was not the usual sort who frequented The Pelican. He stood out just enough to be noticed.

And while Deane was noticing the pair, he noticed some-thing else. He saw the blond man fold some money in his hand and pass it, under the table, to Corey, who took it without looking and thrust it into his coat pocket. They exchanged a few more words, seemed to laugh together at some joke, and then the blond man stood, nodded to his companion, and left. A moment later, Corey left as well.

Out of curiosity, the constable followed him as far as the edge of the village, where the path to the transmitter station and the Poldhu Hotel slanted off across the moor. The moon had risen, and there was just enough light so that he could watch Dick Corey, his hands in his pockets, his head down, trudging through the quiet night.

Deane watched him out of sight, thinking. He had the feeling that he had witnessed something important. It was certainly something that Lord Charles ought to know about. He would look him up tomorrow.

The constable turned and headed for home and Molly.

CHAPTER SIXTEEN

Friday, 3 July, 1903

The Lizard peninsula is well known for its wildlife, especially the many rare birds which inhabit the moors and sea cliffs. The area is particularly rewarding for the serious ornithologist, as there are many bird species—residents, summer visitors, and migrants. Among these are birds which are rarely seen elsewhere in England, such as the Little Bustard, Hume's Leaf Warbler, and the Red-eyed Vireo.

Cornwall Handbook, 1899

After his meeting with the woman calling herself Pauline Chase, Bradford Marsden had spent a very uneasy night. She was not Pauline Chase—more precisely, that was not the name she was using when they were acquainted, some two or three years before. Then, she had been Millicent Mitford, a young woman of substantial means (or so it had appeared), indulging herself in the frivolous pleasures of Parisian night life. Their acquaintance had been brief but intimate and entirely satisfying, at least to Bradford, and, he had reason to believe, to Miss Mitford, as well. That it had not continued had been due solely to Bradford's impending marriage to the lovely and well-connected Miss Edith Hill.

In fact, the relationship might have continued even past his wedding day had it not been for the fact that Bradford had lost touch with the lady. And when he did encounter her again—in Vienna, this time—she was no longer Millicent Mitford, but Francine Sterne, travelling in the company of a very rich American gentleman who was identified to Bradford as Oscar C. Sterne, Miss Sterne's uncle. Bradford obliquely acknowledged their previous acquaintance when they met at a salon, but did not mention the details to Mr. Sterne, or express his concern about the change in Miss Sterne's name and circumstances. He felt rather sorry for that omission when he discovered, some while later, that the poor fellow had died most unexpectedly. Some said it had come about from natural causes, while some were of the opinion that he might have been poisoned. Of Miss Sterne's whereabouts, and the whereabouts of Mr. Sterne's valuable financial assets, no one seemed certain.

These were the worries clouding Bradford's mind on Friday morning as he took his usual brisk before-breakfast walk. He was bound toward Polbream Point, some little way south along the Angrouse cliff path. To his right, the ocean offered a spectacular view, the cliff dropping dizzily into piles of jagged rocks below, where silver surf foamed in great shoals of lather. Sea birds dallied and danced on empty air, while beneath them, the sea shaded from aquamarine to lapis lazuli, the surface lolling in lazy, voluptuous movements, seductive, deceptive, deadly.

Seductive, deceptive, deadly. Exactly the words Bradford would use to describe Pauline Chase, and Millicent Mitford, and Francine Sterne. There was no doubt about it: whether she was out for money or simply for the glamour of being noticed by the world-famous inventor, the woman was dangerous. And if her behavior with the unfortunate Mr. Sterne offered any clue, things might be worse than that. The man was dead, and there were rumors.

But what the devil am I to do? Bradford wondered. Tell Marconi that he's being deceived by a beautiful woman pretending to be someone she's not, a woman with, to put it quite mildly, an unsavory past? That Pauline, or Millicent, or whoever she is had been involved with numerous men, and that, whatever her motive, it was very doubtful that she had his best interests at heart? That was how he should handle the situation, Bradford knew: Tell Marconi everything and dispatch the dangerous and deadly Miss Chase back to London on the earliest train.

The trouble was that it wouldn't work.

Bradford kicked at a rock in the path. Marconi might be a level-headed inventor and an astute businessman, but when it came to women, he was a naïve, addle-brained romantic who flung himself heart-first into one foolish infatuation after another—even going so far as to propose to women whom he had known for only a few days. Worse yet, there was simply no reasoning with the fellow when he was in such an absurd state. Marconi had been known to smash his instruments when they did not work to suit him; if Bradford tried to warn him about Miss Chase, he was certain to explode in a tantrum or dive into a bottomless funk. And either reaction would be disastrous, especially with all the problems facing them. There was the threat of Maskelyne's letter to *The Times,* which was bound to generate a great deal of negative publicity. And the appalling business of Gerard's death, and the missing tuner and diary, which might at this very moment be in the hands of a competitor. And the Royals and Admiral Fisher due to arrive in a fortnight's time, the Prince and the Admiral expecting to see some sort of innovative device. Bradford couldn't afford to be distracted by one of Marconi's mercurial moods. There was too much delicate work to be done, too much—

"Mr. Marsden! Mr. Marsden, yoo-hoo!" A woman's high, brittle voice penetrated his thoughts, and he turned, guiltily aware that she must have been hailing him for some time. "Oh, I *say,* sir! Mr. Marsden!"

Marching toward him was an apparition: a woman of substantial bulk, military bearing, and an air of indisputable authority which would have struck fear into the heart of even the most battle-hardened Boer. She wore a black coat and a black hat the size of a manhole cover. She was armed with a black umbrella and wore a pair of large binoculars slung round her neck.

"Yes?" Bradford snatched off his hat. The woman reminded him of a nanny under whose rule he had suffered as a small child, and a feeling of cold terror congealed in his gut, as if he were eight years old again. "What might I do for you, Mrs.—"

"*Miss* Truebody," the apparition pronounced emphatically. "I have been looking all over for you, Mr. Marsden, and I am very glad to find you *at last.*" The latter two words were delivered with an icy intonation which clearly implied that Bradford, heathen child that he was and disgracefully delinquent, had failed once more to do as he had been told.

"Quite," Bradford said uneasily. "I am very sorry, I'm sure. How may I—"

"You may see to it, young man," she snapped, "that those dreadful telegraphic transmissions remain silent—forever. The wretched noise of those infernal electrical explosions has quite interrupted the nesting cycle of several of our important birds, most notably, that of the red-eyed vireo. Two nests have been abandoned, abandoned utterly. Two!" She gave him a look of dark accusation which let him know that he and he alone was the cause of this lamentable maternal defection. "And what is more, those of us who pursue the peace and quiet of the moor now find it . . . ." She closed her eyes and heaved a shuddering sigh of earthquake magnitude. "We find it quite impossible to enjoy the out-of-doors as we are wont to do." She opened her eyes once more and gave him a narrow, accusing look. "And it is all the fault of the Marconi Company. Your telegraphic transmissions must be *permanently* discontinued, or there will be unspeakable, irrevocable, and intolerable consequences to the wildlife of the Lizard."

Bradford flinched. "I'm . . . sorry," he said. It was the best he could do, but the words sounded banal and inane, even to him, and he knew that they must mortally offend her.

They did.

"Sorry?" Miss Truebody rose on the tips of her toes, as if she were preparing to ascend into the heavens. Her eyes flashed and her voice lifted. She reminded Bradford of an operatic soprano tuning up to sing the role of Queen of the Night. "You are . . . *sorry?*"

"Well, yes. I sincerely apologize for any . . . inconvenience we may have inadvertently caused the . . . er, red-eyed vireo." Bradford took a deep breath. Really, it was absurd to permit himself to be intimidated by this old harridan. He hardened his voice. "However, I must tell you that the transmissions are to be resumed this morning. It has been judged—"

"Resumed?" A look of pure horror suffused Miss Truebody's face, her gloved hand went to her bosom, and her high voice went up yet another octave. Mozart would have been amazed.

"*Resumed?* Young man, you cannot. You *cannot!* It is

entirely out of the question!" She thrust her umbrella at him as if it were a rapier, and he backed up hastily. "The Marconi Company have got to go. The good people of Mullion can no longer tolerate—"

"Ah, Mr. Marsden!"

It was the voice of another apparition, flying at him from the opposite direction, arms spread, flowered hat bobbing, scarves and veils fluttering. Bradford shut his eyes, hoping that he might be hallucinating, but when he opened them, the thing was standing directly in front of him, hands on hips. She was neither as tall nor as broad as Miss True-body—in fact, she barely came up to Bradford's chin—but she, too, wore an indomitable look, and Bradford braced himself.

"I am Mrs. Fitz-Bascombe, Mr. Marsden." Her voice was shrill and strident. "My husband met you yesterday, at the hotel."

"Oh, ah, yes," Bradford said feebly. He put out his hand. "Honored, to be sure, Mrs. Fitz-Bascombe."

Miss Truebody lifted her chin. "I was informing Mr. Marsden," she began in a chilly tone, emphasizing her words with thrusts of her umbrella, "that the citizens of Mullion can no longer tolerate the presence of the Marconi Company. It—"

"Of course, Agatha." Mrs. Fitz-Bascombe gave an impatient wave of her hand, as if she were brushing away a fly. "However, I do not believe that you have heard the latest news."

"Not another abandoned nest!" Miss Truebody cried violently. "I could not tolerate another abandoned—"

"Oh, no, no, no," Mrs. Fitz-Bascombe said. "Oh, nothing like that. Nothing like that at *all,* Miss Truebody!" She inclined her head to Bradford. "Mr. Marsden, speaking on behalf of the Lizard Peninsula Preservation Committee, I can only say that we are honored, deeply honored, that you and Mr. Marconi have so generously arranged for there to be a—"

Miss Truebody stamped one black-booted foot. "What on earth are you babbling on about, Claudia? You cannot possibly—"

"Deeply honored," repeated Mrs. Fitz-Bascombe, with a dark look at Miss Truebody. She turned back to Bradford. "I should very much like to be the first, Mr. Marsden, to extend to you my most heartfelt wish to be of service. And I know that I speak for every member of our committee when I extend their wishes, as well. We shall be delighted to—"

"Claudia!" cried Miss Truebody, her bosom heaving dangerously. "What are you *saying,* Claudia?"

"Agatha," replied Mrs. Fitz-Bascombe, bending forward at the waist and giving Miss Truebody a very severe look, "you have undoubtedly *not* heard the news."

"News?" Miss Truebody asked. "What news?"

Mrs. Fitz-Bascombe pulled herself up to her full height. "That, in only a fortnight's time, our fair little village is to be favored by a visit from . . ." she paused for dramatic effect, and concluded, with a flourish, "from the Prince of Wales!"

"The Prince—" Miss Truebody swallowed.

"Indeed," said Mrs. Fitz-Bascombe smugly. "*And* the Princess. *And* a full entourage of dignitaries, including Admiral Fisher." She beamed. "And it is all on account of the Marconi Company, and Mr. Marsden. Is that not so, sir?"

Bradford was swept by a sudden wave of relief. "Indeed, ladies, I am delighted to confirm that this is the case. Their Highnesses will be arriving Saturday fortnight to tour the station and observe the Lizard transmitter in full operation.

I am not yet privy to the details of the delegation, but I can assure you that—"

"Flowers," said Miss Truebody, with great presence of mind. "There must be flowers, of course. I shall be glad to mobilize the Garden Club, Claudia."

"And bunting," said Mrs. Fitz-Bascombe, opening her purse and taking out a small notebook and pencil. "Flags, to be sure, and a red carpet. And the children." She scribbled busily. "The children shall sing. Miss Lewis will organize a chorus."

"A parade," said Miss Truebody, pursing her lips.

"Luncheon on the hotel terrace, in view of the sea."

"High tea at the vicarage."

"A tour of St. Mellanus Church."

Bradford replaced his hat. "You ladies obviously have a great deal to do. If you will excuse me—"

They did not even notice when he stepped past Miss Truebody and started back to the hotel, walking very fast.

CHAPTER SEVENTEEN

What is the life of man! Is it not to shift from side to side?—from sorrow to sorrow?—to button up one cause of vexation!—and unbutton another!

The Life and Opinions of Tristram Shandy, Gentleman, 1761
Laurence Sterne

Charles Sheridan was halfway through his breakfast when Bradford Marsden came into the hotel dining room, red-faced and huffing, as if the devil were at his heels. Charles gestured to a chair.

"Good morning, Bradford," he said amiably. "Breakfast?"

"Thank you, old chap," Bradford said. He signaled the waiter to pour a cup of coffee, then went to the sideboard and came back with a plate of kippers, scrambled eggs, and toast. "What a vexation!" he said as he sat down. He told Charles about his encounter with Miss Truebody and Mrs. Fitz-Bascombe. "Not the way one would like to begin one's morning," he concluded disgustedly.

Charles sat back with a laugh. "It had not occurred to me that the Royal visit might help you out of a sticky wicket."

Bradford growled something Charles didn't quite catch. He laughed again, and added, "Well, at least the prospect of Royals will keep the village ladies busy. And it sounds as if the event is momentous enough to change their opinions about the Marconi Company. Temporarily, at least."

There was another growl, and then Bradford asked: "Did you locate your friend last night?"

Charles shook his head and pushed his empty plate away. "I drove over to Helford, to the inn where he is staying, but he wasn't there. The innkeeper said he often spends the night on the moor, birdwatching."

Missing Kirk-Smythe had been a disappointment, for Charles was deeply curious about his errand on the Lizard. But he had left a note, and presumably Kirk-Smythe—or John Northrup, as he was calling himself—would get in touch with him if the need were urgent. But the drive, only seven miles or so, had been quite pleasant, and Helford Village had offered its compensations. Charles had spent an hour or two in the pub and had come away with the interesting observation that, even in Helford, people were talking about Marconi's wireless station. Several were strongly opposed to it, arguing that the Lizard's way of life was being altered forever, while others pointed out that the new commerce would boost the district's economy. Without it, there wouldn't be any way of life to preserve.

Then, as the twilight deepened into dark, Charles had walked down to the quay to have a look at the boats—ferries, fishing boats, and pleasure craft—riding gently at anchor on the protected waters of the Helford River. The eastern side of the Lizard was more sheltered than the west (which was open to the ocean and its unpredictable storms) and hence much more hospitable to boaters. If he were sailing a small craft in this area, this is where he would put in.

Somewhere along the Helford River, or in one of its small tributaries.

"The fellow was watching birds at night?" Bradford asked skeptically, applying marmalade to his toast.

"They were night birds, I suppose," Charles said with a shrug. "I left a note, telling him where I'm staying. I'm sure he'll get in touch with me when he has the time." The waiter came around with the coffee pot and refilled Charles's cup. When he had gone, Charles said, "Marconi arrived last night, I suppose?"

Bradford gave him a vexed look, and muttered something unintelligible.

"I beg your pardon?"

"Yes, he's here," Bradford said, and sighed. "With his current paramour."

Charles regarded him. "Did he tell you what problem he encountered at the lecture?"

"The problem," Bradford said with a dark frown, "was Nevil Maskelyne. He jammed the Poldhu-Chelmsford transmission with a message of his own, sent from a Morse transmitter around the corner at The Egyptian." His voice became sarcastic. " 'There was a young fellow of Italy, Who diddled the public quite prettily.' It was followed up by the word 'Rats.' "

"Rats!" Charles could not resist a short laugh, even though he knew that the episode was not at all amusing. "Did anyone in the audience get onto—"

"Luckily, no." Before Charles could say that he was glad, Bradford added, "However, to make up for that deficiency, Maskelyne intends to let *The Times* know what transpired. His letter will probably appear in the next day or two."

Charles was sobered. He could imagine the exchange in *The Times,* with experts and the public weighing in from every side. Marconi was likely to come out looking a fool.

Bradford leaned closer and lowered his voice. "But there's more, I'm afraid, Charles. Arthur Blok was packing up the equipment after the lecture when another unexpected message was received. It was a death threat."

"A death threat! Also from Maskelyne?"

"He denied it, and Marconi believes him. He says it's not Maskelyne's style."

Charles agreed. He was acquainted with Nevil Maskelyne and found him clever, vindictive, and eminently resourceful, but not a man who would threaten to kill someone. He would much rather embarrass his victim publicly—which he was obviously about to do. But if not Maskelyne, who?

"What did the message say, exactly?"

Bradford put down his fork and pushed his plate away. "It said, 'Marconi is dead.' No beating about the bush, you see. Straight and to the point. 'Marconi is dead.'"

"Is he taking it seriously?"

"He didn't say. He seemed upset enough, I suppose." Bradford gave a deep sigh. "Right now, though, he's obsessed with the woman he's brought with him. Pauline Chase." He arched his eyebrows. "That's not her real name, unfortunately."

"You're going to explain that, are you?" Charles asked with a chuckle.

Bradford smiled thinly. "When I knew her in Paris—*before* I was married to Edith, I hasten to say in my defense—her name was Millicent Mitford."

"Perhaps she had a legitimate reason for—"

"And when I saw her in Vienna some time later," Bradford went on, "she was calling herself Francine Sterne. She was traveling with a man who was known as her uncle. A wealthy American." He gave Charles a meaningful look. "The man died rather unexpectedly. The cause was a matter of controversy, I understand, and there was a question about the fate of some of his financial assets."

Charles felt a distinct stirring of alarm. "And now this woman—Pauline Chase, or Sterne, or Mitford, or whoever she is—has set her sights on Marconi." He sipped his coffee, frowning. "I suppose you're going to inform him."

"I don't plan to," Bradford said gloomily. "This is not the first time he's got himself entangled in one of these ridiculous infatuations, you know. I could tell you stories about his romantic escapades which would make your blood run cold. When the fellow is entranced, it's impossible to talk sense to him. If I try, he'll either blow up like Vesuvius or slip into the sulks. And we're facing so many problems right now that I don't dare risk either reaction." His gloom deepened. "I feel as if we're all on a ship with a storm on the horizon and a helmsman who's drunk as a lord."

Charles agreed that Marconi's volatility posed a danger, but doing nothing was worse. There had to be another way to confront the issue. "How about speaking with the woman, whatever her name is?"

"With *her*?" Bradford pulled back. He pressed his lips together. "I don't think I—"

"Why not? Have a private talk with her. Remind her of Paris and Vienna, and extend your deepest condolences on the death of her 'uncle.' And then tactfully suggest that, in the circumstance, it would be prudent if she were to discover an urgent reason to return to the Continent. In fact, if you talked to her this morning, she might just be able to catch the up train this afternoon."

Bradford stared into his coffee cup. "Well, I suppose I could," he said at last, with obvious reluctance. "It's not something I relish, of course. I should not like to—"

"Of course not," Charles said. "However, regardless of her motivation, a woman with a secret past is the last thing Marconi needs right now. As a company director, you must surely agree." He paused. "You'll do it, won't you, Bradford?"

Bradford heaved a heavy sigh. "Oh, very well."

"And there's something else I think you might do, if you have the time for it. You could take the Panhard around Mount's Bay to Porthcurno, and see what you can discover about an aerial which is said to've been built there by the Eastern Telegraph Company to spy on Marconi. I don't know if there's much to be learned, but it might be worth a trip, if you're game."

"You think Eastern might have had something to do with the theft of the tuner?"

"It's possible," Charles said. "If the thing is as important as you and Marconi seem to think, it's bound to be a threat to the cable telegraph companies. At any rate, I think someone should have a look and see what they're up to over there. Don't you agree?"

"Of course," Bradford said. "I shall be delighted to do it." He made a face. "Well, not delighted, perhaps, but willing, at the least. What are you planning for the day?"

"I'm driving down to Lizard Village. I want to take a look at the cliff where Jack Gordon fell to his death, and talk to the operators at the Bass Point station. They worked with the man, and may know whether there's any connection between what happened there and what happened here." He stood. "And this evening, you will recall, I'm to have dinner at Penhallow, with Oliver Lodge. I'll stay the night, I imagine."

"Oh, yes, Lodge. Our friend and friendly competitor."

Bradford grimaced. "I hope you'll give the fellow a good looking-over, Charles. I don't believe his coming to the Lizard is entirely coincidental. He might have put Maskelyne up to his dirty tricks, you know. And he has the equipment to have sent that death threat. I don't suppose I need to remind you that the Lodge-Muirhead Syndicate is promoting its own tuning device as superior to Marconi's. The last thing the Syndicate wants is for Marconi to develop an improved tuner, and especially one which will interest the Admiralty. They—"

"I understand," Charles replied. He grinned. "I'll give Sir Oliver your kindest regards." And with that, he went out to the hotel desk to arrange the hire of a pony and cart to drive down to the tip of the peninsula.

He was standing at the hotel door, waiting for the rig to be brought round from the barn, when Marconi, dapper and well-groomed as always, came down the stairs from the second floor, his hat under his arm, his stick in one hand.

"Good morning, Sheridan," he said. "Where are you off to?"

"To visit the Bass Point station," Charles replied. "I've hired a rig. Perhaps you'd like to go along."

"I would indeed," Marconi said, smiling thinly. "In fact, I was intending to go to there myself. I—"

"Mr. Marconi, a word, if you please, sir." The hotel manager, a short, round man with a bald head and eyeglasses, was hurrying toward them, a look of distress on his face. "It's very vexing, I must say. We have just discovered a . . . a break-in."

"A break-in?" Marconi frowned. "You don't mean—"

"Yes, most, *most* vexing." The little man wrung his hands nervously. "I thought you should know, sir, since it was poor Mr. Gerard's room. I sent the maid in this morning to pack Mr. Gerard's possessions into boxes, to be sent to his brother in Lincolnshire. She found the door forced and Mr. Gerard's things scattered all over the floor. I am dreadfully sorry, sir, but of course, the hotel cannot be held responsible for—"

"I should like to see the room, if you please," Charles put in. He turned to Marconi. "Marsden and I had a look just after we got here on Wednesday, and found nothing amiss." He lowered his voice. "Did Marsden tell you that Gerard's tuner is missing, and his diary as well?"

Marconi's mouth tightened, and he nodded briefly. To the manager, he said, "We'll have a look."

When Charles and Bradford had examined Gerard's room, it was just as the man himself had left it: the bed made, the clothing folded into the dresser drawers and neatly hung in the closet, a box of writing paper and envelopes in one desk drawer, a few personal papers in another. This morning, however, the story was entirely different. The dresser drawers had been emptied onto the floor, the bedding pulled from the bed and the mattress turned askew, the desk drawers pulled open and their contents dumped.

Marconi stood in the doorway. "What do you make of this, Sheridan?" he asked in a low voice. "Was it the same person who took the tuner and the diary, do you think?"

"I don't believe so," Charles said. "Those were taken well before this break-in occurred." He turned to the hotel manager. "It was first noticed this morning?"

"Indeed, sir," said the manager. "It had to have occurred after six yesterday evening. That's when the maid went off duty."

Charles nodded. "Thank you. You've been very helpful." When the manager had gone, he turned to Marconi. "Is Gerard likely to have kept any company documents in this room?" he asked in a lower voice.

"Of course not," Marconi said stiffly. "Daniel Gerard was

a very . . . correct person, who observed company protocol at all times. He kept his notes in his diary and his diary locked in the desk in the company office, as he was instructed to do." He pursed his lips, frowning at the heaps of clothing and papers. "Whoever did this must have been after something . . . well, personal, although I can't imagine what it would be."

Charles began to prowl around the room, poking at things. "Who were Gerard's closest friends?"

"Friends?" Marconi looked puzzled. "We were friends, of course. Otherwise—" He cleared his throat. "I would not characterize him as a man who enjoyed people. He was completely and utterly dedicated to his work, which was why I valued him so highly." He turned away. "It . . . this is all quite distressing, you know. First his death, then the thefts. And now . . . now *this*."

At that moment, Charles caught a glimpse of something on the floor near the window. He picked it up and held it in his hand, a small button, a tiny round ball, covered with cream-colored kid. It looked very much like the button from a woman's glove.

He looked up. "Did Mr. Gerard have any women friends?"

"No, of course not," Marconi said stiffly. "As I said, he was utterly committed to his work, and to the company. That was why—" He looked at Charles, frowning. "What have you found?"

Charles thrust his hand into his pocket. "Nothing of significance," he said easily. He gave the room one more glance. "I'll ask the hotel manager to leave it as it is until I can take the time for a more thorough search." He steered Marconi out of the room. "I think it is time that we were on our way to Lizard Point."

CHAPTER EIGHTEEN

Now what I love in women is, they won't
Or can't do otherwise than lie, but do it
So well, the very truth seems falsehood to it.

Don Juan
Lord Byron

Bradford Marsden did not like the idea of confronting Pauline Chase, and he was not at all convinced that he could accomplish anything. But talking to Pauline was certainly a more productive alternative than discussing the situation with Marconi, and he could not think of a reason not to do it, other than the sheer unpleasantness of engaging in a conversation with the woman. So he settled himself in the hotel lobby with yesterday's *Times*—this morning's edition, which was likely to contain Maskelyne's letter, would not arrive until the afternoon train—and waited for Miss Chase to descend the stairs.

The lady in question put in an unusually early appearance, and Bradford had scarcely opened *The Times* when she came down the stairs. One had to admit, Bradford thought, as he stood to greet her, that she was a very beautiful woman. Her blond hair was piled high on her elegant head, she was dressed in a gray-and-green striped silk cut to show off her delicate neck and stylish figure, and she moved with a languid grace which might remind one of a swan—or a tigress. Bradford rose and went to greet her.

"Ah, Miss Chase," he said, making a little bow. "Ravishing, as always."

She stiffened. "I hardly think that Mr. Marconi would—" she began in a chilly tone, but Bradford took her elbow.

"Marconi has gone down to Lizard Point," he said, and tightened his grip. "Shall we walk along the cliff a little way? The ocean breeze is healthy, and I heartily recommend the view. I'm sure that you will see something in it you have never seen before."

She tried to pull away, but he held fast to her elbow, and she subsided into a sullen silence as they walked through the lobby and out onto the terrace.

When they were well down the cliff path, Bradford remarked, pleasantly, "It was a great surprise to see you, my dear. I had not known that you were in England."

"What do you want?" she asked in a low voice. The green feathers on her hat rippled and she put up a hand to secure it against the ocean breeze.

"Why, Miss Chase!" Bradford said, teasingly. "I want nothing more than the pleasure of your lovely company. Oh, and your attention, of course."

She gave him an oblique glance, her long, thick lashes veiling green eyes. "My attention?"

"Yes. You see, my sweet, I have a proposition to make." She started to speak, but Bradford raised his hand, silencing her. "Hear me out, please. I think you will agree that my proposal is to our . . . shall we say, mutual advantage." He smiled and touched her pouty lower lip with the tip of his finger. "Ah, Miss Chase. A rose by any other name would smell as sweet, and Pauline's lips are even more tempting than those of Millicent or Florence. Perhaps . . ." He leaned closer, as if to kiss her.

Angrily, she turned her head away. "All right," she snapped. "What's your proposal? And hurry up. I haven't had my breakfast yet."

Bradford pulled back. "Oh, it's very simple. I propose that you pack your bags, take the up train to London, and disappear from Marconi's life." He took out his watch. "Let's see. I make it nearly eleven. If you hurry, you will get to Helston in time to catch the one o'clock. I shall be glad," he added, "to arrange a box lunch, so you will not have to go hungry."

"Take the train?" Miss Chase widened her bright eyes and laughed a light, musical laugh. "Now, why in the world, Mr. Marsden, would I want to do *that*? And what would I tell my darling Marky? He's looking forward to our spending time together."

Bradford chuckled in return. "I think you will want to do it, my dear Miss Chase, because if you do not, I shall tell your darling Marky everything I know about you. About Millicent and Florence, too," he added, with a darker emphasis, "and about Mr. Sterne, who died so opportunely. As to what you tell Marconi, I would not presume to make any suggestions. You are entirely free to devise your own explanation for terminating the relationship."

Miss Chase turned away, looking out to sea. "So that's your game, is it?" She laughed again, less musically. "Well, two can play at that one, sir. You're not the only one with a bit of blackmail up your sleeve."

Bradford stared at her. "My dear girl, what are you talking about?"

She turned, lifted a gloved hand, and lightly stroked his cheek. "Why, Mr. Marsden," she said archly, "how very silly of you. You can't have forgotten your letters, can you?" She smiled and fluttered her eyelashes. "Those wonderful, passionate letters which brought such tears of delight to the eyes of a lonely and desolate girl."

Letters! Bradford's stomach knotted.

"Oh, dear," she murmured mockingly. "I see that you really *had* forgotten. How like a man, to love a lady and leave her without a backward glance. But I haven't forgotten, of course. I am glad to say that I have every single one of those sweet, tender letters, tied with a pink ribbon, and kept against the day when I might—"

"When you might use them," Bradford said tautly. "How *dare* you, Miss Chase!"

She shrugged her lovely shoulders. "One keeps one's wits about one, Mr. Marsden, or one does not survive in this unfriendly world. The letters are not with me, of course, but I can produce them whenever they are required." She tilted her head and gave him a knowing glance. "I feel certain that your wife—Edith, isn't it? Quite rich, I understand—would be interested in hearing some of the choicest passages."

"I was unmarried at the time," Bradford said sullenly.

"Indeed. But some relationships are not so easily brought to a close. It would not be at all difficult to suggest that our intimacy continued past the time of your marriage, especially since we saw one another in Vienna." Her smile was admiring. "Really, my dear, it was clever of you to marry so very *well*."

Bradford felt himself coloring. It was pointless to say that he had not married for money, at least, not entirely, and that Edith's wealth had come through a post-nuptial legacy from the estate of her godfather, Cecil Rhodes. He only puffed the air out of his cheeks and said, in a low, angry voice, "What happened between you and me has nothing to do with Edith."

"Of course not," Miss Chase said with a careless toss of her head, "but there it is." She leaned forward, her eyes intent. "I, too, have a proposition to make, Mr. Marsden. I propose that, for our mutual advantage, we forget all about this little conversation. I further propose that you say nothing of it to Marconi." Her voice hardened. "I have no idea of doing a flit, you see. And I doubt very much that you are willing to be embarrassed by those letters. They are very dear and sweet, but I hardly think that Edith would find them amusing." She stepped back and put out her hand. "What do you say, sir? Have we a bargain?"

Bradford thrust his hands into his pockets.

"How very petty of you." She withdrew her hand. "However, I shall take silence for assent. Only a fool would want his wife to learn that he had made passionate love to another woman just a few days before their wedding—and I doubt that you are a fool." The wind tugged at the feathers again, and she put a hand on her hat. "I am going indoors, out of this blasted wind. I expect, sir, that when we meet again, neither of us will speak of this little exchange of views."

Bradford watched her go. The foxy little vixen! Thought she would get the upper hand, did she? Well, he would not let her get the better of him, by Jove. He might be forced to concede this round to the redoubtable Miss Chase, but there would be another.

Yes, by damn, there would be another!

CHAPTER NINETEEN

Tristram in ship lay
With Isolde each night,
Play merrily he may
With that worthy wight
In bower night and day.
All blithe was the knight,
That he might with her lay.

Sir Tristram
Middle English poem,
fourteenth century

At breakfast on Friday morning, Jenna asked if Kate and Patsy would like to spend the day sightseeing on the Lizard. "Mrs. Tremaine can make us a picnic lunch," she said, "and Snood will bring the horse and gig round when we're ready. Sir Oliver isn't expected until tea time, so we'll have the whole day all to ourselves, to go where we like."

"Lovely!" Kate exclaimed, pouring herself a glass of orange juice.

"Where shall we go?" Patsy asked.

Jenna smiled and passed a plate of toast. "I thought we might drive us over to the sea, to Dennis Head, where we can explore to our hearts' content. We can come back by way of the stone circle on Tremorder Hill—if that suits you, of course."

"Wonderful!" Patsy cried excitedly. "I'll take my camera—I have one of those new Ross focal plane cameras, you know, and I've been dying to try it out."

"And as we drive, Jenna," Kate said, "you can tell us all about the history of the place—the Celts and the Romans, and the Cornish fairies and pixies, too. I've heard so many legends about them."

There was a great deal to be seen on the Lizard, and much to be known about its ancient landscape, and Kate was glad for the sightseeing trip. But she was even more glad that Jenna wanted to get out of the house, for their hostess appeared to be under a great deal of strain. Her face was pale, and she seemed anxious and on edge. Kate wondered if her apprehension might have to do with Oliver Lodge's visit. Whatever the reason, though, a day in the sun and fresh air would do her a great deal of good. And Charles would be with them for dinner tonight, which gave Kate herself something important to look forward to.

As soon as they finished eating, they took the basket Jenna's cook had prepared, climbed into the waiting gig, and started off in a southerly direction. The morning was lovely indeed. The horse trotted briskly and the gig was large enough for the three of them to fit comfortably, with the picnic basket tucked securely behind them. The breeze brushing their faces was mild and sweet, the sky was a bright, electric blue, traced with delicate wisps of high white clouds, and there was a great vastness of space around them which made Kate want to throw her head back and shout for sheer joy. Patsy, too, was gay, and even Jenna smiled and laughed and joined in their occasional bursts of song. But Kate thought her liveliness seemed forced, and while the fresh air brought a bloom to her cheeks, it did little to dispel the shadows in her eyes.

They left the horse and gig at St. Anthony-in-Meneage, a gray stone church with a square tower overlooking the little harbor of Gillan Creek. It was the oldest Christian site in Cornwall, Jenna told them.

"It's said that the tower was built," she added, "at the time of the Conquest. A Norman boat was caught in a storm whilst crossing from France to England. The crew vowed to St. Anthony—the patron saint of sailors—that if they survived the shipwreck, they'd build a church at the point where they came ashore." She pointed to the inlet, filled with sailboats and fishing boats. "The story must be true, you know. St. Anthony's tower is built of Norman granite—there's none of that kind here in Cornwall."

Ten centuries! Beryl whispered in Kate's ear. *Think of the stories that tower could tell!*

Leaving the church, they walked a little distance across green fields and over stone fences to Dennis Head, a great headland jutting out into the blue waters of the Channel. The remains of an old fortification were there, erected by the Royalists during the Civil War, in an effort to command the wide entrance to the Helford River, which lay just to the east. Patsy set herself to taking photographs, while Kate used her binoculars to study birds. There was a spectacular view across the Helford, and south, across the Channel, and the breeze was brisk enough to whip their skirts and tug at their hats. The water was the color of tourmaline, shot through with iridescent blues and greens, and the clouds had become more numerous, so that the surface was now bright, now shadowed.

Kate lowered her binoculars. "Did the Romans settle in Cornwall?" she asked curiously.

"Yes, mostly in the areas where there was tin mining," Jenna replied. "But it's possible to find evidences of Roman settlement all over Cornwall." She pointed to the east. "They would certainly have sailed up the Helford, and used the harbor as a shelter from the Channel storms. After the Romans left, the Celts were here, of course, and King Arthur and Guinevere." She shaded her eyes, gazing out across the Channel.

"And Tristram and Isolde," Kate said.

Ah, Tristram and Isolde, Beryl sighed. The tale of a passion which flamed between star-crossed lovers, a tragic romance, for Isolde was the wife of Tristram's uncle, King Marc. Standing here on this windswept headland, looking out across the vast water, Kate did not find it at all difficult to imagine Isolde herself waiting at this spot for her lover to return from the sea, full of hope and eager joy.

"Tristram and Isolde." Jenna's face clouded. "Such a tragedy," she murmured, turning away from the view of the sea. "Such . . . hopelessness."

Kate turned to look at her, struck by the sadness in Jenna's voice and by the sudden and surprised notion that the romance of Tristram and Isolde must echo something deeply personal and profoundly sad in Jenna's life. But what? She had lost her child, but there was nothing of that in Isolde's story. So what was it? A broken marriage? A love affair?

But Jenna's expression was unreadable, and Kate knew it wasn't appropriate to pry into what was so clearly a private sadness. So she linked arms with Patsy and pointed out a small flotilla of ships steaming along fast, not far from shore, heading westward, and after a few minutes Jenna rejoined them with a brighter expression.

They left Dennis Head and found a tiny tea-shop beside

Gillan Creek, where they sat down to enjoy a cup of tea with fresh scones and jam and clotted cream. In the little harbor, boats moved back and forth, chased by screaming flocks of gulls. On the shore, fishermen tended their nets, a pair of men sawed and pounded on a boat they were repairing, and children played a noisy game. Kate lifted her binoculars to study the boats and saw, to her surprise, the birdwatcher—John Northrup, Captain Kirk-Smythe—standing in the stern of a small sloop which was moored to a piling in the inlet. He, too, was studying the boats.

Then, sitting beside Kate, Jenna seemed to see someone she knew. She gave a little gasp, a look of incredulous joy suffused her face, and she flung up an arm in greeting. And then, forgetting all about Kate and Patsy, she was gone, running toward the beach, flying as fast as feet could take her.

"What in the world!" Patsy exclaimed, standing up and shading her eyes. "Why, Kate, it's a man! Someone she knows!"

Kate saw him, too. A tall, blond-haired man in yachting clothes, standing beside a white sailboat beached on the shore. He opened his arms, and for an instant, Kate thought Jenna would fling herself against him, but as she reached him, they both seemed to become conscious that they might be seen. He dropped his arms, and she stopped, and the two of them stood, just looking at one another. It was one of those moments when even the most disinterested onlooker must feel that dangerous forces were at work, like an electrical current which could shock, could kill. A hush seemed to fall over the whole scene. The noise of the saw and hammer stopped, the children's voices quieted. Even the noisy gulls stopped screaming.

Tristram and Isolde, Beryl said ominously. *They're lovers, can't you see?*

"They're lovers, Kate," Patsy said with a note of excitement. She dropped back into her chair. "You can tell from the look of them."

"My goodness," Kate said, not knowing quite what to say. She felt a chill in the pit of her stomach.

Beryl sighed. *I wish we could hear what they're saying to one another.*

"What do you suppose they're talking about?" Patsy asked, propping her chin on her hands. "Wouldn't you love to know, Kate?"

Yes! Beryl exclaimed.

"No," Kate said firmly, and poured another cup of tea. "Whatever they're saying, it's obviously personal and private. Besides," she added, "it would probably embarrass us."

"I don't know why." Patsy's voice was envious. "Love isn't embarrassing. Just look at them, Kate. I wish someone felt as passionate about me as he feels about her."

But why do I have the feeling, Beryl mused, *that this is not a happy passion?*

Patsy frowned. "I wonder whether she came here today to look for him. I wonder—" She rose and picked up her camera.

Alarmed, Kate put out her hand. "You're not going to photograph them, Patsy!"

"Not them, necessarily," Patsy said. "Just the boats. It's a very pretty spot, don't you think? I'll be back in a minute, Kate."

"Really, Patsy," Kate said, "It's not considerate to intrude on such a private—"

You can't stop her, Beryl said. *You know how she is.*

Kate sat back with a sigh. Beryl was right. When Patsy Marsden decided to do something, it was full steam ahead, a locomotive down the track. So Kate took another scone, sat back in her chair, and tried to pretend that she wasn't desperately interested in the small drama playing out on the beach in front of her.

Jenna and the man were standing close together but apart, not touching, as if there were some invisible barrier between them. He was speaking to her earnestly, passionately, his fair head bent over hers. She was answering, her face lifted to his. After a moment, he raised his hand and brushed what must have been a tear from her cheek. Impulsively, she seized his hand and pressed it to her lips, then her breast. Then she pulled away. He took two steps after her, his hand raised, and Kate heard him call "Tomorrow, Jenna!" Jenna did not turn.

Kate watched the two of them, thinking that there was something profoundly tragic about their relationship. What was holding them apart?

Tristram and Isolde, Beryl murmured.

"What do we do now?" Patsy asked, returning to the table.

"I suppose we wait," Kate said. "We certainly can't go off and leave her here alone." And Jenna would have been alone, for the man had pushed his boat out into the water, jumped onto the prow, and unfurled the sails. Kate eyed Patsy's camera. "Did you?" she asked.

"Yes," Patsy said. "I couldn't resist the temptation— although you're right, I'm afraid. I'm sure they didn't know I took the picture, but even so, I'm ashamed of myself. It was an invasion of their privacy. The way they felt was written all over their faces. You could see it the way they held themselves. Anyone looking at them would know." She smiled. "In fact, I wasn't the only photographer. A man on that boat out there." She pointed. "He was taking their picture, too."

Patsy was pointing in the direction of Kirk-Smythe's sloop, and Kate looked toward it. He had cast off his mooring and was pulling up his sail with a great show of casualness. Kate frowned. That he was here—was it a coincidence? It did not seem likely, but she could think of no other explanation. He couldn't have known that the three of them would be here, for they hadn't known it themselves, until breakfast. She would have to tell Charles about it. She wondered if he had got her letter, and whether he had made contact with Andrew.

Jenna returned a few moments later, her eyes red and puffy. She made no explanation, except to say that she had seen a friend and remembered something she had meant to tell him. After that, she fell into silence. In a somber mood, saying very little, the three retrieved the horse and gig. Kate half-expected that the encounter had so darkened Jenna's mood that she might suggest returning to Penhallow. But, still saying nothing, she drove north and west, the narrow road twisting and turning between stone walls and low hedges, the land rising as they passed the village of Manaccan and the smaller hamlets of Choon and Crowns, deeper into the heart of the moor, onto Goonhilly Down. And as they drove, the sky turned gray and a cooler breeze blew, laden with the scent of rain.

CHAPTER TWENTY

Believe me, my young friend, there is nothing—absolutely nothing—half so much worth doing as simply messing about in boats.

The Wind in the Willows
Kenneth Grahame

Affecting a casual nonchalance, Andrew Kirk-Smyth cast off the mooring line on the sloop he had hired in Helford and pulled in the mainsheet. Wolf had pushed off the beach, clambered onto the prow of the *Mistral II,* and run up his jib. Now, he was tacking for the mouth of the little inlet. Kirk-Smythe did not want to let him get too far ahead, but he did not want to be seen as following tack-for-tack, either—and anyway, he couldn't. The hired sloop hadn't near the speed of the larger yacht; it was built for weather, not for speed. So he luffed along until the *Mistral* rounded Dennis Head, sailing east toward the Helford River, then he tightened up on the jib and the main, put the helm down, and sailed as close to the wind as he could.

As Andrew sailed under Dennis's high cliff, the faster, heavier yacht was well ahead of him. But a few moments later, it began to fall off, running downwind with the main and jib out, making for the mouth of the Helford. Andrew relaxed a little and began to enjoy himself. He didn't have to sail hard now, for he knew where Wolf was bound, where he aimed to moor the *Mistral*. Frenchman's Creek.

The early morning—it had just gone seven when they put out of Mullion Cove on the tail of the ebb and began the swing round Lizard Point—had been beautiful: a sharp blue sky over an aquamarine ocean, the water heaving in long, slow rolls, the surf beating against the rocks, the seabirds swooping overhead. As they passed Lizard light, which had stood stalwart against all gales for nearly three hundred years, the southerly breeze was fresh against Andrew's right cheek, and the tiller of the little boat—sturdy, seaworthy, for all its small size—shivered and shuddered like a live thing under his hand. It was a moment of unrestrained, uncompromised, unmitigated pleasure. Whatever his reason for being there, Andrew was glad to be messing about in boats, as his father, a man with a deep love of the sea, had always put it.

But as they beat around Black Head and past the Manacles and then around Nare Point into Gillan Harbor, the clouds had begun to thicken and take on the color of lead. And now, having left the refuge of Gillan, Andrew was glad to be making the turn for Helford and a safer harbor, for the following wind was gaining strength, the waves were higher, and it looked like being rather dirty weather in a few hours. But the run downwind was easy, so he let out the sail, sat far back in the stern, and kept a firm hand on the helm, the prow riding high as the wind hard aft pushed the little sloop forward. This was her favorite point of sail, and she leapt into it with a joyful abandon, planing across the water, skimming the tops of the curling waves like a gull. Andrew felt a thrill strike through him and he gave a wild war whoop.

But Andrew had other things to think about. He had surmised that Wolf put in at Gillan only to take a quick breather and refasten the jib sheet, which had come loose from the clew, leaving the jib flapping. But to Andrew's surprise, Jenna Loveday had appeared, and there had followed that intimate, intriguing exchange between the two of them, a rather unsettling exchange, from Andrew's point of view, although he could not have said why. The scene had been photographed, interestingly, by Patsy Marsden. And by himself, of course, as surreptitiously as possible. While he had other photos, he hadn't one of Wolf and Jenna Loveday together. Although he didn't yet know whether she was an active participant in this business, one never knew when such a photograph might prove useful.

But now there was a further complication, and he didn't like it, didn't like it at all. He had seen Kate Sheridan twice in the company of Jenna Loveday, and it was clear that they were friends, which put him in a devil of an awkward position. The encounter in the churchyard yesterday morning, for instance—it had taken him by such surprise that he'd lost his head and made a major blunder. That foolish remark about Frenchman's Creek had called attention to himself in an entirely unnecessary and amateurish way, when he'd only meant to see Jenna's reaction. Worse, it must have put her on her guard. What had she said to Wolf, just now, about that remark? And had he been noticed, there in the harbor? He'd ducked down behind the sail when he saw the three ladies on the shore, but he was fairly certain that Kate had seen and recognized him.

He gripped the tiller harder as a following sea lifted the stern of the sloop and focused his attention on riding the cresting wave until it subsided. There was something else, too. He had not yet heard from Charles Sheridan—he could only assume that Kate would let her husband know where he was staying and the name under which he was registered. But when Sheridan did contact him, that would be awkward, as well.

Andrew had been acquainted with Charles Sheridan for some years now, and on the two occasions on which they had worked together—at Easton Lodge and in Scotland—they had developed a mutual rapport and respect. He knew Charles to be a strong strategist, courageous in the face of danger, and entirely, unquestionably professional: He would certainly keep confidential anything he was told. But while Kate would not pry into her husband's business, she was a clever and imaginative woman. If she were aware that he and Andrew had met, she might press him for details. And if Charles did not respond to her questions, she was perfectly capable of drawing her own conclusions, which might or might not be on the mark. She might even communicate her suspicions to Jenna Loveday, who might pass them on to Wolf when she saw him next. And if the pair ran true to form, that would likely be tonight, at the boat.

Ahead of him, a quarter-mile farther up the Helford River, Andrew could see Wolf dropping his mainsail, preparing to sail the *Mistral* up Frenchman's Creek on the jib. Andrew knew this because he had been watching Wolf for the past fortnight and talking to people in the little village of Helford, who were as familiar with the creek's twists and turns, its deep holes and shallow pools, as they were with the puddles in the village lanes. A foreigner could believe that he was secure from prying eyes, moored there, but it wasn't true. The local folk knew when he came and when he left, and who visited him—especially when his visitor was the lady of the manor. Jenna's affair with this man had become a matter of village gossip.

Andrew could see the Helford quay, and above it cottages and trees. He pushed the helm down, jibed the mainsail and dropped it, and after a moment nosed the sloop gently into its berth, under the admiring gaze of a pair of pretty day-trippers. He took down the jib and busied himself with the pleasant tasks of snubbing the boat to its mooring, stowing the sails and other gear, and hanging the coiled sheet on the boom. His connection to Wolf over the past weeks had given him the opportunity to sail, and he was pleased to think he hadn't forgotten much. Messing about in boats was just as much fun as he remembered, although he was still pretty much of a duffer, while Wolf was a strong sailor, a sailor for all weathers.

Hands in his pockets, whistling between his teeth, and feeling pretty good about himself, Andrew climbed the rickety wooden staircase up from the river and strolled down the lane to the Oysterman. He was met at the desk by his landlord, who greeted him with the news that a gentleman had called round the night before, inquiring after him. Yes, he had left a name. Charles Sheridan, it was. If Mr. Northrup would like to speak with the gentleman, he could be found at the Poldhu Hotel, on the other side of the Lizard.

Andrew sighed. Now that he knew somewhat more about why Sheridan was here, it was clear that they needed to talk. And after what he had witnessed in Mullion the night before, that need was growing urgent. If Charles didn't come to Helford this evening to look him up, he would have to go over to Mullion again.

This time, though, he thought he would hire a horse.

CHAPTER TWENTY-ONE

No trees, no lanes, no cluster of cottages or hamlet, but mile upon mile of bleak moorland, dark and untraversed, rolling like a desert land to some unseen horizon. . . . They would be born of strange stock who slept with this earth as pillow, beneath this black sky. They would have something of the Devil left in them still.

Jamaica Inn
Daphne Du Maurier

It did not seem the happiest of occasions, now, for a picnic. Kate and Patsy were silent, for they did not know what to say or how to say it, and Jenna herself seemed little inclined to talk. The sky, so beautiful in the early morning, had turned decidedly gloomy and all the color had been washed out of the landscape. The green of the moor had grown gray-black and bleak, as if to match their mood, and Jenna, silent, drove the horse as if the devil himself were after them.

At last, Jenna slowed the gig and they turned onto an almost invisible farm track leading up the side of a brown hill. Looking up, Kate could see three tall stones, each larger than a man, leaning sharply toward one another, silhouetted against the darkening sky. Nearby stood the twisted skeleton of a tree sculpted by the wind. She shivered. There was something wildly, almost frighteningly, primitive about the scene.

"I thought we would have our picnic up there," Jenna said, pulling the horse to a stop. They were the first words she had said since they left the tea shop. "But we should keep an eye on the sky. We may need to beat a hasty retreat if it begins to rain."

"What's up there?" Patsy asked, getting her camera out of the gig. "I can see the rocks. Is it an ancient settlement?"

P'rhaps it's a fairy ring, Beryl suggested, as Kate took out the basket. *Look sharp. We don't want to step on a pixie!*

"It's a cromlech," Jenna said, "a circle of standing stones— *menhir,* they're called. Or rather, it used to be a circle. Those three are the only stones left. Over the centuries, the rest have been hauled off as building material." She nodded toward the north. "This must have been a fairly populated area once. There's a hill fort over there, on the other side of that little valley. And if we drove another mile or two toward the west, we'd begin to find tumuli—mounds of stone piled on top of burial chambers dug out during the Bronze Age."

"So long ago," Kate murmured, feeling the weight of time across her shoulders almost as if it were something physical. So many people, so many generations living and loving and dying in this bleak place, leaving nothing of themselves, no imprint of their lives, no mark of their passing. All that remained was what they had begun with: the rocks themselves.

Tying the horse to a small tree, Jenna added, "Over near Land's End, there's another big circle, called *Dans Maen,* in Cornish—Stone Dance." Her voice was dry, her smile crooked. "The nineteen stones are said to be nineteen women who foolishly went out to dance and sing one Sabbath dawn—at the invitation, it's said, of the devil. They were turned to stone for their sin, and their pipers with them."

"I suppose there's a metaphor there somewhere," Kate said, as they began to walk up the hill. In this bleak landscape, the very idea of frivolity seemed dangerous.

"Not a metaphor, but a moral," Patsy said, frowning. "I don't fancy being turned to stone. Remind me not to do any dancing or singing on Sunday."

"There's a prohibition against almost everything worth doing," Jenna said shortly.

Isolde, Beryl whispered, and Kate did not contradict her.

Taking turns carrying the basket between them, they walked up the hill—not an easy walk, for the moor was rough and they had to detour around impenetrable billows of bramble and gorse. At the top, they set down their basket on a flat, tablelike stone, spread a cloth, and began to lay out the sumptuous feast Mrs. Tremaine had assembled for them: sandwiches and cheese, savory pastries, currant tea cakes, fruit, and a large thermos of tea. The standing stones, their granite skin crusted with blue-green lichens and moss, bent over them like stern schoolmasters listening to the inconsequential chatter of schoolgirls.

But they didn't talk much, really. For a time, Jenna was silent and pale, sitting somewhat apart, her eyes on the southern horizon as if she were straining to see something beyond sight. And then she flushed, stirred, and began to talk quickly and brightly. Kate watched her and was not deceived.

Mrs. Tremaine's food was delicious, but they did not do it justice, Kate thought. They finished eating quickly. Patsy jumped up, took her camera, and hurried off in the direction of a small stream, obviously glad to be gone. Jenna lapsed into silence as Kate repacked the basket, and then they both sat with their backs against the rocks, watching the dark clouds skittering across the sky. Kate was thinking about what had happened at Gillan Harbor, and she knew Jenna was, too.

At last Kate said, "If talking would help, Jenna, I'd be glad to listen."

"I don't know what to say," Jenna said in an exhausted voice. "It all seems so . . . so hopeless."

That's what Isolde must have thought, too, Beryl said. *Hopeless.*

"Who is he?"

There was a long silence. In a low voice, Jenna replied, "His name is Niels Andersson. He's a sailor, from Norway, although he has lived in many places. He sometimes moors his boat in Frenchman's Creek."

Frenchman's Creek? Beryl asked. *Remember that odd remark of Kirk-Smythe's about pirates in Frenchman's Creek? You don't suppose he was referring to Jenna's sailor, do you?*

"Have you known him for a very long time?" Kate asked, thinking of the coincidence of seeing Kirk-Smythe in the little harbor this morning.

"Since . . . since the beginning of the year. He moored his boat in the creek occasionally, and we became . . . acquainted." She looked down at her hands. "I've been lonely, you know, since George died. It's hard, being alone. Niels and I, we became . . . lovers. We exchanged rings." She held out her right hand. On her third finger, she wore a gold ring, cast in a curious twist. A love knot.

There was another silence, awkward and uncomfortable, and then the words began to tumble out, as if, now that she had begun, Jenna couldn't hold them back.

"When Harriet died, I decided to stop going to the boat to see him. I thought . . . I thought her death was a punishment for what I'd done. A punishment for my sin. I wasn't turned into stone—instead, my daughter was taken from me."

"Oh, Jenna," Kate whispered. What an awful burden to bear!

Jenna clasped her arms around her bent knees and began to rock back and forth. "Niels sailed away and I thought I'd never see him again. I thought it was all over, and I resigned myself to being alone. Now he's come back, and he's asked me to go away with him. But I can't, Kate. I can't!"

"Do you love him?"

She turned haunted eyes to Kate. "Yes," she whispered. "God help me, I love him. But there's nothing to be done about it, not after what happened to Harriet."

"I don't understand," Kate said. "What does Harriet have to do with it?"

"I don't know," Jenna said helplessly. "That's the worst part. She drowned in Frenchman's Creek, you see."

Kate frowned. "But I—"

"I don't know why she went there," Jenna said, as if that explained everything.

Ah, Beryl sighed. *She thinks her daughter followed her. She thinks her daughter knew about Niels, but she's not sure.*

"Oh," Kate said. "Yes, I understand."

Jenna nodded numbly. "I went to Niels that night, after I'd put Harriet to bed. It was dark, of course, and I have no idea whether Harriet might have followed me. We were together in the boat for several hours. I came back to the house very late. It was raining, and I was wet through, and all I wanted was a fire and a cup of something hot. I didn't look in on her." She swallowed. "When I went to wake her the next morning for school, she was gone. They found her in the creek."

"Near the boat?" Kate asked.

"Near where the boat had been. It was gone." So low that Kate could scarcely hear, she said, "She must have been there . . . in the water . . . when I left him. It was dark. I couldn't see. I didn't—" Her voice broke, and Kate could hear the anguish in it. "I didn't look. God help me, I didn't even look!"

"Of course not," Kate said softly. "How could you? You didn't know."

"And that's the worst of it!" Jenna cried, with a sudden passionate violence. "I *should* have known! Don't you see? Any mother *would* have known, any mother who wasn't blinded by her own selfish desires!"

How ghastly, Beryl whispered. *How appallingly ghastly.*

"And now he wants me to go away with him," Jenna said. "And I want to, oh, I *want* to!"

Jenna began to shake, and then to weep, and Kate gathered her into her arms. She sobbed stormily against Kate's shoulder for a while, then pulled away and dried her eyes with her sleeve.

"Now that I've started, I might as well tell you the rest of it." She blew her nose. "A few days after Harriet was buried, I began having . . . well, hallucinations, I suppose you'd call them. Sights, sounds, things which aren't there. At first I thought that my nerves were just overwrought. But some of the episodes were—are—really rather frightening. I consulted a specialist, who diagnosed it as hysteria."

Hardly surprising, Beryl said sympathetically, *under the circumstances. So much guilt, so much grief. It would drive anyone right round the bend, wouldn't it?*

"Specialists have to find a name for everything," Kate said, remembering how a dull, debilitating sadness had clung to her for months after she lost her baby, how the sight of every infant had brought her to tears. Work had been her salvation—work and a trip which she and Charles had taken together. "Perhaps you need a change of scene. Sometimes that helps."

"That's what my mother-in-law keeps saying. She thinks the answer is for me to leave this place." She paused. "Sir Oliver believes that there's another explanation. He thinks Harriet might be trying to get in touch with me."

"Oh," Kate said.

Of course! Beryl exclaimed excitedly. *That's it, Kate! That's exactly what's happening. It's Harriet!*

"I think I mentioned that Sir Oliver is an old friend of my family's," Jenna went on, her voice sounding stronger. "He's been involved in psychic research for the last dozen years or so. Perhaps it will sound far-fetched to you, but he says I might be able to receive a message from Harriet." Her slight smile was both ironic and hopeful at once. "Rather like the wireless telegraph, I gather, only using automatic writing."

"Interesting," Kate murmured.

Fascinating, rather, Beryl amended firmly.

"Yes. Well, we're going to try. Tonight, after dinner. Sir Oliver and I had already planned the séance before I learned that you and Patsy were coming. Both you and Lord Charles are invited, of course, and Patsy, too, although I'll certainly understand if you choose not."

We have to do this, Kate, Beryl said in a warning tone. *I shall be very disappointed if we don't.*

"I can't speak for Charles," Kate replied, "but I'd like to be there, if only to see how the process works. I might be able to use automatic writing as an element in one of my novels." The instant she said it, she could feel Beryl's excitement.

Jenna chuckled without humor. "The 'process', as you call it, may not work at all, of course. Sir Oliver might have come all this way for nothing. But I hope . . ." Her voice trailed off.

Does she? Beryl whispered, with just the faintest hint of skepticism. *Does she really hope her dead daughter will tell her what happened? Or maybe it's forgiveness she's seeking, rather than knowledge.*

"I wonder," Kate said slowly, "if you've talked to Alice. About Harriet, I mean."

"Alice?" Jenna frowned.

"A little girl who lives on your estate," Kate replied. "She's about Harriet's age, I think. Her grandmother is your laundress."

"Oh, yes. I know who the child is, although I didn't know her name. Her mother died of consumption not long after she was born, and her grandmother is bringing her up." The frown deepened. "You've met her? You think she might know . . . something?"

"I walked with her yesterday to Helford to post a letter to Charles. She's quite a remarkable child, with an extraordinary imagination. I suspect that she's the one who leaves flowers on Harriet's grave, and the doll, too. She and Harriet were 'secret' friends, she told me."

"Secret friends?" Jenna seemed taken aback. "I wanted Harriet to be friends with the children of the estate, but I didn't—" She colored and looked away. "I suppose you're thinking that I should have known who Harriet's friends were. That a good mother *would* have known."

"I'm not thinking that at all," Kate said truthfully. "If I had a daughter . . ." A hard lump came up in her throat, and she swallowed it and went on. "If I had a daughter, I would do just as you did. I would let her be a child as long as possible, and let her go to school with other children, rather than shutting her up with a governess. I would let her have animals, and time of her own, and friends—yes, and secret friends—and places to roam."

"Thank you," Jenna said. She shut her eyes for a moment. "You'll never know what that means to me, Kate."

Kate cleared her throat. "Would you like me to talk to Alice, Jenna, and see what I can learn? I offered to lend her a book I saw on your shelf—*Alice in Wonderland.* If you don't mind, I could take it to her, try to draw her out."

"Mind? Of course not." Jenna turned to her. "You've already met her, and I . . . well, I'm not sure I'm up to it, actually." A faint pink came into her pale cheeks and she looked away. "Come to it, you see, I'm not even sure I want to know. Oh, I *say* I do, but—"

"You must want to know," Kate said gently. "You've agreed to the séance tonight."

Jenna smiled thinly. "Maybe I don't have any faith in automatic writing." She looked up. "Here comes Patsy with her camera and an armful of flowers."

"Oh, don't get up," Patsy called, coming up the hill. "I've brought flowers for you to hold whilst I take your picture."

The photographic session over, the three women made their way back down the hill to the waiting horse and gig. As they went, Jenna told Patsy about the plan for the evening. Patsy, her usual curious self, eagerly agreed to participate.

"Oh, what fun!" she cried. "Of course I'll be there!"

But in spite of Patsy's and Beryl's enthusiasm for the idea, Kate herself was not so sure. As she picked her way down the hill, between the mounds of gorse and the piles of ancient rock, Kate could feel the stern, brooding presence of the *menhir,* their stone gazes darkly fixed on her retreating back. She did not know what they would think (if they could) of tonight's séance, and of automatic writing, and of efforts to contact the spirit world. It might seem to them to be an invasion of their own sacred prerogative: the power to embrace the unseen, the unknown; the power to commune with the dead.

CHAPTER TWENTY-TWO

The equipping of ocean greyhounds with the Marconi system has taken away part of the dread and mystery of the sea. . . . In April, 1899, the Goodwin Sands lightship off the English coast was struck in a collision, and with her Marconi apparatus was able to send for assistance across twelve miles of ocean. Life-saving stations along the coast of England have received warning . . . that vessels were drifting ashore through the fog, or were threatened by fire on board.

"Commercial Wireless Telegraphy,"
The World's Work, 1903
Lawrence Perry

About the time that Kate, Patsy, and Jenna had set off for their day on the downs, Charles and Marconi were driving a hired rig south along the road from Mullion to Lizard Village. The sun was bright and cheerful and the narrow lane led over the windswept moor, open and empty except for scattered flocks of sheep and small herds of cattle. The silence was broken only by the wind and the birds' musical calls, and Charles understood why this vast tranquility was so highly prized by the people of the moor.

Charles and Marconi did not experience the easy friendliness which Kate, Patsy, and Jenna enjoyed. The two men had been acquainted for five or six years, but while they shared an interest in wireless and a respect for one another's scientific abilities, they had never been especially close. In fact, Charles doubted that Marconi had many personal friends—except, perhaps, for the ladies he courted, and since his romantic relationships never seemed to last very long, perhaps even these did not count. He was not a cordial man; he spoke with an aloof, almost chilly reserve. He did not usually initiate conversation, and he answered questions with a measured caution, as if he suspected his questioner of having an ulterior motive.

Just now, for instance. Charles could not dismiss the possibility of a connection between Gerard's electrocution at the Poldhu station and Jack Gordon's fall from the cliff near the Lizard station some two weeks before. He needed to know more about the connection between the two wireless stations, and he hoped that Marconi would speak frankly. Getting information out of the man was a little like fishing olives out of a bottle, but after repeated questioning, he was finally able to learn something.

The Lizard station had been built some three years previously. The first of eight Marconi stations along the coast, it was located on the high cliff at Bass Point, near the southernmost tip of the Lizard Peninsula, where converging sea lanes funneled the shipping into the Channel. The station was designed to provide ship-to-shore service for the maritime traffic passing Lizard Point, as well as to monitor transmissions to and from the transmitter at Poldhu. And, Marconi reluctantly added, in response to several probing questions, the station was also used to test newly devised receivers, to see if the more powerful Poldhu signal could be tuned out.

"Newly devised receivers," Charles said thoughtfully. "That would be something like the tuner Gerard was working on, would it not?"

"Yes, it would," Marconi said, looking straight ahead. "But the work is very secret, and cannot be discussed with anyone outside the company." He turned, his eyes narrowed. "I am sure you understand, Sheridan."

"Indeed," Charles said. "But you must understand, too, Marconi. I cannot help you unless you are willing to take me into your confidence—not about the workings of the tuner itself, but about the procedures by which it was designed and tested, and who might want it. If I don't know that, at the very least, I'm not likely to be of much use to you."

"I'm sorry." Marconi heaved a weary, beleaguered sigh. "It's just that I have had to hold my cards close to the chest, as the Americans say, for a very long time. Too many people will do anything they can to get ahead of us. The Americans, for instance. The De Forest Wireless Telegraph Company has put out a five million dollar stock offering. Five million dollars, Sheridan! That kind of money can buy anything."

"Even a stolen tuner?" Charles asked.

Marconi's eyes widened. "You don't think—"

"I think it's a possibility," Charles said. "Go on. Who else?"

"Well, the cable companies are still poking around, causing trouble. And there's Maskelyne, of course, with his dirty tricks. And Oliver Lodge, with that patent business." Gloomily, he added, "Even inside my own company, there are disagreements and competition. It isn't easy to . . ." His voice trailed away.

"*Inside* the company?"

"I've been battling the directors since the company was first established," Marconi said thinly. "I had to fight like the very devil to get the money for Poldhu, because the board thought transatlantic transmission was a waste of time—and some still do. I have to fight for every dollar which goes into new stations and new equipment." As he spoke, his voice took on power, as if he had been bottling up his anger and expressing it at last made him feel the strength of it. "The directors worry endlessly about stock prices, and making a profit. As if money were the only reason we're in business!" he added with sudden vehemence.

Charles thought about Bradford. No doubt the hope of a profit was his chief reason for investing in the Marconi Company. If the other directors were like him, no wonder Marconi was feeling the pressure.

"The problem is that they don't really want to spend money on development," Marconi went on darkly. "The kind of thing Gerard was doing, for instance. I keep telling them that development is what we desperately need. It's the only thing that will keep us ahead of the pack." His voice became despairing. "Sometimes I feel I am battling the directors as much as I am battling my competitors. And now that Gerard is dead and the tuner is gone—" He broke off. "It's almost too much to bear," he muttered.

Charles nodded sympathetically. Having a technology as hugely important as wireless in his hands, Marconi must feel as if he himself had to defend it against the whole world. But there were things Charles had to know. "If the Lizard station was used to try out new equipment," he asked, "is it possible that Gerard might have sent the tuner there for testing?"

"He would not have sent it," Marconi replied. "He would

have *taken* it. Gerard would not have entrusted the testing to anyone else but himself." And with that, they pulled up in front of the station on Bass Point, and the conversation was suspended.

The station was little more than a two-room hut, with a hundred-foot mast and aerial alongside. As Charles and Marconi entered, the operator was preoccupied with a flurry of crackling transmissions, punctuated by brief pauses. As Charles's ear adjusted to the stream of Morse dots and dashes and he began to decode the messages, he realized that there were two signals coming in, one strong, the other much weaker.

HANG ON OLD MAN HELP COMING LIFE BOAT STATIONS STANDING BY. That was the stronger signal.

A moment later, the weaker signal came in. FIRE IN MAIN COAL BUNKER IF FLOODING DOES NOT WORK WILL HAVE TO ABANDON SHIP.

The operator began to pound his key, repeating the weaker message, relaying it up the line. When it was sent, he turned and glimpsed Marconi and Charles for the first time. "Oh, it's you, sir," he said to Marconi. "Sorry, I didn't see you come in."

"You were doing your job," Marconi said with the first genuine smile Charles had seen on his face, and introduced Charles and the operator, whose name was Edward Worster. "What's going on here, Worster?"

The operator, small and wiry, with a heavy dark mustache and thinning hair, took off his black Marconi cap and wiped his forehead with his sleeve. "French tramp steamer *La Belle Marie* twelve miles due south, sir. Fire below deck, spreading to her coal bunker. *Marie* can receive Falmouth all right—Falmouth handles rescue dispatches, y'see, sir—but her signal is too weak for Falmouth to pick her up. I've been relaying messages. It's a bit of a problem," he added in an explanatory tone, "because Falmouth drowns *Marie*'s signal when they send at the same time."

"Is rescue on the way?" Charles asked. "And what was that about the coastal life guards?"

"The stations have been alerted to stand by," Worster replied, "but *Marie* is too far out for the lifeboats to be of much use. Falmouth dispatched a rescue ship, but it's going to be a close run thing."

As they waited tensely, the receiver once more came to life with *Marie*'s message: SHIP SOUTHWEST OF US HEADING OUR DIRECTION MUST SEE OUR SMOKE.

Worster dropped into his chair and began to hammer his key: CQD CQD UNKNOWN SHIP SSW LIZARD HEADING NE FRENCH SHIP *LA BELLE MARIE* ON FIRE 49 48 N 5 20 W CAN YOU ASSIST.

The receiver remained silent. "Damn," Worster muttered. "She must not have a wireless."

"Or perhaps not a Marconi wireless," Marconi said, as Worster bent over his key and repeated the message. He glanced at Charles. "CQD is the Marconi code for a ship in distress. Ships subscribing to other systems are not supposed to use it."

Charles frowned, seeing the difficulty created by competing proprietary systems. When it came to desperate situations, such as a ship in distress, competitiveness ought to be set aside. But an instant latter, the telegraph clattered into life, and the doubt was erased.

HMS *HOPEWELL* RESPONDING CQD SMOKE SIGHTED ESTIMATE ARRIVAL 20 MINUTES.

"A British warship!" Worster exclaimed eagerly. "Jolly good, I'd say! She'll have fire-fighting equipment on board. And if all else fails, she can take the crew off." He shook his head. "It would have saved a deal of time if Falmouth could have picked up her first CQD directly, and if we didn't have the interference problem." He glanced up at Marconi. "Not to be critical, sir," he said apologetically.

Marconi patted Worster's shoulder, beaming, his earlier anxiety seemingly forgotten in the excitement of the transmission. "No apologies, Worster. A splendid effort. Splendid!"

"Thank you, sir," Worster said. He took a deep breath. "If you wouldn't mind watching the key for a few minutes, I'd very much like to go out for a smoke. This sort of work is . . . well, you know."

"I know," Marconi said, pulling out the chair. "Have your smoke, old chap, and take your time. I'll keep an ear out for more messages."

Charles had the idea that Marconi was more than happy to sit with the key for a little while—something he might not get to do very often these days. He followed Worster out of the station.

"Mind if I join you?" he asked, as the operator took out a packet of cigarettes and lit one. Worster shook his head with a grin, and Charles took out his pipe. "Gets a bit tense in there," he remarked, filling it with tobacco and tamping it down.

"I'd say, sir," Worster replied emphatically. "Some days, it's very tense. Some days, there's nothing but urgent messages, CQDs, problems with the equipment or the transmissions. Personnel problems, too. Some days, I'd rather be doing something else." He grinned slightly. "Wouldn't want Mr. Marconi to hear that, of course."

"Of course," Charles said. "There's a lot to running a station like this one." He paused. "Actually, I'm here to look into some of the problems you mentioned. The recent deaths, for instance."

"Ah," said Worster, and let out his breath in a long sigh. "Jack Gorden, eh?"

"And Daniel Gerard."

Worster looked away. "Can't tell you anything about Gerard, I'm afraid. I was on duty here at the time it happened. Didn't learn about it until they sent somebody down here to tell me why Poldhu wasn't transmitting." He pulled on his cigarette.

"What about Gordon?" Charles asked. "What kind of a man was he? Given to drink?"

"Drink? Not really. Oh, he'd have his pint or two, like the rest of us. But not to the point where he might just walk off a cliff." Worster narrowed his eyes. "They asked me that at the inquest, y'know. And that's what I said. Of course, nobody knows what happened that night. Nobody saw."

"I wonder," Charles said, "whether he had many friends. Here at the station, for instance?"

"Well, there was only the three of us: Gordon, me, and John Hunt, who came just a week before Gordon died." Worster hesitated, chewing on a his mustache. "Jack didn't know John, and I wouldn't say the two of us—Jack and me, that is—was friends, exactly. We both worked in the same place, o'course, but not at the same time." His grin was crooked. "Marconi operators, we're loners, we are. Rather work by ourselves than with people, by and large."

Charles nodded. Wireless operators must enjoy the solitary life, for the job was known to involve long hours alone in a wireless shack, often at some remote spot along the coast. "Is there anything else?" he asked. "His behavior, for instance? Anything out of the ordinary there?"

Worster screwed up his mouth, thinking. "The weeks before he died, he could've seemed . . . well, preoccupied, you might say. Like he had something on his mind he was trying to work out. And there was a time or two when he asked me to swap shifts with him. Day for night."

"He wanted to work your night shift? Did you find that a bit unusual?"

"Right." Worster answered slowly, as if these thoughts were just occurring to him. "Unusual? Well, now that you ask, I do wonder. I didn't mind, o'course. I like a good night's sleep as well as the next man." He shrugged. "To each his own, though. Jack prob'ly had a good reason. It's a pity it happened when it did, is all I got to say. He was looking forward to his holiday."

"Ah," Charles said. "And where was he going?"

"Back to Bavaria. His mother's fam'ly was there, y'see. He loved the Old Country, and . . ." His voice trailed off and his glance slid away.

"Right," Charles said, as a new thought crossed his mind. "Jack was German, then, was he?"

"Well, not to say German, exactly," Worster replied defensively. "He was born here, same as me. A man can't help where his mother was born, or where his people come from, can he?" He threw his cigarette on the ground and stepped on it. "Worked hard, showed up on time, Jack did. Too bad, that's what it was. Poor chap didn't get his holiday."

Charles changed the subject. "Mr. Marconi tells me Gerard brought that new tuner of his down here for testing."

"Right. Two, three times. Maybe more. I don't know anything about it, though."

"Did he ever leave it here?"

Worster gave a short laugh. "Leave it? Never even let it out of his sight. Afraid somebody was going to steal the secret, I s'pose. He was working on the interference problem, you see. Same trouble as we were having this morning. He was trying to come up with an apparatus which would tune Poldhu out." He paused, then restated his thought. "Which would tune for any specific station."

"A challenge, as I understand it." Charles puffed thoughtfully on his pipe. "Did he succeed?"

Worster shrugged. "Not as far as I could tell. 'Course, I wasn't here every time he brought the tuner here. He may have made it work other times, or in other situations." He grinned crookedly. "I was hoping he'd come up with something, him or Marconi. Guess now it'll have to be Marconi, although he doesn't seem to have a lot of time these days for inventing. But at least he's got Gerard's work, and all he has to do is finish it."

Charles regarded Worster, wondering if he should tell him that the tuner had been stolen. But instead, he said, "This holiday Jack was planning to take. He *was* coming back, wasn't he?"

Worster regarded him for a moment, narrow-eyed. "How'd you know?"

"Just a guess. He wasn't, then?"

Worster shook his head slowly. "Said he'd had enough of telegraph work. Thought he'd do something different." Inside, the key began to clatter. "Time for me to get back to work."

"If you think of anything having to do with either Gerard or Gordon, you'll let me know, will you?" Charles asked. "I'm staying at the Poldhu Hotel."

Worster cocked his head, and a slight crease appeared between his brows. "Think there's something funny, do you? Think somebody's out after Marconi operators?" He grunted. "Should I be worried?"

Charles gave a little shrug. "I doubt it," he said, "unless you have something that somebody wants."

"Well, I don't know what it would be," Worster said with an uneasy laugh. "And that's God's truth."

As the man went back into the station, Charles turned to look out to sea. Daniel Gerard had the tuner and the notes describing its operation.

What did Jack Gordon have that someone might want?

CHAPTER TWENTY-THREE

Alice's foot slipped, and in another moment, splash! she was up to her chin in salt water. Her first idea was that she had somehow fallen into the sea, "and in that case I can go back by railway," she said to herself. . . .

However, she soon made out that she was in the pool of tears which she had wept when she was nine feet high. "I wish I hadn't cried so much!" said Alice, as she swam about, trying to find her way out. "I shall be punished for it now, I suppose, by being drowned in my own tears! That will be a queer thing, to be sure! However, everything is queer to-day."

Alice's Adventures in Wonderland
Lewis Carroll

With the book under her arm and a basket of currant tea cakes left from the picnic, Kate set off down the path to the cottage Alice shared with her grandmother. It was a small cottage in need of whitewashing and roofed with an untidy thatch full of birds' nests. But a bower of red roses arched over the window, red geraniums brightened the window sill, and a half-dozen hens scratched diligently beside the path. The door was partway open, and Kate called out, "Alice, are you at home?"

There was a scurrying noise inside, the door was flung wide, and Alice appeared, wearing the same blue dress and white pinafore she had worn the day before. But her braids were full of twigs and leaves and her pinafore was hardly white. From the leaves in her hair and the red stains on her pinafore, Kate guessed that she had been picking berries and—from the smears on her cheeks and chin— eating them too.

"Hullo," Alice said, with an oh-it's-you-look, and added, "Your ladyship," as an afterthought.

Kate glanced at the table, where a bowl of berries, tins of flour and sugar, and a rolling pin testified to Alice's present occupation. "I've interrupted your baking, I see," she said.

"I'm making a berry tart," Alice said. "It's a surprise for Gram." Her eyes lit up as she noticed what Kate was carrying, and her tone became warmer. "You've brought the book. And cakes!"

"Yes," Kate said, and put both on the table. "I hope you'll enjoy it as much as I did when I first read it. Lewis Carroll has quite a vivid imagination. As a writer, I've learned a great deal from him."

"You're a writer?" Alice asked, frowning skeptically. "You write *books*?"

"Yes," Kate said, pulling out a chair. Sustained skepticism seemed to be the girl's ordinary state of mind, and she was certainly a creature of moods. "I could read a bit of the story out loud, if you would like to go back to your baking. I shouldn't like to delay your gram's berry tart."

"Is it as good as *Treasure Island*?" Her tone implied strong doubt.

"I think so," Kate replied. "Would you like me to read?"

"Oh, I suppose," Alice said, with an elaborately nonchalant shrug which disclaimed any interest at all, and picked up her rolling pin.

Kate began to read the familiar text, while Alice—with a dexterity obviously born of experience—put the berries and sugar into a deep pie pan, rolled out a circle of pastry, fitted it neatly over the top, and crimped the edges. She continued to read as the girl put several lumps of coal into the black iron range built into the chimney, opened the oven, and slid the tart into it. When she finished the first chapter, she glanced inquiringly at Alice, who commanded, "Go on," and began to clear the table. As Kate started the second chapter, "The Pool of Tears," the girl finished the washing up, then sat down on the braided rug at Kate's feet and crossed her legs, still listening.

Kate finished the chapter and closed the book. "Did you like it?" She sniffed the warm aroma coming from the oven. "Your tart already smells delicious."

"Of course I liked it," Alice said indignantly. "I *loved* it." She pulled out her lower lip between her fingers and attempted to look at it. Her eyes crossed. "What sort of books?"

"Pardon me?" Kate asked.

"What sort of books do you write? The boring sort, or good ones like *Alice*?"

"I hope they're good," Kate said with a smile. "Perhaps you could read one or two and tell me your opinion." On second thought, though, perhaps she wouldn't want to hear Alice's opinions. She had the idea that they might be scathing.

Alice rolled over on her stomach and propped her chin in one hand, twisting her hair in her fingers. "P'rhaps I shall write a story." She thought for a moment, then rolled over on her back. "That was a sad one you told me yesterday."

"Yes," Kate said and sighed. "When it happened, I cried so much that I might have drowned in a pool of my own tears, like Alice in Wonderland." She took a currant tea cake out of the basket and handed it to the girl, then took one for herself. "But I expect everybody has at least one sad story to tell. Don't you?"

Alice shot her a look. "About somebody dying?"

"There are all kinds of sad stories."

"The ones about people dying are the saddest," Alice said definitively. She sat up, pulled out her pinafore, and began picking the currants out of her tea cake and dropping them into her lap.

"Yes," Kate said.

Alice picked up the currants and ate them, one by one, slowly. "I s'pose it's not so hard to drown," she said, "especially if you can't swim."

"I suppose," Kate agreed. "And if the water's deep."

"I shouldn't like to drown," Alice said, and ate the rest of the currants and the crumbs.

"Nor I."

"But there wasn't anything I could do, was there?" The girl looked up, and those electric-blue eyes were suddenly bright with tears. "No more than you, when your friend fell off the wall and got killed by the trolley."

"I'm sure there wasn't," Kate said simply, "or you would have done it." She paused, and said, for the second time that day, "If you would like to tell me, I'd be glad to listen."

"It started with the pigeons," Alice said. She dashed the tears from her eyes.

"The pigeons?" Kate asked in surprise.

"There were pigeons in the boat, you see. Harriet was the one who saw them first, and told me about it. We'd hide on the bank and watch the boat, and when the man wasn't there, we'd go and look at the pigeons. Harriet said it was all right, because her mother went on the boat, too."

"And that's when Harriet drowned?" Kate asked in a matter-of-fact tone. "When her mother was on the boat?"

Alice nodded. Her face was pale and pinched. "We'd never gone to the creek at night before, but she came and tapped at my window, and I climbed out. She wanted to know what her mother was doing on the boat, you see. She was curious—Harriet was *always* curious, the most curious person I've ever met."

A picture of Harriet was emerging in Kate's mind: a girl with a passionate curiosity and her mother's permission to explore. She could hardly be faulted for wanting to know why her mother was secretly stealing through the woods to join a strange man on a strange sailboat at night. "I suppose it was very dark," she said quietly.

"Oh, *very,*" Alice said. She shivered. "It was cold, too. I didn't think it was going to be much fun. It didn't seem like a very good idea, either, 'specially since my gram would be very angry if she knew. But Harriet didn't like it when I said no. And it wasn't right to let her go alone, either—at least I didn't think so." She looked anxiously at Kate. "Do you?"

"If I'd been in your shoes, I think I would have gone," Kate replied, reflecting on the difficult moral choice the girl had made, between her grandmother's anger, or her friend's disappointment. It was a choice which would have baffled many adults. She paused. "Did either of you have a light?"

Alice shook her head, and then went on, very fast: "Harriet thought she knew where she was going, you see, but she didn't, and she went too close to the edge of the creek by the big tree, where the water is deep, and she fell in. I tried to reach her but she was too far." Her head dropped and her voice became muffled. "I tried really *hard*."

"I'm sure you tried as hard as you could," Kate said, and reached Alice's hand. The girl's fingers were surprisingly small and very cold, like a doll's fingers. "And then what happened, Alice?"

"And then I fell in myself. But I grabbed a tree root and pulled myself out. I was scared, and I yelled." She pulled in her breath. "I screamed really loud, but nobody came."

"I suppose they couldn't hear you on the boat."

Alice shook her head. "It was around the bend."

"And after you climbed out, you were afraid to run to the boat and tell them?"

A sad nod.

By then, it would have been too late, Kate thought. It was winter, and cold, and the girls would have been wearing woolen coats. Harriet had probably been pulled under the surface by her heavy clothing and drowned quickly. Aloud, she asked, "And you came home?"

"I came in through the window. It was hard to get my clothes dry without Gram noticing." Alice let go of Kate's hand. "I guess I should have told somebody," she said in a small voice.

"You're telling somebody now," Kate said. She reached into the basket and handed over another tea cake, thinking about something she had read recently, about the way pigeons were used during the siege of Paris some thirty years before. And she thought of Kirk-Smythe, and his mysterious disguise, and his interest in the man on the boat.

"Pigeons on a sailboat," she said after a moment. "That's odd, don't you think? But I suppose pigeons have to live somewhere, and a boat is every bit as good as a pigeon loft. Were they kept in a cage?"

"A wooden cage. There were six pigeons in it." Alice wrinkled her forehead. "Sometimes there were only four or five. Or two."

"Perhaps they were let out on holiday," Kate said with a smile, "or to practice flying. Whose pigeons were they, do you think?"

Alice gave her a look. "Why, the man who sailed the boat, of course. They wore bands on their legs, and sometimes little canisters."

"That's interesting," Kate said, remembering that, during the siege of Paris, the pigeons carried important messages from the city to the outside world. She pursed her lips. "You wouldn't have seen what was in the canisters, I don't suppose."

"I did once," Alice said. "Yesterday morning, actually. One of the pigeons came to the church tower while I was up there, feeding the other birds." She wore a serious look. "While you were there, too. In the churchyard, I mean. You and Harriet's mother and the other lady, and the bird-watcher." Before Kate could say anything, she pushed her hand into her apron pocket. "You write things. Somebody wrote this. Maybe you can read it." Frowning, she took out a wad of flimsy paper, about the size of a large pea, and handed it to Kate. "I can't read it, and I can read almost anything."

Kate pulled the wad carefully apart, trying not to tear the paper. What she saw surprised her.

"What does it say?" Alice asked.

Kate laughed a little. "It says: 'I am a very pretty pigeon.'"

"Really?" Alice asked skeptically.

"Something like that," Kate said. She thought once again of Kirk-Smythe, and then of Charles. "May I have this? I'd like to show it to someone."

Another of Alice's elaborate shrugs. "It's of no use to me, I suppose." She gave Kate a shrewd glance. "If I give you the paper, may I keep the book? Until I've finished it, that is."

"Lady Loveday says you may have the book," Kate replied, pocketing the paper.

That brought a smile. "Tell her thank you for me."

"Why don't you tell her yourself, Alice. And I also think you might tell her what you've told me."

Alice looked down. "She would be very angry at me."

Kate leant over and tipped up the girl's chin so she could see her face. "I think you're wrong," she said softly. "I'm sure she would be sad, and so would you. But in the end, both of you would feel better."

"Really?" Alice asked again but this time, there was more of hope than of skepticism in her voice.

"Really," Kate replied.

CHAPTER TWENTY-FOUR

The possibilities of wireless fired the creative imagination. In 1902, for instance, the well-known novelist Rudyard Kipling wrote an inventive story called "Wireless" in which a wireless operator picks up a jumble of unreadable Morse signals from Royal Navy ships.

"Have you ever seen a spiritualist séance?" the frustrated operator asks, as he tries to untangle the garble. "This reminds me of that—odds and ends of messages coming out of nowhere—a word here, a word here and there."

Meanwhile, an elderly man in an adjacent room has fallen into a trance and is taking down stanza after stanza of poetry sent through the ether by the dead poet Keats, whose spirit seems to have been inadvertently contacted by the amateur operator's wireless.

Although people in our time smile at the idea (which is often called "channeling"), a great many Victorians took it very seriously. It was conjectured that the wireless telegraph would allow the spirits of the dead to contact the living.

"Wireless and Psychic Phenomena
in Edwardian England,"
Susan Blake

Charles arrived at Penhallow shortly before seven that evening, and when he was shown into the drawing room, he discovered that everyone was already gathered there for dinner. He greeted his hostess and Patsy Marsden, dropped a kiss on Kate's cheek—she looked especially rosy tonight, as if she had spent the day in the sunshine and wind—and turned with a ready smile and a warm handshake to Sir Oliver Lodge, whom he had not seen for some time.

"Lord Sheridan!" exclaimed Sir Oliver, beaming. He was a tall, distinguished-looking man with stooped shoulders, a balding head, heavy gray mustaches, and neatly trimmed gray beard broadly streaked with white. He shook Charles's hand with enthusiasm. "I am delighted, absolutely delighted to see you, my dear fellow! An unexpected pleasure. And what, if I may ask, has brought you out to the Lizard?"

"I'm here to give Marconi a hand with a problem at the wireless station," Charles said, feeling that he should mention his association with Sir Oliver's rival and get it out of the way, in case there might be hard feelings about it. He was also mindful of Bradford's insistence that Lodge's visit was no coincidence. He did not think it likely that the man had ulterior motives, for he was widely respected as a teacher and scientist. But it was a possibility that had to be considered, especially since it seemed improbable that Sir Oliver would take time from his duties at the new Birmingham University, where he had recently been appointed Principal, to come to the Lizard on an inconsequential errand.

Sir Oliver's eyes twinkled. "Oh, dear me. I do hope it's a *serious* problem!" He chuckled. "There, there. I'm sure you don't want to tell me what it is. After all, the Lodge-Muirhead Syndicate is Marconi's closest competitor, you know. We're negotiating a new wireless contract with—"

He broke off, laughing heartily. "But then, I mustn't let the cat out of the bag, must I? I shouldn't want Marconi to discover what we're up to."

"I've read that your system has some advantages over Marconi's," Charles said truthfully. Sir Oliver was known to have sent wireless signals before Marconi and to have developed a device that—according to some, at least—Marconi had copied and adapted. What was more, his patent on tuning was a strong rival to Marconi's.

"A great many advantages, especially where tuning is concerned." Sir Oliver paused. "I have nothing against Marconi himself, you know—although that patent of his . . . well, I shan't talk about that, either. I'll simply say that the young fellow's commercial advisers have done him a great disservice by making excessive claims and seeking premature publicity."

"It's a difficult balance," Charles said in a neutral tone. Privately, he agreed with Sir Oliver. It seemed to him that the company was promoting a product which was not yet perfected. And if the tuner and Gerard's notes were not found, it might be a much longer time before—

"Those fools on his board of directors can't understand that everything depends on the credibility of the company," Lodge said emphatically. "On the company's ability to keep its promises. They're going to ruin it all for short-term gain. And when Marconi himself is thoroughly discredited, as he was at the Royal Institution night before last—" He shot Charles amused glance. "You know what happened at the lecture, do you?"

"I understand that Nevil Maskelyne indulged in a spot of jamming," Charles replied with a smile.

"And followed it up with a revealing letter to *The Times*," Sir Oliver said, "which will be made much of, in all quarters. In case you haven't yet seen it, I'll lend you my copy.

But I'll want it back." He slapped Charles's shoulder playfully. "It's worth keeping, as far as I'm concerned. In fact, it's worth framing and displaying on the wall above my desk. Not that I hold a personal grudge, mind you. But Marconi has got his feathers trimmed in a most public way, and I for one find it amusing." He chuckled mirthfully. "And I suppose the fellow will reply, and then Maskelyne will reply, and the entertainment will continue for a while, eh?"

Lodge's remarks were more than a little unsettling. Charles had not known that the man bore so much animosity toward Marconi and the Marconi Company for violating his patent—or at least, that's how he saw it. Enough to make an effort to obtain the tuner? Enough to attempt to cause difficulties for the company?

Charles was framing a reply when Kate came up to them, looking extraordinarily beautiful in a silvery dress which showed off her fine throat and the auburn richness of her hair. "I suppose you two are talking about wireless," she said with a smile.

"I'm afraid we are, my dear," Charles said, circling her waist with his arm. "But if you'd rather we change the subject, I'm sure Sir Oliver wouldn't mind."

"Oh, no, not at all," Kate said. "Actually, I wanted to ask Sir Oliver if he's read Rudyard Kipling's story. It appeared in *Scribner's Magazine,* in February, I believe." To Charles, she explained, "It's about a wireless operator who receives nothing but garbled signals, while at the same time, an old man in a nearby room goes into a trance and receives a message from the poet Keats, who is long dead, of course." She turned back to Lodge. "Did you read it, Sir Oliver? Is it too fanciful and far-fetched?"

"Fanciful, yes, but I thought it a delightful story," Sir

Oliver said. "In fact, I have often argued that the ether is just as capable of carrying spirit messages from those who have passed over as it is of carrying wireless signals. Mr. Kipling's tale demonstrates how that might be done—it's quite amusing, too, don't you think?" He beamed. "And to-night, we may have an opportunity to test my theory." As Jenna came up to them, he bowed to her in an avuncular way. "Isn't that right, my dear?"

"We will try," Jenna said, although, Charles thought, not with any great enthusiasm. In fact, he thought she looked tired and pale, a paleness emphasized by the garnet-colored dress she was wearing. She put her hand on Sir Oliver's arm. "Sir Oliver, I have discovered several photographs of you and Father, taken here some years ago. Come and have a look at them." She drew him toward an album laid open on a table.

"What's this about testing a theory?" Charles asked Kate in a low voice.

"Sir Oliver is here to do some psychic research," Kate said. "After dinner, there will be a séance. He's going to at-tempt to get Jenna's daughter to contact her, through auto-matic writing."

"Oh, come now, Kate," Charles said. He viewed the cur-rent vogue for spiritualism with a great deal of skepticism. He had been vaguely aware that Sir Oliver had an interest in spiritualism, but had no idea that he was actually conduct-ing psychic research. Charles's own interest in mediums was of the same order as his interest in Harry Houdini's escape artistry: There was a trick to the illusion, and he was mildly curious to know what it was—but not curious enough to spend any time investigating it.

"I knew you'd say that, you old fuddy-duddy," Kate

replied with a teasing smile. "You don't have to stay, you know, Charles. Everyone would understand if you excused yourself after dinner and—"

"Actually," Charles said, in an apologetic tone, "I thought I might do that anyway, if Jenna and Sir Oliver would not be offended."

"I shouldn't think so," Kate said. "They are both intent on the séance. You might not even be missed." She smiled. "Where are you going?"

"I intended to drive round to Helford, to see if Kirk-Smythe can be found. I received your note," he added. "I tried to see him last night, but—"

"I saw him again today, Charles." Kate leaned closer and lowered her voice. "He was in a little boat in Gillan Harbor. He seemed to have his eye on a sailing yacht that is often moored here in Frenchman's Creek." As Charles listened with a growing surprise, she told him that Jenna had been visiting the yacht the night her daughter drowned. "It belongs to a man named Niels Andersson, who keeps a half-dozen messenger pigeons on the boat."

"Messenger pigeons?" Charles repeated.

"Exactly," Kate said. "Alice, the little girl who was with Harriet the night she drowned, took this message from one of the pigeons." She pressed a paper into his hand. "I have no clear idea what its significance might be, but I thought you should see it."

Charles glanced down at the paper. He frowned. "Why, it's in German."

"In English, it says, 'Item located, negotiations begun,'" Kate translated.

"So it does," Charles said, an idea beginning to stir. "When did the child find this?"

"Yesterday morning. The pigeon came to the church

CHAPTER TWENTY-FIVE

Soon, we believe, the suckers will begin to bite! Fine fishing weather, now that the oil fields have played out. 'Wireless' is the bait to use at present. May we stock our string before the wind veers, & the sucker shoals are swept out to sea!

Lee de Forest, "Father of Radio,"
to his journal, February, 1903

It was past teatime when Bradford returned from his long day's drive around Mount's Bay to Porthcurno, where he had taken a look at the aerial mast Charles had told him about. This was also the place where the undersea telegraph cables made landfall on the British coast. People in England and North America had been able to communicate, via the cable, since the first two submarine cables were laid in 1866. By 1902, when a line was run from Vancouver, British Columbia, to Australia and New Zealand, the globe was at last girdled with undersea cables. A dozen of these cables, owned by Eastern Telegraph Company, came ashore at Porthcurno, where they were linked to land lines which carried the messages to Eastern's main telegraph station in Moorgate, London.

tower while she was feeding the other birds." She looked up at him, puzzled. "What item, Charles? Negotiations for what? What is this about, do you think?"

"I wonder if Kirk-Smythe might have an idea," Charles said, folding the paper carefully and putting it into his coat pocket. "I really must see him tonight, Kate, if at all possible. This message may hold the key to—"

Jenna Loveday clapped her hands, summoning them to the dining room.

"You will have to wait to see Andrew *after* dinner," Kate said firmly, and took his arm. As she pulled him toward the group, she added playfully, in a louder voice, "I'm afraid that you shall have to behave, my dear. You and Sir Oliver must find some other subject of conversation."

"I doubt that will be difficult," Charles said. "Eh, Sir Oliver? We can talk about Nicola Tesla and his latest experiments in electricity. Or those two brothers in Ohio, who are said to be adding a propeller and a gasoline engine to that glider they managed to get airborne last year. Of course, they probably won't succeed. But if they do, theirs will be the first powered flight. Now *that* would be something to see, wouldn't it?"

"Charles is at it again, I see," Patsy teased. "Kate, how *do* you tolerate it? Come on, you two, or we shall have dinner without you!"

It was cable companies such as Eastern, of course, which were enormously threatened by the new wireless. In fact, Anglo-American had got an injunction against the first Marconi station in Newfoundland, based on their fifty-year monopoly on the landing of telegraph cables and the receiving of telegraph messages in Newfoundland. Anglo had decided that transatlantic wireless communication was a major competitive threat. Marconi would have to build his stations somewhere else.

With this in the back of his mind, Bradford would not have been surprised to find a well-organized spying operation at Porthcurno. But he did not. The line from the aerial ended in a small shack nearby, where he discovered one lone operator dozing in his chair, his printer chattering out the messages intercepted from the Poldhu station's very strong transmissions. When Bradford woke him and asked what he was doing, he only shrugged.

"Listenin' in to transmissions, sir," he replied, "although why, I cert'nly can't say."

"What do you do with the transmissions you're intercepting?" Bradford asked, in as neutral a tone as he could manage. The interceptions made him angry, of course, but that had nothing to do with the operator.

"Why, I file 'em, of course," was the answer, "like I'm told to. But nobody's ever been down from the London office to read 'em, or asked to send 'em up. So it doesn't seem to me like anybody much cares." He grinned. "Long as they pay my salary, I don't see how it's any concern of mine."

And that had been that. The operator went back to sleep, and Bradford, feeling that he had learned nothing very conclusive, drove back around Mount's Bay. He arrived a little cross and late for tea, because the drive had been long and tedious, the road dusty, twisting, and narrow, bounded by hedges and high stone walls.

And then, at tea in the hotel's sitting room, Marconi had made matters worse by telling him that someone had broken into Daniel Gerard's room the night before. Since the break-in had happened after Bradford and Charles had searched the room for themselves, it meant that somebody was still searching for something. But who? And what? The tuner was already gone, and Gerard's notebook, as well—what other valuables could the thief be after?

There was more, and worse. The afternoon post from Helston had brought *The Times,* and Marconi put it on the table between them. It contained Maskelyne's sardonic letter describing, in embarrassing detail, exactly what had happened during the Royal Institution lecture, and describing, as well, the equipment his friend Horace Manders had used to generate those humiliating messages. It was an old, simple spark-gap transmitter, which Marconi's system was thought to have made obsolete. The implication was clear: Marconi's vaunted system was not proof against interference or interception. The attack was devastating, and Bradford winced as he imagined how it would be used by the company's rivals. They would launch a campaign to discredit the company, and there was little that could be done to combat it.

Reading the letter again, Marconi had flown into a tirade. "It's nothing but scientific hooliganism!" he cried, throwing the newspaper onto the floor and stamping on it. As he often did when he was angry, he launched into Italian. "The dirtiest of dirty tricks! The lowest of underhanded dealings! The filthiest of filthy dogs!" In English, he added, "I shall write to *The Times* immediately. I shall be revenged! Revenged, I tell you!"

"Steady on, old man," Bradford had said, taking his arm and attempting to quiet him. "A public exchange is only going to whet the public's appetite. Far better to let Maskelyne have his innings and forfeit the game than to drag it out."

"Forfeit the game!" Marconi shrieked. "Never!" he had stamped out of the sitting room and up the stairs, muttering through his teeth. Really, Bradford thought, if the matter had not been so serious, the fellow's pique would have been quite comic.

All in all, the events of the day had been deeply disquieting, and as Bradford went up to his room to change for dinner, he was feeling considerably troubled. His unease had little to do with what he had seen at Porthcurno. It wasn't that business with Pauline Chase, either, although she had certainly been a disquieting, disagreeable presence in his thoughts for most of the day—an unseen passenger, as it were, in the Panhard's left seat. He hadn't come up with a way, yet, to deal with the minx—that is, to force her to break off with Marconi without risking her showing those damned indiscreet letters to Edith. Given the financial situation, things were difficult enough at home just now. The letters would be the last straw.

Bradford finished dressing and glanced into the mirror over the chest of drawers to straighten his tie. As bad as that might be, there was also the threat against Marconi's life to worry about, and that had been on his mind all day, too. "Marconi is dead" was quite a serious matter, and as he smoothed his hair and adjusted his cuffs, he was thinking somberly about it. The company's directors could not afford to take the threat at anything less than full face, especially with two employees dead within the fortnight. But what to do? Cancel Marconi's trip to Paris next week? Employ a bodyguard to shadow the man's movements? Bradford smiled grimly. Now, *that* would be a job, wouldn't it?

The smile became a frown. After dinner, he should have to write a letter to Sir Euan Wallace, the chairman of the board and put him in the picture. Sir Euan would have seen *The Times,* and would want to know the story behind it—and of course, he must be informed about the death threat. And then there was the woman. The frown deepened. How much should Sir Euan be told about Pauline Chase? The woman was clearly up to no good, and her past definitely cast a suspicious light on her connection to Marconi. But without a clearer sense of her motive . . .

Bradford sighed, gave the mirror another glance, and went to the door. He would be having dinner alone again tonight. Sheridan had gone off to Penhallow for dinner with Oliver Lodge—no joy there—and Marconi was dining with Miss Chase, worse luck. He opened the door and stepped out into the hall.

As he did, the door to the room adjacent to his was closing, someone apparently having just been admitted. And through the door, Bradford caught the sound of a light, familiar voice. Speak of the devil, he thought sourly. It was Miss Chase herself. She was his neighbor.

"Well," she was saying. "It certainly took you long enough. I thought . . ." The rest of her words were inaudible but the tone was aggravated and almost shrewish.

A man laughed, not altogether pleasantly. "A pleasure to see you, too, old girl. You're looking quite delightful."

Old girl? Bradford, who had been about to walk on down the hallway, stopped. The man was clearly not Marconi. Was Miss Chase already acquainted with another of the hotel guests? Who?

A suspicion came into his mind. He considered it briefly, then turned, unlocked the door of his room, and went back inside. There was a connecting door between his room and the one he now knew to be Miss Chase's, secured with a bolt on his side and (he presumed) a corresponding bolt on the other. He stepped quietly across the room and applied his ear to it.

"—not quite according to plan, I'm afraid," the man was saying.

"Well, that's hardly my fault, is it, now?" Miss Chase countered crisply. "I should have thought you would make arrangements against all contingencies. Isn't that why White hired you?"

"White hired me to get that tuner," the man said. "Nothing else."

Bradford's eyes widened and he tensed. The *tuner?* Was this the very thief himself?

"That's what I don't understand," Miss Chase said in a petulant tone. "I thought Mr. de Forest had invented his own wireless thingy, whatever-you-call-it. And I thought it was better than Marconi's—at least, that's what they're telling everybody in America. It's in all the newspapers, you know. Those Yanks are awf'ly proud to be ahead of the Brits for a change. So why does White want us to steal Marconi's thingy?"

Bradford, with his ear to the door, barely managed to suppress a gasp of pure astonishment. Abraham White was the promoter of the De Forest Wireless Telegraph Company of New Jersey, which had just recently sold three million dollars of stock. It was the Marconi Company's best capitalized competitor. What a dirty, underhanded bit of business! And just like the Americans, too. Always out for what they could get, with no thought of gentlemanly behavior. Bradford's blood boiled at the thought of it.

The man gave a mirthless chuckle. "De Forest's wireless 'thingy'? Well, my girl, the plain, unvarnished truth of the matter is that there isn't any 'thingy'—at least not one that can be relied on. De Forest's wireless is a flop."

"I don't believe it!" Miss Chase cried incredulously. "Why, Mr. White is selling stock in the company! Millions and millions of dollars of it! And people all over the world are buying it! I've been planning to buy some myself, as a matter of fact."

"Then you'd be as big a fool as all the others," the man broke in cruelly. "You know what they say. There's a sucker born every minute. This wireless mania is nothing but a bubble, that's all. If De Forest Wireless doesn't crash tomorrow or the next day, it'll be gone by next week, or next month, or next year. And all those people who slapped down their life savings, hoping to get rich—well, they'll be broke, I reckon. And so will you, my pretty, if you put any money into it. As for White and de Forest, it'll be tar-and-feather time."

Bradford braced himself against the door, his head reeling. De Forest's wireless company, a fraud!

"And that's why they hired us to get that tuner," the man said. "If you can't invent it, steal it, that's their motto. Why, doncha know, de Forest stole that amazing 'spade detector' of his right off Fessenden's laboratory bench. Hired one of Fessenden's employees, and the fellow brought the gadget with him. Fessenden is suing, o'course. He'll win, too, although little good it'll do him. There won't be a plugged nickel left in the company when White gets through with it. It'll be flat as a busted balloon."

Bradford's heart was pounding and he had broken into a cold sweat. Was it possible that Abraham White and Lee de

Forest had tried to hire Daniel Gerard away from the Marconi Company? And when that didn't work, they had him *killed* so they could steal the tuner? Was he listening to a pair of cold-blooded murderers?

"Well, I don't know anything about those doings," Miss Chase said airily. "And to tell the truth, I don't give a damn. All I know is that I was supposed to make friends with Mr. Marconi and see if I could get that tuner."

The man sighed. "Well, the tuner is one thing, Pauline, but all this other business is something else again. People going over the cliff, people getting electrocuted, people stealing the damn thing right out from under our noses. It's been unsettling, I'll tell you that. All I can think is that there's another party involved."

People stealing the damn thing? Bradford blinked. So this fellow—by now, Bradford was certain he knew who he was—was *not* the thief after all! Someone else had got to it first!

The man sighed again, more heavily. "I even had a look in Gerard's room last night, to see if whoever took the tuner left anything behind. Couldn't find a thing. But I'll tell you, old girl, it gave me a bad case of the jitters to poke around in a dead man's stuff."

Bradford pulled in his breath. The revelations were coming so thick and fast that he could scarcely field them. So this was the man who had ransacked Gerard's room!

There was the creak of a bed, as if someone had sat or lain down upon it. Miss Chase said, with some sarcasm, "Go right ahead. Make yourself comfortable. Take your shoes off, why don't you?" Her voice became heavily ironic. "Take your shirt and trousers off, too, while you're at it. Nobody's looking."

"Oh, go to hell," the man said humorously. "Listen, now that you're here, old thing, and you've got Marconi so neatly twisted around your finger, I've got an idea. I think it's very likely that he's got another one of those tuners, or a pocketful of notes describing it. I can't believe a smart gent like him would let somebody else do his inventing for him. Anyway, I want you to find out."

She laughed. "Me? And just how do you suggest I do that? Ask him?"

"Don't be a ninny. Search his room. If it's there, take it."

Search his room? Bradford was taken aback. Why, the nerve of the man! The idea that they could simply—

"Search his room?" Miss Chase's voice had become chilly. "I don't think so. It's too big a risk. What if he catches me? What if—?"

"I'll see to it that you're not caught," the man said. "I'll cozy up to Marconi while you're having a nice, leisurely paw through his drawers and his wardrobe."

"And how am I supposed to get into his room?"

"Try this," the man said.

There was a metallic clink, as if something had fallen on the floor. Bradford's guess was confirmed in the next moment.

"Where'd you get a *key*?" Miss Chase asked, in admiring surprise.

"Where else? Off the key rack behind the desk. There were two, so they'll never miss one. And if they do, they'll think one of the maids took it and forgot to put it back."

There was a pause. "I suppose I can do it," she said at last, in a half-doubtful tone, "if you'll guarantee to keep him occupied." Her laugh was brittle. "Which shouldn't be too hard. Just talk to him about his favorite subject. Himself. Or that damned wireless of his."

Bradford had to smile. The remark was not far off the mark. Once Marconi began talking about himself and his work, it was almost impossible to change the subject.

"After dinner, then." The bed creaked again, as if the man had stood up. "I'll keep him talking about wireless— I've learned a thing or two about it from de Forest, you know—while you go powder your nose. Now, old girl, what'd'ya say to a little kiss?"

Since she didn't say anything, and since the silence went on for rather a long time, Bradford could only surmise that Miss Chase had allowed herself to be kissed. After a suitable interval, he stepped softly to the door and eased it open a crack.

In a moment, he heard Miss Chase's door open, and he risked cracking his own a bit wider. He recognized the man who passed in front of him, and was not surprised.

CHAPTER TWENTY-SIX

What is called automatic writing, when the pen is held by an ordinary person and appears to write without conscious volition, is a purely psychic phenomenon; for there is no question that the muscles of the writer are used. . . . In the case of such mediums, the brain is as it were leaky, and impressions can get through from the psychic universe which are not brought by the sense organs and nervous network to a brain center, but arrive in the mind by some more direct route.

"Psychic Science,"
Sir Oliver Lodge

Now is the air so full of ghosts, that no one knows how to escape them.

The Psychopathology of Everyday Life, 1902
Sigmund Freud

The dinner party at Penhallow was certainly festive enough. The group—Kate and Charles, Jenna and Sir Oliver, and Patsy—was seated at a damask-covered table set with china, crystal, and silver, centered with a loose, tumbling arrangement of roses and ferns and lit with tall ivory tapers. Kate heartily approved of the flowers, which were a pleasant change from the formal floral displays she usually saw on dining tables. She approved, too, of the menu, for it was a comparatively simple dinner of soup (white and brown); salmon; lamb, ham, and veal; salad and vegetables; a charlotte Russe; and crystallized fruit, and cheese—nothing like the much more elaborate meal they would have eaten at the home of one of their London friends. It was served by Wilson, assisted by one of the village girls; the pair of them did an entirely creditable job, Kate thought.

The conversation was as pleasant as everyone's efforts could make it. Patsy was animated and amusing, full of tales of her travels in the Arabian desert; Charles and Sir Oliver said nothing at all about wireless or other such scientific wizardry, and conversed on any number of agreeable subjects of general interest; and Kate joined in with enthusiasm. But while Jenna did her best to participate, she seemed abstracted and quiet, and rather paler and more delicate than usual, Kate thought, as if the prospect of the after-dinner séance had already depressed her spirits.

After the meal, the entire group (not just the ladies) adjourned to Penhallow's small library, a book-lined room with an oriental carpet laid over the stone floor and comfortable leather furniture, where Wilson served coffee and port. The blazing fire was especially welcome, for the long-delayed rain had begun to fall at last, and an occasional rumble of thunder rattled the windows.

Kate had already explained to Jenna that Charles would not be staying for the séance, and when he rose to leave, his thanks and apologies were accepted without offense. Thankfully, Kate was not asked to explain where he was going, and Jenna's only concern was for his comfort.

"It's raining," she said. "If you're in need of a mackintosh and umbrella, I'm sure we can find them."

"Thank you, but I have mine with me," Charles said, "and the gig has a folding hood and side curtains. It is July, after all, and I shall be dry enough." He bowed to Lodge. "Good night, Sir Oliver. I trust that you will enjoy the remainder of your visit." And with a smile at Patsy and a quick kiss for Kate, he was gone.

Well, then, Beryl said with satisfaction, as Charles left. *Now that His Nibs is gone, we can begin.* Beryl always confessed to feeling somewhat diffident in Charles's presence, a little intimidated by his sometimes stern countenance.

"I'm sorry Lord Charles could not join us for the séance," Sir Oliver said. "But perhaps it is just as well. One never knows, of course, but it has been my experience that overtly skeptical people have a dampening effect on the spirits."

Dampening, Beryl said with a chuckle. *That's it, exactly. His lordship can be dampening.*

"Then we are well rid of him for the evening," Kate remarked lightly. "There was never a more skeptical man than Charles Sheridan. If I were a spirit, I should be totally dampened in his presence." She stretched out her hands to the fire. "Are we having our séance here in the library, Jenna? I do hope so—the fire is awfully nice."

"I thought it would be a good place, if Sir Oliver agrees," Jenna said. "Since there are only four of us, we can all sit at the library table."

The table in question, round and substantial, was made of dark oak, with thick legs curving out from a center pedestal.

"Oh, but it's such a *heavy* table," Patsy objected, regarding it with a mock frown. "It would take an abominably strong spirit to thump it." She looked at Sir Oliver. "I say, Sir Oliver, not to disparage Jenna's table, but shouldn't we have something . . . well, rather lighter in weight?"

Oh, by all means, Beryl put in. *We want a jolly good table-thumping.*

"I wish," Jenna said quietly, "that you wouldn't make light of this, Patsy. It's hard enough without—" She bit her lip and turned away. "I already feel terribly foolish, you know."

Sir Oliver pulled his thick brows together. "If I may be forgiven for saying so, Miss Marsden, the more serious we are about tonight's endeavor, the more likely we are to succeed." He opened a small leather briefcase and took out a stack of paper and several pencils. "Unfortunately, humor can be just as dampening as skepticism."

Patsy raised her hand in a pledge. "No more tomfoolery, I promise. I shall be as sober as a judge. But not judgmental," she corrected herself hastily. "I shan't offer any judgments at all. I shall just—"

"You shall just hold your tongue," Kate said, with a smile, "or the spirits will never be able to get a word in edgewise."

"It's only nervousness," Patsy replied in a whisper. "I really am a little afraid, Kate."

Patsy? Afraid? Beryl exclaimed.

"After all your wild desert adventures?" Kate asked. "I must say, I'm surprised."

"I know," Patsy replied candidly. "It is rather extraordinary, isn't it? But I have a nasty, nagging sort of feeling, you see, and—" She stopped and shook herself. "Oh, I'm just being silly, that's all. Let's get on with it, shall we?"

Yes, Beryl said smartly. *The spirits are eager. Let's get on with it.*

Jenna was clearing the framed photographs, books, and other items from the library table. "Shall we want a cloth?" she asked.

"No need for it," Sir Oliver replied. "The less on the table, the better. Except for—" He picked up a photograph of a small girl in a soft white dress, white stockings, and white slippers, her hair drawn up and secured by a large white bow at the back of her head. "Except for dear Harriet's photograph. We shall put it just . . . here." He set the photograph carefully in the center of the table, and beside it arranged the paper and pencils.

"The lights, Sir Oliver," Jenna said. "What shall we do about the lights?"

"Oh, let's leave them on, by all means," Patsy said hastily. "Otherwise, Jenna won't be able to see to write."

I don't think light is required for spirit writing, Beryl said. *I think the fingers do it all by themselves.*

Sir Oliver gave Patsy a reproachful look, as if to reprimand her for being humorous again. "We must dim the lights at least a little," he said. "If you will allow me, Jenna, my dear."

He took a red silk handkerchief out of his pocket and draped it in front of the lamp which sat on a nearby table, and then extinguished the other two lamps in the room. Now there was just the flickering fire and the ruby-shaded light, which cast an eerie play of shadows in the darkened corners.

Ah, Beryl said. *A perfect setting. Perfectly mysterious.*

"Right." Sir Oliver rubbed his hands together. "Now, ladies, if you will draw up chairs, we shall begin. Jenna, my dear, I shall sit here at your left, Lady Sheridan at your right. Miss Marsden, you shall be our observer, just opposite."

"A silent observer," Patsy said, suppressing a nervous giggle. She sat down.

Really, Patsy, Beryl said reproachfully, as Kate took her place.

Sir Oliver smiled and held Jenna's straight-backed

armchair as she sat down, pulling a garnet-red knitted shawl around her shoulders. He took a large, plump pillow from the sofa and put it to her back so that she could sit with some comfort.

"Now, Jenna," he said. "We shall put the paper on your right"—he shifted the stack of paper—"and ask Lady Sheridan to be sure that you are supplied with it, and additional pencils, if you should need them. As you fill one sheet with writing, I shall take it from you, and Lady Sheridan will slide another in front of you. Once in trance, you see, most mediums write very quickly, and often with a much larger script than usual. We may need a great deal of paper."

Jenna's face looked pinched and very pale, and her eyes were round and luminous. "Perhaps we shan't need any," she said in a low voice. "I have no confidence in my ability to do what you want, Sir Oliver."

"It must be what *you* want, my dear." Sir Oliver sat down and put his hand gently over Jenna's. "Do you want to contact your daughter?" He was looking directly into her eyes and his voice had taken on a different, deeper resonance, Kate thought, almost the resonance of a hypnotist's. "Do you want to reach Harriet, Jenna? Do you want to know what Harriet has to say to you? to us? Do you want to bring some measure of peace to your soul?"

There was a silence. The fire made a soft hissing sound, punctuated by an occasional pop and crackle. Outside, not far away, thunder muttered. Jenna's eyes went to the photograph in the center of the table. She clasped her hands.

"I . . . do," she said simply. "I'm . . . afraid, but I . . . do."

"Very well, then, my dear," Sir Oliver said in a comforting tone, "you have only to relax, close your eyes, and allow it to begin. A sheet of paper and a pencil, Lady Sheridan, if you please."

Kate slid both in front of Jenna, who sat stiffly upright against the pillow, her hands folded on the table in front of her like an obedient schoolgirl, her eyelids lowered, the dark lashes sooty against her pale cheek. Outside, the rain slid down the window with a liquid plashing, while the ruby-tinted light washed the room. Against the wall, a tall clock ticked hollowly: toc toc toc. There was no other sound but the soft in-and-out sighing of four people's breaths, which seemed now to be synchronized. Kate felt the tenseness in her neck and shoulders relax and a kind of fog seemed to settle on her. She was indeed glad that Charles had gone, for she would feel his active, analytic intellect at work, turning and testing, measuring and evaluating and questioning, while the four minds here were merely open, quiescent and receptive.

Beside Kate, the stiffness seemed to go out of Jenna's figure and she softened into the chair, dropping her chin on her breast and becoming very still. After another few moments, as Kate watched, she raised her head and opened her eyes, staring at the photograph of the little girl. But the pupils of her eyes were dilated, her gaze was unfocussed, and there was no conscious awareness in it.

She's in a trance! Beryl exclaimed, and Kate, surprised into alertness, saw that Beryl was right. Jenna's movement was languid as she reached for the pencil and began to spiral it across the paper, not forming words, only drawing a lazy, curving shape. Opposite, Patsy drew in her breath in a little gasp, and Sir Oliver shook his head warningly. There seemed to be a new kind of energy in the room—*A presence!* Beryl hissed—or perhaps it was just that the wind outside had risen, and a tree beside the window had begun to lash the glass.

Another shapeless spiral or two, and the paper was full.

The pencil lagged. Sir Oliver slid the page away and nodded to Kate to supply another. Jenna leaned forward over the clean sheet, her breath coming shorter and harder, her hand moving with a renewed urgency. Kate felt herself pulled forward, watching the flowing marks on the page, still formless, still shapeless. And then, as the pencil moved faster, a word emerged, then another, and another, all curiously rounded, almost childlike:

mother

mother

  dear

mother dear

For an instant, Kate's heart seemed to stop, and a wave of something like fear broke over her. Her senses seemed suddenly heightened. The flickering fire cast a kaleidoscope of colors—orange and red and blue—upon the faces of the people around the table. There was a metallic bitterness in her mouth, and she could almost taste the strong odor of Sir Oliver's pipe tobacco, Patsy's exotic Arabic perfume, the summery scent of Jenna's hair. The wind seemed louder, the lash of leaves against the window more insistent, the thunder more ominous, Jenna's troubled breathing a dire rattle. Kate felt as if she were watching through a telescope held the wrong way round, watching from a great distance but at the same time too near, oh too too near to whatever power propelled the moving pencil. She wanted to push back her chair and run, but something held her there, something—

Sir Oliver had pulled the filled paper away and Jenna was writing on the table, her pencil sliding over its polished surface without leaving a mark. He nodded sharply at Kate. Chastised, she complied, sliding another paper under Jenna's pencil, which continued without stopping.

mother dear dear dear oh dear dear

so so so so sor sor sorry sorry sorry i am i am sorry

Patsy was sitting forward in her chair, her lower lip caught between her teeth, the expression on her face a mixture of terror and astonishment as she watched the swift tracery of the moving pencil. Sir Oliver's eyes were wide and staring and there was a strong tic, almost a jerk, at the corner of his mouth. It occurred to Kate that he had not really expected this to happen, that he had thought tonight would be just another in a fruitless string of dead-end experiments and encounters with mediums who practiced fraud. Now that he seemed to be confronted with the success he had sought—with evidence for the survival of personality beyond the grave—he was so stunned that he could scarcely comprehend the impenetrable, unfathomable mystery of it.

But perhaps this is something else, Beryl whispered significantly. *What do you suppose His Nibs would say, Kate?*

At the thought of Charles, some of the mystery went out of the moment—just as it might have done if he were here. This writing, odd and intriguing as it was, might not be a message from the after-world at all, but only a compelling manifestation of Jenna's troubled mind, her repressed guilt seeking the same kind of release it sought in her hallucinatory moments. It could be rather like what Sigmund Freud described as hysterical manifestations of the unconscious, filling the very air around them with restless ghosts.

But while Kate was considering this in something like a rational way, Jenna—under the spell of whatever forces gripped her from within or without—was continuing to write. Her face was twisted with the effort, her wrist had stiffened, and her fingers grasped the pencil with a white-knuckled ferocity. The sheets seemed to fly out from under her hand, one after another, all with the same repeated words. The writing came faster and faster, the letters less rounded, more angular and slanting, larger and darker:

sorry **sorry** *didn't mean*

not *sorry sorry* **not your**

sorry mother don't be sorry **not your fault**

fault

fault *an accident don't blame sorry sorry*

don't blame yourself mother mother dear dear

Jenna was weeping now, rivulets of tears streaming from tight-shut eyes, her shoulders shaken with suppressed sobs. And then, as Kate watched, there seemed to be something like a struggle, the hand holding the pencil pushing jerkily, producing sharp lines, crooked lines, jagged shapes, but no recognizable words. Jenna was breathing in little gasps, her bosom heaving, her face a sickly gray-white, her head flung back, her eyes open, staring, unseeing, her lips moving in incoherent, inaudible, muttering whispers, as if trying to frame words her pencil refused to write, and all the while her pencil was moving, forming no words at all, only giant, jagged scrawls, like silent screams across the paper.

Patsy put out a protesting hand. "But she's ill!" she exclaimed in a low voice. "Sir Oliver, you must put a stop to—"

"No!" Sir Oliver commanded harshly. "More paper, Lady Sheridan. Quickly!"

Kate supplied another sheet. There was a pause, the space of several breaths, long enough to hear the wind shouting around the corner of the house and feel a searing flash of lightning at the window, followed almost immediately by a bone-jarring clap of thunder. Jenna seemed to gather herself, and began again, forming words, but these were scrawled, almost illegible, and the point of her pencil attacked the paper with such an angry force that it gouged holes.

> aint fair it aint
>
> aint

Ain't fair? Beryl said blankly. *What ghost is this?*

Kate's heart was thumping in her chest as she stared at the words, incredulity turning to fear. It was as if a different mind had seized the pencil, a different, angry energy, a different—

> aint fair
>
> aint fair at all
>
> all i wanted was to to
>
> to to to
>
> go

Jenna's face was twisted, her body writhing, as if she were wrestling with whatever power was driving the pencil, as though a fierce desperate power had seized her hand and would not let it go until it had howled out all it wanted to say, all it could say.

go go back

i only wanted to go back to

only go back to go

back to

bavaria

damn his bloody eyes

damn him

god damn him to hell

BAVARRRRR

beware

There was a loud crash of thunder, so near that it rattled the window. Kate felt her heart stop. Sir Oliver started wildly. Patsy gave a piercing shriek and leapt to her feet, her chair falling backward with a sharp clatter onto the stone floor. On the wall, the clock began to chime, as if it were a pealing bell, although it was nothing near the hour.

Jenna had slumped back in her chair, her head to one side, the pencil fallen from her fingers. She was breathing with long, shuddering gasps, her eyes closed. Kate rose and went to pour a glass of port, but her fingers were cold and her hand shook so that she dropped the glass. It shattered into fragments against the stone floor. By the time she returned to the table with another glass, Jenna's eyes were open and she was struggling to sit up. Patsy had gone to the clock and stopped its chiming with her hand.

"Bavaria?" Sir Oliver muttered, staring at the sheaf of papers he held in his hand. "Back to Bavaria? But—"

Beware? Beryl asked. *Beware of what?*

Patsy joined Kate, and between them, they managed to get Jenna to the sofa, where she lay back exhausted, her breathing shallow, her face very white.

"Is she all right?" Patsy asked worriedly.

"Back to Bavaria," Jenna said, her voice expressionless and dull. "Back to . . ." She closed her eyes. "Harriet," she whispered. "Thank you, Harriet. Thank . . ."

"I'm sure she'll be fine," Kate said, tucking a pillow under her head and spreading the garnet shawl over her. "We should just let her rest." She looked at Sir Oliver. "What happened, do you think?"

"I don't know," Sir Oliver said. "I don't understand any of it. I thought we were hearing from the daughter, from Harriet." He shuffled the papers, and put one down on the table. "You see there? 'Mother dear so sorry not your fault.' Exactly what we'd expect to hear from the little girl, don't you see?" His voice grew excited, and the hand holding the papers trembled. "It's evidence. It's evidence! No doubt about it, it's evidence of the survival of the child's personality beyond the grave!" He gave an enormous sigh. "At last. Oh, at last!"

"But what's that business about Bavaria?" Patsy asked, puzzled. "Harriet was never in Bavaria, at least to my knowledge. Nor Jenna. And the cursing—that's not Jenna. Those aren't her words, nor Harriet's."

"And look at the handwriting." Kate pointed to the page Jenna had written last, its hard, slashing strokes gouging into the paper. "It's not the same at all. If what Jenna received was a message from her daughter, this one must be . . . it must be something else entirely. From *someone else.*"

"But who?" Patsy asked, bewildered. "Damn *whose* bloody eyes?"

And "beware"? Beryl asked ominously. *It sounds like a warning.*

There was an expression in Sir Oliver's eyes of baffled incredulity, as if the thought, the question, was so staggering in its implications that he could scarcely grasp it. "It is another soul coming through," he said, "another spirit. It had such a powerful message to relay that it broke into the transmission of the child's message, exactly as would a powerful wireless signal overmaster a weaker."

Kate thought of the Kipling story she had read. Perhaps, after all, it was not so fanciful and far-fetched. "I hope," she said tentatively, "that you aren't discouraged."

Sir Oliver stared at her. "Discouraged? Discouraged, Lady Sheridan? Oh, no! Not in the slightest. This is proof, do you see? Proof of the survival of the soul—of two souls! And we are all witnesses!"

Jenna moaned, and Kate turned back to her. What was it they had seen? Proof of life after death? Or of some form of hypnotic suggestion, or unconscious wish, or even a communal hallucination?

Beware, Beryl muttered. *What does it mean?*

It was a question Kate could not answer.

CHAPTER TWENTY-SEVEN

Abraham White (the promoter of the American De Forest Wireless Company) had no compunction about inventing the most unlikely successes: to boost his company's share prices he would plant a story in the newspapers saying it had bought out American Marconi. Before there was time for a denial to be issued he would cash in shares whose value had risen momentarily, then keep his head down until the storm blew over.

Signor Marconi's Magic Box
Gavin Weightman

The discovery of the covert relationship between Miss Pauline Chase and Mr. Brian Fisher, both in the employ of the American De Forest Wireless Company, had given Bradford Marsden an enormous lift. There was nothing he could do to soften the impact of Maskelyne's letter to *The Times,* or to keep Marconi from replying to it, and thereby creating an even worse situation. There was nothing he could do to recover the missing tuner and the notebook—he'd had to put that business into Charles Sheridan's hands. But in the last few moments, it had begun to seem that there *was* something he could do to drive a wedge between the rapacious Miss Chase and Marconi, and by damn! he was going to do it.

Bradford stood by the window for a few minutes, his hands in his pockets, his chin sunk on his chest, deep in thought. Perhaps he could . . . No, not that, but alternatively . . . No, not that either—it was too complicated.

He frowned. How about . . . no, that wouldn't do, but what if . . . ?

Yes, by Jove, that just might be it! He turned the idea over in his mind for a few moments longer, looking at it from one angle, and then another, before deciding triumphantly that, yes, indeed, this was *exactly* the way to handle it. Then, with one last glance in the mirror and one more quick smooth of his hair, he went out.

His task was completed in very short order, for all of the pieces were ready to hand. The other business, finding the right place to conceal the thing he had made, was swiftly and privately attended to, and as he went downstairs to the lobby, he had every reason to anticipate a successful outcome of his plan. He paused at the desk for a moment to dispatch a note, and then went in search of Marconi.

"Ah, there you are, old chap," he said pleasantly, finding the man sitting in front of the fire in the lounge, a melancholy look on his face and a Campari at his elbow. Bradford sat down and lit a cigarette. "I trust that you are feeling somewhat better." To the waiter who came to stand beside him, he said, "Sherry, if you please."

"Not a great deal better, by any means," Marconi replied. He shook his head darkly. "Maskelyne is a cad, a bounder. I've made that plain in my letter to *The Times*. And another disheartening matter has come to my attention, in a newspaper clipping I received this afternoon from New York. You will find this hard to believe, Marsden, but De

Forest Wireless is claiming to have bought out our American Marconi company."

"Bought the company!" Bradford exclaimed. Outwardly, he was indignant, but inwardly he rejoiced, thinking ahead to his after-dinner arrangements and hoping that Marconi's anger, already stoked against the De Forest company, would blaze even more brightly when he was confronted with—

"Of course, there's not a word of truth in the report," Marconi went on sourly. "That scoundrel Abraham White planted the rumor merely to boost De Forest's stock prices. But it will cause us a great deal of damage—and do them a great deal of good—before it can be squelched."

"White is nothing but an unscrupulous villain," Bradford growled.

Marconi's sigh was heavy with a sense of personal wrong and injustice. "The world is full of villains, Marsden. I spend far too much time fighting against enemies of the company, when I should be doing more developmental work." He paused dejectedly, glancing toward the window. "Looks to be a foul night, I'd say. Glad I don't have to go out in it."

"Indeed," Bradford said. Outside, the landscape had turned drear, the sea was dull and darkly gray, and it was beginning to rain. There would be no sitting on the terrace tonight.

Marconi glanced at his pocket-watch and stood. "You'll join Miss Chase and me for dinner, won't you? I realize that you are somewhat acquainted with the lady, but I should like you to get to know her better. It's probable that she will be staying here at the Poldhu for a few days—perhaps even until the Royal visit. I believe she would be a delightful addition to our welcoming party, don't you think?"

"I'm sure," Bradford said, in a diplomatic tone. He stretched out his legs to the fire. "But I'll let you and Miss Chase have a private dinner tonight, if it's all the same to you. I'll finish my sherry and have a quick bite, and then be off upstairs. I have some correspondence I must attend to."

But Bradford was still lingering over his after-dinner coffee when Miss Chase and Marconi—deeply engrossed in each other at their intimate table—finished their final course. Outside, there was a flash of lightning, a low growl of thunder, and the patter of rain on the window. It was indeed a foul night.

At that moment, Mr. Fisher, freshly shaven and dressed in evening clothes, appeared in the doorway, looked around, and made a great show of noticing the couple. He made his way toward them, bowed to Miss Chase, and appeared to be introducing himself to Marconi. A moment later the two men were deep in conversation, and Miss Chase had excused herself with a pretty smile and an affectionate pat on Marconi's shoulder.

Bradford gave her two minutes. Then he pushed back his chair, went out to the lobby, waited for half-a-minute, and then hurried back to the dining room. Bending over Marconi, he whispered something in an urgent tone.

Marconi's eyes widened, and he put down his napkin. "Excuse me, Mr. Fisher," he said, hastily pushing back his chair. "A business matter has arisen which requires my immediate attention."

Fisher threw Bradford a curious, speculative glance. "Sorry to interrupt, Fisher," Bradford said apologetically. "Can't be helped, I'm afraid. But do stay and have a glass of wine. Mr. Marconi will be back in a few moments. Until then—" He signaled to the waiter. "Please be so good as to bring Mr. Fisher a glass of wine, and add it to the Marconi company bill."

"Thank you," Fisher said complacently. "Very kind of you, I'm sure. Very kind."

Marconi hurried out of the dining room, and Bradford followed. In the lobby, Marconi put his hand on Bradford's arm. "You say you've found the tuner?" he asked excitedly.

"No," Bradford replied. "I said I've learned something which may shed some light on the matter. But we have to hurry." He went toward the stairs and took them, two at a time.

"Where are we going?" Marconi asked breathlessly, as they reached the second floor landing.

"This way," Bradford directed, turning down the hall which led to Marconi's room.

"But where—"

"Shh." Bradford put his finger to his lips. They were standing outside Marconi's door, which hung slightly ajar.

Marconi frowned. "I'm sure I closed and locked it," he said. "And I turned off the light, as well." He stepped forward, pushing the door open, and stopped just inside. "Paulie!" he exclaimed. "What the devil—"

Miss Chase gave a scream as she whirled from the wardrobe, a wooden box in her hand. She turned pale. "Marky, you startled me! I didn't expect . . . that is, I thought . . ."

"It is quite obvious that you did not expect me." Marconi went into the room and Bradford, closing the door behind the two of them, exulted at the definite chill in his tone. "You will explain what you are doing in my room, and what that object is in your hand."

Bradford stepped forward and took the box out of Miss Chase's hand. When she did not speak, he said, "She believes that this is Gerard's tuner, or a copy of it. You certainly have to give the lady full marks for following instructions," he added admiringly.

"Instructions?" Marconi was imperious. "What instructions?" he demanded. "Who instructed you to invade my room, Miss Chase?"

Miss Chase put out her lower lip in a childish pout. "Oh, please, Marky, don't be angry with your Paulie," she pleaded. Her eyes were wet with unshed tears. "She was only trying to—"

"*Who,* I said!" Marconi screamed. His face was twisted, his jaw was mottled red, and Bradford saw with satisfaction that he had flown into one of his famous Italian tantrums. "You will tell me who, by God, or I—" He seized her wrist and forced her into a chair.

"Ow!" she wailed, rubbing her arm. "You hurt me! You can't—"

"I will do much more than that," Marconi said between gritted teeth. "Do you think I have no influence in Society, no influential friends? I will make it impossible for you to show your face in London henceforward. Who put you up to this?"

"I advise you to tell," Bradford said comfortably. "I am sure that neither White nor de Forest will stand up on your behalf. And as for Fisher, he's in it just as deep as you are, you know."

"How did you—" Miss Chase turned wondering eyes on him. "How could you—"

"White and de Forest!" Marconi cried incredulously. He stamped his foot. "Those scoundrels! And Fisher—the American who was chatting me up downstairs?"

"The very same," Bradford said. "Miss Chase is lodged in the room next to mine. I was able to overhear her and Fisher discussing their assignment. It seems that they were hired by De Forest Wireless to make off with the tuner and—"

"So that's what happened to it," Marconi said bitterly, looking down at Miss Chase. "You and Fisher took it! Why, you are nothing but a . . . a common thief! I shall have you prosecuted!"

"I resent being called 'common,'" Miss Chase replied petulantly, lifting her chin, her eyes flashing. "And we didn't take it, either. It was already gone by the time Mr. Fisher came to look for it." She frowned. "If we'd had the blasted thing, you don't think I would have come up here to your room to look for it, do you?"

Marconi narrowed his eyes and muttered a string of what Bradford took to be Italian oaths. Bradford had to suppress a smile. Really—the situation would have been comic had it not been so serious.

"Anyway," she went on, with an airy wave of her hand, "I don't know what all the fuss is about. So what if the original tuner was stolen? You've got another one. A copy. That box I found in the wardrobe."

"Actually, it's not a copy," Bradford said. He held up the box and shook it. It rattled. "It's only a wooden box filled with—as you so charmingly put it this afternoon— 'thingys.' I placed it on Mr. Marconi's shelf after I overheard you and Fisher planning your search of this room." He turned to Marconi. "I have been hesitant to tell you this, my friend, but our delectable Miss Chase has a rather speckled history of—"

"Mind what you say, Mr. Marsden," Miss Chase hissed. "Remember those letters!"

Bradford smiled pleasantly. "Ah, but blackmail is a game which any number can play. When we're finished, I doubt if you'll have the appetite for it." He turned to Marconi, who was staring at him, his jaw working, his lips compressed into a thin line. "As it turns out, Pauline Chase is not the only name this lovely creature has used. When I met her in Paris, she was Millicent Mitford. In Vienna, she was Francine Sterne, traveling with a wealthy American who had the misfortune to die rather unexpectedly. After the gentleman's death, neither Miss Sterne nor several of his valuable personal items could be found."

"Pauline!" Marconi's voice was filled with a fierce anguish. "You have betrayed me, you *vile* creature!"

And that, it seems, was for Miss Chase the last straw. She rose, gathering her tattered dignity about her, and said, "Well. If you think I'm going to stand here and be insulted, you can think again. Mr. Marconi, I shall take my leave."

Bradford went to the door and opened it. "If you feel you must," he said regretfully.

"Marsden!" Marconi screamed. "Stop her! I intend to prosecute this woman! She was caught in the act of theft! She has joined with my enemies in a conspiracy against me! Stop her!"

Her chin raised defiantly, Miss Chase had swept out the door and was making for the stairs. She did not, however, get very far. For as Bradford and Marconi saw when they went out into the hall, Mr. Fisher was coming up the stairs toward her, a dark scowl on his face. His hands appeared to be manacled in front of him. And behind him, prodding him forward and upward, was Constable Thomas Deane. His hat was thoroughly wet and his mackintosh was dripping.

"Now see what you've got us into," Fisher snarled at Miss Chase. He jerked his head. "This is the constable."

"The constable?" Marconi asked in surprise. "How did he—"

Miss Chase stamped her foot. "What *I've* got us into!" she cried indignantly. "This was all your idea, you fool, and don't you try to duck out of it!"

"I understand, Mr. Marconi," the constable said soberly, "that there's been a break-in." He frowned at Miss Chase. "Is this the burglar?"

"I didn't break in," Miss Chase said haughtily. "I had a key." She gathered her skirt in her hand. "Now, if you will excuse me—"

"A *stolen* key," Marconi snapped. "I gave you no permission to enter my room."

"We'll call it unauthorized entry, then," Bradford said. He held up the wooden box. "And attempted theft. As far as Mr. Fisher's part in the immediate conspiracy is concerned, I can vouch for that. I overheard him confess to Miss Chase that he broke into Mr. Gerard's room on Thursday night, and ransacked it. Moreover, I heard the two of them plotting to steal this valuable object"—he lifted the wooden box—"from Mr. Marconi's room. And Mr. Marconi and I surprised the lady in the act of taking it."

"Valuable object!" Miss Chase said sarcastically. "Why, it's only a little old wooden box filled with—"

"Shut up, Pauline," Fisher said. "You talk too much."

"That's quite enough, you two," said the constable. He motioned to Fisher with his head. "Come along, now, both of you. We're going into Helston."

"Into Helston?" Miss Chase's eyes were large and round. "But . . . but what for?"

"You're off to gaol," said the constable.

"You can't do that," Fisher protested. "I'm an American citizen!"

"Rubbish," said the constable sternly. "You have broken a British law. Here in Cornwall, we do not take attempted theft lightly. At the last assize, a man and a woman earned five years each for doing what you've just done."

"Oh!" cried Miss Chase, and put the back of her hand to her forehead.

"It's no good fainting, my dear," Bradford advised callously, as she showed every sign of doing just that. "We'll only let you lie until you pick yourself up off the floor." To Thomas Deane, he said, "Will you need any help with this pair, Constable?"

"Thank you, but I've brought someone with me. He's waiting with the horses. They'll be taken to Helston, where the accommodations are somewhat more comfortable." The constable regarded Miss Chase. "I certainly shouldn't like to handcuff a lady, but I will be forced to if she—"

"I hardly think that will be necessary," Bradford said. "Miss Chase understands, I believe, that her cooperation is critical to clearing up this business." He smiled at her. "Would you like to borrow my mackintosh, my dear? I'll drive up to Helston tomorrow so we can have a little talk. You can return it to me then."

"Talk?" Fisher asked in alarm. "What do you want to talk to her about? I'm the fellow who—"

"Oh, rather, quite," Bradford said. "Well, I certainly see why you would not want me to discuss these matters with *her*. But now that you've mentioned it, I believe I might find time to have a chat with you, as well."

The constable glanced at Bradford. "Lord Sheridan, sir. I've been trying to find him. Is he in the hotel this evening?"

"No. He's been out all day, and isn't expected until tomorrow morning," Bradford said. "Shall I ask him to stop in at your office?"

"Please do," Deane said. "Tell him it's important." To Fisher and Miss Chase, he added, "Let's be off now."

"How did it happen," Marconi asked, as they watched the constable shepherd his reluctant charges down the stairs, "that the constable appeared on the scene just after we encountered Miss Chase? And how did he know that Fisher was involved with her?"

"I sent him a note before dinner," Bradford said, "telling him what I thought might be up. Not that I didn't believe that you and I could apprehend them quite handily," he added hastily. "I simply felt that we didn't want to go to the bother. Sheridan might have done, but he is otherwise engaged this evening. Thus, the constable. Sheridan says he's a good chap, you know. Quite cooperative and all that."

"I see," Marconi said. He frowned. "Although I don't know why you want the trouble of interviewing that pair tomorrow. You might just as well let the law take its course."

"I intend," Bradford replied, "to require each of them, as a condition of their release, to sign an affidavit stating who employed them and why. If nothing else comes of this wretched affair, we may be able to force De Forest Wireless to leave off their dirty tricks."

" 'Wretched affair,' " Marconi said with an anguished sigh. "Too true, I am sorry to say. How could I have been so blind? I believed, oh, I honestly believed she *cared* for me!"

"I dare say, old chap," Bradford said, putting his arm around Marconi's shoulder. "But you must buck up. You'll find the right girl, just you wait and see. And in the meantime, there's plenty of work to be done." Tomorrow, he thought, Sheridan would be back from his evening on the other side of the Lizard. Perhaps he would have dug up a lead on the missing tuner, or an idea about Gerard. It was imperative that they get the bloody business completely cleaned up before the Royals put in an appearance.

"Ah, yes, work," Marconi said listlessly. "I suppose I shall have to spend some time in the laboratory, trying to sort out Gerard's progress. Perhaps I will be able to . . ." His voice trailed off.

"I'm sure you will," Bradford said encouragingly. "But there's nothing more to be done tonight. Shall we go and see if we can find someone to pour us an after-dinner drink?"

CHAPTER TWENTY-EIGHT

At the turn of the century German spies were still being disregarded with an almost criminal indifference by Britons in high places, both among politicians and Secret Service chiefs . . . From time to time warnings were given about the presence of (German) spies in Britain, but people who volunteered information on the subject were liable to be treated as at best nuisances and at worst as obsessed lunatics.

A History of the British Secret Service
Richard Deacon

Andrew Kirk-Smythe was summoned from a restless sleep by an insistent tapping at the door of his room. "Mr. Northrop, Mr.Northrop—are you there? A gentleman t'see you, Mr. Northrup."

Groggily, Andrew lit the bedstand candle and looked at his pocket watch. Going ten, it was. He didn't usually retire so early, but he'd been up nearly all night the night before and after a day on the water, he was tired to the bone. He pushed himself out of bed and padded barefoot to the door. "Who is it, at this hour?"

"Lord Charles, he says, Mr. Northrup."

"Show him up, then," Andrew said, knuckling the sleep out of his eyes. "Oh, and would you be so good as to send a boy up with a bottle of Scotch and a couple of glasses? Your best, if you please. Oh, and some coffee, too."

He lit the lamp, put on shirt and trousers, and combed his hair. Outside, thunder muttered across the Lizard and rain rattled the window. He doubted that there was any point in going out tonight, after all. Wolf wouldn't leave his mooring in such rough weather, and if he and his lady chose to tryst in the rain, Andrew would not presume to interfere.

By the time he was decent, Lord Charles was at the door, whiskey and glasses in hand. "Hullo, Northrup," he said with a twinkle. "I understand you're here to do a spot of bird-watching."

"Come in, m'lord," Andrew said, and closed the door behind him. "Very good to see you." He frowned at the bottle. "Sorry, sir. I told the landlord to send the boy with that."

"I volunteered. And we can dispense with titles." His guest, whose mackintosh was dripping on the floor, put the glasses on the chest of drawers, unstopped the bottle, and poured them each a drink. "Cheers, old man," he said, raising his glass. "Here's to all those *rarae aves* you've come to spy out."

Andrew raised his. "Take off your coat and have a seat," he said, pointing to the only chair, chintz-covered, beside the window. "Boots, too, if you like," he added, seeing that they were wet. "Pity there's no fire." He had chosen one of the dingier room at the back of the inn, next to the back stairs, rather than a larger, better-appointed room with a fire. He hadn't much money, and anyway, in a situation like this, he didn't like to call attention to himself. One never knew who might be watching.

"Not to worry," Sheridan said, hanging his mackintosh on the back of the door. "I'll soon dry out."

Andrew sat down on the edge of the bed, feeling awkward and ambivalent about the meeting, at the same time knowing it to be necessary. Sheridan might have information which could help him do what he had come to the Lizard to do. But how much he should tell of what he had already learned—well, he didn't know that yet, did he? It would depend on Sheridan, and he hadn't seen the man since Scotland. It might not be smart to tell him anything. The man had connections in Whitehall. Word might get back.

Before Sheridan sat down in the chair, he picked up the book lying there. *"Riddle of the Sands,"* he murmured. "A fascinating tale. Are you enjoying it?"

"Yes, although I must say that parts of it are rather sobering," Andrew replied. Erskine Childers's book, recently published, told the story of a pair of young adventurers, sailing off Germany's Frisian and Baltic shores. They uncovered a German plot to land an army of infantry armed with field-guns in a flotilla of sea-going lighters, towed by shallow-draft tugs to Britain's vulnerable east coast. The book was so detailed and well-documented that many readers had taken the fiction for reality.

"And perhaps not far off the mark," Sheridan said. "I have the feeling that people are going to be discussing this book for quite a time. Fiction or not, it certainly raises questions about how much we know of our German cousins' military intentions." He gave Andrew a narrow glance. "Are we free to talk here?"

Andrew frowned. Sheridan had a way of getting straight to the heart of the matter. "We're at the end of the hall, sir. The door opposite opens onto a stair, and the room next door is unoccupied. I think we can speak freely."

"The room next door is occupied now." Sheridan set his glass on the window sill, pulled off a boot, and dropped it with a thump onto the floor. "I've taken it for the night. I don't propose to go out into that storm again." He pulled off the other boot and leaned back, stretching his legs out in front of him and rubbing one stockinged foot against the other. "Tell me, Andrew—are you still handling cryptography for Military Intelligence?"

"In the main, although not at the moment," Andrew said guardedly. "I've . . . taken on an additional duty. The world is fast becoming a rather interesting place." He gave a little laugh, meaning it to sound careless but feeling that he had not quite brought it off.

"Isn't it," said Sheridan, wiggling his toes. "Wireless, and all that. The Germans appear to have quite an interest in it—and especially in Marconi's system." He took out his pipe and began to fill it with tobacco. "I'm told that the Kaiser doesn't have a great deal of confidence in the German wireless." He glanced up, arching an eyebrow inquiringly. "Perhaps you've run across this attitude, in the course of your . . . additional duty."

A great many possibilities flew through Andrew's mind. Perhaps, although he had been as careful as he could, he had somehow slipped up and revealed himself—not, he supposed, a difficult thing to do, especially with Sheridan watching. Perhaps Sheridan had been alerted by someone in the Admiralty; he didn't think so, but in that labyrinthine maze, one never knew who might have picked up a word here or a word there. Perhaps Sheridan had somehow managed to go round behind, through the Germans—such a thing was definitely possible, given his contacts on the Continent. Or perhaps Sheridan was merely probing, stabbing for reactions, for sensitivities.

But whatever the explanation, it was clear that Sheridan was fishing for his reasons for being on the Lizard, and he resolved to hold fast.

"Before I reply," Andrew said casually, "I hope you'll be good enough to answer a question of mine. Lady Sheridan told me that you were having a look into that accident at the Poldhu wireless station. The electrocution." He hesitated. "Is there . . . is there anything more to it than that?"

Sheridan struck a match and put it to his pipe. "Anything more? What more might there be?"

If there was a roundabout way to ask the question, some means of discovering it other than asking, Andrew couldn't for the life of him think what it was. He found himself simply blurting it out. "That is to say, have you a Royal commission? Are you here on behalf of the Crown?"

Andrew was well aware that Charles Sheridan had received such mandates in the past, having been tapped by the Palace for one task or another. They had first worked together when Andrew was serving as a personal bodyguard for the Prince of Wales, now King Edward, and their second job had involved a missing Royal in Scotland—a rather ticklish business which included a spot of espionage. On both occasions, Sheridan had done very fine work—and there may have been other such assignments of which he was unaware. It would undoubtedly make his own job a great deal harder if the man were here on a commission from the Palace, but there was nothing he could do about that.

"No Royal mandate, I am very glad to say," Sheridan remarked, pulling on his pipe.

Andrew tried not to look as relieved as he felt.

"In fact, quite the reverse," Sheridan went on. "I'm sure that Marconi would prefer not to call Daniel Gerard's electrocution to the attention of the Royals." He blew a ring of fragrant blue smoke and added, in an explanatory tone, "Marconi needs to know whether Gerard's death was an accident or something more, but fears that if the police got into it, the story would show up in the press, with negative consequences for the company. That's why I agreed to have a look."

Andrew was frowning now, almost completely at sea. "The Royals?" he asked blankly. "Why should the Royals pay any attention to a death on the Lizard?"

Sheridan cocked an inquisitive eyebrow. "You're not aware that the Prince and Princess of Wales will be here in a fortnight? The plan is for them to visit the station, have a look at the electrical works, and trade wireless hellos with the Tsar of All the Russias, or something like that."

Andrew stared. The Prince and Princess, *here?* Then perhaps he was wrong about the reasons for Wolf's presence on the Lizard. Perhaps there was more to it than he had thought. Perhaps—

Sheridan was grinning. "I didn't really think you were here as an advance scout for the Royal party, Andrew, but it did seem a plausible explanation for your presence."

Andrew grimaced. "Smashing," he said, with a gloomy sarcasm. "Just smashing." The personal protection of Royal persons was no longer up his line, and the Admiralty didn't know he was here, so he'd not known of the plan. "A fortnight, you say?"

Well, with any luck, his business would be over and he would be out of here by that time. Unless of course, there was some connection between Wolf and the Royal visit. He shivered. Good God, now *that* would be something, wouldn't it?

"Yes, it's to be Saturday the eighteenth," Sheridan said. "I'd like, if I could, to get this unfortunate business at the wireless station wrapped up before then, but it's beginning to look doubtful." He paused, eyeing Andrew. "I take it, then, that you have nothing to do with the Royal visit?"

"Hardly." Andrew regarded him, feeling rather more comfortable. "And you have no Royal commission?"

"None at all," Sheridan said, and chuckled. "Well, then. Now we've cleared that up, we can be straight with one another. Why *are* you here, Andrew? Does it have anything to do with the fellow you were watching in Gillan Harbor today?"

The thunder rumbled again, and the rain beat harder against the window.

Well, if he knew that much, Andrew thought with resignation, there was no point in trying to dodge the rest of it. "Yes, it does," he said. "I have reason to suspect that the man may be somehow involved with that 'unfortunate business,' as you put it, at the Poldhu station. After the fact, perhaps."

Sheridan leaned forward, pipe in hand, elbows on his knees. "And I have reason to believe that Daniel Gerard's death might not have been an accident, although I have no proof. Gerard was developing a new tuner, you see—a rather critical piece of wireless apparatus, designed to solve the problem of interference and interception. He'd been working on the device in the laboratory in the Poldhu Hotel, adjacent to the company office, where he also kept a diary of his designs and experiments. Both the tuner and the diary are gone. And last night, somebody broke into Gerard's hotel room and ransacked it."

"Gone!" Andrew exclaimed, sitting forward. His equilibrium, which seemed to have steadied over the last few moments, took on a precipitous tilt. "You don't mean to tell me that the tuner . . ." He stopped. He hadn't intended to go that far.

"Ah," Sheridan said. "You know about the tuner, then?" When Andrew bit his lip and did not reply, he took one or two more puffs of his pipe and went on. "Of course, it's possible that Gerard died accidentally, and that someone who knew about the existence of the tuner and the diary took them for his own purposes. But it is also possible—quite possible, unfortunately—that Gerard was deliberately pushed into the electrical works, either to put an end to the tuner project, or to steal the tuner itself."

"Well, then," Andrew said, feeling that he had better tell all he knew. "I think I might be able to offer you a bit of help. I suppose you know about Jack Gordon—the Marconi operator who went over the cliff at Lizard Point about a fortnight ago."

If Sheridan was curious about the connection, he didn't reveal it. "Yes," he said. "I spent part of the day at the station. As I understand it, nobody saw the accident, if that's what it was. But I've spoken with the other wireless operator, who disallows the possibility of Gordon's walking off the cliff in a drunken state."

"He didn't," Andrew said simply. He emptied his Scotch and got up to pour another. "I know, because I saw what happened." He turned, lifting the bottle. "Another for you?"

Sheridan replied by holding out his glass. Andrew filled it and sat down on the bed again, settling himself to his story.

"I've had this fellow—the man who appeared in Gillan Harbor this morning—under surveillance for some time. He's known as Wolf, although of course that's not his real name. He came to the Lizard around the middle of June. He's a sailor, you see. Has his own boat, which has posed a bit of a challenge for me. I caught him up the first time among the Frisian islands—how that came about is a rather long and involved tale, and I shan't bother you with it now. Enough to say that I got onto him when I was in Kiel, doing a little job for the Admiralty."

"But not in cryptography?" Sheridan asked.

"No, that's become rather a sideline, although I do keep my hand in." Andrew took a swallow of Scotch. "Anyway, when I connected with the fellow again, his yacht was berthed in Mullion Cove, and he was spending most of his time hanging about the village. It was not, as I learned, his first visit to the area—he had been here back in the winter, while I was cooling my heels in London with a different assignment. On the night Gordon died, Wolf went down to the pub in Lizard Village, and the two of them—Wolf and Gordon—shared a pitcher of ale."

"Was this the first time you'd seen them together?" Sheridan asked.

"Yes, but Wolf had been here for a few days by the time I arrived, and it's possible they'd met during that time. But as I say, it was a new connection for me." He crossed his legs. "Anyway, I followed Wolf to the pub, and got as close as I could to the pair of them. He and Gordon—I found out his name by asking the barman—talked for a while, amicably at first, and then they seemed to get into a disagreement. I got the idea that Wolf wanted Gordon to do something he wouldn't, or couldn't do. After a bit, Wolf shrugged—the sort of disgusted shrug that says, 'I'm done with it'—and left the pub."

"And you followed him?"

Andrew nodded, remembering that night, and the feeling that he'd had about it, the feeling of something about to happen, and of wanting to watch it, and not wanting, at the same time. "It was a bit of a delicate business. I went out to the privy and watched through a crack. Wolf hung about behind a nearby shed, and waited until Gordon came out. Then he followed him, trailing not far behind. I kept to the shadows behind the both of them. When Gordon got to the high point of the cliff, Wolf caught him up and they talked for a moment or two. The discussion seemed to be entirely friendly, but then—" He swallowed. He didn't like telling this. "One shove, and that was it."

"You didn't try to stop it?" Sheridan asked.

No, he hadn't tried to stop it, because interfering would have put himself in the picture—the last thing he wanted to do. At the time, that had seemed right. Now, he wasn't sure. But now, it was too late for anything except explanations, excuses.

"I'm sure you understand the circumstance. If I had intervened—well, the game would've been up, wouldn't it?"

"I suppose that was the reason you didn't attempt to have Wolf arrested for murder."

Now they were getting a little closer to the uncomfortable truth, and Andrew spoke more cautiously. "My eyewitness testimony would've been the only evidence against him at inquest. He would've been bound over for trial, of course, which would have put my quarry out of my reach. And when the case came to trial, his defense council would surely have uncovered my interest in the matter." He grinned ruefully, although not altogether honestly. "That would be the end of my usefulness as an operative, and I'm not quite ready to quit."

"Yes, I suppose that news of your activities would get back to Wolf's colleagues here in England, and to the person they're working for." Sheridan paused. "Do you know who that is?"

"I have some suspicions," Andrew said evasively. In the

end, of course, that was the chief issue. "You're right. Convicted of murder, my man would be out of the game, and so would I. And his associates would know we are on to them and I . . . we should have to start all over to ferret them out." He shook his head. "I . . . we must keep an eye on them, so that in the event of hostilities, they can all be swept up together."

"I suspect that Gordon was working for your man Wolf, in one capacity or another," Sheridan said. "I was told that he had been planning to take a holiday—to visit family in Bavaria."

Bavaria! That explained a great deal, didn't it? But it also pointed to the weakness of his own methods. He should have thought to look into Gordon's background for a clue as to how Wolf might have been using him. "But I thought the Marconi Company refused to employ Germans," Andrew said, as if to explain to himself why he hadn't dug any deeper. "That's what I heard after the Germans tried to break into the Nova Scotia station last summer." And that's what they had told the Admiralty, he added to himself.

"So I understand," Sheridan said with a shrug. "But if a man can pass himself off as British, I imagine whoever is doing the hiring takes him at face value."

Andrew stared at the opposite wall, thinking. "So Gordon was in league with Wolf," he muttered. "I suppose he was killed because he knew too much, or was threatening to reveal it, or wouldn't do as he was told." He could think of a dozen other reasons, none of them pretty, why one spy might murder another.

Sheridan puffed on his pipe. "And what about this chap Wolf?" he asked after a moment. "Is he of great importance to . . . to whoever you're working for at the moment?" He eyed Andrew. "And who is that? Army Intelligence?"

Andrew shifted uncomfortably. This was the tricky part. "If you must know, I've been seconded to Naval Intelligence. Unfortunately, the Admiralty by and large don't seem to think that intelligence is vital to the defense of the realm, and they behave as if wireless were no more important than any other technology. They don't view Wolf and his sort as significant enough to warrant attention. In fact, they don't seem at all concerned about spies. Somehow, German agents just are not on the horizon."

"I've encountered that attitude," Sheridan remarked. His gaze lingered on Andrew. "French, Russians, but not Germans." He grinned around the stem of his pipe. "Probably has to do with the Kaiser being Victoria's grandson, and her commissioning him as an honorary Admiral of the Fleet. I understand that he told the British ambassador in Berlin that the thought of wearing the same uniform as St. Vincent and Nelson made him positively giddy."

The old queen's grandson, Andrew thought with bitter amusement. As if blood relations had never in the history of the world gone to war. As if the men who worked in Steinhauer's German Intelligence were all gentlemen, and wouldn't dream of spying on British soil. Steinhauer—who had previously been a private detective for the Pinkertons!

"Of course," he said sarcastically, "it might be a different story entirely if one of Steinhauer's fellows were caught copping the key to Jackie Fisher's office, or passing design details out of the Portsmouth shipyard. That might make our side wake up and take notice."

Andrew's move to Naval Intelligence had come not long after Jackie Fisher was promoted from Second Sea Lord to Commander-in-Chief, Portsmouth—assignments which were established stepping stones to the office of First Sea Lord. It was common knowledge that Fisher viewed Germany as Great Britain's most probable naval opponent, and that he was already developing a strategy to combat the Kaiser. He had raised the Home Fleet—now called the Channel Fleet—from eight battleships to twelve by withdrawing four ships from the Mediterranean Fleet, and instructed his commanders to think in terms of fighting alongside France, rather than against her. And there were rumors that as soon as he was officially named First Sea Lord (surely no more than a matter of months), he planned to build a ship so formidable that it would strike terror into the heart of any nation which dared to challenge Great Britain on the high seas. Fisher already had a name for it: *Dreadnought*.

"Wake up our side indeed," Sheridan remarked thoughtfully. "Still, the Admiralty are very much worried about keeping the tonnage and gunnery secret, not to mention the potential speed. They wouldn't like any of that sort of information to somehow get to the Kaiser."

Andrew pounded his fist on his thigh. "But all the *Dreadnought*s in creation won't be worth a bloody farthing," he burst out, "if we don't have some better means of communication! I've been studying wireless, and it seems to me that Marconi's system offers our best hope of developing a reliable ship-to-ship and ship-to-shore communication. I'll be damned if I'll let the Germans steal it from us, whatever the Admiralty thinks!"

There. It was out, and the devil take it.

Sheridan gazed at him for a moment. "Ah," he said finally. "So this is your own private patch, is it? Your own bit of personal espionage?" He paused. "I suppose that's really why you couldn't report Gordon's death as murder. You were afraid that word of your doings might get back to the Admiralty."

"I've taken furlough for three months," Andrew muttered. "They bloody well can't tell me where I can go or what I can do on my own time. If I want to keep an eye on one bloke or another, or track down a few leads of my own, that's my bloody business, and none of theirs."

"Oh, I'm not censuring you," Sheridan said mildly. "Not at all. In fact, I quite agree with you about the problem of the German spies, and especially where it comes to this wireless business. If we find ourselves at war, particularly a naval war, wireless may well hold the key to victory. But the transmissions have got to be secure against interception and interference—and the German wireless system hasn't a prayer of achieving that." He leaned forward, his brown eyes intent. "Is that what Wolf is after, do you think? The tuner Gerard was developing?"

"Yes," Andrew said emphatically. "I think they got word of Gerard's work in Berlin, and Steinhauer set Wolf on him. The fellow was a natural choice—he worked for Slaby and D'Arco on that duplex wireless of theirs. He understands what's involved." He frowned. "He didn't steal the tuner— I'd swear to that. If he had, he'd be gone from here by now. But I can suggest someone else."

"Oh?" Sheridan slanted a questioning look. "And who would that be?"

"I was in Mullion last night, keeping a watch on Wolf. He spent some time at The Pelican, talking to Dick Corey, from the wireless station. Of course, it's possible that Corey hasn't a clue, and that Wolf is simply probing—especially if he's also got word that the tuner is missing. He's not a man to leave any stone unturned, no matter how unproductive." He paused, thinking. "You may have already questioned Corey in Gerard's death, but it warrants another go. He may be simply trying to get rid of stolen property, or he may be deliberately practicing espionage." Either way, Andrew thought, Corey could very well be in danger. Two men had died already. Corey could be the third.

"I see," Sheridan said, and reflected for a moment. "Of course, as you say, Wolf may simply be exploring all possibilities. But perhaps we had better arrange a little test for Mr. Corey. What would you say to participating in a bit of counter-espionage?"

"You can count me in," Andrew said promptly. "What did you have in mind?"

Sheridan looked up at the ceiling, blowing smoke rings. After a moment, he began outlining a strategy. Andrew offered other ideas, and they turned them over for a time, finally agreeing to a plan.

"Very good," Charles said. "I suggest you sail round the Lizard to Mullion tomorrow, first thing, and we'll put the business into operation." He paused again. "How is it, do you suppose, that your man Wolf is communicating with his colleagues?"

"I don't have to suppose, I know," Andrew said, with a dark humor. This was the most amusing part of the whole thing. "The damned fellow is using messenger pigeons." He chuckled ironically. "Isn't that something? Doesn't that impress you with his ingenuity? The man is one of Slaby's proteges, he's out to steal the most advanced of communications technologies, and he's passing the word to his associates via messenger pigeons!"

Sheridan shrugged. "Perhaps. But in the circumstance, it's a more sure means of communication than any other. Pigeons are generally proof against both interference and interception. If Wolf were operating a transmitter on board that boat, his messages would certainly be picked up." He glanced at Andrew. "I don't suppose you have been able to intercept any of the pigeons."

"Not a chance," Andrew replied. "I've only seen him release two, one a week or so ago, the other one yesterday morning. I doubt he can be keeping more than a few on that yacht of his."

"Six," Charles said.

"Six?" Andrew stared at him. He knew that Charles Sheridan was a genius at uncovering information, but—"How the devil do you know how many pigeons Wolf keeps?"

Sheridan regarded his pipe as if wondering whether it had gone out. "A little girl told my wife."

"Told . . . Lady Sheridan?"

"Yes. It seems that the child—in the company of Jenna Loveday's daughter, Harriet—climbed onto the boat when they knew the coast was clear. This happened in February, before the daughter's drowning. They found six pigeons in a cage."

The child. Andrew had seen her over the past few weeks, watching the boat. So Lady Sheridan had befriended her. It was not an idea which had occurred to him, although it should have done.

"There's more," Sheridan said. "It seems that the pigeon whose release you witnessed yesterday morning did not immediately fly off to its destination. It detoured by way of the church bell tower, where the girl—her name is Alice—happened to be feeding the birds, as she does regularly. Kate says she is a very clever child. Clever or simply curious, Alice relieved Wolf's pigeon of its burden."

Andrew was dumbfounded. "She—what?"

Sheridan reached into his pocket and took out a scrap of

flimsy. "I assume that you read German," he said, and handed it over.

Andrew read it at a glance. "Item located, negotiations begun," he whispered. "By God, Wolf has located the tuner. And this is *proof!*" Holding the flimsy between his fingers, he felt an exultant, victorious surge, which died away as quickly as it arose. Proof was of no use at all, in the circumstance, for there could be no trial, no justice. That tuner was their sole object now. It couldn't be allowed to fall into German hands.

"Indeed," Charles said. He paused. "If it's of any use to you, the name he's given to Jenna Loveday is Niels Andersson."

Andrew felt a surge of deep compassion for Jenna Loveday. "When I saw him first in Kiel, he was calling himself Hans Rhinehardt. There's no particular reason why he should have told her his real name."

Sheridan nodded. "Kate didn't say it in so many words, but I got the distinct impression that Wolf and Jenna Loveday are—or have been—lovers."

"I know." Andrew turned away. He took a small leather-bound book from the drawer of the bedside table, opened it at the back, and slipped the paper Sheridan had given him into a kind of pocket between the leather cover and the stiff paper which lined it. He returned the book to the drawer. "She was apparently visiting him on the yacht the night that her daughter drowned," he added in a matter-of-fact tone. "At least, that's what they're saying in the village. The affair seems to be a matter of common knowledge, and common talk."

"Ah," Sheridan said regretfully. "I doubt if Lady Loveday knows that people are talking. Kate seemed to think the affair was a closely-held secret."

"The lady is not terribly discreet," Andrew remarked,

and was surprised at the pang which came with the words. "I saw them together myself today, in Gillan Harbor. Both Miss Marsden and I photographed the scene," he added, and went on to describe what he had seen. "I think it was an accidental meeting, but I've been concerned that she might become an unwitting participant in whatever plot Wolf is hatching. He will use her if he can."

He thought of the scene at Lizard Point, the quick, hard shove, Gordon's scream as he went over. If Jenna Loveday got in Wolf's way, something of the sort could happen to her. He thought of Jenna—slim, delicate, vulnerable Jenna—in Wolf's arms, and of a sudden fierce twist, a broken neck, a body disposed of at sea. He shuddered, suddenly afraid for her.

"Wolf's a very dangerous man."

"And love is a dangerous passion." Sheridan's smile held a slight amusement, but his glance, Andrew felt, was penetrating. "I shouldn't think spies are immune to it, any more than the rest of us. Love would explain his being here, wouldn't you think? On this side of the Lizard, I mean. So far, at least, all the action has been in Mullion and at Lizard Point. If all the man wants is to get his hands on the tuner, he should be staying over there."

"Love or lust," Andrew said, pushing away the thought, and the unexpected anger. "But you're right. He could far more easily tie up in Mullion, or at one of the other little harbors nearer by, instead of sailing all the way round Lizard point to the Helford River. She has to be the reason he comes to Frenchman's Creek."

He frowned, uncomfortably aware that there seemed to be more here—more in his feeling for Jenna Loveday, that is—than he himself had wanted to admit. He had thought it was merely compassion for her loss, perhaps mixed with admiration for her courage, and certainly for her beauty. But . . . more? He did not want there to be more. It would only complicate what he had to do. Don't linger on it, he thought to himself. Focus on the task and ignore the feelings. They will go away.

"I picked up one other bit of village gossip," he went on. "Some of the folk here in Helford are saying that Wolf might have had something to do with the child's drowning. It seems that he weighed anchor and left very early on the morning she was found dead, in the creek."

"If that's true," Sheridan said, "if he had something to do with her child's death, and if she loves him, it's another tragedy for her."

Andrew could taste the sourness in his mouth. "Any involvement with the man is a tragedy, if you want my opinion." He paused. He hated to bring this up now, but now, if ever, was the moment. "I hope you will not take it amiss if I say that it's best not to let Lady Sheridan know anything about this business."

Sheridan regarded him. "Why?"

"Because if Lady Sheridan spoke of it to Jenna—to Lady Loveday—word might get to Wolf, even if she did not mean to tell him."

"That's so," Sheridan said easily, and smiled. "You can count on me to keep it a secret from the ladies, Andrew."

Andrew relaxed. He'd been dreading having to say that, and there had been no need. He wished the other problem— his feelings for Jenna—were as easily resolved. "Another Scotch?" he asked.

Sheridan wiggled his toes again. "I believe my socks are dry. It's been a very long day, and I am ready for bed. Are you watching birds tonight?"

A flash of blue lightning lit the sky outside, and thunder

rattled the windows. "I doubt if Wolf will be going anywhere in this weather," Andrew said, thinking that if Jenna had gone to him, if the two of them were alone on the boat together, making love, he did not want to know about it. "I believe I'll stay in tonight."

"Good," Sheridan said, and tossed off the last of his drink. "I wouldn't have wanted you to go out in this storm alone, but I wouldn't have wanted to go, either. I'm glad you have taken the decision out of my hands."

He stood, picked up his boots, and retrieved his mackintosh. In his stockinged feet, he opened the door. "Goodnight, Andrew. Don't stew over all we've said. Just go to bed and get a good night's sleep. There'll be plenty to do tomorrow."

"Goodnight," Andrew said, and was left staring at the closed door. Go to sleep, when he had so much new information to turn over? The stolen tuner, an inquisitive child, six pigeons, and an intercepted note. And now, Jenna Loveday.

Jenna Loveday, Jenna Loveday.

If Andrew knew himself at all, he knew he'd be awake half the night.

CHAPTER TWENTY-NINE

Saturday, 4 July, 1903

It is seldom very hard to do one's duty when one knows what it is, but it is sometimes exceedingly difficult to find this out.

Note-Books
Samuel Butler

Charles rose just before dawn, breakfasted with Andrew, and drove back across the Lizard to Mullion—a pleasant drive in the cool, bright air of the early morning. The road was muddy, but the night's rain had freshened the moor, the sky was a vault of unclouded blue, and diamond droplets of dew sparkled in the sun's first light. The horse seemed energized by the cool breeze, and in spite of the mud and mire of the road, they made good time across the peninsula.

It was just after nine when Charles drove into Mullion. Thinking about what lay ahead for the day, he decided to have a brief talk with the constable, upon whose help he and Andrew might have to rely. He hitched his horse to the railing outside King's Chemist's Shop and went down the narrow alley to the office of the Devon-Cornwall Constabulary in the rear. The constable's red bicycle was there, the door was partly open, and from within came the sound of a broom being vigorously wielded. Charles knocked, and the sweeping ceased. A moment later, the constable came through an interior door, broom in one hand, the terrier at his heels.

"Good morning, Lord Charles," he said, standing the broom in a corner. "I'm glad you received my message."

"Message?" Charles shook his head. "Sorry, no. If it was left at the Poldhu, I wasn't there. I've just come from Helford, where I spent the night."

"I see." The constable dusted his hands and went to the kettle steaming on the gas ring. "I was about to make tea for myself. Will you have a cup?"

"Yes, indeed." Charles sat down and took out his pipe. The terrier, as if this were a familiar routine, retreated to his blanket in the corner, turned twice, and settled down with his nose on his tail. "A message, eh? Something new has turned up?"

"You might say so." Deane grinned. "Two things, actually," he replied, getting out the pot and spooning in tea. "If you haven't been to the hotel yet this morning, I take it that you haven't heard about Miss Chase and Mr. Fisher."

"No, I haven't." Charles took out his tobacco and began the ritual filling of his pipe. "Miss Chase's name is certainly familiar to me, although I've not yet had the pleasure of meeting the lady." He thought of Bradford's pained expression as he'd related the ominous tale of her manifestations in various places, under various names, all different. "But who is Fisher?"

"Fisher? He's the American I mentioned to you when we talked last—the man who said he was here to play golf but has spent all his time poking about the village."

Charles lit his pipe and listened with growing surprise,

mixed with amusement, as the constable related the events of the night before. It sounded as if Bradford had been supremely successful, or very lucky, or both.

"You say that Miss Chase and Fisher are in the Helston gaol?" he asked, when the whole story had been told. "What's to be the charge?"

"Attempted theft. As you heard, the lady was caught red-handed, with what she thought was the tuner. Of course, it was only a wooden box, but she wasn't to know that." The tea now brewed, the constable poured. Handing Charles a cup, he added, "Don't think there's any direct proof of it, but Mr. Marsden overheard Fisher boast that he had ransacked Gerard's lodging." He sat down himself and lit a cigarette.

So that was it, Charles thought. He reached into his coat pocket and took out the small round button covered with cream-colored kid he had picked up off the floor in Gerard's room. He put it on the table beside his tea cup.

"What's this?" the constable asked, picking it up and looking closely at it.

"I found it in Gerard's room after the break-in," Charles said. "I suspected that it might be a button from a woman's kid glove, but it might just as easily have come from a golfer's spats. It should not be difficult to check Fisher's spats—assuming the man wears them—and see whether they are lacking any buttons."

"I shall do just that." The constable took possession of the button. "Too bad you couldn't have been there last night, sir. It was what you might call an interesting scene. Full of drama."

"I'm sure," Charles said, thinking that however Bradford Marsden had managed the business, he seemed to have successfully accomplished his mission: to separate the dangerous Miss Chase from her victim. "I am truly sorry I missed it." He paused. "Was that what you wanted to talk with me about?" He rather thought not, since the constable would likely have assumed that Bradford himself would report the news about Miss Chase and Fisher.

"No," Deane said. "Not directly, anyway." He tapped the ash off his cigarette into a cracked cup half full of cigarette butts. "It has to do with the tuner that's gone missing, y'see. Not the fake which tripped up the lady last night. The real one."

"Well, then." Charles leaned forward. "You have news of it?"

"No, sir, but I have a suspicion. I was in The Pelican night before last, and so was Dick Corey. He was talking with a foreign-looking chap, the one who sails in and out of here on occasion. Danish, the man might be, or Swedish. I saw the sailor slip Corey some money, under the table."

Money, Charles thought. Kirk-Smythe had missed that— but then, the constable was sitting in a different place, with a different angle of vision. "Were you close enough to hear their talk?"

"No, I wasn't," the constable said regretfully. "So I can't be sure what the money was for. A gambling debt, maybe, or even a bit of procurement, although I'd have to say I haven't got wind of anything like that going on in the village. Up in Helston, maybe, or Penzance, but not here. However, I know that Corey was one of the men who worked with Gerard, and I did just think—" He stopped and eyed Charles. "Am I off the mark here?"

"I think," Charles replied, "that you might just be spot on. That sailor has a compelling reason to acquire the tuner.

I think you'll understand when I've told you the story, which also involves the murder of Jack Gordon."

"Murder, eh?" said the constable thoughtfully.

"Yes," Charles said, "although it can't be proven in a court of law. But listen—" And he related as much of the story as he felt he could, without compromising Kirk-Smythe or his mission.

Deane listened with attention and with a growing seriousness. "I see," he said, when Charles had concluded. "Well, that's a bit of a facer. What can I do to help?"

Charles stood and began to pace. "I'm afraid we are working against the clock in this matter, Constable, and time is growing short. Here's the plan I have in mind for—"

"Oh, Constable Deane!" a woman's voice cried shrilly, and a female figure of substantial bulk darkened the door. She wore a black coat and a large green hat, which was decorated with a mound of fearsomely colorful raffia flowers. She carried a black umbrella, which she brandished like a spear. "Oh, good, very good. I am so glad to find you in. I have the most important news, you see, and we must discuss it straightaway. There are a great many decisions being made, and you should be informed."

"Good morning, Miss Truebody." The constable rose to his feet. His voice, Charles noted, was resigned, and he made no effort at introductions. The terrier, who had been jarred out of a sound sleep by the woman's cry, stood and shook himself. "Unless your errand is urgent, I must respectfully ask that—"

"Urgent!" cried Miss Truebody in a very loud voice, enthusiastically gesturing with her umbrella. "Urgent! Why, my dear man, of course it is urgent! We in Mullion are facing one of the most significant challenges in the history of our dear little village! You will have the duty and honor of protecting two of the most august Presences in the land, for we are expecting—" She stopped, having noticed Charles, who had withdrawn to a distant corner of the room. "Pardon me," she said distantly. "I did not know you were engaged."

The terrier, with the clearest intimation of disdain, trotted past Miss Truebody and out the door.

"Don't mind me," Charles said. "I—"

"That's alright, then," boomed Miss Truebody, bowing in Charles's general direction. "I would not interrupt, of course, but time is growing short and the committee must take decisions of enormous significance on very short notice. You see, Constable Deane, our little village is to be the site of a most unusual, most magnificent event. Their Royal Highnesses, the Prince and Princess of Wales, are due to arrive on—"

"Eighteen July," said the constable.

Miss Truebody's eyes narrowed. "Indeed. Eighteen July. You are aware? You have been . . . informed?"

"I have been informed," said the constable. He stood. "Now, if you will excuse me, Lord Charles and I are discussing a rather important matter. If you would be so good as to return—"

"I am sorry, Constable Deane," she said, her eyes flicking to Charles with rather more respect, now that she understood that he was a lord. "But it is your duty to listen to what the committee—"

"—return tomorrow," the constable concluded, as though she had not spoken. He frowned. "No, that won't do, tomorrow's Sunday. Come by on Monday morning, Miss Truebody, and we'll have a talk. No, best make it Monday afternoon. I have a pair of prisoners in Helston, and I shall need to see the magistrate."

"But sir! Your duty!"

"Monday afternoon, Miss Truebody," the constable said firmly, crossing his arms.

"Oh, very well," the lady muttered, and swept out of the room, leaving a raffia flower behind on the floor.

"Good show, Deane," Charles said with admiration, picking the flower up and placing it on the table. The terrier stood on the threshold, surveyed the room as if to be sure that the lady was gone, and found his corner and his blanket again.

"Thank you, sir," the constable said. He grinned. "I do know my duty. Once the rooster lets the old hens take over the coop, he's done for." He took out another cigarette. "Now, where were we?"

"We were talking about Dick Corey," Charles said. "Let me tell you what I have in mind."

It took only a moment to outline the idea he and Kirk-Smythe had worked out the night before. When he had concluded, the constable nodded. "It might just work," he said. "And if it doesn't, I suppose there's nothing to lose."

Yes, there is, Charles reflected grimly. He thought of the wireless tuner in the hands of the Germans, and shivered at the possible consequences. They had better work fast, and they had better do it right. There was a great deal at stake, and a very great deal to lose.

CHAPTER THIRTY

Of all the facts presented to us we had to pick just those which we deemed to be essential, and then piece them together in their order, so as to reconstruct this very remarkable chain of events.

"The Naval Treaty"
Sir Arthur Conan Doyle

Bradford Marsden, feeling smug and self-congratulatory, was breakfasting rather later—and rather more elaborately—than usual, with a glass of the hotel's best champagne beside his orange juice, and the bottle nestled in a bucket of ice. It was by way of celebration, he told himself, for the success of last night's little game. Marconi was cured of his ridiculous infatuation with Pauline Chase, the De Forest Wireless Company's nefarious plot against the Marconi Company had been foiled, and with any luck at all, Sheridan would shortly locate the missing tuner. Then Marconi could finish the job of making the bloody thing work, and they could all get on with the plans for the Royal visit. And then—

But at that moment, a shadow fell across the table, and Bradford looked up.

"Good morning, Charles," he said heartily. "Just back from Helford, are you? Well, well. Pull up a chair and join me for breakfast."

"Thank you, but I've eaten," Charles said, and sat down.

"Well, then, a glass of bubbly." Bradford hooked his finger at the waiter, who hurried over with a second glass, took the champagne out of the bucket, and poured. Bradford lifted his glass. "To success," he said, "and the *absent* Miss Chase." He tilted his head. "Have you heard?"

"I've heard," Charles said, as the glass rims clinked. He added, to the waiter, "I'll have coffee, please." To Bradford, he said, "I stopped at the constable's office. He told me what happened, and the outcome. But he couldn't tell me how you managed to set it up."

"Right," Bradford said. "I didn't bother to let the constable in on the initial gambit. Sufficient for him to appear at the ultimate checkmate—the moment we nabbed pretty Paulie with the tuner in her dear, dainty hands." He pushed his plate away and leaned back in his chair. "Not the real tuner, of course. Just a wooden box with a generous selection of 'thingys' in it. They rattled quite satisfactorily."

"Thingys?" Charles asked, with amusement.

"Her word." He took out a gold cigarette case, an engagement present from Edith, and extracted a cigarette. "I overheard Miss Chase and Fisher—the American who claimed to be here to play golf—talking in her hotel room, which, most conveniently, was adjacent to mine. During the conversation, it emerged that they were both employed by the American De Forest Wireless Company. Both had the same assignment, to steal the tuner."

"So they gave themselves away," Charles said thoughtfully.

"They did indeed. From that point on, it was merely a matter of stage management. I concealed the fake tuner in Marconi's room, without his knowledge, of course. I contacted the constable and arranged with him to make the arrests. And then I took Marconi upstairs to witness the nefarious doings." He smiled complacently. "Miss Chase did not disappoint. Really, Sheridan, I do wish you had been here to observe."

"I congratulate you, Marsden," Charles said. "A splendid job." His coffee arrived and he added cream and sugar. "Marconi is going to prosecute?"

"I doubt it," Bradford said. "The negative publicity, you know, although the pair is not to know that just yet. I plan to drive over to Helston this morning to have a conversation with Miss Chase."

"About those letters?" Charles grinned.

"Yes." Bradford chuckled, in anticipation. "I imagine the lady will agree that a batch of letters is a small price to pay for freedom. Shouldn't you?"

"Most likely," Charles said. "I wonder—what were you able to learn yesterday when you went to Porthcurno? What's the purpose of that aerial over there?"

"The purpose is spying, without a doubt," Bradford said. "Eastern Telegraph—which owns the cables which come ashore in Porthcurno Bay—has built a shack and installed a wireless receiver. I talked to the operator, who told me that the messages are merely intercepted, printed, and filed. And that appears to be the end of it. Nobody has ever bothered to examine the printed tape of the transmissions." He paused. "Which seems to me to eliminate Eastern as a possible suspect for the theft of the tuner. I shouldn't think they'd go to the trouble, unless they were deeply interested, which appears not to be the case. Would you agree?"

"I would," Charles said. He considered. "Sounds as if Eastern has concluded that Marconi Wireless is not a competitive threat to its business."

"More fool they," Bradford growled. He pulled on his cigarette. "What about your evening, Charles. How did it go, eh? What about Lodge? Why is the man at Penhallow? Do you think he's after information?"

"Oh, he's after information," Charles said with muted irony, "but not the sort one might expect. It appears that he came to conduct a psychic experiment, with our Lady Loveday as the medium. He was hoping she would be able to contact her daughter, and thus put to rest her feelings of guilt for the daughter's death."

Bradford stared. "A medium! A *medium?*" And with that, he threw back his head and laughed, long and loud. "I heard that the fellow—for all his vaunted intellect—has an interest in that kind of spiritualist clap-trap. And if that's truly what he has in mind for his visit here, I think we can count him out as a suspect."

"That's truly his motive, as far as I can tell," Charles said. "He was, of course, delighted to read Maskelyne's letter in *The Times*." He picked up his coffee cup. "I hope you were able to dissuade Marconi from answering. Lodge says he is anxious to follow the exchange."

"Not a chance," Bradford said glumly. "He's already written." He regarded Charles curiously. "Did Lodge and Jenna succeed? In raising the dead, I mean. Not," he added hastily, "to be irreverent about it."

"I seriously doubt it," Charles said, "but I must confess that I left before the séance began. Spiritualism is not my cup of tea. I'm sure Kate and Patsy will tell us all about it." He paused. "Since you're going to Helston this afternoon,

I wonder if you would be willing to do a spot of investigating for me."

"Investigating?" Bradford asked doubtfully, remembering the tedious drive he had taken the day before, which had turned up nothing.

"Yes. We are in need of a few facts, and you can gather them for us. I should like you to locate a certain person—the town is small, and one or two inquiries will likely turn him up. Then ask him a question or two, perhaps three. And tell me the answers."

"And that's it?"

"That's it."

"All right, I'll do it. Who shall I be looking for?"

When Charles told him, he was surprised. "I don't quite see," he began.

"Neither do I," Charles said. "But perhaps we both will, when you've done this bit."

Bradford shrugged. "I'm willing to take you at your word. What are you doing today?"

"I'm planning a little welcoming party," Charles said, and stood.

CHAPTER THIRTY-ONE

Alice laughed. "There's no use trying," she said. "One can't believe impossible things."

"I daresay you haven't had much practice," said the Queen. "When I was your age, I always did it half an hour a day. Why, sometimes, I've believed as many as six impossible things before breakfast."

Alice's Adventures in Wonderland
Lewis Carroll

Jenna Loveday woke up on Saturday morning with a slight headache, as if she had slept too hard and too long, and with only a vague recollection of what had happened at the séance the night before. But her spirits felt curiously light, and she got out of bed with the unaccountably happy thought that, somehow, something had changed—although what it might be, she certainly couldn't say. Glancing out the window, today seemed brighter than yesterday, the sky a brilliant cerulean, the trees green and lush, the flowers in the garden glowing like gemstones. But surely she didn't feel better—happier, more light-hearted, as if she had been freed of some terrible burden—just because the night's rain had cleansed and freshened the world. Had she had a wonderful dream she couldn't remember?

Whatever had changed while she slept, she was glad, and as she dressed in a white shirtwaist and dark skirt and tied her hair back with a blue ribbon, she thought happily ahead to the day. Since Sir Oliver would be leaving tomorrow, today would be a good day to go sightseeing. They could drive across the Lizard to the west, to Mullion and Mount's Bay, a trip Sir Oliver might enjoy. They could have a late luncheon at the Poldhu Hotel, and—she smiled at the thought—perhaps he might visit the Marconi station.

Dressed, she went down to the breakfast room, where she found Kate Sheridan alone at the table, Patsy and Sir Oliver having already eaten and gone off together for a morning walk.

"I hope you're feeling well this morning," Kate said, with evident concern. She poured a cup of coffee for Jenna.

"Just toast and juice," Jenna said to the maid. "Thank you," she said to Kate. "I'm feeling very well, actually. Better than I've felt in a long time."

"I'm so glad." Smiling, Kate glanced out the window. "It looks to be a beautiful day, doesn't it? The prettiest since we came."

"Yes," Jenna replied, mindful of the maid's presence. One always had to be so careful what one said in front of the servants. "I thought we might go to Mullion today, for some sightseeing." When the girl had brought her toast and juice and left the room, Jenna lowered her voice. "Now you must tell me, Kate. What happened last night? Was Sir Oliver very terribly disappointed? Was it an awful waste of time?"

Kate looked at her in some surprise. "You don't remember?"

The orange juice tasted very good, Jenna thought, and

the toast was done exactly the way she liked it. She added marmalade before she spoke.

"No," she said with a little smile, "not a thing. I vaguely recall drawing circles on a piece of paper—more to please Sir Oliver than out of any other urgency, I'm afraid. And then—" She laughed. "The next thing I remember is your helping me off to bed. To tell the truth, I think that last glass of wine I drank at dinner was too much for me. I was already feeling a little giddy before we began, and wondering whether we should go forward with it. I hope I didn't disgrace myself, or embarrass the rest of you."

"No to both," Kate said quickly. "In fact, Sir Oliver is mightily pleased with what happened. He considers the evening a great success."

"A success!" Jenna looked up, surprised. "You mean, I actually *wrote* something?"

Kate nodded. "Pages and pages."

"I don't believe it," Jenna scoffed. "I'm sure I would remember something like that!"

"Do believe it," Kate said. "It's true."

Jenna stared at her. "Well, then, where are the pages?" she demanded. "I want to see them. Does Sir Oliver have them with him?"

"No," Kate said. She nodded toward the sideboard. "He left them there, in that envelope. But are you sure you want—"

"Of course I'm sure," Jenna said firmly. She pushed back her chair, went to the sideboard, and took up a large manila envelope. Back at the table, she poured another cup of coffee, opened the envelope, and pulled out a sheaf of papers.

"All *this*?" she asked in surprise. "I can't have written all this and not recall a word of it! Why, there must be more than a dozen sheets here."

"All that," Kate said. "Sir Oliver has numbered them, as you can see."

"Well, these," Jenna said decidedly, flipping through the sheets of paper, "are nothing but scribbling, my pencil going in circles. And this—"

She stopped. She was looking at a page where the words "mother dear" were written over and over, first in her normal hand and then in a round, childish script which was not her own. And then a full page of "sorry I am sorry" and on the next page, "not your fault." She felt the skin on her arms prickle.

"I wrote this?" she asked in astonishment.

"Yes," Kate said simply.

Jenna looked at the page. "Do you believe . . ." She stopped, swallowed, and began again, but she could barely muster a whisper. "You were there, Kate. What did you think . . . did it seem to you that those were Harriet's words?"

Kate was silent, and Jenna felt both awkward and penitent. She shouldn't have put her on the spot in that way. She put her hand on Kate's arm.

"You don't have to answer," she said. "It's not a fair question. I have no right to—"

"Of course it's a fair question," Kate said, regarding her with a steady gaze. "I'm just not sure how to answer. It did seem to me, honestly, that you would not have written as you did—you yourself, I mean. It was clear that you were in the grip of something other than your ordinary self. Whether the messages came from within or without, though, I could not be sure." She smiled a little. "Sir Oliver is very sure, though. He's convinced that these words came from Harriet, communicating through you."

Jenna sat very still, trying to settle her breathing as she struggled to make sense of her jumbled feelings. Trickery was impossible, since she herself had done this, and she was no trickster. It had to be true. She had to believe it. But again, if it were true, where did it come from? Within herself, or from another source?

She looked again at the pages in her hand. "If this truly came from Harriet," she said wonderingly, "it must mean that she has forgiven me."

"Yes," Kate said. "I should think it does."

Jenna looked up, meeting Kate's compassionate gaze. "And if it came from within me, it means that I have forgiven myself."

"That, too," Kate said, and smiled. "And to tell the truth, one may be just as important as the other."

Jenna's vision blurred, and she closed her eyes, feeling the swirl of emotions within her, the sadness and loss and grief she had felt ever since Harriet's death. But the swirl was not a storm, and she was not seized by the overwhelming helplessness which always accompanied the sadness, the grief—the helplessness which usually presaged one of her hallucinatory moments. Had the séance, whatever else it accomplished, put an end to those moments? Had it settled the ghosts, put the past to rest?

Well, there was no way to know the answer to that, except to go forward into the future. Perhaps, if she were truly able to forgive herself, there might even be a future for herself and Niels—if he loved her enough to settle at Penhallow. Of course, they could go off on yachting trips as often as he liked, and perhaps spend part of the year in Norway, where he came from. He hadn't told her much about himself, and she hadn't asked. Now, perhaps, things could be different between them. They could start over, as if nothing had happened. They—

She opened her eyes. There was no blurring. Everything seemed clear and extraordinarily bright.

"Thank you," she murmured, although she was not clear to whom she spoke. She felt that she had been given a great gift, and she was grateful.

Kate gestured at the papers. "There's more, Jenna. Perhaps you'll know what it means."

"More? Oh, yes," Jenna said, recalling herself to the pages in her hand. There were other sheets, and she began to glance through them. She stopped, staring blankly at the page.

" 'Ain't fair'?" she asked. "I wrote this?" She raised her eyes from the page, frightened, feeling cold at the pit of her stomach. She began to shiver. "Where did it . . . who *wrote* this, for God's sake, Kate? It's not in my hand—or in . . . in Harriet's, either."

"You wrote it," Kate said. "I watched you. But it was different. It wasn't the same as the earlier pages. It was another sort of energy altogether. I wasn't the only one to notice, Jenna. We all did."

"But . . . but *Bavaria*? I have no idea what that means. I've never . . ." She swallowed, feeling the gooseflesh rise on her arms.

Kate pointed to the bottom of the page. "There's one more word, dear."

Beware.

" 'Beware'?" Jenna's eyes widened. "Beware of what? Who should beware? And these other words, these cursings. Who in the world—"

"Damn his bloody eyes." And then, as Jenna read the words on the page, she heard in her ears the echo of a voice speaking them: a man's voice, rough, uncultured. But more than just the words, she felt his anger, his fear, his—

"Jenna?" Kate asked.

Her fingers were cold, so cold, but the paper on which

she had written the words felt hot, scorching. *Damn his bloody eyes*. She could hear her voice whispering the words, but it was thin and faint and came as if from a distance, and the voice in her ears was louder and harsher, filled with a knifelike fear and hatred.

Damn him god damn him to hell.

She could hardly breathe now, as if something was cinched tight around her middle, squeezing the breath out of her. She heard someone breathing in choking gasps and knew it was she. The room was growing dimmer, filling with a dark, chilly fog, wisps and tendrils twisting around her. *His bloody eyes, god damn him* . . . She could feel the eyes on her, bright and hard, peering through her, searching, searing her soul. *bloody eyes damn his eyes damn* . . .

And then, suddenly and breathtakingly and terrifyingly, Jenna was seeing *through* those eyes. She was watching a scene being played out before her, no farther away than arm's length. She was balancing on the brink of a steep cliff, the midnight ocean black beyond, the surf booming against the rocks, the moon silver and cold as ice, and the man in front of her was falling backward, pitching over, arms flailing, as if in slow motion, and as she heard the scream, the long, anguished cry, she knew that she was watching a man die, and that she had pushed him off the cliff. But not she herself. It was the person, the man through whose eyes she was seeing, the man whose hands were now raised in front of her, whose *hands* she was seeing.

And with an incredulous, frozen horror, she knew whose eyes they were, whose eyes—*damn his eyes damn*—and whose hands. She knew, because she saw the fingers, saw the—

"Jenna?" Kate's voice pulled her out of it, recalled her from the cliff, and back to the room. "Jenna?" Kate was standing beside her, her hand on Jenna's arm, her voice urgent. "Jenna, say something to me, Jenna. Are you all right?"

Jenna grasped the edge of the table, trying to speak. The room was turning around her, the chair was tilting, and she too was tumbling, like the man, the doomed man who had gone over the cliff. "No!" she moaned dizzily. Her head dropped back and she felt herself half-fainting into a gray, bottomless fog.

"Jenna!" Kate spoke in a commanding voice, and slapped her cheek lightly. She wet a napkin in a glass of water and patted Jenna's forehead. "What's happened, Jenna? What did you see? You're as white as paper!"

"I'm . . . terrified," Jenna whispered, with an unsteady candor, as the room stopped spinning around her, the chair stopped tilting. "But I'm all right."

"Have a sip of coffee," Kate said, and pressed the cup against her lips.

Jenna drank, glad for the hot liquid, and grateful for the firm chair under her and the four walls around her, for Kate's sturdy, practical presence. Her mind was whirling, the thoughts and feelings swirling and turning. She heard a loud, thudding noise, wondered what it was, and realized that it was the pounding of her heart.

"Tell me, dear" Kate said, pulling her chair closer. "Tell me what you saw. You were reading the words on the paper and . . ."

Jenna gripped Kate's hand and spoke through numb lips. "I was reading the words on the paper, and suddenly I saw . . . I saw a man . . . a man murdered."

The words. The words she had written but had not written. The words which had come through her pencil onto the paper, the words of the murdered man. And reading those words just now, she had been drawn back into the dead man's last moment of life, his last fearful breaths, before—

"Murdered!" Kate was staring at her. "How? Who?"

"I don't know who," Jenna said helplessly. "A man. He fell—he was pushed off a cliff. I saw . . . Oh, God, Kate, I saw the hands that pushed him!" She took a deep breath and let it out, and with her breath, the words, the awful words: "I know who did it."

"You know? How do you know?"

"Because he wore a . . . ring," Jenna said miserably. She shook her head. "Please, don't ask me about it now. I don't think I can bear to tell you." She stood, felt herself swaying, and put her hands flat on the table to steady herself. "Just . . . come with me, Kate."

Kate stood too, and put a steadying arm around Jenna's shoulders. "But you're not well, my dear. Come upstairs with me and lie down. You can't go out in this state."

"But I have to!" Jenna cried frantically. "I must go now!" Sobbing, she pulled away from the comfort of Kate's arm. "And you must come with me, Kate. Please. Oh, please! Just . . . come."

CHAPTER THIRTY-TWO

I am two fools, I know,
for loving, and for saying so.

"The Triple Fool," 1633
John Donne

Andrew Kirk-Smythe had risen before dawn to breakfast with Charles Sheridan. After Charles had driven off to Mullion, Andrew went down to the Helford quay, where he climbed aboard the hired sloop, checked the rigging and sails, and cast off. The sea was calm, with a fair wind blowing from the south, rippling the water in a fine, friendly way. It was a perfect day for sailing, and as he tacked down the Helford River and into the fresher breeze around Nare Point, he found himself whistling cheerfully. The foam rushed under the lee-bow, the salt spray splashed on his fingers and misted his face, and the sun as it rose warmed his back and sparked from the tops of the great blue waves.

Grand sport, sailing, Andrew thought. He should do more of it—and the Lizard, with its bays and inlets, its deep rivers, was the perfect place. When all this was over, he would come back here, and drop round at Penhallow, and see how Jenna Loveday was getting on, and whether she had—

He frowned and tightened up on the jib. See Jenna Loveday? He was a fool. The lady was in love with someone else, someone who would inevitably break her heart. Even if he warned her, if he told her to beware of the fellow, she would not listen. Even if he told her who he himself was, and why he was watching Wolf (or Niels or Hans or whatever name the man had given her), it would make no difference. Even if he told her about the man Wolf had murdered, about—

The luff of the mainsail rattled as the wind shifted forward by a point, and Andrew fell off a bit to fill it, sailing farther in toward the rocks, then putting the helm down and tacking back to starboard. Settling himself, he took out a cigarette and lit it, turning his shoulder against the wind and cupping the match in his hands. He was a fool twice—once for loving her, and once again for imagining that he could change her mind and her heart. He would stop thinking of her, forthwith. Instead, he would think about the plan he and Charles Sheridan had discussed the night before, and this morning at breakfast. He would review its details and devices, try to see where it might go wrong, or how it might be improved. He would—

But of course, Andrew did nothing of the sort. He tried to concentrate on the plan, and failing that, on the magnificent cliffs and the booming surf and the seabirds flinging themselves joyously into the clearest of clear blue skies. But he could think of little else but Jenna Loveday as he sailed past The Manacles and Black Head, past the wireless station on Bass Point, past the light at the tip of the Lizard, and far enough out into the gray waters of Mount's Bay to jibe and let the mainsail full out for a fast run past Mullion Island and into Mullion Cove.

It was only as he began to occupy himself with dropping

sail and the tricky business of maneuvering around the sea wall into the shelter of the cove that he was able to give his whole mind to the task at hand. He secured the painter to one of the iron mooring rings fixed in the sea wall, dropped the fenders over the side, and made sure that everything was stowed below. Then he climbed the stone stairs and followed the track which led past the lifeboat station, up the cliffside to the top and along the edge of the cliff, around Pollurian Cove, to the Poldhu Hotel. It was lunchtime, or perhaps a little past, and he was guessing that he'd find Dick Corey in the hotel pub.

He was right. Corey was sitting by himself, a glass of ale at his elbow, greedily tucking into a fragrant shepherd's pie. Andrew leaned over the table.

"Mr. Corey?" he asked pleasantly.

Corey looked up, and wiped his mouth with the back of his hand. "Aye, Corey. That's me."

"Good," Andrew said, and without waiting for an invitation, pulled out the chair and sat down. "Wolf sent me," he said. "I'm to tell you that there has been a change in plans."

CHAPTER THIRTY-THREE

Rule, Britannia, Britannia rule the waves.

James Thompson, 1700–1748

Kate would not have thought that Jenna had the strength to walk, after her fright, but she was running—to the French doors, out onto the terrace, and through the garden. The blue ribbon which tied her hair had come loose and her long locks flew around her shoulders.

"Where are we going?" Kate cried, running after her.

"To Frenchman's Creek," Jenna said, over her shoulder. Her voice was high and breathless. "Don't ask questions, Kate. And please, don't say anything."

Frenchman's Creek! Beryl exclaimed. *It's the pirate, Kate! The man she's in love with. Niels!*

Niels? Kate thought blankly, as a branch whipped across her arm. Does she think Niels has been murdered?

No, you ninny. She thinks he's the murderer!

"Oh, God," Kate whispered. "But then who . . . who did he kill?"

The man who wanted to go to Bavaria. Whoever that was.

Kate's breath caught. Beryl's leaps of fancy were often wrong, but in this case, she had to be right.

The path angled more steeply as they neared the water. Kate held her skirt up out of the leaf-litter and grabbed at a sapling to slow her forward momentum. The trees were thick around them, the leaves like a green vault overhead, shutting out the sky and throwing an eerie shadow, like a green veil, across everything. An unnatural stillness seemed to have fallen over the woods. No leaves stirred, no birds called, no squirrels chattered. The only sound was the rustle of their passage along the path, and the sound of their breathing.

Then Jenna, ahead of her, stopped and put up a hand. Kate stopped, too. Through the trees, she saw the bright glimmer of sunlight on water, and off to the left, a little distance away, the outline of a sailing yacht, moored to the bank under an overhanging oak.

"Shall I wait here?" Kate asked in a low voice.

"No," Jenna said. "Come with me, please." She turned with a brittle smile. "Oh, he's not going to hurt us, if that's what you're concerned about. I wouldn't put you in danger, Kate."

Kate shook her head. "I only thought you might want . . . privacy."

"No," Jenna replied, and held out her hand. "Actually, I need you with me to keep me true to my purpose. What I've come to do is painful. I'm afraid I won't be able to do it."

Without a word, Kate took her hand. The path leveled out and made a turn to the left, to follow the shoreline. As they came within ten yards or so of the boat, Kate smelled the rich odor of coffee brewing and bacon frying. Jenna raised her voice.

"Niels," she called. "Niels!"

A moment later, a man in a gray woolen shirt, sleeves rolled to the elbows, put his head and shoulders out of the galleyway and turned in their direction. Kate got a good look at his face. He was blond and sun-browned, and his eyes beneath the brim of his yachting cap were an almost brilliant blue. His face crinkled into a smile as he saw Jenna, but the smile faded when he realized that she was not alone.

"Jenna," he said, in a foreign-sounding voice. He turned to look full at Kate. They were standing on the bank, now, within arm's reach of the boat's mooring. He studied Kate. There was a fierceness behind his eyes, she thought, and something so cold that she felt chilled through. Then he seemed to dismiss her, as if she were of no consequence. He turned back to Jenna. "You've brought a friend. Well, good." The smile was back. "You can both join me for breakfast. The coffee is ready, and there's—"

"No, Niels." Jenna's hand tightened on Kate's. "I've come to tell you that you must . . . go. Today. Now."

He came up another step out of the galleyway, and his face showed the first signs of emotion. But it was not deep concern, or disappointment, or even regret. He was, Kate thought, merely puzzled. "But I thought we had agreed—"

"No," she said.

The man's eyes, now wary, went to Kate, as if he were considering what he could say in her presence. "Is it your daughter's death? I've told you I had nothing to do with that." His voice became stern. "It was not your fault, either, Jenna. You cannot—"

"I know," Jenna said. She cleared her throat, and Kate could feel her trembling. "That isn't the reason, Niels—if that's your name. You've killed a man. There's blood on your hands."

"Blood?" He looked at his hands, then held them up, palms out, as if to show her that they were clean. Kate caught the flash of a gold ring. She could not be sure at this distance, but she thought it was a match for the ring Jenna wore. He tilted his head. "How melodramatic. Really, Jenna, I hardly think—"

"The man on the cliff," she said. "You pushed him off. I *saw* it."

His smile, suddenly vivid, showed very white teeth. "Oh, come now, my dear. You could have seen nothing of the sort. You weren't . . . it didn't happen."

"You're right," she said. "I wasn't there. But it did happen and I saw it, Niels. All he wanted was to go back to Bavaria, and you killed him."

"Bavaria!" The man's mouth hardened and he took another step up the galleyway, into full view. Kate suddenly found herself wishing that they were somewhere else. Jenna might be confident that they were not in danger, but she was not so sure. He wore a holstered pistol on his hip.

"If you are so confident of the facts," he said stiffly, "I suppose there is no point in attempting to argue, to make you see reason." His eyes flicked to Kate and back again to Jenna. "What do you mean to do about it, my dear?"

Jenna spoke with a surprising authority, Kate thought, especially considering the gun. "You have until noon to leave, Niels. After that, you'll have to deal with the constable. I don't want to, but I'll tell him everything."

"An empty threat, without proof," he said dryly, as if he were amused. "So. You are giving me fair warning. Is that it? Slip my mooring and be gone, or else?"

"I *am* giving you fair warning. Because I . . . loved you once."

"Past tense, is it?" He sighed. "I am truly sad, Jenna. I

hoped you would come with me, when my work was done here. We could have had at least some time together. It would have been . . . such a pleasure."

Jenna appeared not to have heard. "But only until noon. Do you understand?"

His face hardened into grimmer lines. "I do. But you don't, you know. There's a great deal at stake here, my love, and much more to this than you can possibly—"

"Yes," Jenna said, and now the fierceness was all in her. "And I don't *want* to know it. All I want is never to see you again, Niels."

There was a faint trace of feeling in his face now, but whatever emotion he felt twisted his mouth into a wry shape and brought a deep bitterness to his voice. He put his hands on his hips, the tips of the fingers of his right hand brushing the gun.

Kate tensed, ready to flee. But he could aim and fire faster than they could run. If Jenna was wrong about him—

But she wasn't.

After a moment, Niels dropped his hands, shrugged, and half-turned, taking a step backward down the galleyway. "Very well, my dear," he said lightly. "I'm not the sort of man who outstays his welcome." He raised his cap. "Good-bye, Jenna Loveday."

And then he disappeared down the galleyway. In a moment, they could hear him whistling cheerfully.

The tune was "Rule, Britannia."

CHAPTER THIRTY-FOUR

"What do you know about this business?" the King said to Alice.
"Nothing," said Alice.
"Nothing whatever?" persisted the King.
"Nothing whatever," said Alice.
"That's very important," the King said, turning to the jury.

Alice's Adventures in Wonderland
Lewis Carroll

Bradford's visit to the Helston gaol was a brief and entirely satisfactory one. The gaol was ordinarily used to confine the drunken and disorderly, and the Helston constable, Mr. Clifford, confessed to Bradford, in an apologetic tone, that he was unable to provide proper accommodation for a lady.

"Oh, that's all right," Bradford said carelessly reaching into his pocket and taking out a cigar. "Miss Chase is no lady."

"Ah," said Constable Clifford. "Ah, yes, I see." He accepted the cigar with a knowing look. "You're wantin' to have her released, then."

"Not at all, not at all," Bradford assured him. "I should like to see her, alone. I shall stand surety against her escape."

The constable was now more certain of Bradford's intention. "You'll be wantin' privacy."

Bradford laughed shortly. "Not that sort of privacy. Only the sort required to write a letter. Shouldn't take more than a few minutes."

Bradford's errand did, in fact, require only a few moments. The lady was so chastened by her experience in the gaol—"Rats!" she exclaimed in undisguised horror. "The place is simply crawling with rats!"—that she agreed to his demand without any argument. She sat down and wrote, at his direction, to her cousin in London, describing the box in which the letters were kept and instructing her to send the entire box and everything in it, posthaste, to Mr. Marsden, at the Poldhu Hotel, Mullion, Cornwall.

"Very good," Bradford said with satisfaction, watching her address the envelope.

Miss Chase stood. "Well, then," she said eagerly, attempting to smooth her disheveled hair. "I can go now?"

"No, my dear," Bradford said, with a shake of his head. "Not until I receive the letters." He smiled significantly. "Just in case, you know, that your cousin is not able to locate them from the description in your letter."

Miss Chase fixed him with a silent, narrow-eyed gaze. Then, without a word, she ripped open the envelope and pulled out the letter-paper. She sat down, scratched out several words, and added a sentence at the bottom of the page before returning it to the envelope.

"Thank you," Bradford said courteously. He pocketed the envelope and raised his voice. "Constable! Your prisoner is ready to return to her cell."

"Oh!" cried Miss Chase, shrill with vexation, and stamped her foot. "Oh, you wretch!"

"Do unto others, my dear," Bradford said. "I shall arrange

for your release as soon as I have received them. *All* of them." He watched with a smile as the constable escorted her away. When he returned, Bradford put the query with which Charles Sheridan had supplied him, although he had to confess that he still did not understand why it was worth the bother.

The constable frowned, scratched his head, and wrinkled his nose. "Corey? I know nothing about a Corey in Helston."

"No Corey?" Bradford asked in surprise. "But I'm told, on good authority——" He took out another cigar. "Perhaps a little incentive——"

"Incentive or no," the constable said, gazing covetously at the cigar. "I can't tell you how to find a Corey when I don't *know* a Corey, now, can I?"

Allowing in a regretful tone that this was so, Bradford handed over the cigar anyway. "Where else might I inquire?"

The constable, satisfied, tucked the cigar into his pocket. "Well, I'll tell you. Walk straight down Coinagehall Street to the Post Office, and ask Miss Clara Standish to tell you whether there are any Coreys in Helston. She's been puttin' up the post for three decades, you know. If there's a Corey living in Helston, she'll tell you, straight off." He grinned. "Miss Standish don't smoke cigars, but she do like a bit of chocolate now and then. Moyle's Confectionery, on your right, just before the Post Office."

Forewarned was forearmed, Bradford thought, so when he presented himself at the Post Office and inquired for Miss Clara Standish, he was supplied with ten-pence-worth of chocolate drops. Miss Standish proved to be a rotund, white-haired lady with wire spectacles perched on the end of her nose. She accepted the chocolates without hesitation, listened to Bradford's query, and shook her head.

"Never been a Corey in Helston," she said definitively,

opening the bag and taking out a chocolate drop. She frowned. "Mrs. Moyle didn't have any chocolate mints, then?"

"I'm sorry," Bradford said penitently. "I didn't know you had a favorite." He paused. "You've never heard of a Richard or Dick Corey, who works at the Marconi wireless station in Mullion and comes to visit his brother, who lives here in Helston?"

She put the offending chocolate back into the bag and closed it, her mouth set. "If there was a Corey in Helston, I should know him," she said firmly, stowing the bag under the counter. "And since I don't, there isn't. Now, do you want a stamp for the letter you have in your hand, or is that all your business for the day?"

"I'll have a stamp, please," Bradford said meekly, and gave a great deal of attention to applying it properly.

It was too bad, he thought, that he had not been able to carry out Charles Sheridan's errand. That small failure aside, however, he had certainly accomplished what he had come to do. When he dropped Miss Chase's letter to her cousin into the post box and drove off in the Panhard—which, parked, had become the town's most intriguing attraction—he felt he had every right to be pleased with the outcome of his errand.

CHAPTER THIRTY-FIVE

"Oh, I've had such a curious dream!" said Alice, and she told her sister, as well as she could remember them, all these strange Adventures of hers which you have just been reading about; and when she had finished, her sister kissed her, and said, "It was a curious dream, dear, certainly: but now run in to your tea; it's getting late."

So Alice got up and ran off, thinking while she ran, as well she might, what a wonderful dream it had been.

Alice's Adventures in Wonderland
Lewis Carroll

A lice had spent as little time as possible with the washing up and sweeping and dusting that morning, for she was bent on finishing *Alice's Adventures in Wonderland*, in order to start reading the book all over again. She had quite forgotten *Treasure Island* and *The Water Babies* and felt that there was no book in the world quite as marvelous as *Alice*. So she took a packet of biscuits and an apple and clambered into the willow tree beside the cottage, where she often went to read on a dreamy summer's day, comforted by the sound of the wind in the leaves, and the birds wheeling overhead, and the fragrance of the roses which climbed the cottage wall.

Alice was so deep in her reading that she failed to hear the crunch of footsteps on the gravel path. It wasn't until she heard someone knocking on the cottage door and calling out "Alice, are you at home?" that she looked up.

Or rather, looked down. "What do you want?" she asked, peering through the leaves. And then she saw that it was Lady Sheridan, and that Lady Loveday was with her, and regretted her peremptory tone. "Hullo," she said, more nicely.

"Oh, there you are," Lady Sheridan said, looking up. She smiled. "The tree seems a perfectly wonderful place to read a book, but I wonder if you wouldn't mind coming down and having some tea with us."

"I suppose," grumbled Alice, "that you'll expect me to make the tea." But she tucked the book under her arm and began to climb down anyway.

"I rather thought," Lady Loveday said, when Alice reached the ground, "that we might have tea at Penhallow. I understand that you are fond of Mrs. Tremaine's currant cakes." She held out her hand. "My name is Lady Loveday. I am Harriet's mother. And you must be Alice."

Alice, of course, did not need an introduction, for she had been keeping a close eye on Lady Loveday since Harriet died. But she was pleased at the unexpected possibility of currant cakes, and there was also the matter of the book. "Thank you for *Wonderland*," Alice said, and bobbed as brief a curtsey as possible.

"Well, then," Lady Sheridan said cheerfully, "Now that we've had our introductions perhaps we can all go and have tea." With a smile, she put her arm on Alice's shoulder. "Lady Loveday told me just now that she would very much like to hear your story about Harriet."

"Really?" Alice gave her a doubtful look. "It's very sad, you know."

"I am sure it is," Lady Loveday said. "But sometimes it does one good to hear a sad story, particularly if it answers questions which have been plaguing one for months and months." She held out her hand. "Will you come, my dear?"

For a second or two, Alice hesitated, and then she took Lady Loveday's hand. "Yes," she said. "I rather think I will."

CHAPTER THIRTY-SIX

He who is embarked with the devil must make the passage in his company.

Dutch Proverb

Charles Sheridan settled himself in the heather which edged the bluff overlooking Mullion Cove. His elbows on his knees and his field glasses to his eyes, he scanned the small harbor some forty feet below. Down and to his left was the lifeboat station, the pilchard cellar and net store nearby. The small harbor itself was embraced by two massive stone arms of the seawall. Several fishing boats, dinghies, and rowboats were pulled up on the shingle inside the wall, above the flood tide, and a white sloop was moored at the end of the north arm: Kirk-Smythe's sloop.

Crouched beside Charles, Constable Deane pointed to the breakwater. "Built in the last decade," he said, "by Lord Robartes. The pilchard fleet had bad years, back-to-back— the whole fleet nearly wiped out by storms. The fishermen are glad of the breakwater."

"I'm sure they must be," Charles said. On this pleasant July evening, with the warm scent of heather rising around them, the calm sea a turquoise blue, and the sky clear above, it was difficult to imagine the ferocity of the winter gales which must lash Mullion Cove. The little harbor would be at the mercy of the sea for months on end, and boats left in the water, or even pulled onto the beach, would surely be broken by the waves. The breakwater would provide a fair measure of protection in the worst of the weather.

Charles took out his watch, glanced at it, and put it back. "He should be here shortly, Constable, if things go according to plan." Of course, sometimes they didn't. The man they were waiting for might prefer to delay until after dark, which would seriously complicate their scheme. Or he might have got the wind up, and not appear at all.

The constable nodded, his attention fixed on the track which led from the village down to the seawall.

Charles looked to the west, out past Mullion Island. The sunset promised to be stunning. The red-orange clouds banked above the horizon were pierced with the golden shafts of the setting sun. And beyond the horizon, below the curve of the earth and so far to the west that it was still bathed in the light of midday, the wireless station at Glace Bay might at this very minute be receiving the Morse dots and dashes sent from the transmitter at Poldhu, now back in operation. He shivered as he thought of the staggering immensity of the distance and the threadlike fragility of the electromagnetic signals cast out into the void—and the remarkable, perhaps even miraculous fact that they could be received and converted into human language. "Marconi's miracle," as it was called, might be just a small first step, but it could lead to other inventions which would change the world.

"Look there," said the constable, and a light tap on his shoulder brought Charles back from his thoughts, "That's our man, isn't it?"

Charles trained his glasses on a small figure with a Gladstone bag in his hand, trudging down the track toward the harbor. "Indeed," he said, and got to his feet. "Time to move into position. We need to be close by and ready when Kirk-Smythe gives the signal." And with that, they scrambled down the heather-covered hillside and made their way onto the breakwater.

Their quarry did not look back. He walked rapidly out to the end of the sea wall, climbed down the stone steps, and stopped beside a moored boat. "Ahoy," he called, somewhat tentatively. "Anybody here?"

Kirk-Smythe appeared above deck, beckoned, and went below again, and the man, glancing apprehensively around, climbed over the deck rail and boarded the sloop.

Charles and the constable moved out onto the sea wall and waited. In a few moments, Kirk-Smythe came up the galleyway carrying a bucket of water. He glanced in their direction, tossed the water into the harbor, and disappeared again.

"That's the signal," Charles said, with some relief. "The fellow has it with him."

So much, at least, had gone as they hoped. From the camera bag on his shoulder, Charles took out the Webley revolver the constable had lent him and tested the action, gently lowering the hammer against the frame. It wasn't likely there'd be a need for the gun, for the constable was armed with his stout wooden truncheon, and Charles hoped that it alone would be sufficient to dissuade their man from any rash action. But when the trap was sprung, the fellow would be desperate—and if armed, dangerous.

He looked around. There was nothing to be seen but a pair of fishing boats making for the leeward end of the island, and a sailing yacht running in toward the sea wall on a fair west wind, its mainsail out and jib luffing.

"Let's go," he said crisply.

"Right behind you, sir," said the constable.

At the end of the wall, they descended the stairs and stepped onto the sloop. Charles nodded to the constable, who rapped the deck rail smartly with his truncheon. "Police! Up top, smartly, now. Show yourselves!"

A brief, angry exchange could be heard below, and the galley door opened. Kirk-Smythe climbed up, holding a wooden box. He was followed by Dick Corey, who wore a frightened look on his round face.

"The box—is it what you're looking for, sir?" the constable asked Charles, as both men came on deck.

Charles took the box from Kirk-Smythe, slid the wooden lid to one side, and studied the interior. "It appears to be," he replied cautiously. There was no way to tell until Marconi himself could examine it, but it certainly looked to him like a wireless tuner, surely the one Dick Corey had taken.

"Dealing in stolen property, are you?" The constable glowered at Kirk-Smythe and Corey.

"Thank God you're here, Constable," Corey cried. He pointed a wavering finger at Kirk-Smythe. "This fellow offered to sell me the tuner, and I pretended to go along with his game in order to get it back for the Marconi Company. Arrest him!"

The constable folded his arms. "Well, now, Mr. Corey, if that's what you intended, it would have been smart to have let me in on the secret. Dealing with a thief is dangerous. And you've certainly put yourself into a compromising situation."

Corey licked his lips, his glance skittering from the constable to Charles, whom he clearly recognized, and back again. "There . . . well, there wasn't time, you see. He approached me with an offer to sell, and I had to move on it right away, or lose the chance." His voice rose a notch, and Charles heard the bluster in it. "Arrest him, Constable! Don't let him get away!"

Deane patted the palm of his left hand with his truncheon. "Well, now, that's queer," he said, with apparent relish. "This fellow—" nodding at Kirk-Smythe, "*he* had time to contact me." He paused, and Corey blanched. "But according to him, it was the other way round. You were offering to sell the thing to him. And you must have thought it was valuable, seeing how much you demanded for it." He glanced at Kirk-Smythe. "Is that how it was, sir?"

"Yes," Kirk-Smythe said. "That's exactly how it was."

"Oh, no," Corey cried. "No, no, that wasn't it at *all*! This man came to me at the hotel while I was having my lunch! He said he—"

"Do you have any proof, Mr. Corey?" Deane asked.

"Proof?" Corey looked around, as if he were searching for something. "Proof? Well, no. But I—"

"Thank you, Mr. Corey," Deane said. "I think we've heard enough." Turning to Charles, he said, "I don't quite see how we sort this out, sir. Seems like one man's word against the other's, and that's always the worst sort of thing. Hard to prove, either way."

"That's very true," Charles said gravely. "I appreciate the difficulty." He frowned. "I suppose we could put both of them in gaol while we see if we can get to the bottom of it."

"We could. But you have your equipment back, so there's no real harm done. I propose to keep this fellow here," he nodded at Kirk-Smythe, "who isn't one of the Lizard folk, and let Mr. Corey go." He cocked his head to one side. "What do you say, sir? Shall we release the fellow?"

"Right," Corey said eagerly, and took two steps backward,

toward the deck rail. "Splendid solution, Constable. That's exactly the way to handle it. You've got the tuner, and that's what's important."

"I suppose you're right, Constable," Charles replied, in a thoughtful tone. "Although I can't help but wonder whether Mr. Corey will still be alive at this hour tomorrow— if you don't take him into custody, that is."

"Well, there is that, I suppose," the constable said regretfully.

Corey froze. "Alive?" Alarmed, he stared at Charles. "Why shouldn't I be alive? Mr. Deane said I could go. You can't—"

"Oh you have nothing to fear from us," Charles replied. "We're perfectly willing to let you go. The problem is your friend Wolf, you see—the foreign fellow who paid you some money when you met him at The Pelican night before last. Wolf is a hard chap, he is, very hard. He takes a dim view of the double-cross." He eyed Corey. "Perhaps he didn't bother to tell you that he has already killed one man for this tuner."

Corey straightened. His look of dismay was genuine. "I don't believe you," he said. "Who did he—" He stopped and licked his lips nervously, the tip of his tongue flicking in and out. "I don't know anybody named Wolf."

"He killed Jack Gordon," Charles said.

"No!" Corey's eyes opened wide. "That was an accident! Jack—"

"It was no accident, Mr. Corey," Charles replied regretfully. "Your friend Wolf was seen shoving Gordon off the cliff."

"You're lying!" Corey pointed wildly to the constable. "If it was murder, Constable Deane there would've arrested him! He'd never let a killer go free!"

"I'm afraid it's not that simple, Mr. Corey," the constable

said in a practical tone. "I couldn't arrest the fellow. The witness refuses to testify. And Wolf, well, he's a foreign national, working for his government. He's German, you know."

"Danish," Corey said.

"German," Kirk-Smythe put in firmly.

The constable shrugged. "Those Germans—well, you know how they are. If we nab one of their fellows, they'll shout bloody murder, and we'd have an international incident on our hands. And with Royalty coming in a fortnight, too." He sighed. "The Marconi Company will never stand for that, you know."

"Anyway," Kirk-Smythe said, "you'd have to catch the fellow." He grinned wryly. "And Wolf is the very devil to catch. He comes and goes just as he likes. Dangerous, too, bloody dangerous. If he wants to kill, he kills. There's no stopping him."

"Kills!" Corey cried desperately. "But he can't just go around killing innocent people!" He appealed to the constable. "You've got to keep me safe, Constable. It's your responsibility. It's your duty!"

The constable gave a rueful shrug. "You should have taken account of the devil's claw, Mr. Corey, before you slept with the fellow. If I were you, I would do whatever I could to keep out of this man's way."

Corey tried to speak, but couldn't. He looked, Charles thought, like a trapped animal, searching frantically for a means of escape. It was time, he decided, to offer the man another alternative.

He spoke quietly. "There *is* one way, Mr. Corey, that you might save yourself."

"How?" cried Corey desperately.

"By telling us what happened to Daniel Gerard."

"Daniel . . ." Corey's mouth worked. "I don't know what happened to Daniel Gerard," he said. "I wasn't there. I was with my—"

"Yes, your brother in Helston—a brother who doesn't exist. It is a dangerous lie, Mr. Corey, since it suggests that you had something to cover up, and the likeliest thing is Daniel Gerard's death. It was so easy, wasn't it? After all, you had access to the station. And—" he held up the tuner, "you had a motive."

"No, not the tuner. That wasn't the reason!" Corey seemed to shrink. "I didn't plan it." His voice was thin and high-pitched. "It was an accident."

"Perhaps it was," Charles said. "Perhaps you and Gerard merely had an altercation."

"Yes, that was it," Corey replied eagerly. "An altercation. He . . . he was trying to ruin me with Mr. Marconi, you see, and I told him I couldn't let him do that. And then he . . . well, he stumbled, and fell into the—" He broke off, almost sobbing. "It was awful, I tell you. Like a flash of blue fire, and a horrible . . . a sizzle. And a smell. The smell of burning flesh. I haven't been able to sleep since."

"If it was an accident," Charles said, as if he were puzzled, "why did you take the diary—and the tuner?"

Corey wiped his nose with his sleeve. "I took the diary because I was afraid he'd written something terrible about me. I told you—he was trying to ruin me with the Marconi Company. It wasn't right, what he was saying about me, all those lies! And then I saw the tuner and . . . well, I thought—" He gulped. "But I always meant to give it back. At least, until—"

"Yes," Charles said. "In fact, you took the tuner with the

intention of recovering it, and of being applauded as a hero. Just as you put the tower right after you cut the guy wires and the wind brought it down."

"How . . . how'd you know?" Corey asked wonderingly.

"Criminals follow patterns. You're not the only one to have done this sort of thing. And it might have worked, too—if you'd been content to stop with that. But then you discovered that someone else was willing to pay for the tuner." He sighed. "Pity you didn't know that he would also kill for it."

"Kill!" Corey cried, and covered his face with his hands.

"I think," said the constable, "that I may have a solution to Mr. Corey's problem."

"Very good," Charles said approvingly. "And what is that?"

"If he'll sign a statement setting down all he's just told us, I can see he's kept safe in the Helston gaol until the Assizes. When the judge hears that Gerard was killed by accident, and that Mr. Marconi's property has been returned, I'm sure he'll—"

"A statement!" Corey gave an hysterical laugh. "Not bloody likely!"

And then, with a manic energy, he bolted between them and across the deck, vaulting the rail awkwardly and half-diving, half-falling into the water. In the next moment, he had broken the surface and was pulling for the opposite sea wall. But he wasn't making much headway. He was obviously not an expert swimmer, or strong, and his strokes were poorly coordinated.

Charles pulled out the constable's Webley and aimed it. But after an instant's reflection, he lowered the revolver. It would have been an easy shot—too easy, and stupid and pointless. Corey was thrashing, more than swimming. He gestured to the rowboats pulled below the sea wall.

"Launch one of those and fish him out," he directed. "I'll go up on the end of the wall."

While Charles climbed up the stairs to the point where he could have a clear view, Andrew and the constable sprinted toward the rowboats, leapt into the nearest, and laid on the oars. It wasn't going to be much of a contest, Charles saw. Despite Corey's lead, the man could not swim nearly as fast as his pursuers could row. But he might have hoped he would shortly be free, for he could not see the rowboat behind him. He was making for the gap between the two sea-walls. He obviously aimed to reach the shingle beach beyond, and the sloping cliff, which was not too steep to climb.

But then, just as Corey cleared the end of the sea-wall, a white yacht—the same one which Charles had seen earlier—came into view. The main was down, and the boat was moving easily and lightly under the jib, as if the captain—a blond-haired man, bent over, his hand on the tiller—were preparing to sail in behind the sea-wall and dock for the night. But then the captain straightened and appeared to take in the scene: Corey swimming frantically, the rowboat pulling forward, and Charles standing watch.

Corey, too, saw the yacht, and appeared to recognize the yachtsman. He flung up one arm and shouted, and as the boat bore down on him, shouted again. The yachtsman picked up a round life preserver. As the distance between the boat and the swimmer closed, he heaved it in front of Corey, who grasped it frantically and clung to it as the yachtsman pulled it in.

"Stop!" shouted the constable, seeing that Corey was about to be rescued. "Stop, in the name of the law!"

And then, just as Corey was about to reach the safety of the boat, Charles saw the yachtsman raise a pistol and take quick aim. There was a single loud report. Corey lost his grip on the life preserver and fell back into the sea. In the space of a breath, he had disappeared beneath the surface. Without a glance, the yachtsman reached for the tiller, put it down hard, and swung up into the wind.

"Stop!" cried the constable again.

Charles, watching, knew what he had to do. He raised the Webley, cocking back the hammer with his thumb. His elbow locked. As the front and rear sights came into perfect alignment on the blurred silhouette, he squeezed the trigger.

CHAPTER THIRTY-SEVEN

It is a truth universally acknowledged, that a single man in possession of a good fortune must be in want of a wife.

Pride and Prejudice
Jane Austen

Kate and Charles had remained in Poldhu just long enough to attend the coroner's inquest into the deaths of Richard Corey and the adventurer known to the people around Helford as Niels Andersson. Bradford had decided to bring his wife, Edith, to the Lizard for the Royal visit, so that Kate was able to escape the irksome task of paying court to Princess May. Feeling relieved at having been excused from that duty, she had said a fond goodbye to Jenna Loveday and returned home with Charles, to the farm, her school, and her garden.

It was now high summer, a fortnight after their return. If the fine weather held, the haying would be done in a day or two and after that, the sheep-shearing. Kate was on her way from the dairy barn, preoccupied with an assortment of busy thoughts: the milking arrangements that she and Mrs. Bryan had discussed, the tree that had fallen across the rhubarb patch, Meg O'Malley's long-anticipated arrival the next week, and the letter she had received in the morning's post from Jenna Loveday, which mentioned Andrew Kirk-Smythe three times. That had made Kate smile with pleasure, for Jenna's tone seemed light and optimistic. She was still thinking of Jenna and Andrew when she heard the chug-chug of an approaching motor car and turned to see Bradford Marsden's new green Royce coming up the drive. Bradford pulled the motor to a stop and got out, stripping off his goggles and gloves as Kate came through the gate.

"Ah, Kate, my dear," he said jovially. "Good morning, good morning! I just dropped by to put Charles in the picture about the Royal visit. It went off very well, I'm pleased to say."

"I'm sure he'll be glad to hear that," Kate said. "It will cheer him up."

"Not upset about the shooting, I hope." Bradford said carelessly.

Kate bristled. "Yes, he is. Charles doesn't go around shooting people as a matter of course. The whole affair disturbed him deeply."

Bradford harrumphed. "I should have thought that someone who'd shot all those heathenish Dervishes in the Sudan wouldn't cavil at killing a Hun. He was doing his duty, after all—and it was clearly self-defense. That's what the constable testified, wasn't it? Had your husband been a split second slower, he'd have been a dead man."

Kate knew there was no point in discussing this matter with Bradford and hoped he would have the sensitivity not to raise the matter with Charles. As to the Dervishes, she knew that Charles had great respect for their courage and faith and saw little difference between defending one's king and country and defending one's God and prophet. And as for the German spy, Charles had told her that he had shot the man to keep him from escaping and with the knowledge that, had he been captured, he could not have been brought to trial. The constable had testified to self-defense in order to bring the matter to a speedy and sure close.

But it was probably the spy's weapon that had swung the coroner's jury, Charles said. The Luger recovered from the deck of the yacht was unlike anything the jurors had seen before. This pistol had no cylinder, just a long, bare barrel with a swept-back handle and two round finger grips in back. It held eight rounds in the handle, automatically reloading as fast as the trigger was pulled each time it was pulled, so fast that no human eye could follow the movement. It was clearly capable of killing as many as eight men in rapid succession, and the jurors were not comforted when they learned that the German Navy was about to make this vicious weapon their regulation sidearm. Incensed that a foreigner would have the temerity to bring it into peaceful Britain, it took them only a quarter-hour to reach their verdict. They found that the man known as Niels Andersson had murdered Richard Corey when Corey failed to deliver the stolen Marconi tuner. Andersson's death was ruled a justifiable homicide, Lord Charles Sheridan having acted in self-defense.

With all that in mind, Kate only said, "Charles will be pleased to hear your report. He's up in the attic, running some tests with the Chelmsford Marconi station. I'm sure you can find your way."

Charles had cleared away a corner of the large, dusty attic to use as a transmitting station, placing a table for his telegraphic equipment under the gable window and installing a wire to an aerial attached to a chimney. The window gave him a good light, a cool breeze, and a wide view of the orchard and meadow at the foot of the garden, a view that he enjoyed while he worked at his telegraph key. He had put on his headset and was so absorbed in his transmission that he did not hear Bradford's halloo and looked up only when his friend placed a hand on his shoulder. When he completed the message, he removed the headset and sat back in his chair.

"Hullo, Marsden." He gestured to a stack of wooden boxes. "Pull up a seat and tell me how things went in Poldhu last week."

Bradford turned up a box and sat down on it. "Everything was splendid, simply splendid," he said with enthusiasm. "The Prince was deeply impressed by Marconi's demonstration, and the Princess was delighted by the fanfare. The whole countryside turned out: flags, bunting, bands, choirs, the lot. The Prince actually climbed one of the masts and pronounced the view smashing."

"And the Admiral?" Charles asked eagerly. "What did Fisher have to say about the tuner?" That was his only regret about missing the Royal visit—that he had not been there to see the look on Jackie Fisher's face when Marconi demonstrated Gerard's tuning device and the Admiral understood what an advance on the present technology it represented.

"Oh, that." Briefly deflated, Bradford took out a cigar and lit it. "Well, as to that, it was a good thing the Admiral wasn't able to come."

"Not able to come!" Charles exclaimed in surprise. "But I thought that was the whole point of the exercise!"

"Quite," Bradford replied, puffing on the cigar. "As I said, however, it was a good thing. Marconi has not yet been able to make the tuner work properly." He made a wry mouth. "Gerard was rather ahead of him, it seems, in certain technical matters. His death is likely to be very unfortunate for us. However, we shall recover. We shall recover."

Charles sighed regretfully. "If we had been able to find the diary, it would be a different story. That's where all the experiments are recorded." He paused. "The thing hasn't turned up yet, I suppose." They had not found it when they searched Andersson's yacht, and Corey had given no clue to its whereabouts.

"Sadly, no. Whatever that bloody Corey did with it, he took the knowledge with him to his death." Bradford blew a cloud of smoke. "But Marconi will piece it all together eventually. Once you scientists know that a thing can be done, it's just a matter of trying out different ways of making it work. Give Marconi some time for experimentation, and he'll get it right. Although," he added carelessly, "the company is doing so well—in terms of new contracts and installations, I mean—that we hardly need the damned thing."

"At least for the moment," Charles murmured, thinking that for all his friend's shrewdness as a businessman, he was a fool about some things. The tuner was a vital part of the new technology that would have to be developed if the Marconi Company were to stay ahead of the pack. It was a pity that Bradford didn't seem to fully grasp its importance, and that the Marconi board was more interested in employing Marconi on the marketing front, rather than in research and development. But he only smiled and remarked: "The Royal visit was good for business, then, was it?"

"Rather!" Bradford exclaimed expansively. "The press turned out in force, and the newspaper reports were glowing. I must say, the publicity didn't hurt the price of Marconi shares one bit." He paused. "Marconi is most grateful to you, old man. We all are. If you hadn't got to the bottom of those deaths, the Royal visit would certainly have been cancelled, and the adverse publicity might have spelt the end of Marconi Wireless."

"There's one thing that troubles me, though," Charles said thoughtfully. "The death threat that Marconi received at the close of his lecture at the Royal Institution. Obviously, someone out there has a grudge against him, and it needs to be taken seriously. I would very much like to find out who—"

"Haven't I told you?" Bradford said. "That turned out to be the work of Maskelyne's assistant, the one who was transmitting the message."

"Indeed!" Charles said.

"Yes, the fellow threw it in *gratis,* it seems." Bradford waved his cigar. "And when Maskelyne found out what the chap had done, he was so chagrined that he withdrew his planned attack in *The Times*. So even that unfortunate bit of business worked to the company's advantage."

"So it would appear," Charles said dryly, thinking that the Marconi Company certainly seemed to lead a charmed life. He changed the subject. "I wonder—do you happen to know whether Kirk-Smythe is still on the Lizard?"

"I heard that he has taken possession of Andersson's yacht until the authorities decide what to do with it. No one has stepped forward to make a claim to the boat, and she might well become his." Bradford gave him a meaningful look. "He's moored her in Frenchman's Creek, I understand."

"Really?" Charles remarked.

"Yes. He seems to be seeing a great deal of the beautiful Lady Loveday."

So Kate had said, having heard the news from Jenna herself. Charles smiled. "Well, I've certainly seen worse arrangements. Kirk-Smythe is a good man, and Jenna must lead a lonely life, out there on the Lizard. They may be right for one another."

"They may, indeed," Bradford said. "Certainly, a wife like Lady Loveday would do wonders for the fellow." He gave Charles a wink, "It is a truth universally acknowledged, that a single man in want of a fortune must possess himself of a wife with a good one. At least, I have found it true in my case."

Charles glanced out the attic window and caught a glimpse of Kate, hair blown by the wind and skirts whipping, carrying a basket into the garden. He was suddenly overwhelmed by his feeling for her, and his gratitude for all she gave him: her warmth, her understanding, her support, her love. "I don't know about the fortune," he said quietly. "But a man without a good wife must be a lonely man, indeed."

AUTHORS' NOTES

By Christmas Eve (1906, Reginald Fessenden) was ready to give his first broadcast. That night, ship operators and amateurs around Brant Rock (Massachusetts) heard the results: "someone speaking! . . . a woman's voice rose in song. . . . Next someone was heard reading a poem." Fessenden himself played "O Holy Night" on his violin.

Though the fidelity was not all that it might be, listeners were captivated by the voices and notes they heard. No more would sounds be restricted to mere dots and dashes of the Morse code.

Empire of the Air: The Men Who Made Radio
Tom Lewis

Bill Albert writes about Marconi and wireless:
    Susan and I had considered writing a book on Guglielmo Marconi for over a decade, ever since we learned about his wireless factory in Chelmsford, less than ten miles from our fictional Bishop's Keep. Given Charles Sheridan's interest in science and military background, it stands to reason that he would have been an avid follower of the developments in wireless that revolutionized existing communications technologies in the early 1900s, and that

he would have made Marconi's acquaintance soon after the young Italian came to England.

Until we actually began the research for the book, however, I found it difficult to see how we could create a compelling fiction about Marconi's life and work. My doubts disappeared when I realized just how ferocious the commercial competition in wireless really was—much fiercer, even, than the competition in the early motor car industry, which we described in *Death at Devil's Bridge.* While motor cars were initially viewed with an exasperated humor as toys for the idle rich and nuisances for everyone else, the public at large easily and enthusiastically grasped the possible applications—commercial, military, governmental, and scientific—of a fully-operational wireless telegraph system using the familiar Morse code. A number of inventors quickly jumped on the wireless bandwagon, while the undersea and landline cable companies (with their colossal investments in infrastructure) were doing everything they could to stop the advance of the new technology. Governments saw the enormous advantage of wireless, and armies and navies were eager to adopt it. Great Britain, which claimed Marconi, might have held a slight lead, but Germany, the United States, France, and Russia were all anxious to benefit—without, as far as possible, paying royalties to the Marconi Company. In fact, on all sides, the historical record shows decades-long attempts to copy ideas and infringe on patents. Some of these suits were not settled until the Second World War.

When writing historical fiction, Susan and I are occasionally challenged by the conceptual divide that exists between our characters and our audience: that is, a concept which would have been familiar to our characters in their period is unknown or alien to our readers—or vice versa. (An example of the latter: One reviewer of *Death in Hyde Park,* a prisoner of contemporary technology, thought that by "wireless" we must be referring to cell phones!) Readers of this book will have to recognize that in 1901, when Marconi sent the coded letter "S" from his transmitter at Poldhu to a receiver in North America, neither he nor anyone else foresaw the use of wireless in broadcast mode. ("Broadcast" was the agricultural term for casting seed by hand). In fact, Marconi envisioned only transmitter-to-single-receiver applications; the ability of multiple receivers to intercept a message from a single transmitter was viewed as a major problem, in terms of security and signal interference, not as an asset that might translate into a whole new technology. Once past its initial inventive phase, the Marconi Company was never again in the forefront of technology or experimentation.

But the technologies that Marconi inspired evolved swiftly. In November of 1906, Lee de Forest created a tube that he called the "audion," which made it possible to transmit the human voice. And in December of the same year, only forty-one months after the time of our book, Reginald Fessenden broadcast his first epoch-making program of voice and music. The world of mass communications was born—and the future did not belong to Marconi.

A personal note: I have one regret about this book—that is, that my father, Carl Paul Albert, did not live long enough to help with it. He would have been a wonderful source of information and inspiration, for he knew and understood the apparatus we describe in this book. He became a ham operator as a teenager in the early 1920s, and was a life-long radio enthusiast. I loved to hear him tell the story of the proud day when he had finally saved enough to buy and install a single tube in his radio receiver—the tube burned out after only an hour. And I can still remember watching him test and replace the tubes in the family radios in the late 1940s. After his death, as I dismantled his forty-foot radio tower and gave away his stash of circuit boards, resistors, and transistors, I couldn't help reflecting on the technological change in the space of his lifetime.

I hope for Pop's sake that there are radios in heaven.

There is no doubt that the day will come, maybe when you and I are forgotten, when copper wires, gutta-percha coverings, and iron sheathings will be relegated to the Museum of Antiquities. Then, when a person wants to telegraph to a friend, he knows not where, he will call out in an electro-magnetic voice, which will be heard loud by him who has the electromagnetic ear, but will be silent to everyone else. He will call "Where are you?" and the reply will come, "I am at the bottom of the coal-mine" or "Crossing the Andes" or "In the middle of the Pacific"; or perhaps no reply will come at all, and he may then conclude that his friend is dead.

Professor W.E. Ayrton, the Institution of Electrical Engineers, in a lecture at the Imperial Institute, 1897

Susan Albert writes about Oliver Lodge:

"But even if his friend were dead," Sir Oliver Lodge would promptly respond, "he might still be able to answer!"

Sir Oliver—at the time of our book, the president of the Society for Psychical Research—was one of a large number of Victorians (Sir Arthur Conan Doyle prominent among them) who were interested in demonstrating that it was indeed possible to communicate with the dead. Lodge's early wireless work and his tuning patent made him a strong and active rival of Marconi, and in 1906 the Marconi Company was forced through a lawsuit to buy out his company (the Lodge-Muirhead Syndicate), pay Lodge a thousand pounds a year for the seven years until his patent had expired, and hire him as a consultant for five hundred pounds a year.

But Lodge seemed to care less about wireless communication than he did about communicating with the spirits of the beyond, and throughout the remaining four decades of his life, he became one of England's most prominent scientists in the field of psychical research. "At an early age," Lodge wrote, "I decided that my main business was with the imponderables, the things that work secretly and have to be apprehended mentally." He was intrigued by the idea that the human brain could function as a receiver for messages from the spirit world, much as the wireless receiver intercepted electromagnetic waves traveling through the ether. He was especially interested in automatic writing, and was present at hundreds of séances (like the one described in our book), where different kinds of spirit communications were attempted and carried out with varying degrees of reported successes and failures.

Oliver Lodge summed up his feelings on the afterlife in his last book, *My Philosophy*: "The universe seems to me to be a great reservoir of life and mind. The unseen universe is a great reality. This is the region to which we really belong and to which we shall one day return." Before his death in 1940, Lodge gave a sealed message to the Society for Psychical Research, hoping that—once departed—his spirit could send a duplicate message through a medium, thus proving the existence of life after death. It was not a successful experiment.

As Bill and I worked on this book, I came to see Lodge and Marconi as two ends of a fascinating spectrum: Marconi, the talented tinkerer who could assemble physical objects and make them work, even when he didn't fully understand the science; and Lodge, the far-seeing, far-ranging scientist who was more interested in the "imponderables" that lay beyond the physical realm. They are wonderful examples of the kinds of men produced by a wonderful era, when all seemed possible and the sky—literally—was the limit.

REFERENCES

Here are some of the books we found helpful in creating *Death on the Lizard*. If you have comments or questions, you may write to Bill and Susan Albert, PO Box 1616, Bertram TX 78605, or email us at china@tstar.net. You may also wish to visit our website, http://www.mysterypartners.com, where you will find additional information and links to Internet sites having to do with various aspects of this book.

Childers, Erskine, *The Riddle of the Sands*, originally published in 1903, available as a Dover reprint.

Gordon, John Steele, *A Thread Across the Ocean: The Heroic Story of the Transatlantic Cable.* New York: Walker & Company, 2002.

Kipling, Rudyard, "Wireless," *Scribner's Magazine,* August, 1902.

Jones, Jill, *Empires of Light: Edison, Tesla, Westinghouse, and the Race to Electrify the World.* New York: Random House, 2003.

Lewis, Tom, *Empire of the Air: The Men Who Made Radio.* New York: Edward Burlingame Books, 1991.

The Lizard, Falmouth & Helsen: Ordnance Survey Explorer Series 1:25000 # 103. Southampton: Ordnance Survey, 2003.

Marconi, Degna, *My Father, Marconi*. Toronto: Guernica Editions, 2001.

Perry, Lawrence, "Commercial Wireless Telegraphy," *The World's Work*, March, 1903.

Standage, Tom, *The Victorian Internet: The Remarkable Story of the Telegraph and the Nineteenth Century On-line Pioneers*. New York: Berkley Books, 1999.

Tarrant, D. R., *Marconi's Miracle: The Wireless Bridging of the Atlantic*. St John's, Newfoundland, Canada: Flander Press Ltd., 2001.

Weightman, Gavin, *Signor Marconi's Magic Box*. New York: Da Capo Press, 2003.